A Town of Empty Rooms

A TOWN OF EMPTY ROOMS

Karen E. Bender

COUNTERPOINT
BERKELEY

Interior design by VJBScribe
Cover design by Charles Brock at Faceout Studios

Library of Congress Cataloging-in-Publication Data

Bender, Karen E.
A Town of Empty Rooms / Karen E. Bender.
pages cm
ISBN 978-1-61902-069-6 (hardcover)
ISBN: 978-1-61902-145-7 (ebook)
1. Marriage—Fiction. 2. Families—Religious aspects—Fiction. 3. Belonging (Social psychology)—Fiction. I. Title.
PS3552.E53849T69 2013
813'.54—dc23

Paperback ISBN: 978-1-61902-274-4

COUNTERPOINT
2560 Ninth Street, Suite 318
Berkeley, CA 94710
www.counterpointpress.com

Printed in the United States of America

To Robert, Jonah and Maia
With love

Part One

Chapter One

....

SHE DID NOT INTEND TO steal anything that day. Serena Hirsch was walking through midtown Manhattan on her lunch break; it was one week since her father had died, and it was her first day back at work. It was a bright April afternoon, and people were gathered in loose, happy groups outside, sitting on concrete walls and benches, turning faces to the cool pale light. Others seemed relieved, released from the confines of winter, certain of the damp promise of spring. Serena walked with the crowd marching down the sidewalk, hoping she would feel she was one of them again, but now the clear sunlight, the blaring cabs, and the groups gathered on the sidewalks all seemed to exist in some world that she did not inhabit. Her father was not part of this world anymore, and now, just back from burying him, she did not know how she belonged to it as well.

She watched people head down the sidewalks, clutching crisp bags from Saks, and she turned into the store. Customers walked politely through the golden, unearthly light. Everything seemed carefully arranged so as to create longing. Her own parents, middle class and both bitter and hopeful about it, had always viewed Saks with a kind of defensive disdain. "Thieves," her mother had said. "How much are these things worth? Look at the markdowns during a sale." It made the store seem perplexing and a little unsavory when Serena was a child, even as she admired the silk-sheathed mannequins, frozen in air, as she walked by the glass cases that held silver lipsticks that gleamed in white spotlights.

Sales. There was the theater of customers looking, buying; of sales-people coaxing; of the warm hum of life. There was the bustle of sales-girls tenderly applying makeup to customers' faces; there were the walls thick with leather purses. She walked. Customers leaned over glass cases and gazed at the watches, scarves, jewelry, inside. Serena

3

felt as though her body were walking by all of this, without her. "Our new Pearlessence lip liner is just right for you!" a woman said to Serena with great confidence. She was surprised the salesgirls were talking to her; their chipper greetings, their assurance, made her feel somehow released from commerce's usual rules.

She stopped in Fine Jewelry. Her father had liked this section, for he could point out appropriate jewelry that one could store for future pawning. He was not interested in how a diamond necklace might be purchased for a fancy outfit but in how it could be slipped into a pocket and carried to another country to be sold if America fell apart. This could, in his mind, happen at any moment. Once, when she was eleven, he leaned over the glass case and chatted, for a half hour, with a salesgirl. Serena remembered her name: Kathy. She held out a diamond bracelet, $1,298. "How would you rate the color and symmetry on this one?" he asked, in great seriousness, though he really had no intention of buying anything. "Will it hold its value more than this ring?" Kathy discussed clarity and depth. Serena's father listened intently and then suddenly said, "Thank you," and headed off. Serena hurried after him, feeling a little bad for the salesgirl, but the briskness of his walk told her that he was embarrassed and didn't want the salesgirl to know that he couldn't afford to buy the item. "You," he said, putting a hand on her shoulder, "you will be able to buy these things, and save them, and you will know when to leave."

She wondered what he would want her to buy today. It made her feel better, purposeful, to imagine this. There were bracelets and earrings and necklaces, the white diamonds, rubies, sapphires, unearthly, the hard, clear stones aglow in the pure light. She stopped and looked at them, all set out on wrinkled squares of black velvet.

"That's a beauty," said the salesgirl. "Do you want to try it on?"

The silver bracelet was extremely smooth around her wrist. Serena touched the clear hard surface of the diamond. Its solidness was shocking, seemed the weight of all good things on earth; she wanted it. She leaned against the case trying to seem casual, as though she was the sort of person who, in fact, purchased these objects. The bracelet's price tag said $890. This price made her dizzy.

"Is this the price?" she asked, as though there could be another one.

The salesgirl nodded.

"It's beautiful," Serena said.

At a certain point, standing here, she would be a potential consumer to be flattered, and at another point she would be a loiterer, and at another point, not too much farther along, the nice salesgirl would call security on her. Suddenly, Serena was aware, as she was aware of the fragility between life and death, the fine line between civility and criminality, as thin as the silvery threads on a spiderweb. Serena wanted the bracelet. Her mouth was dry. She was alive, and her father was not. She had not been ready for this wall to come down between them—as if anyone was ever ready—but she was also thinking about the fact that she had not brought him the success he had wanted for her, and their last phone conversation had, in fact, involved his threatening to call her superior to demand that she be given a raise. What could she offer him? She was trembling; she wanted to give this bracelet to him, wherever he was, hand it to him and say: "Here. Let's go."

She would buy it.

Lightly, casually, she handed the company credit card to the salesgirl. "Here," she said. What was she doing? It seemed that the walls were vanishing, that they were melting away like butter. She felt almost as though she were falling backwards, but she was only standing still. The air was soft, unreal with notes of vanilla, rose, and lemon from the fragrance counter. The girl innocently swiped the card. It was approved. The girl smiled, approving of her. She put the bracelet into a box and then into a stiff fragrant Saks bag with silver tissue flaring up the sides.

"Thank you very much," the girl said.

Serena was startled at herself, embarrassed; she was about to tell the girl that this was a mistake, that she was not the sort of person who could afford this, but that fact was so deeply shaming there seemed no other choice than to walk out. Her throat tightened as she strode toward the door, and she closed her eyes, not knowing what would happen when she left with the bracelet. She stood on the crowded sidewalk, in the sunlight, blinking, her heart enormous.

. . . .

IT TOOK HER THREE DAYS to rack up eight thousand dollars on the company card. She went into Saks again, Tiffany's, Bendel's, and she asked the salesgirls about the symmetry and clarity of the diamonds, tried to imagine what would be best to transport. "Something for a new outfit?" a salesgirl, Tania, asked her, and the disconnect between this assumption and her purchase was so profound that she bought a bracelet and a ruby ring, too. She walked out, her heart in her mouth, surprised each time the card swiped, but it made her feel better to leave with these items, made her, oddly, feel as though she was being good. Her father had been worried about the nation. It was late 2002, he had been outraged about Bush, his disregard for rules, and he had told her to prepare to go to another country if Bush started expanding the Patriot Act — she was, she told herself, buying diamonds to pack away to sell, the way her father wished his family had done. Plus, Earl Morton owed her, after that terrible health insurance plan, after not covering dental, for god's sake, after taking her ideas and not giving her credit, after asking her to pick up coffee again and again. He had laughed at her request for dental coverage one time too many; he had demanded she come back to work three weeks after giving birth; she had staggered back, leaking milk, so tired she was nauseous, missing her infants so deeply her skin ached. "It's America," he said, tipping back in his chair, smiling as she held a clipboard against her chest, trying to keep the cotton nursing pads from slipping out of her shirt. "We all have to contribute."

Now he was contributing. To her.

Her father had been overjoyed that she was at Pepsi, a Fortune 500 corporation, as though that implied that she would somehow absorb the riches that they created, but she spent the better part of her conversations with her father trying to make up what she actually did. Her father had ideas. "Pepsi should invent a juice drink with no calories," he said. "Healthy. Tell them." He only bought Pepsi products, and in large quantities, as though that would somehow increase her stature at the organization. She remembered him sitting in his garage, staring at his model train landscapes. Once he had started a landscape that was intended to show a large Pepsi plant and trains that would leave it, bringing bottles of soft drinks to the cities beyond. He had searched far to find the tiny plastic bottles that would fill the trucks; he found plain ones and carefully dotted the Pepsi colors on the caps; in the window of a large office building, he put a tiny brown-haired figure, looking out the window, gesturing masterfully to the outside world. "That is you," he said, proudly, and she went home and wept.

She hoped that no one would notice. Perhaps the money she spent would fade into the coffers of Pepsi, into the supply budget, the travel budget. She had seen the travel receipts, the first-class airfare, the lunches at Le Cirque and the Four Seasons; she saw the fruit baskets, the golf clubs that her boss Earl Morton sent to associates for the holidays, and this was okay while she and Dan had a fight every time the insurance co-pay went up? A part of her could not believe that accounting would notice. She marked it down: *Morton: Travel Expense.*

During her childhood, her father was up at the first light, sitting at the table, flipping pages of the *Los Angeles Times*, but not reading it, as though trying to emulate what a regular person would do in the morning. He was searching for stories on Nixon, on the cover-up. "Republican fascists," he muttered. Days when he found something particularly egregious, he brought out something from his bathrobe pocket—a surprisingly valuable silver key chain, or a 24k gold link chain. He kept something valuable on his person at all times.

"Keep something with you that you can sell," he told her once, when she was nine, when she wandered, sleepy, into the quiet dawn of the kitchen.

"Why?" she asked.

"Just in case. Good to have it. So you can sell it and move."

"What's going to happen?"

"You never know," he said. "Remember. When things are falling apart around you, be ready to go."

When she had received twenty S-chain gold necklaces for her Bat Mitzvah, the delicate offerings from teenage girls who had all purchased them at the same jewelry store in Westwood Village, he bought her a special jewelry box where she could keep them. She had wanted something with a ballerina, with lavender adolescent froufrou, but her father proudly presented her with a jewelry box that was a small, armored safe.

One day he drove her around to identify pawnshops in the Los Angeles area. He had familiarized himself with them, the ones that paid the best prices, the ones with the friendliest proprietors, and she sat in his car as he drove them by the storefronts that announced, in enormous letters: CASH NOW! WE TAKE GOLD, SILVER, STUDENT LOAN CHECKS, INCOME TAX REFUNDS! INSTA-CASH HERE!

"You're the oldest," he said, "so you should know this. This is my advice."

She was proud that she was getting this advice, that she was deemed worthy of it, but she looked at the stores, shabby, with enormous, overly enthusiastic signs, and she shuddered.

"I don't want to go in there," she said.

"Good point. On a regular day, don't. But think ahead of the pack. Be a wolf, honey, not a sheep."

"How do you know who's who?" she asked.

"What?"

"A wolf. Or a sheep."

He scratched his neck, which was pink and spackled; he never wore sunscreen, as though believing himself immune to the effects of the sun. Her father and his family had left Germany in 1936, not long before the rest of their relatives had been herded off and sent to the camps, and he had a particularly fierce awareness of the preciousness of life. He stocked antiviral medication and antibiotics in preparation for future epidemics, once cancelled her seat for a flight she was booked on because he had heard about thunderstorms in the flight path — she had not found out about the cancellation until she was standing in the check-in line. He wept aloud at newspaper stories of untimely death — the teenager who was shot by the police, the mother who drove the wrong way down a one-way street and was killed. As a child, she often found him at the kitchen table, the newspaper neatly folded beside himself, a Kleenex crumpled in his hand. "Don't look," he said, his eyes red, as he tried to pour her some cereal. "It's something bad."

It was a fresh, bright morning in Los Angeles, and a few young women were jogging, faces gleaming with sweat. "Don't trust her," he said, pointing to one blonde girl smiling to the music playing in her ears.

"Why?"

"Sheep don't have their eyes open. You can have your eyes open. You can lead the way."

She was nine years old. How did anyone know how to lead the way? He claimed to have known, when he was three years younger than she wa then, of the end of his world. He had told his parents, who had not wanted to leave, that they had to leave Berlin in 1936, and finally they had listened to him. If everyone has one age, one moment, in which they are stuck and that shapes them forever, it was this time for her father. It was his bravest moment. She sat with him in the car, the blue vinyl warm on her back, and she cared mostly that he had decided to impart to her this information.

"Serena," he said. "I trust you. You'll know what to do."

Here, at forty, she strolled absurdly down Fifth Avenue. She imagined where she and her family could go. Quebec. Israel. Japan. Really, she wanted to go where he was, she wanted to talk to him one last time; she looked at the phone, waiting for it to ring. And later, when the security guards showed up at her office, when the lawyers hammered out a deal, when they asked why she had done this, for she had never done it before and did not think she would again, she did not know how to tell them how natural and free it felt, buying up the world with fake money; she could not explain how it felt like a final conversation with her father, like a deep and uncontrollable act of love.

THREE MONTHS LATER, AFTER WORD had gotten out about her and she was unable to find a job in marketing at any corporation in New York, after the lawyers' fees depleted all their finances, she and her husband Dan hurled their resumes all over the nation and took the one job that was offered; it was to Dan. They piled everything into a U-Haul and drove six hundred miles to Waring, North Carolina.

The first month, Serena found herself, consistently, embarrassingly, getting lost. She had not yet found a job, so she was trying to get to know the city of Waring with their children — Zeb, five, and Rachel, three — toting them to playgrounds, parks, but she was having trouble negotiating the streets. Her heart marching, she hunched over the steering wheel so that they would not see her trembling hands. Waring was the kind of town where people seemed to wash up when their luck grew thin, a place that people picked off a map at a moment when the creditors were closing in or the divorce papers were filed. She drove down the main drag of the city, a former port in the Civil War, where one now noticed a longing for bargain electronic equipment, discount shoes, and cheap burgers. Marble antebellum mansions now stood deified as museums, and placards outside the churches declared, without irony: *If God Is Your Co-Pilot, Switch Seats*; *Democracy Is Nice, but the King Is Coming*; *Choose Your Future: Smoking or Non-Smoking?* She tried to find the best route home.

They did not know anyone here. It was a city of pickup trucks perched on tires the size of inner tubes, of SUVs humming along ribbons of asphalt. There were the billboards by the highway: *Honesty, Caring, Responsibility, Faith*, as though the simple declaration of these traits on the wall would cause them to be absorbed by the people driving by; she passed *Jesus says: I will make my home with you*; *Free Coffee: Everlasting Life*; *Don't Be So Open-Minded: Your Brains Will Fall Out.* The purpose behind them all was so puzzling that she actually missed the half-naked underwear models looming over any given corner in Manhattan.

ONE DAY SERENA WAS COMING back from the supermarket, made a wrong turn by a church placard which held the distracting message *His Blood's For You*, and ended up in a web of streets that wound through a development with no trees, the sky an impassive, enormous blue. The houses appeared to have been built all at once, with five different design plans, the streets were unnamed, identifiable only to those who understood some private code, and she felt herself become afraid. The world seemed the consistency of paper, first from her father's abrupt death, and then from the incidents with the credit cards—everyone had asked her over and over what she had been thinking, and, really, there had been no thought at all. She had been borne on a wave of feeling, a desire to be close to him in this new, shocking state of who he was. The action had revealed some tawdriness in her, and she did not know what would happen next. The children still saw her as good, and she wanted to do right for them, but she still could not find her way through these streets. "Hold on, hold on," she murmured to the children, handing them handfuls of cheese goldfish as they sat in the back, innocent and cantankerous and hungry. She swung the car onto a side street and then back onto a main road and onto Tenth; she knew that if she called Dan, he would not want to hear from her, knew that in a moment the goldfish she was handing to the backseat would be rejected, and she was afraid of herself, of her children's imminent outrage, of the sheer and surprising number of Bojangles' and Hardee's, and of the fact that anyone in the world could, at any moment, disappear.

She passed a building, a plain, concrete box with deep blue stained glass windows and golden doors. The name Temple Shalom was written over the doors.

The royal blue of the stained glass windows and the gleaming gold door lent the simple building the exaggerated, grand aura particular to all religious institutions, as though its structure could somehow contain the varied, raw longings of its congregants. It was the only synagogue she had seen in the city, surrounded by the vast, modern church compounds—Baptist, Catholic, A.M.E. Zion.

She drove past the building once, paused, turned around. She did not feel Jewish, or interested in God at all, really, and in New York she would have walked by this building without another thought. But this was the only building here that seemed at all familiar to her. She stopped the car, unbuckled the car seats, and coaxed Zeb and Rachel out. Stepping into the converted basement, she said, "Hello?" to the air.

A man wearing a yarmulke walked in. He was a tall, taut man, and his hair was a lush, glossy brown. His skin was the color of caramel. The room was dim and quiet; he looked surprised that anyone was coming inside.

"Rabbi Josh Golden!" he said, as though he had just decided this. He looked to be about forty-five, though there was something in his face that looked younger; his arms appeared stiff and muscular under his blazer, as though he was preparing to combat his congregants' myriad spiritual doubts. "Who are we welcoming here?"

"Serena Hirsch. This is Zeb and Rachel. I just need directions to Old Oak Street," Serena said. "The kids are hungry and—"

"Hi, hungry kids," he said, kneeling beside them. He rose and stepped into a closet and brought out some chocolate coins. "Leftover gelt. Can they have some?"

"Sure," she said.

The children grabbed the gold coins and began eating them, ravenous.

The rabbi stood and smiled at her. He regarded her in a peculiar way, as though she were both right in front of him and a window, and through her was a place unexpected and beautiful, a pristine outline of a lake. She turned around to see what he was looking at, but she saw only a slightly peeling wall.

"Where are you from, Serena?" he asked.

"We just moved from New York," she said. "I'm trying to find Old Oak."

"You're almost there," he said. With a pencil, he drew a little map on the back of a Temple Bulletin. "You just have to turn back onto Sycamore and make that left on Haynes. That's a left that a lot of people miss."

"Thank you," she said, and meant it.

"You're welcome," he said. His eyes were dark and blue and so intent she looked away from them briefly. He smiled. It was as though he contained something, not sunlight, but an essence just as illuminating. "You should come and join the festivities!"

They all stared at the dim, silent room.

"Where?" asked Zeb, squinting.

"Maybe," she said. "Thank you again."

He shook her hand. His grip encased her hand completely for a moment, and then he released it.

....

THEY KNEW NO ONE IN Waring, and now she and Dan did not know each other. Once the children were asleep and the house had settled into a sort of quiet save the shudders of the dishwasher and dryer and the children's mournful calls for juice, she and Dan assumed the grim, silent chore of avoiding each other. That night, after she had sent out another resume, she stood by the kitchen door, watching Dan read his files. She wanted to go to him, to touch his shoulder, his hair, but there was a warning, a stiffness in his shoulders that had become more pronounced, a wall against her, in the last year. He had had a loss of his own eight months before; he had learned of the death of his older brother. Harold had not been in contact with the family for years. He had been wandering the globe and was in a car accident, and after Dan found out, he, a publicist, a tall, talkative, optimistic man, seemed encased in ice. Serena had tried to figure out what might comfort him, tried to help him talk or not talk, remember Harold or not, but he did not want to engage with anyone at all. She tried to hold him at night, and sometimes they clutched each other, silent, but the sun rose and they stumbled forward, separate, into their days.

And then she had walked into Saks. She had tried to explain that she had thought perhaps that the gathering of diamonds and silver might actually help them when the country fell apart, that she had been nobly preparing to take all of them as they resettled in some new country, but now this plan did not sound practical as much as insane. He had no idea why she had done this, and neither did she. She had not been able to stop herself those few days with the credit cards; she had not been able to think about the regular rules of commerce because the death seemed to break every rule she knew. But Dan seemed to be waiting for something to answer his outrage, and, unfortunately, it was this. He became silent after the credit cards, the move, as though with this action, she had betrayed him.

She stood, by the door, waiting for him to look up; he stared at his files, determined. "Dan," she said, feeling his name, familiar, but flat, just a word, on her lips. "Would you like to go to services Friday? There's a temple here. I thought we could go."

She heard herself and was embarrassed; it sounded ridiculous, as though she were asking him on a date. It occurred to her that marriage was, in its distinctive currents, almost like dating, but with the same person, over and over; they had each shifted over the years, in ways both hopeful and otherwise, and now this person sat in their kitchen, in this house where they both lived, and it was almost as though she was introducing herself to him for the first time.

He glanced up. The yellow kitchen light shaded his face. "Why would I want to do that?"

"It's somewhere to go," she said. "Maybe we'll like it." She was oddly shy saying *we*.

"You can go."

"You don't want to?" she asked.

"Why would I want to?" he said. All right — that was clear. There was a deflation in her chest, the fading of hope that he would say something that would remind her that he harbored some sort of love for her — but he did not, and she crossed the room in the silence that made it seem that there was no one there.

SHE WALKED IN, ALONE, TO the Temple that Friday. In the front room there was a silk shawl with a Chagall print spread over a section of water damage — an attached note said that the damage was from Hurricane Fran and they had not yet been able to repair it; she looked at the framed glass pictures of the tiny Bar/Bat Mitzvah classes — sometimes with just one child a year. The room had an elaborate feeling of cleanliness, as though what the room lacked in grandeur would be made up for in soap. An ancient hunched man with a nametag was handing out mimeographed services. "Welcome," he said, handing her a blank sticker, marked VISITOR. "Write your name."

She was not a religious person, but now she needed to be here. There were fourteen other people scattered among the pews. The sight of a dozen or so Jews dressed formally for the Southern evening, waiting for services to begin, startled her. This synagogue was a simple, beige, boxy room, much smaller than the sanctuary where she had sat as a child, a temple in the San Fernando Valley that in its vastness and girth resembled a spaceship; there was a thoughtlessness, a brash optimism, to that temple, with its membership of six thousand and the sparkling black lake that was its parking lot. Her father, who grew up, after Berlin, in a small town near Sacramento, had never gotten over the expanse of their Los Angeles temple; he walked through its parking lot slowly, taking pleasure in methodically counting the cars. Once he walked through it, turned to her, and smiled. "Three hundred and twenty-seven," he said, with a kind of awe. "They all came."

Stepping into this room was different; it was a declaration.

She stood in the back, wondering where to sit; there was no lack of available seats here, but she wanted to find a good spot. She stepped forward, not too close to the front, hovering near the middle, and then she sat down, quickly.

"What's your name, darling?" asked a woman in front of her with a nametag that read BETTY B, notable for a silk hat with an eerily realistic azalea branch on the front.

"Uh. Serena," she said, briefly, ridiculously, forgetting. "We've been here a month."

"Welcome," said Betty. "We need y'all. We need new blood." She laughed. "How many are you? You married?"

"Yes," she said, carefully. "Four of us."

"Well, where are they? How many families do you think we have?"

Serena tried to come up with a number that would not be insulting. "Two hundred?"

"Ninety-five!" said Betty. Her face became almost maniacally hopeful. "But growing."

"There are 5,045 families in that cruise ship across the street," said a squarish man in a silk navy suit; his voice sounded as though he were speaking through a microphone. "That's just First Baptist."

"According to the international Jewish mailing list," said Betty.

"You may ask, compiled by who?" said the man in the navy suit.

"Norman. Please. We have about 263 Jews here. We have a county of one hundred thousand people."

Rabbi Golden ascended the stairs to the maroon-carpeted bima. An organist began to play softly on the second level of the synagogue. The congregants settled quickly into their seats.

The rabbi began the service. Serena did not listen to the prayers exactly but was moved by the straggly red velvet cushions on the pews, the clear jingle of the silver crowns of the Torah. She was in the one place in this city that reminded her of her youth. Or—three decades removed from it, a nostalgic youth, not one that she had actually lived. Her family's attendance at services was erratic—her mother never went, and her father attended only when he needed to drive her for services required for her Bat Mitzvah. Her father would grab a yarmulke and bolt into the synagogue, slumping shyly in a seat near the back, like a student unprepared for class. He stammered through the prayers, lost his spot on the page, cleared his throat; Serena sat, reciting each prayer slowly so he could copy her. He sat, leg jiggling, and she tried, with her concentration, to keep him still. She was ten years old. Suddenly, she had a purpose.

Now she found herself glad for the moments in the service during which she could stand up and see the rabbi more clearly; she wanted to watch him. She noticed this about the rabbi: how tightly his hands gripped the sides of the lectern where he gave his sermon, and the hard, bright confidence of his gaze as he looked out at the congregants, as though he were taunting all of them.

THE RABBI CAME STRAIGHT TO her during the oneg, the ode to lemon squares and dry brownies that followed the service. The other congregants gathered around a foldout table, arranging desserts on paper plates. "So, you've enlisted," he said, leaning toward her. "New York. I was an army chaplain. I'm here from Fort Myers. Five years before that, Brussels. Akron. Sarajevo. San Diego. Iraq. Camp Lejeune." His words tumbled out as though he was trying to catch his breath. "Now I'm here." He grinned—that sunlight again—and held out his arms. "Forty years old and I've made it to my first pulpit!"

"You've traveled a lot," said Serena.

"Always traveled," said the rabbi. "Hobo as a child. A kind word for what I was. Then life in the military. I've seen everything. Jews in India! Morocco! Alaska! You wouldn't believe how glad they were to see me. They wanted to see what I brought with me. Matzos. Dreidels. Hamantaschen. These were things that reminded them of home." He paused. "What do you think of the Jewish community here?"

"Is this it?" asked Serena.

He laughed. "My point exactly. I want two hundred families here in the next five years." He punched his hand into his fist. "Watch me! Two hundred!"

His voice had the tininess of a game show host's, a controlling cheeriness — it was as though he could not quite perceive his own volume. But Serena heard something in his voice that got her attention; his words were expansive. "Where are you going to find them?" Serena asked.

"I have plans," the rabbi said. He bounced on the balls of his feet so he seemed to be half-floating in the air. "The Southeastern North Carolina Jewish Community Center. Five thousand square feet, with classrooms and lounges, and outside, baseball diamonds. The Baptists have it, the Catholics have it. We should have it. The elderly in one room, reading to the little kids. The teenagers playing basketball outside. Everyone steps in and is welcomed. Everyone has a place to go."

They stood, clutching their tiny plastic cups of wine. The rabbi's breath smelled like a child's, cherry-sweet.

The rabbi cleared his throat. He looked at her with the strained desperation of a suitor. "Serena Hirsch. Join. I can tell you are board material. You are going to help lead us."

He knew nothing about her. Serena was grateful to him, his ignorance, his assumption of her goodness; she was also glad that no one was there to contradict him.

"Thank you," she said.

"Shabbat shalom," he said, and stepped back. "And don't try to get away from us."

At another moment in her life, she would have found that statement a little cloying and false; but at this particular moment, she wanted him to go on. After she had been fired from Pepsi, after she had said she was guilty, after she paid the fine, after they landed here, in this strange city — perhaps this person could help her. She stood amid the small, talkative group and found herself following the rabbi's orbit around the table, positioning herself so she could hear his conversations with the other congregants.

"Jackie," he said. "Is your brother out of the ICU?"

"Not yet," said a woman whose bright blue eyeliner matched her purse. "Maybe Thursday. Still on the ventilator."

He put a hand on her shoulder. "That is hard," he said.

Jackie's eyes were teary. "I don't know what to do, Rabbi."

"He's in all our prayers, Jackie. Day by day. We'll keep him on Mi Sheberach."

He stood beside his congregant in his crisp suit, looking down, hands clasped. It was a posture he had clearly refined through the years. His arms made a triangle in front of his body, one hand gripped the other, his head was lowered; if he was not a rabbi offering comfort to a congregant, he could be a movie executive considering an enormous deal. He was listening. It seemed to require a large effort on his part to remain this still. Serena noticed he was, very softly, deliberately, tapping his foot. It was as though he was allowing Jackie to borrow him for a moment, accessing some supreme power that rose from him.

She watched the rabbi move around the table. He knew everything. His mind contained information about the sick, the wayward or ungrateful grown children, the hip surgeries, the upcoming trips to Israel, the divorces, the new grandchildren, the children's marriages to spouses the parents did or did not approve of, the SAT scores, the jobs gained or lost, the untimely deaths. His navy rayon suit shone bleakly in the overhead light; it needed to be ironed. She watched the expressions of the people as he barreled around the table toward them, everyone affixed with nametags, clutching cups of soda or coffee; they were all, in one way or another, waiting for him.

After a while, she said good night. On the way to the car, she looked back at the small building on the corner. The stained glass windows burned amber and blue in the darkness. It was impossible to see who was inside; the building simply stood there. Above the city, the deep sky stretched, the clouds floated overhead, great gray ships lit through with the moonlight, gleaming—throughout the day, the clouds had shuddered with light and thunder. Her soles floated on the sidewalk as though on ice. She looked back at the Temple, the pure golden light in the windows. She wanted to go back inside.

Chapter Two

THE CHILDREN DID NOT KNOW why they were here. They had moved to Waring in July, as soon as Dan received word about the job, and Zeb woke up each morning asking if they were going back to New York, or if they were going on to Alabama, or England, or any place he had heard about; he and Rachel jumped out of bed, going about their days finding ways to dismantle the house. They reached into a corner and found the spot where the floors detached from the walls, knocked against a door and watched it fall off its hinges, stuck a finger into a hole and came out with a fingernail streaked with mold. They moved through the house with stealth and relentless fortitude, on a mission to locate the nail or spring that would either make their parents move back to a place they knew or bring the whole house down altogether.

The task of moving had absorbed Serena and Dan, their conversation those days brisk and utilitarian. But the night they had moved into the new house, when the boxes were all inside and when the children had passed out, he had reached for her under the blanket. It felt like it had been weeks since they had made love; his hand was urgent, slipping her nightgown off, and, without a word, they had wound into each other quickly, as though here, in their bodies, in the quick rise of desire, they would find a place to hide from the world. In the morning, when she awoke, she had hoped that he would mention it, that the silence between them would subside, that they could talk as they always had, but he had retreated back into himself. He whisked forward to the morning. She felt, after eight years of marriage, strangely, a little cheap.

Now she watched him move through the kitchen, briskly making a sandwich, throwing himself into the appearance of order, when they both knew there was none. He played with the children after breakfast, swinging them up around himself for a few minutes; he approached them like a hostage who paid tribute to his captor by doing animal imitations. She was grateful for the chaos of the morning, for the way the children filled the room, like smoke that prevented the parents from seeing each other. Now she watched Dan load Zeb and Rachel onto his back, ride like a horse across the floor, pretend to be a chimp, a lion, stirring them into a froth of excitement. It was almost time to go. "Mommy, ride now!" Zeb shouted.

Serena was rinsing the dishes. She saw Dan on all fours, Zeb jumping up and down. Dan lowered his head in a gesture of parental abdication. His shoulder twitched.

"Mommy, ride the horse!"

Dan slowly stood up and shook out his arms. The children thought this was hilarious, the idea of reducing their parents to workhorse and rider, but they sensed something—that Dan was playing with them out of love but also, perhaps, to avoid her.

"This is just a kids' game," said Dan. "Got to go!" He stood up, grabbed his lunch off the table. "Got to go," he said again. His voice was almost apologetic. He looked at her and stopped.

"What?" she asked.

"Well," he said.

She wondered if he was going to offer her a ride on the horsie and, if so, if this was progress.

"Can you pick up some milk?"

"Okay," she said.

"One percent, not whole. You got whole last time."

"Got it." She paused. "Anything else?"

"No," he said. "We just can't run out of milk." He seemed a bit too determined about this.

"That would be bad," she said.

"Yes," he said. He looked at her, as though embarrassed, like he wanted to add something to this, but he picked up his briefcase. "Bye," he said.

The children rushed to the door like a tide. Serena opened the back door, and they ran into their yard, a square of dirt with grass like thinning hair and one impossibly tall green pine tree. They all drifted toward the tree; it was the one beautiful part of the yard, and its branches reached up like human arms making a plea. Serena began to pick up the pinecones scattered below it, and Zeb and Rachel gathered sticks and began to decorate the tree with them. The neighborhood had once been a pine forest, and the tree was one of the few remnants of it. They stood near the tree and she scanned the other yards, wondering who the other people were around them.

THE THIRD WEEK OF AUGUST was Zeb's first day of kindergarten. The school was a neat, stolid public school with the low-slung beige shabbiness of a community college. The dark hallways held the subdued patriotism and despair of any public institution, the corkboards displayed the cheerful propaganda of school: *Dream and You Will Become! You Can't Achieve Unless You Try!* There was the astringent smell of fresh paint. The children, Tyler and Shakira and Juan and Mary Grace and the others, were escorted by their parents, often startlingly young, to their seats. There was the remarkable spectacle of the populace, with nothing in common except for their occupying the same precise developmental stage, a situation one finds a few times in life: nursing a newborn in a hospital, watching toddlers in a playground, moving into a college dorm. The parents tended to say hello and then shy away from each other as though supremely aware of how their lives had deposited them at different places in terms of economy, happiness, love; they did not know how they had ended up in these places, whom they should thank, or, more frequently, whom they should blame. The senior teacher, a slight, redheaded woman who Serena thought looked about sixteen, stood in front of the classroom, smiling wanly, as though already predicting this blame; her assistant, Miss LaChawn, shook each parent's hand firmly as though welcoming them to a company. The children, not yet sorted or labeled, found seats sized for fairies.

The senior teacher, Miss Donna, was dressed in a business suit, as though borrowing the adornments of the corporate world would defuse this morning of its high emotion. She had an air of embattlement about her, as if she expected the children or parents to stage a coup. The room was filled with elaborate behavior charts, of colored sticks in pockets with the children's names, boxes where children's names would be written if they had not done their homework. Homework? "If you don't turn in your homework, you get a silent lunch!" she exclaimed. The children fidgeted, picked their noses.

"This year we'll learn about insects, weather, and the holidays," she said. "We'll learn about Christmas around the world."

Serena stepped forward to address this last point and then stopped. When the bell rang, she was the only parent left. She felt unable to leave the room. She stood in the corner, clutching Rachel's hand. Miss Donna looked at her with trepidation. "Run along now," she said, smiling. "We'll see you at two thirty!"

Zeb looked up at her with his dark eyes, then he looked down again. Miss LaChawn smiled at him, waiting; Serena squeezed her daughter's hand and ducked out. She lurked around outside the school for a while, standing guard. There was a police car parked at the front of the school. The officer was watching her.

"Any problem, ma'am?" he asked.

"I have a child in there," she said.

He nodded. He was chewing gum and flipping through a copy of *People.*

"Why are you here?" she asked.

"First day of school," he said. "You never know. Always good to have an extra pair of eyes."

"You never know *what*?" she asked, trying to stand upright.

"Nothing," he said. He chewed his gum thoughtfully. "Go home."

THAT NIGHT, SERENA DREAMED ABOUT the rabbi. She was sitting at a pew in the synagogue; the light was dim, and the room was shabby but had, in the antique light, the ashen majesty of a castle. She heard him come up behind her. "Serena," he said. She knew it was him without looking; she was surrounded by the sweet and dark odor of a swamp. "Hold still," he said, and he put his hands on her hair. He began to stroke it; he was trying to braid it. She felt each finger stroke her hair, as though he understood how to touch every cell in her body. His smooth, clean fingers brushed against her scalp. It was almost too much to feel each finger against her skin, as though if one of them pressed too hard she would explode. "Look," he said, and she felt like the inside of a mountain, the foam on a sea, the dampness underneath clouds in the sky. She wanted to be surrounded by and to surround him; his fingers worked carefully until he had finished, occasionally brushing her neck. She had never been touched in this particular way, with this miraculous softness, this attentiveness. "There," he said, in his low, sweet voice. It was as though she were now ready for some important event, and she reached back, touched her neck, her hair, lightly with her fingers, tried to feel the braid there, to see how he had arranged her hair. Her skin was cool, alive, but she could not feel any difference, and when she turned around, he was gone.

She awoke. Her husband slept beside her, and even in his physicality, the soft avocado muscles in his shoulders, the brown skin of his arms, there was the disorienting sense that he was an intruder. She was sweating, her heart was racing, and she felt somehow ashamed; she stumbled out of bed and into the living room. The air conditioning worked badly, and the air was thick as cream on her arms. She opened a window and looked out on the dark street. The scent of the magnolia and honeysuckle filled the room, and, all at once, it held the fragrance of honey. The sweetness of the air saddened her. The trees swayed in the soft blue wind. She held the edge of the windowsill and, slowly, she breathed.

SHE WENT BACK TO THE Temple—a few days after she had had the dream about the rabbi, for she had wanted it to fade—and sat on a wall outside, looking at it. She felt foolish sitting there, for she had never liked going to Temple, but she had a sense that once she walked in, she would be, in some way, forgiven.

She thought of the last conversation she had had with her father. There had been three calls from him that morning. He had wanted to know why she wasn't demanding more money from her employer.

"What are you getting? You're worth more than that paltry sum they're paying you." He was touchingly wounded by the concept of the world's lack of wonder for his children; less touchingly, he planned to correct it.

"I'm actually making a good amount for a speechwriter," she said. She had lied to him for fifteen years, sitting in the gray-lit cubicle at Pepsi, pretending that she was a successful speechwriter. She had, admittedly, written a couple good lines: *Ladies and gentlemen. I submit that you are the most computer-literate generation that has lived in this country. And you are about to become the lucky few who are going to take the next step.* Or: *We do not see the glass half-full. We are going to fill the glass!* Or: *Our finish line is every line we step!*

Her father had thought the fact that she was working for a big corporation meant that she would instantly have money, a lot of money, which would ensure safety through any national crisis, strife, impending war. He liked the fact that she was permitted to carry her boss Earl Morton's credit card, as though this implied her high ranking there; the fact was that she was allowed to hold onto it to occasionally pick up his coffee or a gift for his kids. She had been surprised, ten years before, when she had been hired as an assistant to the speechwriting team, and was elated when her boss, Earl Morton, promoted her soon thereafter. But while they used her blather to inspire the sales force, they were not raising her pay, and while others in her group got lavish promotions, rose to accompany the executives on their journeys to Paris, to conferences in Rome, she did not. Earl Morton used just enough of her material to make her feel she was contributing, raised her pay once, to give her hopes that it could happen again, but otherwise he ignored her efforts. And the time she had sent out her resumes to other companies, the city was sliding into recession, and the opportunities for her skills had dried up.

Her sister Dawn bounded forward, holding fundraisers for Oxfam, for the United Way, to combat global hunger; she posed on red carpets with celebrities, smiling steadily into cameras. How had they become so different? Dawn had absorbed their father's adaptability; Dawn, somehow, knew how to get out and use the world. Serena didn't know what she was doing wrong. Was it the wrong job or the wrong employer? How did anyone know how to create luck? She went in each day and sat at her desk writing impassioned speeches, while Earl Morton used her ideas and didn't pay her more; she sat in her cubicle, imagining that she was somewhere else.

"How much are you making?" he asked, softly; it was a question that came up too often.

"Fifty." She paused, inflating it. "Thousand."

"That's not enough."

"I think it's pretty good." She bit her lip.

"The fools. You should be getting two hundred. Ask," he said, and hung up.

The second call was two hours later. "I have good news," he said. "Dawn met Angelina Jolie. They were raising money for a Ugandan orphanage. She said she was very nice. They may get together with the kids."

"Great, Dad."

His voice always assumed a deep, theatrical pride when he discussed Dawn, as though someone else was listening. "She showed me a picture. Arm in arm. They're flying the orphans out. What are you doing? Did you ask?"

"No."

"By four o'clock, you're asking. One hundred thousand. No less. They're robbing you."

"No."

"What are you waiting for? The clock is ticking—"

"Dad. This is not how it's done."

"I'll call for you—"

"Dad!" Her voice cracked, like a fifteen-year-old's. The vice president of marketing looked over at her and laughed.

"I'm calling," he said, haughtily. "His number is 839-0958."

Amazingly, he had it right. He was good.

"Dad. Let's not talk about me for a sec. Tell me about your trains." Though he was always creating elaborate sets of distant cities, right before he finished his creations, he would dismantle them. "How's Paris?"

"I can't find a good Eiffel Tower."

This she could help with. "I could look online for one . . . is there a type you want?"

"I'll find it. Now ask. Or I'm calling your supervisor. Honey. Believe!"

"Dad, please!" She hung up and then stared at the phone, aghast; she had never hung up on her father before. But she did not call back when he phoned the next time.

The caller ID said his name: Aaron Hirsch. The call had come at 2:00 PM. Later, she pressed the button over and over but could not access the message; he had died at four.

NOW SHE SAT ON A low brick wall that marked the compound of the First Baptist Church of Waring across the street from the Temple, which had been erected in 1902. The building seemed slanted just slightly, and there was a crack in the stucco on the left side. The building had the brushed, antiquated look of a Disneyland castle, as though the stucco on the outside had been redone recently and in haste.

She pushed open the door and walked down the stairs to the office, a tiny room with half-opened cardboard boxes. There was the sour odor of old coffee and copier fluid. The only person in the room was a small, distraught-looking woman who stood before a large Xerox machine, the copier light flashing green repeatedly on her face.

"What do you want?" said the secretary, flatly.

It was not stated with malice, just as a point of order. She was a squat, sharp-eyed woman with a froth of gray hair who had the job of controlling the concrete in an institution that prized the invisible and metaphoric.

"Uh. When does religious school start?" Serena asked.

"You have to join first," said the woman. She handed her a membership form. "Rates are $700 per year."

"Seven *hundred?*"

"We like you to use black ink," said the secretary. "The copier can read it better." She said it wearily, as though her travails with the copier were a long and arduous romance in which she had ruefully adopted the role of appeaser. She handed her that form as though Serena had said yes.

Serena sat down, clutching the form. "I don't know my Hebrew name," she said.

The secretary approached the copier and slapped pieces of paper onto it.

"Make one up. You're number 127. That'll make him happy. We just lost one, Saul Huffenberg. He died last night. Not that he was such a prize. Always thinking I took his check. Meaning stole. I misfiled it. He blamed me. They all did. Kick Georgia! I hear things. I didn't cry when Harold Levitt passed away, or Joanna Schwartzman. I didn't want this job. It was Trey, my husband, who died after twenty-eight years of marriage. I thought I was getting a retirement community in Florida, and instead I get this Xerox machine."

She heard footsteps on the hardwood floor before she saw him; the footsteps sounded like someone running.

"Serena Hirsch?" said Rabbi Golden. "We've been waiting for you."

He had remembered her name. She stood up, as though before a dignitary. He lunged in, grasped her hand, and shook it. He laughed, as though she had said something funny. His grip was fierce, and it felt to Serena like he was not shaking her hand as much as clinging to a rope. "Finally, Georgia!" he said to the secretary, who had returned furiously to Xeroxing. "She's here! What did I say?"

He seemed more pleased with his prediction of her arrival than with her actual presence; he swerved around the office, gathering rubber bands, paper clips. He turned around and looked at Serena. "Come in," he said.

His office was full of half-filled boxes; it looked like a photo gallery. There were photos of the rabbi in military gear and a yarmulke, standing by a tank in Bosnia; on the steps of a synagogue in Akron; shaking hands with Jimmy Carter at a Habitat for Humanity event. He was posed with groups of Jews, military and civilian, by national landmarks: the Eiffel Tower, the Coliseum, the Wailing Wall.

She perched on the edge of the chair in front of his desk. He had the complex innocence of someone who had been included in another's internal life—perhaps many—and seemed unaware of it; he immediately busied himself with shuffling a variety of papers, as though her function was simply to wait. She glanced at his hands; his fingers were slim, and his fingernails were very short and slightly uneven, as though they had been chewed. "Hadassah needs bodies," he said. "Now."

"Excuse me?"

"The Caring Committee needs someone to drive the elderly to services. Darlene Green needs someone to coordinate the Passover candy fundraiser. How about it?"

"I'm sure I can be of use to the Temple," she said, trying to figure out how to avoid these particular activities. She did not want to actually do anything. Now that she was in his office, she just wanted to sit there; she felt safe there, included for no good reason, and she wanted to stay for a moment with him.

"What are your talents?" he asked.

She sat up. "I was, uh, a top speechwriter for Pepsi. In New York—"

Why was she saying this? She stopped.

"Maybe you could write the Temple Bulletin," he said, tapping his pen against his desk.

"Excuse me?"

"You know. Writing the birthdays, whose anniversary it is, what Hadassah did last month, what the religious school's up to."

"Aha."

"It would be good for a journalist! You have expertise."

"Well," she said. "I'm not exactly a journalist—"

"All right, then," he said, shuffling some paper.

He was sitting half out of his chair; his forehead glowed, as though lit by something hot within. He flashed that smile again, that brilliant light.

"You look busy," she said.

"Just with empire-building," he said. "Brick by brick!" He paused. "How are your kids?"

She took a breath. "Fine."

"Your son's the only Jewish kid in his school. Am I right?"

Her stomach tightened. "Yes."

"You want him to belong to something big?" he said. "The Southeast North Carolina Jewish Community Center. I need someone to coordinate it. You can be the president. It will be for everyone. Your son will never feel alone."

She misheard him, for a moment thought that he had said she was alone, and was startled that he had responded to her own sadness so fully; her face got hot, and she looked away, quickly, at his posters of Israel, at the cascade of photos of him.

"Who's she?" she asked, noticing a woman in a photo.

"The first Mrs. Golden."

"First?"

"Series of three," he said. He looked around. "First one. Leah. Other two—where are they—right. Diane. Jeanette. There they are."

She looked at the photos of the three women. They looked ordinary, and there was no discernible pattern among them: a lithe blonde, a heavier redhead, a plain brunette. It was an intriguing display; she wondered who had left whom.

"You still display their photos," she said.

"They were part of my life," he said. "I include anyone who is part of my life. My wives. My soldiers. My congregants. They're all here. Soon I'll have a photo of our congregation. You can be in the photo. We can have a picture of you and me. Serena, who will lead Temple Shalom to the future. You can see yourself up on the rabbi's wall."

He looked right at her, his blue eyes deep, sapphire, and set on her. She was aware of the depth of colors of the room—the clear, lemon glass of the Chai sculpture in the corner, the dark brown of the wood paneling on the walls—which shimmered, almost cold against her skin. She shivered, looking away, as though his eyes could see what she felt.

"You've lost someone," he said softly. "Is that why you're here?"

"Yes," she said. "My father. How did you know?"

"I always do," he said. "I am truly sorry. How long?"

It took her a moment to speak; he had said the word *sorry* beautifully, in a deep, melting voice, in a way that was palpably different from the way others said it. It was not even a matter of being professional—it was as though the rabbi actually fooled himself into experiencing her father's absence, as though anyone's feelings were his own.

"Three months," she said. She clasped her hands; they were shaking. She, who had made some sort of living with her words, was reduced to this, this sensation of muteness. "Tell me something," she said. "What do I do?"

He nodded. He stood up, slowly, regally, and came around the desk. He sat next to her, hands clasped, and said nothing.

She waited.

"Why don't you say anything?" she said.

"At times like this, the Torah takes refuge in silence," said the rabbi.

His phone erupted, shrilly, into the room. He ignored it.

It seemed to be taking him great effort to sit with this level of quiet; one of his feet tapped, insistently, on the floor. "Would you like me to say Kaddish?"

"No," she said.

He nodded as though he understood; he still did not move from beside her but leaned forward on his knees, clasping his hands. He closed his eyes. She noticed a muscle twitch in his shoulder. It seemed the most intimate interaction she had had with another person in weeks; it acknowledged that there was nothing that one could do but sit beside another. There was nothing but the slow, living breath of another human. She listened.

In another few minutes, she stood up. Then so did he. She wondered how long she could have sat there with him.

"Thank you," she said. There was a lightness in her chest.

"We hope to see you soon," he said. He waited until she had stepped into the hallway, and then he turned back to his desk.

Georgia was holding her application. "Seven hundred dollars," said Georgia.

Her heart tumbled. "What?"

"How do you think we keep this place up?" said Georgia. "The electric bill, the flyers, the machine?" She slapped the copier as though it were a horse. "You can also help out a little each week for reduced dues."

"How reduced?"

"Four hundred dollars."

"My god."

The rabbi peered in. "You need an assistant, right, Georgia?"

Georgia shrugged.

"We could use you," he said. "Every morning. Fifteen dollars an hour. Free membership. A deal."

Fifteen dollars an hour? She wanted to laugh but then stopped herself. She couldn't laugh at this point. Her resumes were not being answered. But it was something; it was a way to be here.

"Will be good to have some help," said Georgia. Serena filled in the application.

She walked out into the sunlight. She turned around, and she saw Rabbi Golden through the window, holding his cell phone to his ear and bursting into a torrent of speech. She saw him standing, looking out the window, extending his arm out with emphasis, gazing intently at the street outside, and she wondered what he was looking for.

Chapter Three

DAN SHINE DID NOT WANT to tell anyone this: He was afraid of his wife. He did not want Serena to know that he still watched her in the morning while she slept, that he sometimes put his fingertips on her hair, as though trying to relearn her by the familiar softness of its texture. It still surprised him that they could be married to one another, that they wrestled naked in the darkness and had kissed every rise and crevice of each other's bodies, that he had seen the first child they had created, *they* had made together, the neatest trick in the universe, pushed out of her, two people (well, plus the doctor) in the room and then three, and yet his wife slept, her eyelids quivering, and he could not fathom what she would tell him when she woke up. It seemed that all the rather arbitrary rituals of matrimony—the rings, the shared names, et cetera—were meant to distract you from that fact. Her breath had the sourness of someone he had just met; he had not felt this until she had called him from her office in April. "They're escorting me out," she said, a strange, shocked calm in her voice, as though she had, in some way, been waiting for this, and all he could hear was the fact that she had done something so surprising that he had never, ever predicted it. He had married her partly for this—he had loved the fact that she was transparent.

Now he drove through the streets of Waring, looking for a place he had been thinking about. The Boy Scouts of America was a large building with the high, alpine roof of a roadside Denny's. Dan was on his way to work when he saw it, the sign: PHYSICALLY STRONG, MENTALLY AWAKE, MORALLY STRAIGHT: JOIN THE BSA TODAY! When he saw the sign, Dan thought of his brother Harold, whom his father had taken to Scouts. He saw the two of them heading out the door, Harold crisp and proud in his uniform. "Next," his father had told Dan. "You'll go next." It was just three months before his father left them.

It was twenty minutes before Dan had to be at work. He had time. He got out of the car, smoothed his hands on his suit, and walked inside.

There were many accoutrements of boyhood—they were all inscribed with the universal Boy Scout insignia, like the mark of a great nation. The insignia was there on night lights and tie tacs and crystal boxes; there were desk sets with clocks and rubber wristbands with words like DUTY and DISCIPLINE, and on navy and beige caps, on leather belts, on coffee mugs, on flashlights, on cufflinks, and on socks.

He walked around all of the items emblazoned with the Boy Scouts logo. The store had just opened; he was the only customer there. It seemed comically early for anyone to be purchasing Scout merchandise, but there he was. He glanced at himself in a mirror and was startled; he was old. How had this happened? His skin was riddled with the large pores of an older person, and there were deep lines radiating around his eyes. It was a joke. Annoyingly, it could not be stopped. He tried to peer at himself again, from another angle, but it was even worse. He stepped away from the mirror and turned, with renewed interest, to the Scout items: the neckerchiefs, the visors, the water bottles, the Swiss Army knives, the ponchos, the slingshots, the guidebooks, the pamphlets, the faceless mannequins with arms lifted, trim and crisp in their blue or beige uniforms. He felt like an idiot standing there, but he was captivated, surrounded by the armaments of a childhood that he had not had.

Dan saw a man dressed in a Scout uniform standing near the register. He had never seen a grown man wearing a Scout uniform. The man also wore an expression of purpose. Dan would not have noticed him but for the dignity, the peculiar comfort, with which he wore the child's uniform. The man looked as though he had slipped into the Boy Scout garb at age seven and worn it for the last seven decades. He wore a brown sash covered with a variety of medals. A woman came over to him and touched his arm.

"Forrest," said the woman, "Oakwood Elementary's on the line. They want you to do a Cub Roundup next Friday at six."

"Thanks," the man said, picking up the phone. His brow furrowed. His voice was suddenly practiced and hearty. "Hey there! Forrest Sanders here! Can you get those Cubs in next Wednesday? You got signs? We're Pack 287. No, thank *you*, ma'am, we do appreciate it!" He hung up.

"Next Wednesday?" asked the woman.

"Yep. Can you bring the snacks?"

She sighed briefly and made a note on a pad. Forrest touched her arm with a casual intimacy, and Dan knew that they were married. They appeared to be in agreement. They made it look simple, a commercial demonstrating an agreeable couple. Dan watched them; they seemed to exist in a secret zone from which he had recently been banished.

The old scout's eyes lit on him. Forrest blinked; he seemed to be making a sort of evaluation. Forrest's face swung into a big smile. "Howdy, sir! Looking for something?"

Dan stepped toward the counter.

"Brings back the old days, doesn't it?" asked Forrest. "The badges, the trips . . . where you from, buddy?" He regarded him. "Morocco?"

Dan laughed; then he saw the question was serious. "No. New York. Dan Shine," said Dan, as they shook hands. Forrest's grip was both papery and intent.

"Yankees," he said, a little grimly.

"Well," said Dan.

"I know where you live."

"Excuse me?"

"We're neighbors. You live at 108 Maple Drive. I'm 104. Right next door!"

Dan looked more closely at the man. He had seen someone resembling him puttering around the front yard.

"I'm here working at the Chamber of Commerce," said Dan. "We're putting Waring on the map—"

Dan's career was doing public relations for cities that no one visited, trumpeting the beauties of forgotten lakes, unused hiking trails, empty museums, lonely battlegrounds. Prudrock, Virginia; Shell Run, Georgia; Tall Palms, Florida. They were the towns on the way to the more notable ones—Orlando, Myrtle Beach, Richmond, Atlanta—that wanted a cut of the tourist business, and they hammered on Dan Shine's door.

Waring was like the other overlooked towns he had promoted, and he found them all a little awkward and touching. They all wanted to be visited. They all wanted to be part of people's vacation maps. There was a part of him that loved the yearning in the towns, even the abject desire for attention; the Chamber of Commerce members, the mayors, would shake hands with him and plead for help, and, over and over, he could give it.

"We are already on the map," said Forrest. He gazed at Dan. "So, what brings you to our headquarters this morning?"

"Well," said Dan, wondering himself. "You know, couldn't wait any longer—you know. I, uh, missed the old troop—"

"He old enough for Cubs? Scouts?"

"Who?"

"Your boy."

"Right," said Dan, reddening. Zeb. "Five."

"Old enough," said Forrest. His eyes gleamed; he was a recruiter.

"Of course," said Dan, trying to conceal the fact that he did not know what a Cub was. *He* wanted to wear the uniform; that was what he felt he shared with Forrest.

Forrest's wife was donning a blue vest that said *Welcome to Walmart. May I Help You?* "I'll be back at seven," she said, gloomily.

"Have a great time!" said Forrest. He watched her leave. "Hard worker," he said to Dan. "Best Walmart greeter there is." He paused. "A lot to do to make this pack the best ever. We're all volunteers here. Work for the good of our boys and our country—"

"I could help," said Dan, eagerly.

Forrest blinked. "Sure," he said. "Provide guidance for our young boys. Lead groups in crafts. Just put in an application. Easy. Just pass the background check and you're in." He paused. "Gotta check out you New Yorkers!" He laughed and slapped Dan on the arm.

"Right," said Dan, glad it was not Serena applying. He took the form from Forrest.

"Your son will never forgive you if you don't," said Forrest. "I'll be watching you."

Dan walked through the aisles, then back into the heavy summer air. He felt he had fooled the man, this neighbor; suddenly he was material to be a troop leader. It made him feel giddy, that he had tricked him, because really Dan wanted to be this — a man who could turn into a boy, a man who could belong to the Boy Scouts of America. Any man could belong. It sounded simple and beautiful.

Chapter Four

ZEB DID NOT WANT TO go to school. One week after school started, his reasons were sudden and numerous. He had a headache, then he said he was too tired, then he said his stomach hurt. In the morning, they had to lift him out of bed, where he feigned limpness, and they had to carry him to the breakfast table. He kept his eyes shut as they dressed him, like a rajah or a baby. It was as though each morning over breakfast Zeb was rehearsing all the sadness he would feel in his life.

They all sat, worried, frightened, around the table as he wept. Serena pulled him onto her lap, and they tried, in pained voices, to come up with possible reasons for his anguish. Perhaps it was a mean friend. Did a teacher berate him? Pull a colored stick with his name on it from his file? Did someone steal his lunch? Trip him in the hallway? The morning discussion became a litany of all the ways they themselves had been maligned as children, and Zeb listened with interest, collecting ideas. No. No. No.

Dan sat at the kitchen table and held his son's hand. He had taught himself to walk into a room and say, "Dan Shine. Pleasure to meet you." He had learned how to look into the pupils of his clients' eyes, how to grip their hands a beat longer than they held his, how to clap men on the shoulder, how to touch women lightly on the lower back, to convince them; he had learned how to nod, absently, when clients said something grandiose or laughable, nod just enough so they felt taken seriously. He had walked into the Chamber of Commerce in Waring and burst out, "Let's get this town on the map!" and watched their faces light up.

He had wanted Zeb and Rachel to have no hesitation. He wanted them to know—intuitively, easily—everything he had not known. He had spent too many years watching, envying, trying to catch up. This was something he believed the moment he held Zeb—his tiny, damp, rubbery body—in his palms; he wanted his children to have an easier time than he had.

When Zeb was a baby, when he woke up screaming, Dan sometimes walked him around in the middle of the night, the baby's small, hard head pressed against his throat. Dan was surprised by the monumental burning in his chest. *Please feel this*, he thought; he would love Zeb so thoroughly, so much more than he himself had been loved, that his son would have no fear.

Now Dan could try to do what he did day in and day out; he would mount a campaign.

"You'll have a great day!" Dan announced. "Remember yesterday? Remember Grayson? He gave you his brownie at lunch?"

"No."

"You'll play a great game of tag."

"I'm not going."

"You'll find a great new book. You'll learn to read!"

"No."

Zeb clung with fortitude to his misery; Dan backed away. Serena carried Zeb into the car and strapped him in. Rachel would sometimes shriek with an unfortunate sympathy, and then Serena was rushing up the grass with two children screaming, trying to walk her son into the next stage of his life. The parents marched their children across the gray, trampled grass to deposit them into the flimsy classroom trailer. Zeb was the only one who screamed. The other children filed inside, and the other parents looked at Zeb, bemused and grateful for their own luck. The teacher grabbed Zeb's hand and pulled him in, as though rescuing him from a kidnapper. "Bye!" Miss Donna said brightly. "Have a good day!"

Serena stood outside the classroom, in the parking lot, listening to the screams. The police car was still there, protecting the school against vague and numerous insurgents: the parents' inevitable disappointment in their children, the children's balking at their loss of freedom, the teachers' frustration at their meager pay. The screams subsided a few minutes after she left. She stood, waiting for them to begin again, but they did not. The policeman was watching her.

At the end of school, she stood on the sidewalk, waiting for Zeb to emerge. He skipped out, now calm, inhabited by atstonishing new desires. "I want a new pack of YuGiOh cards," he said, his small face intent. "I want Obelisk the Tormentor."

ONE NIGHT AS THE CHILDREN slept, Dan watched Serena fold laundry in the living room. Dan picked up a pair of socks and began to roll them. He looked at her, and the tension he felt in his jaw now, most of the time, subsided for a moment; he wanted to know what was wrong with Zeb.

"What is happening with Zeb?" he said.

He looked adrift, standing there, wondering about their son. The silence between Serena and Dan had been so weighted and wounding, the fact he was asking for an answer, to anything, made her look up.

"Maybe it's something at the school," she said, carefully. "Maybe his classmates—"

"Maybe his teacher?" he asked. "What's her name—"

"Miss Donna. The CEO of kindergarten."

He laughed. She stopped folding and listened; he had not laughed at anything she'd said in a while.

"Is it her?" he said. "Is she too hard on her product line?" He was restless, folding up the small shirts and tossing them on the sofa. "What do you think? Who do you think is upsetting him?"

They were both afraid. The heater thunked, alarmingly; they stood in this flimsy house that held the odor of dirt; the low-echoing sound reminded her where they were. It felt like nowhere. She wanted to go to him and touch his cheek, the hard, clear slope of it; she wanted him to reach forward and touch her arm, softly, the way he used to, to feel his hand slip gently beneath her shirt. He looked so frightened pacing the room, and she could hear some crumbling in his voice. There was something pure in the knowledge that here was the only other person in the world who bore the same fear that you did about your child. They had shared other things—the idea that the other person said things that seemed infinitely smart and important, the sensation of being asleep together, flesh against flesh, over years, the shudder of sex, the sounds they made into each other's skin during orgasm, the odd understanding that all these pots and pans and utensils were theirs, the perception, over the last decade, of the shift and startling fading of youth, and then this, this emotion that began five years ago. The moment Zeb was born, they were united in love for him but also in this profound and utter fear.

"I wish I knew," she said.

He sat on the couch; she sat next to him. She could sense his restlessness in the way he was tapping his foot, and she put a hand on his leg, gently.

She remembered the day that they had brought Zeb home from the hospital. They had sat in their living room, this unbelievably small, pink person wrapped in a blanket, in her arms, and after the relatives and friends had brought their casseroles and left, when there was finally silence, they remained seated and looked at their son. They were alone, the three of them. Suddenly she was aware of the sound of the city roaring below them, the whine of a wet, gray April New York City morning, the sounds of people going to work, impassive through birth and death. Sitting in this small room with this tiny being, she felt, acutely, the sense that they had all been thrown there, carelessly, that the continents and the oceans clung to the earth by the most fragile gravity, that they could grip this child tightly and he could still fall through their arms. She understood, more fully, her father's fear of what could happen to her. She stared at the boy and she wanted to surround him, and she saw the way Dan's large hand set the blanket around the child's face, the way his hand trembled. She loved him for his helplessness, for the way he, too, was now a prisoner.

She felt him pause for a moment when she put her hand on his leg. They sat for a moment, like this, as though they were testing it. Maybe now they could move on from the standoff between them. Dan looked up at her for a moment, and, as though her face was too bright, like the sun, he jumped up and started walking around the room. They had eight hours before the shrieking began again. She knew that walk, its briskness; he wanted to fix this. Now.

"It's not the teacher. Not the students. Maybe it's something else."

"Like what?"

"What do you say to him?"

They had not begun accusing each other when Zeb was first born; that happened over time, when the endless sleeplessness made their brains feel like cotton, when the children, inexplicably, flew into demonic rages in supermarkets, when she counted to three and no one had any desire to do what she asked, when it became clear they were, as parents, as helpless and sometimes ineffectual as castaways thrown into an ocean on a raft. Someone had to have gotten them into this mess. You. How could happiness feel this bad?

It began then, the occasional moment of blame, the desire to squeeze out of the chaos and find this—an escape. But now she saw something new in his eyes: desperation.

"I tell him, 'Go inside.'"

"What about saying, 'Kindergarten will be fun! You'll be the star!'"

"Like that will make it happen?" she asked.

They wanted their child to walk into school, happy, even carefree, the way other people's children seemed to be—how did the other parents engineer it? He rubbed his hands together the way he did when he was about to make a presentation.

"But why do other kids just walk in?" he asked.

"Maybe they've lived here longer. He's just been here a month."

"Maybe you're saying something that's scaring him," he said.

Something hardened in her. "Me? Why does it have to be me?"

"It has to be something," he said, folding a child's pair of jeans, as if that gesture would reveal some innocence.

"Well, keep thinking," she said. She walked to the other side of the room, annoyed.

SHE REMEMBERED THAT, AT THE beginning, he had seemed devoid of fear. The first time she and Dan walked down the street, she felt like she wanted to capture him, like a butterfly. The longing became wide inside her, like a net. It buoyed her up so she felt like her feet were light on the sidewalk. He walked, but what she loved about him, what she wanted to absorb, was his eagerness, which he had manufactured, somehow, to reside in every part of himself—his large, slender hands, which reached up to gesture through the air when he made a point, which reached forward, gently, to tuck a strand of her hair behind her ear. She saw it in the way he rushed into a restaurant and moved them three times until he had found the right seat. She saw it in the way he pressed the waiter for the best year for the Cabernet. She saw it in the way he took her hand later, the way he leaned in and kissed her. Early on, he seemed to believe their life together was determined; it was a certainty that startled her.

Dan had specialized in creating glossy press packets, strategies for the small cities and regions that had been overlooked, ignored: He dragged out the Museum of Handmade Potholders in Gelman, Virginia, *Two hundred and thirty years ago, colonial women were faced with a question: How to pick up a steaming pot? This museum is the answer.* Or the botanical garden that held the one coconut tree that produced a pink coconut. *Come to Tall Palms, Florida, home of the rare pink coconut tree.* Or simply the state park that no one visited: *Come see the unmarked beauty of Gorges State Park in Georgia!* "I can raise any town's tourist traffic twenty percent," he said, and he was right; they came from small, midsized cities along the Eastern seaboard to get his expertise, to be well-regarded, a destination where strangers wanted to go. During one of their first dinners, he said, "Burgo, South Carolina. What kind of name is Burgo? A bunch of chain stores, a mucky lake. But Burgo is home to a group of the most dedicated troll doll collectors in the country. They had to put together a museum! That led to a revival of the local handmade donut store. No one believes they have anything valuable to offer. They just want Walmart, Target, Old Navy. That's not how they'll bring people in. America. I'm sick of hearing about DisneyWorld; I'm sick of hearing about the Mall of America. They're attention hogs. You have to find what is unique in a town. I can tell them what's worthwhile about themselves. I can help *spread the love.*"

He knew everything about the promotion of small towns, but he did not tell Serena that he felt he was improvising his family. Serena took it for granted that her family, with its flaws, would not vanish. He did not tell her that he felt a cool gratitude blow through him when he opened the door, lugging plastic bags of groceries, to see her sitting at the table, bent over her laptop, casually expecting his arrival; he could not believe it when he crawled into the bed they shared and she was there; he could not believe it when the children ran to him in a tide of sound, their small, fierce arms embracing him. It was gorgeous and disorienting, and in New York he had walked through midtown and had felt like he was part of the world. As a boy, he had not imagined he could ever be part of it.

He remembered when he was five, walking into the parking garage under their building with his brother Harold. He saw his father pressing up against a woman, her long arms wrapped around him, her fingernails sharp and red. Dan remembered the sudden rapid pace of his heart; how his father's knees buckled, as though he'd been shot; how his father turned toward him, how he pushed the woman into the car, how he heard the trilling and awful sound of her laugh; how his father walked toward them, his footsteps ringing through the dank parking garage, and stared at them, his face icy and incomprehensible. Dan believed, at that moment, that anything could happen: Their father could drive off with that woman or, perhaps, kill them.

"You saw nothing," their father said. "Go." Dan barely spoke the whole year he was five; his tongue felt like a wild fish in his mouth. He barely got through words the next year or the next, until his mother, distraught after their father left them, finally noticed and hired a speech therapist for him.

"My first client was in Mississippi," he told her, and laughed. "I remember how slowly I said the name. Perfectly. Mississippi."

There is, in finding your beloved, the belief that this person answers a question that resides in you, a question that you did not know has always lived inside you. Dan answered Serena's question—how can you move through the world while sometimes closing your eyes to what surrounds you? She loved in Dan what seemed to be an endless hopefulness. She liked the way he believed in clichés; he seemed to believe in the goodness of the world even after growing up in a family that wanted to disregard him. It seemed so generous, this eagerness, so fearless in a way. She answered the question for Dan—how can you move through the world while allowing yourself to see everything in other people? He had loved the fact that she could not hide anything about herself and could spend large amounts of time talking about her fears, that she regarded the world with a clarity that he did not; he admired that. He had spent his life trying to find people who would not surprise him at all.

After their wedding, they drove, with the cavalier machismo of the newly married, all night to a flimsy, plastic motel by the highway just off the Delaware Memorial Bridge, a place they had chosen just because they were too tired to move. There was such a glorious naiveté in that drive, that rush in their rental car down I-95, by the rattling trucks, by the people hunched over the steering wheels, for the cool pure hope that, by finding each other, they had fled some basic sadness. They spent their marital night at a truck stop, the long, white beams from the headlights sweeping through the plain room, the trod-on blue carpet, the sharp odor of Lysol, the guttural grinding of the engines outside. She gazed at him, sitting naked against the pine headboard, one knee bent, looking out at the semis lined up in the parking lot, and the headlights fell upon his face so that he looked as though he expected to be swallowed into them, into pure light. She moved toward him, wanting, too, to be brought into his longing. He wanted to fall into her breasts, her thighs, the way she cupped her chin in her hand and peered into the darkness outside as if waiting to see something else come out of it. She loved his hope, and he loved her fear. They fell into each other, grateful for each other's arms and legs and lips and for what they could grab from each other, and they woke to the sour, damp sheets, the pink light of the sun in the shabby room; she looked at him asleep beside her, and she felt that particular brief melting pleasure—she did not want to be anywhere else.

The flaws were already sown, as they are with any union.

....

HE HAD THOUGHT SHE WAS joking when she called to tell him that she had been escorted by security out of her office at Pepsi. He laughed, but when she was silent, he could not speak for two days; he did not trust how he would form the words. He put on a good face for the lawyers; he watched their small savings vanish; then, a few weeks later, when he walked with her out of the lawyers' office, after they had settled with Pepsi and the company had agreed not to press charges, he leaned toward her and asked why she did it.

"I missed my father," she said.

He stared at her. "What do you mean?"

"I wanted money so we could get out of town."

She said this in a normal voice. He picked up a fork and began to twirl it slowly, a simple, ordinary action; he hoped it would keep his hands from trembling. "Out of town? Where?"

"He always told me, 'Be prepared to leave.' We talked about it. It was a kind of bond."

He nodded, quickly, as though to prove he understood. Her hands felt warm, but he was aware of their physicality, the bones in her knuckles, the rubbery tendons under her skin, how delighted he had been when they held hands before and he could not distinguish between her hands and his own. Now he squeezed them for a moment, but then he let go.

"Just then — I missed him so much I could barely breathe."

He closed his eyes; she would think he was saddened, but he was thinking of something else.

The truth was that at his brother Harold's funeral, a few weeks before, he had been unable to feel. He was surrounded by the members of his family, weeping, his father standing back, gray, the first time he'd seen him in years, and Dan felt a hollow sensation in his chest. Harold had been the only other person who had seen their father in the garage, and Dan remembered the rise and fall of his eight-year-old brother's breath, Harold's hand gripping his shoulder, and how they felt like one body walking out of that shadowed garage into the golden light emanating from the lobby's chandelier. The chandelier looked like a cluster of icicles, and they stood beneath its dim burnished light, stunned.

He waited for Harold to do something, and his brother lunged toward the light switch and switched off the chandelier. The lobby darkened; people turned toward them; Harold laughed and switched it on again. They took turns, switching the chandelier on and off, and he loved Harold then, intensely, for this, the way they controlled the lobby, the two of them, until they were sent upstairs.

Serena was looking at him, waiting; he needed to speak quickly. This was why he did not want to feel; it was clearly dangerous.

"Yes," he said.

DAN NOTICED FORREST SANDERS, THE aging Boy Scout, puttering around his garden in the evening. Forrest lifted a hand in greeting but did not have time to talk. Dan wanted to talk to him privately in the Boy Scout office; his desire to belong to something, to be welcomed into this seemingly happy group, felt too precious to reveal across the wire fence. He noticed when Forrest gunned his pickup truck and drove off wearing his Scout uniform: It appeared to be Mondays. The next Monday, Dan waited a few minutes, got into his car, and followed him.

He reached the office at 8:00 AM, when it opened. He stood for a moment, gazing at the building. The sign outside the building said: TODAY'S WORDS: SCOUTS LIVE UP TO THEM! BRAVE CHEERFUL CLEAN REVERENT OBEDIENT

Forrest was restocking Scout navy caps on a shelf. He looked up.

"Howdy, neighbor," he said. "Up early."

"Early to bed, early to rise," said Dan, which was the sort of thing he imagined Forrest might like to hear. He looked around the room; the Scout items, in their outdoorsy innocence, seemed to be mocking him.

"How's your boy?"

"Wanted to see if I could enroll him. And to see if I could apply to be a troop assistant leader. If you need one." He heard himself make this offer and was suddenly afraid that Forrest would turn him down. Forrest grinned as though a lever had been pressed in his head.

"Why not? Come in the back. We'll get you the forms."

Dan followed Forrest to the back of the store. Forrest went to a metal desk surrounded by posters. There was a poster of a Scout leader pinning a badge to a beaming boy. There was a poster with a picture of a desk and large brown shoes. It said: *Father's Office: Where you can fix scraped knees and hurt feelings.*

"Your son will never forget it," he said, gravely. "Those moments when you stand with him, as he receives his badge, as you see the firelight on his face, as you kneel beside your boy, sharpening a stick . . . the moment he looks at you and sees you there, his father. Beside him." He looked at him. "What's your best Scout memory, Mister Dan?"

Dan rubbed his hands on his slacks. "Best memory," he said. He leaned forward. "Hard to choose, Mister, ah, Forrest. Maybe when . . ." He glanced at the posters on the walls. "When my father taught me to make fire. Rubbing the sticks together. In our backyard. That spark."

"I made fire, too," said Forrest. "I remember when a spark flew off the stick and landed on a pile of leaves. It took but a second and everything was ablaze. My poppa fell onto it and rolled. He rolled out that fire with his shoulder. One second and it was out. Let me tell you. True story."

"Sounds like a great man," said Dan; he sensed that Forrest wanted to be admired.

"A giant. I'm telling you." His voice was suddenly fierce. "Don't even try to measure up. Don't even think about it."

"I won't," said Dan, leaning back.

"Good," said Forrest. His eyes were sharp and blue, taking him in. "So. Your boy's going to be thanking you the rest of his life for this, Mr. Dan Shine. He's going to be a good Southern gentleman after we're done with him."

"Let's hope he can make a fire," said Dan. "And put it out with his shoulder."

"Amen," said Forrest.

Chapter Five

....

THREE WEEKS INTO THE SCHOOL session, Zeb made a friend. Serena stood on the patchy wet grass outside his bungalow with her son, who held her hand with a violent, bone-crunching grip until Ryan showed up. Ryan was six years old and almost five feet tall. He was the son of a former football star and already ran with sportsmanlike grace. When Zeb saw this boy, he lit up, beautifully, pink rising from his cheeks to his hairline. It was as though he was trying to recognize himself.

Ryan's mother was a blankly cheerful woman whose main project seemed to be maintaining silence; Ryan was the oldest of four, and she was constantly bent over, stuffing a pacifier into someone's mouth. When Serena offered to have Ryan over, she nodded, abruptly, "Sure. Sure. Take him. Please."

Ryan was a gigantic, garrulous six-year-old whose head was full of numbers and rankings. She listened to his conversation with Zeb in the backseat:

"What's your favorite hockey team?" Ryan asked.

"What's yours?" asked Zeb.

"Oilers. Who's your favorite basketball player?"

There was silence. "Who?" Zeb asked.

"Michael Jordan." He paused. "How fast can you run fifty yards?"

"Five seconds," blurted Zeb.

"I can do three."

Ryan's mind was wrapped around one consuming task: to rank the world and to come out on top. Zeb was smaller, lithe, but less brutally athletic, and his relationship with Ryan's quest for superiority was to try to absorb it. If he could not be Ryan, he could borrow him. Ryan competed in terms of his reading level in school; his height, weight; the statistics of the Oilers, his favorite hockey team; the Braves, his favorite baseball team; the exact size, to the inch, of his father's plasma TV screen. He had a demeanor that switched by the minute, both slap-happy and aggrieved, as though trying to figure out which persona lent him the best advantage. Zeb owned a large and complex collection of YuGiOh cards—that was part of what, it seemed, Ryan liked about him, besides his devotion. "I have 328 YuGiOh cards," Zeb said with a beautiful confidence. "And many power cards."

Ryan was quiet. "I want to see," he said.

How did you pave the world for your child? Perhaps the route was through other children. Serena watched them sit in his room, whispering over the shoebox of cards. Then she watched Ryan toss a football to Zeb outside. Ryan came over and lifted Zeb's arm, and her son beamed. Ryan was now his escort into kindergarten, his guide to the world.

She drove Ryan back to his house. The boys ran inside. Ryan's mother stood, dazed, among the wreckage of the toddlers, one of whom lurched around slurping a can of Diet Coke. The house was modest, dusty, and sparsely furnished except for the living room, where the biggest flat-screen TV Serena had ever seen took over most of a wall. The rest of the room was arranged in homage to this screen. "Ryan's dad is a big football fan," she said. "After church, this is where we live on Sunday." She paused. "And during the week."

Ryan and Zeb bounded into the living room. "Did you see our screen?" asked Ryan. "It's the biggest in Waring." He stood, on tiptoes, trying to touch the top.

When they left, Serena asked her son, "Did you have a good time?"

"Yes." He paused. "He has a big TV."

"He does," she said.

"I know who created the world," Zeb said.

"Who?" she said.

"Jesus," he said.

"No," she said, quickly, "It was the Big Bang. This is proven. There were a lot of gases swirling around, and then they went *bang*, and there were all the planets, then Earth and everything."

"How loud was it?"

"I don't know. Loud." This appeared to be a selling point, so she added, "Really loud."

"Who made it happen?"

Was this the purpose of any theology? To answer the unanswerable from five-year-olds?

"I don't know. It just happened."

He looked out the window. She glanced at the back of his head, the full head of brown curls.

"Maybe Jesus made it happen."

"No," she said, sharply. "Jesus wasn't born then. Besides, he wasn't the son of God. He was — uh, just a man. A very nice man."

"Ryan said his mother would get him ten packs of YuGiOh cards. Now he has more than me. He won six games of kickball and I won zero." His face was slack with envy. "Jesus gave Ryan more YuGiOh cards than me. I want another pack of YuGiOh cards," he said. "I want Obelisk the Tormentor. Then I will be the champion of everyone."

She heard the silvery yearning in his voice, the desire for mastery. "Of course," she said, and reached over and held his hand.

THERE WAS, WHEN A MARRIAGE was good, a deep romance to lying beside a spouse in bed. There was a comfort in the sameness of this body beside you, of knowing the precise softness and hardness of these legs, this cheek, of feeling these arms around you in the dark, of knowing the different ways you could touch each other and the effects it would have, of knowing what worked, what didn't, and what didn't and then did, of knowing that you each remembered the other when you were younger, more beautiful, and could, in some ways, locate that in a way no one else could, of feeling the other's arms around your shoulders, of feeling fingers against skin, of knowing the two of you were located somewhere that seemed, briefly, safe.

And there was, when a marriage was not good, an awareness of the brevity of one's life when lying in bed beside a person who was angry at you. There was the lonely feeling of staring at a naked back, of wanting to reach for the other but being afraid that you would be turned down, of feeling, beside the beloved, the startling sensation of being alone. Serena lay beside Dan and often she could not sleep.

Sometimes she got out of bed, walked around the bluish living room. She sat on the couch and stared into the darkness; sometimes she felt as though she would disappear.

In the morning, she took Zeb to school and Rachel to a playground across the street, and then she headed to the Temple office. She could make calls for the Ladies Concordia Luncheon, or make flyers for the Religious School Picnic, or organize the bus to take a group to see a Chagall exhibit in Raleigh. The office was a place to go; it was a little bit of money. Her mother and sister would laugh at this, her father would have told her to ask for $100 an hour or quit, but no one else was hiring her at the moment, so this was what she would do for now. She sat with Georgia and listened to who had paid their dues and who was late again; she shuffled through the requests mailed in for relatives to be mentioned in the weekly Yahrzeit; she got through her day.

Serena did not want to admit the other reason she was there: She wanted to see the rabbi. It was not a thought she held consciously; it was a thought that shimmered, alive, under her skin. When she got out of her car to enter the synagogue, she was aware of the presence of his dented orange Buick, whether it had gotten there before she did, or not. She measured time by his schedule; she knew that he came in at nine fifteen, that he returned his phone calls the first hour, that he rushed out to visit the ailing at eleven. She attended to the day's work but was aware of his movements in the unknowing but supremely knowing way of planetary bodies, as a planet making a slow orbit around a sun. There was a pleasure in this, this waiting; it gave a shape to her longing.

Once he stopped her and held out his calendar. "Look at all this," he said. "They all want me." At 8:00 AM, he had to go to the hospital to visit Gloria Steinway, who had a broken hip, and Morris Schwartz, in a coma; at 10:00 AM — if Morris had not died, for, if so, the rabbi had to tend to his family — he had Torah study, at noon a meeting with the Ladies Concordia, at 12:30 PM a meeting with the Cemetery Committee to look into a new plot of land to house (in the future) the growing population of aging Jews, at 2:00 PM a meeting with Jennifer Gold and her fiancé, Colin McHenry, a lapsed Catholic, to talk about the road to conversion, at 3:00 PM a meeting with Josh Hofstein to practice the prayers for his Bar Mitzvah, at 4:00 PM a pause to sign birthday cards for everyone with a birthday this month. "Look at this," he said. "Look at all of these clowns. Josh Hofstein. His parents forget to up his dose of Ritalin before he comes in. They want me to speed up his Bar Mitzvah process. Teach him everything in six months. Insta-Mitzvah. What can I say? Can I say no?" He sighed, sharply. "Sadie Straun calls me every night to remind me to pray for her hip. At 2:00 AM sometimes. You wouldn't believe how many calls I get then." When he was not wearing sunglasses, his eyes had deep gray shadows underneath.

She did not tell him that some of the late night calls had been from her. She called the phone company to change the caller ID on her phone to read *Out of Area*. One night, pacing the living room, her breath shallow in her chest, she went to the phone, picked it up, and called the rabbi.

She was perfectly still when he picked up.

"Hello? Hello?"

She barely breathed.

"Morris?" he said.

She said nothing. The moment was full, brimming as a raindrop.

"Morris?" he said. "I can talk to you later." He slammed down the phone.

It was Morris only once. Then it was Audrey. Sadie. Simon. There were apparently many of them bothering the rabbi in the middle of the night. It was as though they were involved in a large and secret conversation. She tried to imagine them all across the county, sitting in the darkness, sad, afraid, ear to the phone, waiting for the rabbi to say something to them.

"Hello," the rabbi said, and this in itself was somehow enough.

SHE PRETENDED TO IGNORE HIM while he bustled around the office, but she was aware of him. He smelled of cheap aftershave, an astringent tonic that had undertones of a swamp — when he walked by, it opened your eyes. His corporeal presence, the way he flew through the office, was startling; she thought of the dazed huskiness of his voice when he said hello in the middle of the night, as though they had woken up together; there was his invisibility, in all of its strangeness and glamour; there was the vivid ghostly presence of his arms in the dark, the way she imagined they would feel if she touched them, the curiously magnificent presence of the imagined over the physical, the living.

Now, here he was, in the office. Her midnight calls embarrassed her in daylight. Perhaps she could ask him a question that would establish her as a person who was more normal, less desperate, than she actually felt. One day, after her son's discussion with Ryan, she knocked on his door; she had something to ask.

"Come in," he called.

His office gleamed with a violet light, as though all the lights were about to go out. Georgia had offered to get him new bulbs, but he refused. He seemed to prefer working in this darkness, as though he liked having others squint to see him. She sat down.

"How did the world begin?" she asked.

He looked up and put down his pen.

"My son thinks Jesus did it," she said. "His friend told him. He's not a good friend, but he's his only friend. He helps him walk into school. I want to know about another version so Zeb can say something back."

The rabbi laughed. It was a beautiful, mocking laugh. "Listen to these words: Let there be light." He sat up in the dimness of his office. "What is better than that? What is light? You don't see it. It reflects off people, things. We don't see it but it's there. Look!" He raised the blinds on his window — the pale sun gilded the air. "Where is it coming from? We're all stardust. It's everywhere, but we don't know it's there." He crossed his arms.

"But who said, 'Let there be light'?" she asked.

"No one said it," he said. "No one was around to see it, so no one really knows what happened. But you know what's here now?"

"What is here now?" she asked.

He blinked. "Look around you," he said. "It's all a miracle. God is in your heart, your face, your arms, in everything you do. Look in the mirror and you see your mother, your father — you carry them everywhere with you; your father lives still in your memory, your heart, Serena." Her throat tightened; again, he acknowledged what she was thinking. "And the parts that are not from your mother and father, the parts you can't identify, they are from God." He was talking faster, walking back and forth. "Listen. I was an orphan. At three years old. I didn't remember my parents' faces. I looked in the mirror and I touched my nose, my cheeks, thinking, *Where did this come from? Who am I?* I was no one. I was floating. You know what? I am God, Serena Hirsch." He paused. "No. That does not sound right—God is me."

He stood, grinning slightly, in the swath of sunlight on the floor. "Well," he said. "More later." He clapped his hands together. "Just tell him this," said the rabbi. "BC, Before the Common Era. But some people also call it Before Christ. Before! That means it didn't come first. The Sunday School teachers at these churches are sometimes confused."

"Okay," she said, relieved for this tactic. "Thanks."

"I want to ask you something," he said, and smiled.

She froze. She tried to analyze his tone.

"We have an opening on the board," he said. "Darlene Braunstein is dropping out."

"Why?"

"They stopped paying their dues. Not even the fifteen dollars a month that they promised. My services are not free. They are, but they are not. Fifteen dollars and he owns a Toyota dealership!"

"They were paying fifteen dollars a month?" she asked, surprised.

"Correction. They were *not* paying fifteen dollars a month. They were—" he caught his breath. "I see it in you! Leadership qualities."

"What do I have to do?"

"Say yes," he said.

SHE RECEIVED A CALL FROM Norman that night. "Would you like to join the board?"

"What do I need to do?"

"Are you alive?" asked Norman.

She paused.

"I heard a breath," said Norman. "Tell me I heard a breath."

"Yes," she said.

"You qualify. Show up tomorrow night. Social Hall, 7:00 PM," he said, and he hung up.

SHE WAS ODDLY HAPPY ABOUT it. The Temple Board. Her announcement to her family that she was going to be part of the Board of Directors of Temple Shalom was met with a huge and crushing indifference. "Does it pay?" Dan asked, a pointless question—he knew it did not. So what? Her father had been enamored of titles; she wanted to tell him this, even if he would not hear. It was a position on the Board of Directors; she would help lead the congregation. It felt like an important, useful thing to do; plus, there was the happy fact that, here, no one knew what she had done.

Betty Blumenthal noticed Serena coming into the meeting. The new girl had, touchingly, outfitted herself in a business suit and came in clutching a clipboard; she looked as though she were walking into a law firm instead of the sweaty and desperate volunteer effort that was the Temple Board. Betty was relieved to see this, for she hoped it distinguished Serena from the others whom she had been working with here—Norman, Tom, Tiffany; none of them held the vision for the Temple that she did. Betty had belonged to the Temple since she was a child, longer than anyone here—she had been a member for fifty-six years. She had been the first female Bat Mitzvah, the first woman president; the Temple had evolved because of her. She was a pioneer. She liked showing people what she had done for the Temple. As a girl, the Temple had prepared her, she thought, for her later achievement—her catering service. Norman, Tom—they had to just think beyond the small and embrace the potential grandness.

Lately, she had lots of ideas for the Temple. Betty spent a great deal of time thinking about the Temple and its future. She thought about it when she sat in her home, trying to become accustomed to the immense silence; it had been six months since her husband had left—suddenly, after thirty-three years of marriage. After Pearl came to her, eight months ago, she had begun compiling the list. Betty wanted to find someone who would understand the gravity of the complaints on it.

Norman Weiss had been at the Temple second to Betty in terms of time. She had grown up here, and he had come here by choice, when he moved from the North after the death of his first wife. He had seen so many others join and drop, leave and die. He was still here. He had run the most sought after pediatric practice in the western part of Long Island; he did not even know why the children had liked him, or why the stocks he had picked had risen. He could never quite trust the good luck that befell him. He wanted to spread it around this place. If people looked around, they would see him everywhere. He had bought back the second Torah when he returned from Israel in 1979. He had paid for the new and elegant gold-plated Eternal Light that hung over the Ark. If the others knew what he had bought for the Temple, they would appreciate him. Now, with the news of his throat, after the doctor had sat down with him and told him what the results of the biopsy could mean, he wanted anyone to walk into Temple Shalom and know that Norman Weiss was the most generous member of the congregation—that he was somehow essential.

Tiffany Stein understood immediately why Serena had dressed in a suit; it was to show respect for the board. This was why Tiffany wore the large golden Star of David, the Chai charms around her neck. Her husband joked that she looked like a Jewish gangster, but she was trying to show the others her respect for the religion and also to convince them that she belonged. Her life as a Jew dated two years and seven months—it had coincided with her marriage to Harvey Stein. She had been recently divorced and had not believed she would ever marry again. Harvey loved her, but he wanted her to be Jewish, and she had never felt particularly attached to her Methodist upbringing, so she studied with Rabbi Moshe Rappaport in Tampa, and then the couple moved here. She came to Temple Shalom a fully certified—or however one would say it—Jew. And then, a year into her membership, she was invited to become a member of the Temple Board. She had cried when she had been asked; she believed they took her seriously.

Serena walked into the Temple basement to join the eleven members of the board hunched around a folding table. The room gave the general impression of a cave. The fluorescent lights let out a long, aching buzz, and there was the undersea gurgle of the coffee machine. Betty Blumenthal was smiling at her.

Rabbi Golden saw her and clapped his hands together. "We're all here," he said. "Let's begin. Tom, do you want to lead the opening prayer?"

Tom sat up, visibly brightening to have been singled out by the rabbi. His face assumed a blank expression that concealed something infinitely more complicated. The board members lowered their heads.

"Dear God," Tom said, lifting his hands. His eyes were closed. "Watch over us tonight as we perform our duty of leading our congregants. Inhabit us with wisdom and the vision to care for all of us, young and old, sick and healthy, those who attend and those who do not. Let the Torah guide us in its wisdom. Amen."

Everyone looked up. Norman reached to snag the last piece of pastry.

"First item on the agenda," said Norman. "We have a new board member. Serena Hirsch. She's been a member of the Temple for five weeks. I say that's long enough!" He paused and looked up, grinning. "Georgia says she does a great job in the office. I say she can represent the youth."

There was quite a bit of business to discuss. Marty Schulman, sixties, board treasurer, a former auto mechanic from Morristown, New Jersey, told them that the organ had come of age and that they needed to choose a birthday for it, as it was turning one hundred this year.

"I put down two thousand dollars as seed money to celebrate the organ's birthday!" announced Norman. "I will research the organ's history and choose the day of its birth."

There was a silence.

"Two thousand?" asked Marty, making a note of this. "No offense, Norman, but why do we need two thousand? The religious school needs money—not to mention financial aid for members—"

"It is rumored that this is the oldest organ in any religious institution of North Carolina," said Norman. "This will bring fame and renown to our Temple. I have even begun organ lessons—"

"Is it *your* birthday, Norman?" asked Betty.

"If you want to donate two thousand dollars," said Marty, "we could get all new books for the religious school, plus actually pay the teachers—"

Norman was annoyed by Marty's attempt to distract him. The organ was what he wanted to fund. The organ people could hear. They could see. They would think of him. "My birthday is November ninth. I will be seventy-nine," said Norman, smiling. "Betty, I can hire you to cater my organ bash, if you're nice to me—"

"Schedule's full up," said Betty. "But thank you."

Serena noticed a tense cheeriness in Betty's voice. They established a task force to create the birthday celebration for the organ. "Our next item," said Tom, "is the new Jewish cemetery."

Serena noticed Rabbi Golden standing slightly apart from the board. His job, he explained, was not to serve on the board, for that was the job of the Temple congregants. He would be available for advice. He was pretending to ignore the workings of the group, but she noticed his reaction to everything that was said. It was almost as though he was having a personal conversation with each member of the board. He rolled his eyes, he smiled briefly, but he mostly wore a floating expression she could not place for a moment, then recognized as disdain.

"The cemetery," said Tom. "I am head of a committee entrusted with creating a new Jewish cemetery for the Jewish residents of Waring. The land was a donation from the Selzer family. We are happy to say that it contains 152 plots, which we will put on sale when we have the area measured and cleared."

The group applauded, which seemed both the right response and not.

"Someone has *got* to call the mortuary to stop doing what they do to the bodies," said Saul.

"What do they do?" asked Serena.

"Put makeup on them!" said Saul. "They started an embalming process on Myron Steinway—without asking."

"Why did they do that?" asked Serena.

Tom tapped his fingers together as though he were trying to be patient. "Because they didn't know the rules for cleaning the body," he said. "Saul, you call them. Our other point of order is the status of non-Jewish spouses in the cemetery. We have, at last count, forty-three families in the Temple who are intermarriages."

Tiffany looked up. "Some of us have converted," she said softly.

"This is about the Christian spouses, Tiffany. Do we want to reserve spots beside their Jewish spouses? Or," he cleared his throat, "should they be buried in a spousal section of the cemetery, specially designated for non-Jews?"

There was a silence as everyone considered the implications of this statement. "You mean segregate them?" asked Tiffany.

"They could have converted," said Norman. "They had every chance to do that. Up to their moment of death. They made that decision not to. I don't want the non-Jewish spouses taking up the hard-won spaces reserved for Jews."

Serena was a little too familiar with the idea of burial to contemplate forcing anyone to bury their beloved anyplace other than where they wanted; she suddenly wondered why she had believed that joining the board was a good idea.

"Plus, we don't have a lot of room in the cemetery," said Norman. "What are the dimensions, Tom?"

"About an acre and a half," said Tom. "It is adjoining the Walmart parking lot."

"Is that where the non-Jewish spouses will go?" asked Tiffany, her voice hardening. "In the Walmart parking lot?"

Serena had had enough. She began to stand up.

"Where are you going?" asked Betty.

"I have to go," said Serena.

"We need your vote," whispered Betty. "Stay."

The general resemblance of the Temple members to her own family, to people she had known, was like looking into a funhouse mirror. Serena's neck was getting warm.

"Why can't it be for anyone who wants to be buried there?" burst Serena.

She stopped, startled by herself. Betty was beaming at her. Norman's face stiffened in alarm.

"Rabbi," said Norman. "Get over here."

Rabbi Golden clicked off his cell phone and walked over, slowly.

"What are the rules for burial in a Jewish cemetery, Rabbi?" Norman asked. "Wouldn't it make sense that the buried would have to be — Jewish?"

"Rabbi, thirty percent of our congregants are intermarried," said Betty. "Isn't the true spirit of religion to be inclusive? To make everyone feel welcome who wants to belong —"

"All I'm asking is a little room for me," Norman said. "All I'm asking —"

"And why wouldn't there be room for you, Norman," said the rabbi, clapping Norman on the back. "You! Norman Weiss! You don't just need a cemetery, you need a statue."

She was surprised by his tone, its light, almost merry quality. He seemed to sense the tension in the room, and he was skating over it, somewhat joyfully.

"Set up a task force," said the rabbi, lightly. "Jewish cemeteries. How to design it for everyone's, um, needs. Norman, Betty, you head it. Vote."

They all voted to establish a task force. The rabbi smiled and stretched, as though he had just come in from a refreshing jog. Serena was impressed with his ability to change the tone of the room; the air had been simmering a moment before and now was calm.

"Thank you, Rabbi," said Norman.

"Meeting adjourned," said Tom.

As they headed out, Betty caught up with her. "See, we need you," she said. "A voice of reason."

THE NEXT DAY, SHE HAD a discussion with Zeb about the concept of BC, and he was eager to try it out on Ryan.

Later in the week, she was driving the two of them home in the car.

"Do you know what BC is?" Zeb asked.

"No," said Ryan.

"The time of earth before Christ was born," said Zeb, sounding pleased to have claimed this era.

"Well, that would be a *very* short time," said Ryan, "because Christ was here first. He invented the world."

Zeb was quiet. "No, he didn't," he said.

"Yes, he *did!*" said Ryan. "He was here before anything! He was here before the *sun!*"

"He was not," Zeb said. "God was. Sorry to say. It started with Let there be light."

"But who said it?" asked Ryan.

"We're made of a star," Serena said, quickly. "All of us. The Big Bang theory. A big star exploded, and here we are."

"I am not," said Ryan. "I'm skin."

"I'm made of star," said Zeb wistfully, holding out his hands and examining them, and then they were home.

Chapter Six

DAN BELIEVED HE HAD THE solution to helping Zeb become part of this community. He walked into the bedroom one night and held up a manual.

"We're doing this," he announced.

The book was titled *Boy Scouts of America: A Guide to Pack Leaders.*

"Zeb can learn to make anything out of anything. He can make a burner out of a tin can. On Eskimo Day, he can make a blubber mitten. He can make a knight helmet out of an ice cream carton."

Serena wanted to join his enthusiasm, but she thought this sounded ill-advised.

"How is that going to help?" she asked.

"I never learned to do any of this. I never belonged to any group. Most people belong to groups."

"That's why we should join the Temple," she said.

Dan flinched. She was intent on this. Her father. It was some tribute to him. It made him jealous, he had to admit, this endless tribute to the great Aaron Hirsch. He had liked Aaron, liked particularly the way his father-in-law grabbed Dan and hugged him, fiercely, when he saw him. Aaron had escaped the worst calamity the Jews had faced, which meant, according to Serena, that they had to honor the religion in some endless celebration of him. Although in Dan's opinion, it seemed the smarter strategy would be to avoid Judaism altogether. It was the one area in which he agreed with his parents. His own parents had been Jewish in name only. They stayed away from the temple with a sense of entitlement—his mother, before the divorce, said they were too successful to need such magic.

And here they were, where people proudly flew Confederate flags on their front porches, where Forrest's first question was about his "affiliation," where he walked into the office and suddenly everyone saw the dark curl of his hair, the olive tone of his skin, and thought he was from Morocco. Forget it. He had always felt separate enough from other people; now it made him shudder, this idea that they would look at him without his saying a word and decide what he was.

"Boy Scouts. It's easy. He fits in. They all do. See? He'll be a Cub, a Tiger, all will be fine."

"I think he's crying because he's afraid," she said.

"He's crying because he wants to be one of them," he said, softly. "How can he be one of them?"

"He is one of them," she said. "He can just be this other thing, too. I mean, there's his heritage," she said. She could not believe she was saying this word, *heritage*, but she was.

"Screw the heritage," he said. "Why do we need it?"

He flinched; he wished he had not said this. But he also wanted Zeb to walk into school proudly, not to be this other thing.

She sat down. She felt as though he were telling her to vanish. It was not that his goals were not noble — he wanted to believe in ease, in the beauty of shared motion, of a group of boys marching down a shiny street all wearing the same uniform. It was a lovely little dream, but it was one that did not sit well for obvious reasons.

"I keep thinking about how my father took Harold to Scouts," said Dan, suddenly. "You should have seen him in his uniform. Age nine. Harold couldn't wait for Boy Scout night. He said maybe I could come when I was older. I watched them walk out the door. I wanted to go."

She was still, listening; it was the first time he had talked about his brother since his death.

"Sometimes, after they left, I went upstairs and put on his old uniforms. They were too big, but I walked around, pant legs dragging, determined to wear them." He paused. "Zeb's not going to have to do that."

She put a hand on his shoulder; a sorrow of being married was that you could not dive through time and comfort the child your spouse had been or, perhaps less noble, fix his troubles before they reached you. Dan's muscle twitched under her hand. He looked at her as though he sensed this desire in her and stepped away.

"I just want to try," he said.

THE NEXT NIGHT, DAN WALKED into the kitchen. He had purchased the beige uniform. It was crisp and fresh with an embroidered badge that said "Troop Leader" on the right side of the chest. The children were delighted with the costume; they applauded.

"I have been approved!" He picked up Zeb and swung him around, as though they had just met after a long separation. "I'm going to help lead your troop. We're going to be part of the Cub Scouts! You're a Tiger Cub!"

Dan put his hands on his hips. Zeb gazed at him with an expression as open as a cup; Serena saw in his face the absolute force of parental authority.

He looked at their son with a hope that went beyond mere parenting and went to the idea of the child as something else: a solution. It was the secret that lurked inside many of these homes. There were the mothers who slunk out of their marital beds to sleep with their toddlers, who dressed identically to their daughters, the fathers who stood in their Boy Scout uniforms, desperate to teach their sons the survival skills that they had never learned. There was a fragile line between giving to a child and appropriating one. That night, Serena saw her husband and son model their new uniforms.

They rehearsed the promise. "I promise to—"

Her son looked at him, hesitant.

"Do my best."

"And obey the laws of the pack."

"Obey laws of the pack."

"Remember the wolf call," Dan said.

They howled.

THE NEXT MORNING, SERENA PICKED up the phone.

"Serena. It's the rabbi," he said. "It's your lucky day." His voice sounded strangely distant and tinny, as though he was shouting, from a great distance, from inside a cave. "We're looking for a new building. Betty and me. The place where all the generations can come together. Unprecedented in Southeast North Carolina. It is your—" he paused, "sacred duty to help us. Plus, don't leave me alone with Betty." He let out a hollow laugh. "I can pick you up in half an hour. Say yes."

Yes. She said yes. This was what she would do.

Serena had never willingly dropped by the Jewish community centers in the cities where she had previously lived—after her Bat Mitzvah, she had had enough—but now she liked the idea of this: creating a castle. It didn't even have to do with Jews, particularly, but with this most ineffable yearning: having a place to belong. The Southeast North Carolina Jewish Community Center would be a three-story building fashioned entirely out of glass. It would contain a baseball field, a swimming pool, a library, a basketball court, a conference room, a ballroom. She imagined the glass windows (bulletproof) stretching floor to ceiling, the building a pure, glowing cube of light. Now the Jews of Waring wouldn't have to drive by the elaborate compounds set up by the churches in town, wondering what went on inside.

The rabbi drove up in a large, dented orange Buick of indeterminate age. "Forgive this," he said. "I'll upgrade when you all give me a raise."

She sat in the back; Betty was in the front. The backseat of his car was not particularly clean. There was a variety of sandwich wrappers on the floor. He seemed to have a democratic and inclusive taste for fast food: McDonald's, Chick-fil-A, Bojangles', Hardee's. The backseat also functioned as a sort of travelling library, with magazines strewn all over it: *Time, Reform Judaism, Tikkun, Muscle and Fitness, Marines.*

They were going to look at three properties. The rabbi drove with a flexible interpretation of stop signs, with a tendency to brake hard for speed bumps and then clatter painfully over them.

"In Atlanta, Jews ask you, 'Where are your people from?' In Charlotte, they ask, 'What bank do you work for?'" said the rabbi.

"Here, they ask, 'Do you attend?'" said Betty.

"Twenty-five last night," said the rabbi. "Up from sixteen the week before."

"Could have been thirty," said Betty. "If you had let me be in charge of the food."

"That's not all that draws people."

"A few dry carrots, stale Chips Ahoy! They don't feel taken care of, Rabbi." She paused. "Bring in some decent rugelach, they will come."

"You can feed them other ways," Rabbi Golden said. "It's not all about food, Betty. Once I went to a service led by a rabbi on a base in Sarajevo, and he was so good, so uplifting, I didn't need to eat. Twelve hours later, I still felt full."

This was an intriguing statement, but he did not elaborate on it.

There were only a few properties within the current budget. They stopped to investigate a plot of pine forest off the interstate, a crumbling mansion with eight bedrooms, an abandoned elementary school dark with mold. The three of them wandered through one building that the rabbi had chattered about excitedly; it was a private school that had recently been foreclosed. It had been damaged in a storm, and there were brown clouds of water damage on the walls. There were ten, fifteen large rooms, and they all smelled as though they were sinking into the earth.

Betty walked through each room, slowly, marking down each bit of damage. The rabbi flew through the rooms like a deer.

"Look at it," he said. "Room to grow. It's perfect!"

"Rabbi," Betty said, looking concerned, "it's a dump."

"Great! We get it cheap!" he said. "Come on! We're this close to signing the Rosens. The father owns the biggest toy store in town. They have five cars!"

"Rabbi," said Betty, softly.

"What's wrong?"

"There are too many rooms," said Betty.

"We'll fill it up," he said.

"With what?" asked Betty.

"With people fat on your rugelach," he said. She stepped back. "Act now. Put down an offer. We can always withdraw."

"The committee has to vote," she said.

"The commit-tee. Hide behind the commit-tee."

He was smiling, a tight smile, but his tone copied Betty's; she reddened.

"Rabbi," Betty said, pressing her clipboard to her chest, "we want to do things right."

He grimaced. "Oh, we," he said. He stepped toward her, then paused and turned away quickly, shooting through the halls. He motioned for

Serena to walk with him. He whispered to her, "The grande dames of the Temple. They don't want to act. All they want are their names on plaques. All they think about is themselves." He was bending toward her conspiratorially as they walked through the moldy building, which smelled so green and bitter that she felt a stinging in her throat. "Serena. Come on. I have to sell this to the board. The future. Let's go. Are you with me?"

She listened to the peculiar shift of his voice—his annoyance at the "grande dames" and then the husky romance of this voice in a room where the walls seemed to be the consistency of flannel. The floors were warped and soft as cardboard; the building, frankly, needed a wrecking ball. The rabbi stopped in the middle of the room and gazed at the sunlight falling onto the rotting wood floor. The sunlight seemed thicker here, a pale, transparent band falling through a hole in the roof, the dirt glinting in its path. The rabbi stepped forward and put his hand into the warm swath of sun. His face was bright and solemn with an extravagant hope. She understood that hope, had felt it when she began her work speechwriting, loved the sensation of wanting to release something significant onto other people—her father had been so certain, so sure of her.

"I love the idea," she said. There was a glint of this new, fresh entity, the future—how she wanted to be part of it. They made their way to the car. Betty was waiting there.

"I think my father would like this," Serena said, though she didn't know if he would have, particularly.

"A man of good taste," the rabbi said. "You see? Do it for him, Serena. Let's get it for him." He stepped back and clasped his hands. "We need this building for everyone," he said. "The dead are not gone. They are not here with us, but they are not gone. Serena," he put his hand on her shoulder, "the Jewish community includes the living and the dead."

SUDDENLY, HE WAS IN A hurry to get back. He bolted to the car and sat there, gunning the engine, which gurgled and spat in an alarming way.

"We have to start somewhere," said Betty, brightly. "We made a good—"

"Start? We're finished," he said. "Don't sit on this. Get up, everyone! Get up!" He was doing about forty-five in a twenty-five-mile-an-hour zone, hunched over the wheel.

"Rabbi, slow," said Betty, pressing her hand against the dashboard.

"Slow! Enough slow. Full speed ahead."

When he stopped for gas, Betty, face damp with sweat, leaned over to whisper, "Listen. I want to tell you. I'm not one to gossip. I'm just saying—" Betty fanned herself with her hand. "We're losing people because of that man."

"What are you talking about?"

"He's going to fill that place with people? Ha! He's going to bankrupt us with his schemes. Who in god's name among us is going to pick up a saw to fix that place? Norman? Open your eyes, Serena, just wait and see."

Serena stared at Betty, her dark maroon lipstick gleaming like new paint. Betty had the same feathered gray haircut as Serena's mother, who lived in Los Angeles along with Serena's sister, Dawn, and had, for no reason she could fathom, been remiss in returning her phone calls. A part of her liked being around Betty, but Betty was different in that she seemed to be the sort of person who rose into the day, perfectly groomed, possessed of unwavering certainty.

The rabbi slid into the driver's seat and Betty stopped. "Speed limit only, Rabbi, or I'm reporting you," she said, trying to make her voice sound light.

"No time to lose," he said, but he seemed to hear a warning in her voice. He slowed down.

The rabbi was stopped at the gate of Betty's community, which was surrounded on all sides by pointed evergreen bushes. It was called Windsor Plantation. The guard halted the rabbi's car with a concerned expression until he saw Betty inside. "Miss Blumenthal," he said, in a tone of respect and bewilderment. The rabbi drove to her house, an enormous brick mansion with a slanted Tudor roof; it looked like it could house a German restaurant.

The rabbi drove out, waving to the guard, who lifted his hand warily at the old Buick. As the rabbi continued on, he smacked his head. "I forgot my sermon!" he said. "I have to finish it. It's at my apartment. Do you mind if I stop on the way?"

She did not mind. She wanted to see where he answered her calls in the middle of the night.

The rabbi rented an apartment in the Sweet Briar luxury complex. *Luxury* was a word loosely used; the apartments looked as though they had risen through some hasty and questionable marriage between developer and city council. They were slapped together with paste and cheap lumber, and there was a vaguely toxic odor of resin in the air. The sounds of heavy metal thumped through the heat. No one appeared to have a job here, or at least not during daylight hours: People were hanging around on porches in an equal-opportunity display of paralysis or unemployment. No one appeared to have heard of the benefits of sunscreen. There was the vigorous and sour smell of beer.

She felt protective of the rabbi in this enclave, striding through the grounds in his suit and pale blue yarmulke, but he seemed supremely unaware of the circus around him. The rabbi stomped toward his apartment past a pale blue swimming pool that was inhabited only by a leathery, heavily tattooed couple floating in the water. Actually, it took Serena a moment to discern that there were two people: They were kissing with exhuberance, and it was not quite clear whether they were having intercourse or not.

He opened his door. She stood at the doorway for a moment. "I'll just be a sec," he said.

She stepped inside. His apartment was dark; rust-colored curtains hanging on a sliding glass door let a faint tangerine tinge of daylight into the room. There was a brown couch, an oval coffee table, some bookshelves. The room looked as though it belonged to a college student, with the feeling of someone's floating on the haphazard froth of his life.

He walked out and closed the door. "It's all right," he said, "until, of course, the board votes me a raise. But the pool is heated. There are lots of screaming fights at all hours." He laughed. "Makes me feel at home."

"Your home was like this?" she asked.

"One of my homes. I had a few." He coughed. "I was an orphan. Parents killed in a car accident. Drunk. Plowed into a truck. I was in the back. They pried me out. I was three."

She let out a breath. "I'm so sorry," she said.

"Look," he said. He flipped open his wallet. "My parents. Jill and Saul Silverman. Or, ha ha, the chauffeurs who almost killed me."

The Silvermans stared out through the plastic. It was a wedding picture, a man who resembled a young Rabbi Golden clutching a dark-haired woman in a white gown.

"I was put in foster care with the Eisenbergs in Tucson. Father managed a Denny's. They thought they wanted kids. They didn't. They wanted things. He had a used Mercedes with a license plate that said *True Love*. Someone had died in it; that's why he got it cheap. When I was seven, they had had enough, and they sent me to the Schwartzes. They took me on and put me in Hebrew school when I was nine."

He told her all of this rapidly, in a somewhat practical, matter-of-fact tone, as though he had simply been purchased at a supermarket. His sorrow floated through the room, disembodied; he did not appear to feel it, but she was acutely aware of its weight. There was no way to comfort him in this, but she placed her hand on his smooth brown arm. The muscle in his forearm twitched; she quickly lifted her hand off.

"What helped you get through all that?" she asked, wondering.

He laughed. "Hebrew school," he said. "The sounds of the words. They sounded like they were spoken in a different universe. I said them, and I felt like myself." He paused. "Listen to these words. Sh'ma Y'srael Adonai Elonaynu Adonai Echad. The Lord is one. I said them without knowing what they meant, and then one day I knew. One. Everything is one. I was part of everything."

"I see," she said. She closed her eyes.

"The Schwartzes couldn't pay for college, so I enlisted. ROTC. I was one of those guys you probably made fun of in high school. I was with the troops in Afghanistan. The first night of Passover, I got the Jews together—there were six of them in five hundred. I had an entire Passover seder shipped in from a Hadassah group in New Jersey.

Charoset packed in ice. They were in shock. It actually got them off their PlayStations. You know? I still remember their names."

He was sweating slightly; he wiped his brow with his sleeve. The chemical smell of chlorine rose off the pool.

"This was what they told me in Hebrew school. God is intangible. You can't run into Him; you can't feel Him. I loved that. He's in all of us."

"What does that mean?" she asked, looking away. He knew she needed to hear this, somehow. She blinked; there were tears in her eyes.

"It means He is whatever you imagine," he said.

Chapter Seven

"WELCOME TO THE NEIGHBORHOOD," HE said.

It was a warm, late-September day, the first cool breath of autumn in the air. She was in the backyard, and the man standing on the other side of the wire fence was talking to her. She had noticed him before; he headed to his backyard every afternoon, armed with one sharp building tool or another, to cut wood and hammer pieces onto the two-story shedlike building that he was constructing in his yard. A Confederate flag fluttered from the shed.

"We haven't met. Forrest Sanders here."

"Serena Hirsch," she said.

"Hi, Miss Serena. Been waiting to meet you since you moved in. I've met your husband. Mister Dan. He's going to help out our pack."

"Aha," she said. "That was you."

"I've been here for thirty-four years. It's been a fine neighborhood. I have one guiding philosophy. I'll be good to you if you're good to me."

"Oh," she said.

"Hiya, son," he said to Zeb. "Come on over." Before she could stop him, Zeb hopped the fence and careened after Forrest. They all headed into the structure in his yard. Zeb was too fast to stop; Serena grabbed Rachel and followed them. The room held various dangerous pieces of machinery for cutting wood — large, vicious blades waiting to slice into plywood, fingers, hands — and on the walls were guns from the Civil War era; daggers; indeterminate rusty devices that looked like they could be used for torture; a poster with the Confederate flag that said, "If you find this offensive, you need a history lesson"; a red, white, and blue banner that proclaimed, "One Nation Under God." There was the general disquieting potential for tetanus and violence. Forrest beamed, as though he had just invited them into a living room furnished with expensive and delicate antiques.

Zeb gazed upon the sharp tools, the machinery, as though they spoke to some desire he had not realized was there. "Let me try!" her son shouted.

"Hon, wait—" she said, watching his face; she saw it was hungry. Forrest strode in between her and Zeb and stood beside him. "Not too close," he said, and he put a piece of wood under the blade; he held his hand over Zeb's and used a lever to cut the wood. Then the wood slid off. "Good job, son," he said. It was such a studied demonstration of neighborliness, of almost professional good cheer, that she let out a breath; perhaps he was, in some way, trying to be nice.

"I had six children," said Forrest. "Raised 'em up in that house. How old do you think I am?"

He seemed to have been waiting to ask this question. He stood, hands on his hips, beside his extensive collection of saws.

"Sixty?" she said, trying to aim lower than she actually thought.

"I am seventy-eight years old," he chortled.

"Good for you," she said, a little tiredly.

"My secret is that I'm resourceful," he said. "You know, a good scout. I see what I need out there, and I don't waste it. I built this," he said, indicating the large shed. "All materials I found on the street. In the dump. This building cost me . . . I'd say twenty-three dollars in nails. Can you believe it?"

She looked at Forrest Sanders, his joy in self-aggrandizement. Was this the only way any human really related to another? She was tired, suddenly, of everyone proclaiming the grandness of their ideas, their particular schemes.

"Can I cut another?" Zeb cried. "Please!"

"Sure, son," said Forrest. "Can practice for your woodworking badge." He guided Zeb to another machine. It seemed they were the same age, their fascination with the murderous tools a happy bond. Forrest chopped off another piece of wood for him. Now the boy had two; he gripped them lovingly.

"Two," she said. "That's enough."

They walked out of the workshop.

"So, where do you folks go to church?" he asked.

"We don't go to church," she said.

"Oh," he said.

"We go to Temple Shalom," she said, cheerfully, watching him. "Have you seen it? Downtown — Seventh Street."

He blinked. "I haven't seen it," he said. "We attend First Baptist. I recommend it. You can walk in anytime. Say Forrest sent you."

And what was this, ultimately? Could it be perceived as nice? Was he saying, 'I like you, and I want you to be in heaven with me'? Or was he saying, 'You are damned, and I will get points for recruiting you'? Or was he saying he would like to say hello to you on Sunday mornings? Or was he saying he wanted to erase you? What?

"On Camellia Street," he said. She knew the building — it had a plaque that said, *We win through tenderness and conquer through kindness.*

"Well!" she said, briskly, clapping her hands. "Time for homework!"

"Don't go," said Forrest. "Wait."

He reached over on his side of the fence and brought out a seedling of a tiny maple tree.

"What is this?" she said.

"One of my seedlings," he said. "My maple. You can plant it in your yard. It will grow. I'm a good neighbor," he said.

"Thank you," she said. She smiled and stepped back over the fence.

FORREST SANDERS, HAVING MADE INITIAL contact, waved to her whenever she walked into her yard. He wanted her children. Forrest Sanders loved children in the showy way people do when they are trying to hide some moral or emotional deficiencies in themselves. It was as though by talking jovially to the children, he was constantly trying to trumpet his innocence; they were the mirror to his better self. He had mastered the art of tricking children with his booming cartoon-like voice, his activities with the saws that held the thrill of violence; Zeb loved crossing the fence into the land of someone else.

"Who wants to see me cut a board in two!"

"Me! Me!" called her son. "We're going to Forrest's shed!" Zeb announced, leaping over the fence, and she leapt over the fence with Rachel as well, and a couple afternoons a week, she found herself lurking in the workshop. "Five minutes," she said to her son, while Forrest stood, brandishing a saw and free-associating his dreams for the neighborhood and his displeasure with people who interfered with the purity of his dream.

"I'll tell you what I want for the neighborhood," said Forrest Sanders. "A group of people who help each other. Watching each other's houses. Having potlucks. Luminaries on the sidewalk at Christmas. Easter egg hunts. Fireworks on the Fourth of July."

Forrest's own house, a small bungalow streaked with mold, was silent. His six children all seemed to have fled; no one ever came by. His wife, Evelyn, who looked to be in her seventies herself, rose at dawn and drove off in the day's first light to Walmart, where she spent the next ten hours on her feet working as a store greeter. She came home, her face gray, and collapsed. Serena heard shouts sometimes through the windows when the wife returned home. "No. I can't," she heard; Forrest yelled back, his words indecipherable. There was a clattering of dishes, then silence again. Serena left her window open so she could hear them; she wanted to keep track of what was going on. She caught an edited history of their grievances: Forrest had run a lawn care business into the ground when his employees had sued him for nonpayment of wages; he had been fired as a manager at Jimbo's when a customer had found rat droppings in his omelet, and Forrest, instead of replacing the food, poured the omelet over the customer's head. "You're no man," Serena heard; "you're a child." On the weekends, Evelyn knelt in the dirt in the front yard, silent, potting pansy after pansy, their garden a voluptuous wave of color, while Forrest hid in his shed, cutting wood, the saws screaming.

Forrest seemed eager to prove his credentials as a decent man bullied by the ignorance of the rest of the world. Serena pretended she wanted to chat while she tried to keep her son from losing his hand in a woodcutter and her daughter from putting her head in a steel vise. Forrest went on about how the other neighbors had let him down.

"Let me tell you about our neighbors. The other neighbors here . . . they're not . . . neighborly. Let me tell you. Number 2287 was renting out a room. You know, it's not zoned for renting. Plus, the guy parked the wrong way every day on the street. I called the city on them and got him out! Number 2298 parked their car facing the wrong way. In the space in front of my house. I called the police! Got him ticketed! Number 2273, right over here, was mad because my creation here went over the line of their property. Two inches. I built it when this was just an abandoned lot. How was I to know? They had a survey done. There was no survey before!" He was not talking to her as much as to the air. His breath smelled like mouthwash, medicinal and sweet. He terrified her. It was time to go.

"Why do you do any of that?" she asked, stepping back.

He looked at her, unblinking. "Listen. One day, their kids were out playing in the front. They were sitting on the roof over the porch. You know how much I love children. I couldn't let that slide. So I called Social Services. I didn't care that Mister Ron was in a custody battle. I have no problem calling the authorities if someone's out of line."

Forrest Sanders stood, a sprightly five-foot-two, and smiled. His two dogs, large, savage-looking Akitas, circled him. "We have to go," she said.

"I want to use the saw," said Zeb.

"You can play with it anytime," said Forrest. "You hear that, son? You can come to see old Forrest anytime. I'm always here."

Her son brightened. Forrest's voice had a monotone edge of pleading in it, which sounded, first, abrasive, but which, upon listening more closely, had a plaintive tone. It seemed that he was used to begging. He stood, armed with his rusty, broken weapons. Serena was aware that the distance between their homes measured about thirty feet.

DAN LIFTED HIS HAND IN greeting to Forrest when he came home. He liked seeing the man standing in his front yard, trimming or pruning one plant or another. "Hello, Mister Dan!" called Forrest. It was a robust, hopeful hello, which seemed particularly intended to welcome him; Dan needed that greeting, he was embarrassed to say, needed a nice word from someone, for it made him feel that they were part of this enterprise, the neighborhood. He admired Forrest's energy; the man seemed never to rest. He was standing by the low wire fence between the properties and was fingering the branches of a camellia bush.

"Ready for the meeting tonight?" asked Forrest.

"Absolutely," said Dan.

"Badge night! One of my favorites," said Forrest. "Wait'll you see their faces. The light in their little eyes. You'll remember. One of the best moments of my life, it's true, getting those badges, giving them . . ."

"Right," said Dan. The fraudulence of his claim of boyhood involvement in Scouts made him feel somehow beholden to Forrest, wanting to prove something to him.

"Yessir," said Forrest. Dan noticed that he was gripping one of the leaves on the camellia bush. Forrest held up a leaf. "Nice camellia bush you got here."

"Oh, that," said Dan. "We haven't really looked at the yard since we got here—too much to take care of right now."

Forrest blanched slightly and said, "Y'all ever thought of pruning this?"

Forrest was stroking the bush as though it were a lion's mane. There were a few glossy green branches extending into Forrest's yard.

"Is something wrong?" asked Dan, alarmed.

Forrest laughed. "Not wrong, just look. *This* is your side. *This* is mine. Do you see how—"

"Sorry. I'll get to it, soon as I—"

"Here. Take these. See what you can do. Be at the meeting at seven." Forrest handed him a large, rusty pair of garden shears and went into his house.

Dan felt slightly admonished; he looked at the bush, clipped a couple branches away, and then, clutching the shears, walked up to the house. He opened the door into the yellow light.

They had already started eating. There was the warm, bready smell of frozen chicken nuggets. It was all the children ever ate. The water heater, stuck in a corner behind a pink sheet, gurgled. Zeb was standing at the table, his palm covered in ketchup. Rachel walked around the room chewing a nugget, a doll pinned under her arm. Serena was rushing around, peeling carrots that the children would certainly ignore.

"Daddy!" yelled Zeb, and he rushed toward him. Dan felt his son and then his daughter bang into his legs. The children came toward him, utterly ignorant of their beauty, seeing some value in him and their mother, both of them stooped and worn in comparison. Why did they love him? Why did they even like him? Their intensity made him grateful and suspicious. The children seemed to sense this and began hurtling around the kitchen.

"Everyone, sit," he said, in what he thought was a stern voice. Neither of them seemed to hear this. Zeb was jumping on the floor. Children did not understand that was their true power: that their parents actually did not know how to make them listen. "Sit!" he said, more sharply. Rachel crawled under the kitchen table and laughed.

"What is going on?" he said, louder.

"I've been trying," said Serena. "It's been a long day." Her face was pale; she looked as though she had been emptied out.

"Everyone, sit!" he shouted. His voice had the absurd tone of pleading. The children regarded him with an expression of bemused judgment.

"Come here," he whispered to them. He held out his hand. He had bought a bag of Hershey Kisses on the way home. That worked. Dan unwrapped a few Hershey Kisses, the children opened their mouths, and he put a chocolate Kiss in each one's mouth. They laughed, delighted. They were like tiny seals.

"What?" said Serena.

"Nothing," he said. "They're enjoying their dinner."

Their tongues were coated with chocolate. Zeb fell onto the floor laughing. Perhaps this was the answer—force chocolate into them? Bribe them?

"Okay, done," he said, grabbing whatever nuggets were left and tossing them into the trash. "Let's get in the uniform!" he called to Zeb.

The children ran off into the other rooms. Serena came over, clutching peeled carrots.

"They weren't finished," she said.

"I thought they were," he said.

She could sense that he was lying; he liked to come in sometimes and side with the children, as though he wanted, briefly, to join their ranks. She stood and ate one of the carrots.

"Hey, Forrest offered us his garden shears. He wanted our camellia bush to stay on our side."

This seemed an odd statement. "He's always trying to give us things," she said. "He likes to make trouble with the neighbors. I think he's weird."

"It was growing onto his side," he said. "We want to make sure it doesn't."

"Well," she said, wondering why he cared.

"He gave us that tree," he said. "He's helping us be part of the Scouts. Who do we know that would just give us a tree? For nothing!"

"I think he's a menace," she said.

"We have to find a way to get along," he said. His forehead was damp with sweat. "Tonight's a big night. Zeb's getting his first achievement badge. We all need to go to the Scout meeting."

The Cub Scout meetings were at the First Baptist Church. It was an enormous compound, the meeting held in a room with a Gothic, Disneyesque quality, with thick, bleary orange stained glass windows and arched stone doors. The boys sat in their crisp navy blue shirts while a few fathers, wearing the long tan shorts of the official leaders, instructed them on the evening's work. There was a general feeling of bemusement about the boys, their antics, their own attempts to be seen. Serena was struck by this: The fathers could not become their children, and the children could not climb out of their small selves to adulthood. There was, at middle age, the concerted desire to stop thinking. The parents were all trying to stop thinking—of the ways in which they'd failed, realized they weren't all that good at their chosen careers, found love lonely and bruising, buried the people who had given them life. There was a lot to try to stop thinking about.

It was Knight Night, and the boys were trying to make armor out of the plastic loops that held together soda cans. The boys and their parents were huddled over long swaths of plastic. The parents had mostly taken over. The spectacle of the parents trying to urge their sons to chop up plastic trash to construct a noble outfit was somehow compelling, but Zeb wanted instead to join a rogue group swiping sugar packets from the church coffee machine and pouring the sugar into their mouths. Most of the parents made halfhearted pleas with the boys to return to the project, and Dan seemed relieved that Zeb was having a good time, so finally the parents finished the plastic armor themselves.

Forrest circled the room like a jovial drill sergeant, offering tips about the best position of the stapler on the plastic rings, and then he saw a boy run out of the kitchen clutching a sugar packet.

"What's going on here?" Forrest said. "We can't have our scouts raiding the church kitchen. Boys! What's going on?"

He looked around at the other parents, who were mostly chatting—his eyes settled on Dan.

"Troop assistant, what are you doing?"

"Sorry," said Dan, reddening. He stood up. "Zeb! Come on—"

"What's one of our words for the week?" Forrest said. "Reverence?"

"Sorry," said Dan. "I didn't—they had just a sugar packet each, right? They were having fun—"

"They are supposed to become knights," said Forrest, "not hoodlums." He crossed his arms.

"Okay, boys!" Dan stood up and clapped his hands. "Everyone! No more sugar! Time to become noble knights!"

At the end of the night, Forrest bestowed the first badges on the scouts, for they had completed the requirements for mastering the details of flag etiquette. Forrest announced each name, and the families duly applauded. Dan watched as Zeb ran up, and Zeb was so excited that he grabbed the badge out of Forrest's hands before Forrest could hand it to him. The crowd laughed.

After, the crowd packed up. Dan was cleaning up the leftover plastic rings. Forrest was chatting with some of the parents. Serena noticed that Forrest was watching Dan; it was a brief, careful glance, as though he was trying to keep track of him.

....

WHEN SERENA ATTENDED THE SECOND meeting of the Board of Directors, Norman led that night's opening prayer. "Let us clear the path of Temple Shalom through the wilderness and to the sunlight of the future," he said. "And let us remember the organ, to turn one hundred in February, and to find a way to give it the accolades it deserves." He then distributed pens that he had had made. Their inscriptions read, *Board of Directors, Temple Shalom, 2002*.

"How nice, Norman," Betty said wryly, looking at it. "What is the occasion for your generosity?"

"I would like to take this opportunity to announce that my biopsy was positive," he said. "I have stage I cancer of the thyroid. I am going in for surgery in two weeks."

There were utterances of sympathy and then silence. Betty blushed, as though her general animosity toward Norman had taken physical form.

Norman sat up, pale; Serena noticed a new weariness in his face. "I have all reason to believe that this will be resolved quickly," he said. "I did have a sudden urge to make some personalized pens. Please enjoy them. Think of me as you write. Now. On to regular business."

Everyone tried to live up to the sobering nature of Norman's announcement and his generous gift of the pens. They discussed the distribution of High Holy Day tickets and the poor water pressure in the kitchen sink. "Rabbi Golden would like to address the third item on tonight's agenda," said Tom Silverman.

Rabbi Golden stood up. He had worn a burgundy suit made of a thin, shiny material; he looked as though he was about to deal cards in a casino.

"I would like to propose the site of a lifetime," the rabbi said. "The old Williams School on Third Avenue. Behold, Temple Board, the glorious future of Waring's Jewish community. A place to walk in, to be welcomed. A place to start some social action, to reach out to the poor. A place to celebrate who you are. A place where no one says, 'You're the first Jew I've ever met!' It's a place—" he stopped and paused, looking at them, and said, "where you can be proud to be yourself."

They all nodded—there was a feeling of purpose in the room. The rabbi was on to something: that the group could actually create this elusive thing, a community; that they could gather lonely people and give them a destination; that the Temple could even do something productive for the poor, heal the world somehow; that finally something useful could be done. Serena sat up, tapping her pencil on the table, ready. Then Rabbi Golden handed out photos he had taken of the moldy school. The photos were shot from across the street so that it was impossible to see the place where the roof was damaged; the photos of the interior were made at such clever angles and in such a pristine light that it occurred to Serena that they could have been doctored.

"All we need is a down payment of one hundred thousand dollars, and the future is ours," said Rabbi Golden.

"Objection," said Betty, "I have been to this quote, unquote, site of a lifetime. These photos do not show the fact that it is a heap of junk."

"Hey!" said Rabbi Golden, clutching the rest of the photos to his heart.

"It's a nice idea," said Betty. "But this site has severe water damage. Mold. Rabbi, it will take months to fix. It will bankrupt us."

"Look at this! Opportunity!," said Rabbi Golden. He peered at a photo he was holding. "We could have a big Temple cleanup day. Everyone bring a scrub brush—"

"But no one's going to *do* that," said Tiffany. "Barely anyone comes to services."

"I like the rabbi's vision," said Norman, tapping his pen on the table. "Big."

"Listen to Norman," said the rabbi. "Hurry! How long are we going to be sitting here? Betty? How *long* do you want to keep sitting on your—" He walked toward her and then changed direction suddenly, as though he had forgotten something in his bag. Serena noticed his hands balling into fists and then releasing, as though he were trying to hold something. She saw Betty and Tiffany exchange glances. He turned back, his face a little damp, and walked up to her. He said, "Serena. You were there. Tell them what they are going to miss."

She did not remember much about the building—mostly its unripe smell and the constant, aggravating sensation that she was about to cough. They had walked together through the rooms, and she, too, could see the Southeast North Carolina Jewish Community Center, could see the ways in which the rooms transformed into shining glass. The rooms could be anything, and she, Serena Hirsch, could help build them. "Now look at that picture," he said, handing her a photo of a clean white room. It could not possibly be of the building they had seen. Was he kidding? Did he simply substitute another photo? Unsettled, she put the photo down.

He wanted more; that was a longing that also billowed within her. He wanted the center to be enormous, and beautiful, and full of people who would gather—reasonable, even loving—all the time. They would open their doors to feed the hungry of Waring, they would tutor the uneducated, they would use themselves to do good. He was not satisfied with the ordinary world. It was what she had felt walking out of Saks a couple months before, those diamonds in the shopping bag, the cool, unrelenting desire for transformation.

"I like it," she decided. "I think it was in that left wing." She was in with him, quickly, before she could stop herself.

"Yes!" the rabbi said. "That's where it was."

"Serena, there was no left wing!" said Betty.

"There were areas we didn't all see," she said. The rabbi nodded at her briefly, stormed to the other side of the table, and placed his hand on Norman's shoulder.

"Who moves to vote?" he said. "Establish this building as the future site of the SENCJCC—"

"Not yet!" said Betty. "It's a toxic dump!"

"It's not a *dump!*" he said, his voice rising. He was talking faster, stepping closer to Betty; he was sweating. "Why can't you just trust me?" he said, his voice rising. "What's the damn problem—why can't—" Then he stopped, turned, and ran out the door. It slammed so hard the building shook.

They all sat around the foldout table in silence.

"Should somebody go after him?" asked Tiffany.

"Why?" asked Betty crisply, making a note.

"Rabbi Golden is a man of strong opinions," said Tom, carefully. "That is not a crime."

"I move that we table this issue until next meeting," said Norman. "And, Betty, I want my pen back."

"But, Norman, it is such a nice pen."

"I want it back."

Betty silently handed it over. Norman scribbled a line on a pad to see if it still worked and then pocketed it. "My surgery is scheduled for a week from Friday," said Norman. "Four days after Rosh Hashanah. Not a sweet New Year. Think of me."

They walked, clutching their pens from Norman, into the night. The rabbi had slipped into the darkness. Betty was striding next to Serena.

"There was no left wing," said Betty. "I didn't miss that. Those were not pictures of that building."

"Maybe there was," Serena said. She was annoyed at Betty now, to question this quality . . . vision. She was seeing it now, the glass community center, a radiant structure rising out of the ruined building. Who cared how they found their way to it? "It's a great idea. It would be a beautiful building. Why can't we just go ahead and do it?"

"We all have our own ideas," said Betty. "My ex-husband was a master at telling me I was crazy when I was sad, or demanding when I was mad. It's taken me years to figure out what is real."

Serena sensed that Betty wanted to say something more, but instead the older woman hugged her, briefly, and got into her car.

ROSH HASHANAH FELL ON OCTOBER 3; Serena told herself it was her duty as a board member to attend services, but somehow she wanted to go. The general and complete ignorance of the entire county to the fact of the Jewish New Year made her determined to attend. She had taken her son out of school at noon to attend the children's Tashlich service. "Doctor's appointment?" the secretary asked.

"It's Rosh Hashanah," Serena said. The secretary looked up.

"What?"

"The Jewish New Year."

The secretary paused and then stamped *Excused* on a slip. "Lashane tov," the secretary said.

"L'shanah tovah?" asked Serena, surprised and touched.

"I had a Jewish friend once," she said. "My best friend, third grade. She was Jewish. I'm not. I consider it—a privilege." She coughed. "We've come a far way, don't ya think? Excused. Have a good day."

At 2:00 PM, the rabbi took a small, ragged band of children to the river for the Tashlich service—they would be writing down things they wanted to change about themselves on (biodegradable) rice paper and releasing it into the river. The parents were wearily trying to throw out suggestions about what the children might want to improve in the coming year, and the children were ignoring them.

"How about not tormenting your brother?" said one mother.

"How about not leaving the room a total mess?" said another.

The children's responses were beautiful in their innocent greed.

"I want long hair," said a tiny girl who had a pixie cut.

"I want a new Nintendo," said a boy, eyeing those of the other boys who had snuck them in. "Red."

They reached the wide gray river in which they would throw their sins. The rank smell of fish, industry, and gasoline rose into the air. The rabbi swooped into the cloud of children. They had all been dressed formally, the girls in princess dresses, the boys in button down shirts; they had no idea why they were here.

"How do any of you feel connected to God?" he asked them. No one had an answer to this. He rubbed his forehead. "Okay. How do you feel when you are connected to people?" he tried.

"Like Siamese twins?" asked one girl.

"God is nice. He made us. You know, Adam and Eve? Duh. So he made us," said another girl.

"He made me?" asked Zeb.

"Okay, how do you feel when a friend's mad at you?" asked the rabbi. "Or how do you feel when you're disconnected?"

"Like, say I'm talking on the phone to someone," said a boy, "and there's a thunderstorm and I'm having an important discussion where I'm telling them some Nintendo cheats, and then suddenly the power goes out and *boom*—"

"Right," said the rabbi, looking a little lost.

They all stood, overlooking the gray river, which swept by, currents cutting through the water like long, graceful sashes.

"Serena," said the rabbi. "Do me a favor. Turn around. Link arms." Suddenly, she was back-to-back with the rabbi, feeling the back of his torso pressing against hers; they were locking elbows. "Okay. Move." He tried to walk forward, and she tried to walk the opposite way; they were frozen, struggling. She felt the ripple of his muscles in his back, the ridge of his spine; it was too close, suddenly. She held her breath, glad she was linked with him, and afraid the others would see her gladness. The kids shrieked, laughing.

"Watch!" The rabbi called. "Can we move this way? What happens? Are we stuck?"

"Jump!"

"Move to the side!"

They tried to follow the kids' orders; they were really stuck. He was strong. So was she. Suddenly it occurred to her that he had somehow chosen her, that he also wanted to feel this confinement.

But he was clever; he changed the subject. "If you feel too many rules from God, if you feel too stifled, if you can't really be your best self, then you and God are like this."

"Kids," she said. "Watch what happens now."

She slipped her arms out from his and jumped free; they both fell forward. "Kids!" said the rabbi. "Use your best selves. You can get rid of your bad twin and find your good self. Now let's think about what we want to throw into the river." He started passing out pencils and rice paper. She stood, a little far away, looking at the children, reaching up and grabbing the pencils, writing down the things they wanted to throw away.

THAT NIGHT, AROUND 7:30 PM, there was a knock at the door; it was Brittany, a fifteen-year-old who lived across the street. Dan held the door open, puzzled.

"Yes?" asked Dan.

"I'm scheduled to babysit," said Brittany.

"For us?"

"Come on in," Serena said to the babysitter. Serena was wearing a black silk dress and coat as though they were going out.

"Where are *you* going?" asked Dan.

Serena looked at him. "I thought we might go to services," she announced brightly.

"We?" he asked.

"It's Rosh Hashanah," she said.

"So?"

"Why don't you come with me —"

He rubbed his face. "Come on, Serena," he said. "I'm busy. No."

He was surprised that she seemed to dim at this. "Please," she said.

They stood in the doorway, the babysitter shifting from foot to foot, smiling, but also aghast. She had signed on for her $5 an hour, and she did not want to see this display of marital discord. Serena wanted him to come. It was Rosh Hashanah, the start of the New Year — there was a logic to that, in a way. They could just decide it was time to start over. Perhaps they could pretend that they were as they had been, as they thought they would always be.

Dan looked away. He did not want to go; he did not want to admit to her how he dreaded the feeling he would get in the Temple. It made no sense to him, first off, the muttering in Hebrew, the marching around with the Torah, the standing up and sitting down for no apparent reason. But mostly he feared the sensation that others were part of this, of this and of everything, and he never would be, and, secretly, that his wife was solidly part of this, had figured all this out. It was one reason that he had been drawn to her — her assumption that she belonged in her family, that she belonged here, even at Pepsi, even if they didn't appreciate her — but marrying her didn't mean that he absorbed this quality; he was merely spectator to it. Now he felt left out and sometimes, embarrassingly, competitive. How could he feel competitive over the Temple, of all places! It was not a feeling one was supposed to have in a marriage, he thought. But there it was.

"It's the New Year," she said, and she seemed so intent, and she sparkled in a way that caught at his heart, for she looked beautiful and nostalgic, and the babysitter stood there, polite, shaming them into an outing. He threw on a jacket and they left.

They rode together in the car. It felt strange to be going somewhere formally dressed, as though they had been hurled into civility. She had purchased this dress seven years ago, off the sales rack at Macy's, a black sheath with glimmering threads thrown in. Dan was wearing the navy jacket he had always worn to corporate parties. The radiant purple dusk spread out across the city; it was as though they were impersonating themselves in an earlier life.

The car was quiet. "You look nice," he said, as though they were on a first date. Perhaps, in a way, they were.

"You, too," she said.

Serena wanted to sit in a pew near the front. Dan turned this down, as he felt his reluctance was naked, so they settled on the fourth row from the front. The day's dying light fell through the stained glass windows, creating radiant colored squares on the floor. The congregants stepped through the translucent light gently, as though through pools of water. There was the melodic engine of the almost hundred-year-old organ rolling, heavy, through the room.

Dan watched her expression when the rabbi strode up onto the pulpit. He was wearing an almost blinding white suit, the sort of suit that advertised purity so slavishly it seemed ridiculous, fraudulent. Clearly, he had consulted no one on this. He noticed that Serena was watching the rabbi intently. The light through the windows was darkening. The rabbi looked at the congregation arranged in front of him, his face suddenly, brilliantly, awake.

The rabbi stood on the bima. He gazed out at all of them. Showtime.

"L'shanah tovah," he said.

When he turned to face the Ark, he lifted his arms to indicate that the congregants were to rise, his arms coming up with a slow stateliness; it seemed that wings were rising from his back. It was a gesture of the deepest confidence, that he knew the others would follow him, but, more, that he believed that his role was to be followed.

He turned and, clutching the Torah by its wooden handles, held the scroll up before all of them. It was heavy, but his arms did not tremble. The gesture threw her back, fully, to her childhood, and her eyes filled with tears. She had sat with her father, watching the rabbi of their Los Angeles temple lift the Torah; that moment was gone, vanished — there was no way to recover it. The service, the sight of the sanctuary, was a trick; it was a way to remember him, and it was like a hall of mirrors, distorting the air. She missed her mother and sister, who lived in Los Angeles and whom she had not seen since the funeral. She touched her eyes, embarrassed. Dan noticed her crying. He put his hand in his pocket and lifted out a Kleenex. She took it.

Serena watched Rabbi Golden lower the Torah onto the lectern. She watched his hands grip the brown handles, watched his arms tense under his suit. "This is our covenant," he said. "This is what has bound us for five thousand years."

The rabbi gazed out at the congregants all standing in the sanctuary; it was as though he understood all of them.

Chapter Eight

....

SHE TRIED TO KEEP HER children from going into Forrest Sanders's yard, but it felt impossible; the three-foot-high chain-link fence could be hopped in a moment. And Forrest wanted to talk to them. After his initial enthusiasm, his attempt to advertise himself as a decent man, Forrest seemed intent on one activity: lending her things. He kept an eye on their backyard to gauge what she needed. When her yard filled with leaves, he loaned her his rake and green plastic tub; when a branch was dangling off her azalea bush, he showed her how to use his garden clippers to take it off. She took the sharp things offered over the fence, thanked him, returned the tools, and hoped that would comfort him. She did not understand why he constantly tried to lend her things until she realized he wanted to incur a debt.

One afternoon, he waved to her. "Can you spare a moment?"

He was artfully posed with a hammer against his hip.

"Well, Miss Serena," he said. "I've been wanting to ask you a favor." He pointed to the tall, grand pine standing in her yard. "Take a look at your tree."

She looked up at the pine tree towering into the blue sky. It reminded her of a tree that had grown in her parents' backyard—that was not a pine, but a tall, strange palm that swung over their own small stucco house—that tree, too, had been startling in its grandeur. Sometimes now, in the evenings, she came outside and sat under the pine tree, looked up at the way its branches stretched out against the dark sky. They had a small, broken house, but that tree rose and rose out of the sparse grass of the yard, perhaps fifty feet high into the white morning mist.

"What about it?" she asked.

"It's leaning. During a hurricane, it could fall on my shed. Smash it."

She stepped back and examined the tree, its green needles hard against the bright blue air. The tree shot up into the sky, perfectly straight.

"I don't think it will," she said, slowly.

"You need to cut it down," he said.

An insistence in his voice, an assumption that she should listen and obey him, made her mind slam shut. She tried the folksy, wheedling tone he had assumed a moment before. "Mister Forrest, sir, it looks like a nice tree to me."

He was not fooled. In fact, this attempt at banter galled him; he knew what she was doing.

"I don't want to say this, but—" he laughed.

"What?"

"Y'all want to destroy my shed," he said, in an almost cheerful voice.

"No, I don't," she said. "I really don't."

The air suddenly was perfectly clear, the sky a deeper, closer blue, and Forrest himself so precise and white-haired he resembled a doll. Her heart began to march.

"Why," she asked, trembling, "would I want to destroy your shed?"

"You tell me," he said. "*You* tell *me* why you don't want to think about me. This is my shed. I worked on it for months. Years. It cost me almost nothing. You don't know what the hurricanes do here."

She took a deep breath. She walked over to the tree and banged it with her hand. Then she faced him. "I'm not cutting down the tree," she said.

He blinked and stepped back from the fence. She was aware that it was a flimsy wire fence, no protection against anything.

"Well," he said, and reddened. "Well, Miss Serena. Are you sure about this?"

She paused. "I'm not cutting it down," she said.

"Then I'm sorry to say that you just lost the best neighbor you ever had."

These words had the ringing, solemn tone of a statement that had been made before.

"What?" she asked, stepping back.

"You don't care about my property. You want to see it smashed. Ruined! Gone!"

"I do not!" she said. Her hands were shaking; he saw this and smiled.

"Then cut it down," he said. He looked more animated than she had ever seen him. It was as though he had deciphered the nature of humanity—that everyone was out to take down his shed, and then him—and he had finally found some clarity! "Until you can do that, stay away. Keep the kids off my property." He snapped his fingers at his dogs. They looked up and barked, as though they were aware of a sound neither of the humans could hear.

"Come on, boys," he said, sweetly, to his dogs. He turned around and went into his house.

SHE HELD THE DISCUSSION IN her head the rest of the day, reliving it over and over, a banal, hopeless type of rehearsing—it was as though Forrest would utter something new in it the fifteenth time she went over it, or she would have figured out the right thing to say, or she would shoot him down with the perfectly phrased retort that would make him step back and say, "Yes, what was I thinking? Leave the tree alone." Perhaps she could have been calm or jokey or beguiling or authoritative or anything else, but she could not decide upon any other way she could have responded. She didn't know what made him so mad about it. But she did not want to cut down the tree.

She knew what Dan would say when she told him, and so announced it quickly, almost blasé, when he was brushing his teeth—by the way, Forrest had told her they were not on speaking terms and they were supposed to stay off his property.

He dropped his toothbrush. "No. He didn't say that."

"Yes, in fact, he did."

"Was he kidding?" he asked.

"No," she said.

He blinked; he looked bereft for a moment, as though his careful idea that everything could work out, everything could be simple, was ruined.

"What did you do?" he asked. "Maybe he's right. Maybe it could fall on them and then—"

"The tree's fine. Look at it. Something else is going on. I don't know what—"

"I'll tell him we'll think about it."

"But we're not going to—"

He stood, staring at the curved porcelain basin. He seemed to be contemplating something deep; then he said, in a flat, knifelike voice, "What if this gets Zeb kicked out of Scouts?"

"Why should this get us kicked out of anything?"

"This is not how you deal with people," he said crisply. "We have to fix this now."

The next morning, he went to talk to Forrest. He came back a little pale. "He said he made a nice and friendly request and that down here people think about each other."

"Really? They do that? Cut down trees for no reason?"

They looked at each other.

"We need to do the right thing," he said.

The houses sat side by side across the wire fence; she told the children that they should keep a distance from Forrest. "Let's not go over to his house anymore," she said. "He's in a bad, uh, mood." They had seen the discussion, the fragility of the adult masks in the chilled fall afternoon; now they were interested in knowing the precise boundaries of engagement.

"But he's nice at Scouts," said Zeb.

"Well, I bet he will be nice there. Just be careful."

They were sitting at the kitchen table, eating breakfast cereal, and she was telling them that another human was dangerous; they nodded and absorbed this, and it was suddenly deeply sad.

Whenever Serena went into the backyard, whenever she backed the car out of the driveway, the two muscular, wolflike Akitas began to bark. They pressed up against the low wire fence, their mouths wet and black. "Shh," she said to the dogs, trying to soothe them, even once secretly slipping them a piece of bologna, but they continued, and she saw Forrest Sanders in his shed, chopping some wood, letting them.

She looked up articles on the Internet — *How do you tell if a tree might fall?* She printed out photos of trees that appeared dangerous, none of which resembled the pine, and left them in his mailbox. Zeb tried to make friends with the dogs. "Here, boy," he said, approaching them, absurdly, beautifully hopeful. He tried to whistle, a low, moist breath. The dogs stood up, paws on the fence, their barks puncturing the air. Rachel ran away from them, her hands over her ears. Worried they would hurt her flowers, the girl spread Kleenex over some of them so that they would not hear.

At the Scout meetings, Forrest's enthusiasm for the other scouts' achievements seemed to be knocked up a notch. "Would you all believe that Carson McNulty collected eighteen different leaves on his nature walk last week! Let's all give him a big hand!" She believed that he was taking a circuitous route in the church social hall, walking a wide circle away from them, with Dan following him, carrying various ceremonial doodads. During a meeting, Forrest posed in his beige uniform, pale and worn out over the years but lavishly adorned with badges. He walked grandly through the expanse of boys, as though they were awaiting his opinions on their projects, badge progress, necktie knots. In actuality, Serena noticed, the boys and fathers did not really talk to him; they nodded and smiled when he came by, and occasionally asked him questions from the Cub Handbook, but they were all involved in their own projects, and the conversations quickly melted away. Forrest was trying — he thrust himself into conversation after conversation, with plenty of backslapping and high-fives to the boys. She watched him circle the room, and in his walk there was the floating intensity of a hawk, a bright hunger in his eyes. He smiled at Zeb at the meetings, and he gave extensive instructions to Dan, who was helping to organize the loud, chaotic pack of boys, but Forrest did not acknowledge her at all.

....

IT WAS A PURE, GLORIOUS day in mid-October, and Serena watched Zeb and Rachel toss rocks toward the pine tree. Each rock flew through the air and chipped off a small piece of bark. They had the cavalier, crooked aim of small children. The rocks were small. They flew toward the tree. One. Two.

A rock flew over to Forrest's side of the fence.

The three of them stood and watched the rock slowly arc through the air.

"Oh, no," Rachel said with an utter calm, as though she had predicted this all along.

The rock flew through the blue sky and fell into Forrest's bed of Gerbera daisies.

Serena hoped, for a moment, that he had not seen anything, but that was absurd. That was his job, to notice and address injury done to him. He was hammering away at his shed but had taken note of everything—the way the child threw the rock, the speed with which it tumbled through the air, the spot where it landed. She thought she heard him cough, and then she thought she saw him nod at the dogs.

Did he nod at the dogs? Or did he just look at them? What did they sense from him, so that they felt suddenly unrestrained? In a single, floating leap, they were over the fence.

SERENA COULD SMELL THE DOGS. They smelled dark and wet, and one of them bounded toward Zeb. She heard a high-pitched shriek from Zeb; he was trying to run, a spastic crooked run, and the dog ran around him, its tail whipping against his arm, and then ran off. She lunged toward Zeb, grabbed him by the hand, and hoisted Rachel under her armpit, like a football, and ran to the house. The dogs were barking, as though they were shouting, the sound so loud she could feel it vibrate in her throat, and she felt wetness, a dog's tongue, on the backs of her legs. "Stop," she called to them, but they did not. She heard the guttural growling in their throats, and Forrest did not call them. She and the children were at the door. She grabbed the knob, her hand shaking, pushed the children inside, and shut the door. Forrest stood there, watching.

"Get your dogs!" she screamed.

He whistled. The dogs turned and leapt back onto his side of the yard.

She closed the door to the house, the children inside, and ran down to the fence. "What the hell was that?" she said.

"They were playing."

"They were not."

"How's Zeb going to get his animal care badge if you don't understand dogs?" He had his arm around a dog and was scratching its furry neck. He had a talent for making himself resemble a Hallmark portrait. "Man's best friend. Dogs play."

"No. No." She was shaking. "Tell the truth, Forrest. You wanted them to scare us."

The dogs' tails bounced in the air; suddenly, they were transformed back into pets. She stepped away from the fence. He was petting his dog. It whimpered and rubbed against him.

"Dogs play," he said, and went into his house.

SHE RETURNED, TREMBLING, TO HER house. The children's faces were damp with fear and a kind of outraged excitement. "They would have chewed off our legs first," said Zeb. "After they ate them, they would eat our arms."

"They would eat our heads," said his sister.

They looked at her to check the validity of these statements; Serena took a breath. She cleared her throat a few times, pretending to cough, as she was afraid to hear how she would sound, and when she spoke, it was a cool voice, utterly false. "Enough," said Serena. "We're fine. Let's go — get dinner. Let's get out."

She drove down the streets until the children shrieked with joy at the radiant yellow sign for Golden Corral's all-you-can-eat buffet. The expanse of food, the pretense of order, was calming. Everyone here was just interested in shoveling as much fried okra or pot roast or corn bread as possible onto a plate. She was grateful for it, the feeling of distraction and abundance. Mostly, the children made repeated visits to the dessert buffet. The desserts were set out on glass shelves, lit up: brownies with icing dark and artificial as an oil slick, whipped cream rising in buoyant waves off the banana pudding.

"I want to come here for my birthday," said Rachel, "and I want them to call my name."

She looked at them, scooping up whipped cream with their spoons, their faces dazed with the pleasure of sugar. She remembered the moment she and Dan had brought Zeb into their home, and then Rachel, the understanding that they were to create the world for them, and here they had ended up in this strange town living beside this awful man. They had ended up here because of her sorrow, her impulses, and she did not know how to begin to solve this. They kept eating. The children finished one round of desserts, had another, and returned to discussing the chase, trying to figure out what had happened, until they were all suddenly exhausted.

Later, when she was putting them to bed, Zeb threw his thin arms around her neck. "I want to move," he said.

DAN WALKED UP TO THE house at eight, his jacket clinging to him, his shirt damp; he had been in two meetings in a row and had not had a chance to eat. He was hungry. The house was silent, the lights off, as though no one was inside it. When he opened the door, the room was silent; the children were already asleep. Serena was sitting at the kitchen table, the light gray in the room.

"How's it going?" he asked, taking his jacket off and hanging it on a chair.

She looked at him; her face was animated, intent. She had been waiting.

"He sent the dogs to attack."

He had hoped merely for a plate of spaghetti.

"What?"

"We were playing, and a rock accidentally fell into Forrest's yard. They were barking at us for days and then —"

He sank into the chair beside her. It was cheap, and the metal rods dug into his back.

"Forrest? What?"

"They leapt over the fence. They chased us to the house —"

"What?" The words felt disembodied, unnatural, in the room. He heard himself asking, "Did the dogs bite anyone?"

"Almost," she said. "They wanted to —"

He stared at her. The dogs. What was she talking about? He had not heard them barking. He got up suddenly and went into the bedroom to look at the children; they were asleep, their faces smooth, untroubled — nothing appeared to be wrong. Something in his chest contracted; he could not take on another strain. Was she making this up? She had lied to him that week when she was buying the jewelry, lied for the first time in their marriage — that lie had disoriented him so that he had forgotten to attend Rachel's sing-along at the preschool, forgotten to pick up Zeb at a child's house; he couldn't keep track of anything, suddenly. Couldn't she see how her actions had destroyed his sense of the structure of the world? Now she appeared to be herself, sitting in the dark light of the kitchen, but could Forrest really have sent dogs over the fence? Anxiety coursed through him, staticky, and he could not help thinking what this would mean for them, for him. What would that mean for them, now that they had tried to finally set up a home?

He swallowed and said the one thing that would make sense to him.

"It was a mistake."

She was still, looking at him.

"Dan. You're not looking. It happened. It's true —"

There were so many ways one could look at the world. You could look at the waterfront at Wayne Beach, Virginia, and say it was a ruined old port, or you could say it was beautiful — perhaps authentic. You could walk into the dusty rooms of Mrs. Donna Hayworth's McDonald's Happy Meal collection in Davenport, Iowa, and see it as a collection of commercial trash, or you could see it as a careful preservation of items she loved. You could look at your mother, tearful whenever you opened your mouth, and think she was disappointed by you, or you could pretend she was thinking of something else. You could believe your father was fleeing you when his car roared out of the garage with the woman who was not your mother, or you could believe he was maybe giving a stranger a ride home. You could decide whatever you wanted; that gave you power. Dan stood up. The dogs were just pets, and you could get along with anyone. He wanted to believe this.

"I'll test it," he said.

Serena's eyelids flickered. "What kind of test?"

"Maybe they were trying to play," said Dan. "I'm going to test it. I'll go see what they do." He opened the door into the cool night.

He stepped into the darkness, among the softly rotting smell of the white onion flowers that appeared on the dry grass like foam on an ocean. Dried sycamore leaves roared under his feet. The dogs trotted on the other side of the fence; they were pale, muscular. Their tails lifted, and their breath rumbled. Dan's feet were light. He marched over to the fence. "Here," said Dan, snapping his fingers. The dogs stood on their hind legs, watchful, their red tongues slick. He stepped closer.

Forrest's house sat perhaps twenty feet from him; the kitchen lights burned yellow inside. Were Forrest and his wife leaning toward each other, having a similar discussion about them? What did Forrest and Evelyn see in the way Dan and Serena looked at each other, the air between their faces? Suddenly, he wanted an answer. The dogs stood, muscular tails afloat. Dan took a deep breath. "Miss. Is. Sipp. I," he whispered, slowly.

The dogs waited, muscles twitching beneath their fur.

Dan stood, a tired, worn man in his office suit, arms dangling, while the animals stared at him with sweet, glassy eyes. Something unbuckled in his chest. He reached over the fence and put his hand on the bigger dog's head. It whimpered, and he felt its skull press up into his hand. The dog looked at him, tail wagging.

"Be good," he whispered to the dogs.

Chapter Nine

SERENA WATCHED THE RABBI MOVE around the office; he wandered in and out of rooms, as if about to utter a proclamation, then he retreated back to his office. When his door was shut, she heard him on his phone, talking rapidly. He was making plans.

He opened the door.

"Serena Hirsch. How are you?"

"All right," she said, though she was not.

"Come on in!" His voice was suddenly hearty, friendly.

She walked in, now wary, and sat at the chair by his desk.

"I want to ask you," he said, leaning forward at his desk. His hands were carefully clasped. He inhabited a posture, an expression, that was perfect in its erasure of him and in its acknowledgement of the listener's anguish; he was a cup ready to receive what she would pour into it. "You're upset about something. I've noticed, Serena," he said. "The last week."

He had a talent for looking at the person in front of him as though he was surprised by their originality and goodness.

"You know," she said. "What I told you. My father—"

"Of course," he said. "But there's something more." He pressed his palms together. "Can I help?"

She looked at him; someone, finally, had noticed. She had carried the argument with Forrest, and Dan's disbelief, around with her for the last few days. The rabbi spent his time attuned to the sorrow of others, but his eyes were open. He had noticed something that no one else had.

"Our neighbors hate us," she said.

"Why?"

"I think because we're Jews."

This wasn't exactly true; she just suspected something like it. "He asked me to cut a tree down, and I wouldn't, and now he's trained the dogs to bark at me. Just at me and the children, not at my husband. Then the dogs jumped over the fence—"

The rabbi tilted back in his chair and looked at her. He nodded. "How has he shown he hates Jews?"

"I don't know," she said. "He's always asking us to go to church. I can't say it definitely. I just sense it. You need to help me," she said. "He won't talk to me. Dan won't believe me—" she could not stop herself, but here she went, and it felt like a sweet relief to tell someone. "He says it's me. But it's not. Forrest told the dogs to bark at us."

Her armpits felt damp; she was both glad and appalled that she had said this, that she had revealed this awful rift between her and her husband, to the rabbi, who was, after all, a stranger.

He got out a pencil. "Well," said Rabbi Golden, sitting up. "We can't have that. What is his name?"

He wrote it down. The ordinary quality of the action, the simple taking down of names and addresses, soothed her; it was like she was filing a police report.

"You'll be happy to know I'm an expert at this. Team building, shall we say. I've done it in Ohio. Germany. Kuwait. Albuquerque. I come, I conquer!"

"Okay," she said.

"What does he like?"

"He likes Boy Scouts. He also likes to steal materials and build a shed with it."

"What else?"

"He raises maple saplings. He gives them away."

The rabbi noted this on his pad.

"When is he home?" asked the rabbi.

"All the time."

She was aware of the peculiar slowness of time in this room; time was pooling, like caramel, and they were trapped in it, soft and golden, as though all one craved from another person was the slowing down of one moment to the next. He had listened to her, with the simplicity of complete attention; it was a gift. She sat, nervous, not wanting to leave. Rabbi Golden, hands behind his head, his voice rich, warm, said, "Four o'clock tomorrow. Be home, Serena Hirsch. We'll take care of this, you and me. Watch."

A LITTLE BEFORE FOUR, SHE set the children in front of the TV and picked a window where Forrest would not be able to see her. Forrest was raking some leaves in his front yard. The garden around Forrest was raked, the pansies potted, stone birds and dwarves placed there to an elaborately cute effect. It could have been the entrance to Snow White's cottage. There was nothing that had not been trimmed, controlled, mowed, fertilized, transplanted, and contained. Serena's family's yard was, comparatively, a wreck: bushes spread out, unchecked; the lawn sprouted up, weedy, ragged. There was a competitive nature to the gardening, a battle that Serena's family was clearly losing.

She had had it with talking to Forrest. She wondered how he would respond to someone else. At four, the rabbi parked his car at the other end of the block and began to walk toward Forrest's home. He was wearing a suit, dressed for official business on par with a wedding or funeral. The blue shadows of the autumn afternoon stretched out on the white sidewalk.

"Sir," said the rabbi, "the word in the neighborhood is that you raise some beautiful maple saplings. Are they for sale?"

The rabbi had almost perfected a drawl, a rhythm of speaking similar to Forrest Sanders's own. Forrest stopped raking.

"I do raise some saplings," said Forrest Sanders.

The two men stood in the low afternoon light.

"Let me introduce myself. Rabbi Josh Golden."

"Pardon?"

"Rabbi Josh Golden." The rabbi held out his hand.

She saw Forrest studying his yarmulke. She did not know if he even knew what the word *rabbi* meant. What Forrest did detect was the flattery. His hand rose up and shook the rabbi's.

"Forrest Sanders. Well, Mister Josh, those are my babies. I can show you the beauts." Forrest Sanders took the rabbi to the side of the house. She watched the two men walk beside the house—the rabbi trying to control his brisk stride, Forrest ambling by, observing him. The rabbi had mastered the art of imitation, of matching the physical style of whoever was beside him.

"How much do you want for one?" asked Rabbi Golden.

"I don't usually charge," said Forrest Sanders, smiling.

"That's a crime! I'll give you twenty dollars," said the rabbi.

Forrest slowly lifted his hand and scratched his head. "You always pay for what you want?" he asked.

Rabbi Golden smiled, a pained smile. "I want to honor the work you have done," he said, sounding a little tense.

"What's the name of your church?" Forrest asked the rabbi.

"I don't lead a church. I lead the Temple. Temple Shalom," said the rabbi. "My first pulpit. Got here from San Diego. Before that I was with the forces in Kuwait, Korea, Camp Lejeune."

"Marines?" asked Forrest, also attuned to this form of authority.

"Army chaplain," said the rabbi.

"Sir," said Forrest Sanders, "Army chaplain. What is your opinion of that tree?"

Serena thought she could see the rabbi's shoulders relax at the fact that the stranger acknowledged if not his religion, then his rank as a spiritual leader. It seemed that Forrest was deeply trained to honor that role.

"Which tree?" asked the rabbi.

"That tree in their yard. It's going to fall."

Serena watched as Forrest walked toward their pine tree. Forrest was convinced of the hostility of the tree, as though the tree itself had reached out and slapped him.

Rabbi Golden surveyed the tree. "I don't think it will fall."

"Look," said Forrest Sanders. "Close. One good hurricane, another Hazel, and kaboom! It's going to fall and destroy my shed!" He paused. "Guess how much it cost to make it?"

"Tell me."

Forrest put his hands on his hips and said, "Twenty-three dollars and forty-seven cents."

"No!"

"I find things. In the street. In Dumpsters. I have an eye." He paused. "Twenty-three dollars and thousands of hours. Of dedication."

"Have you read Deuteronomy, chapter 20?" asked the rabbi.

"Certainly," said Forrest, crossing his arms.

"Do not destroy or waste," said the rabbi. "I see it as this — the way of the righteous is that nothing should be lost to the world."

"Why that tree and not my shed?"

"The Torah specifically tells us not to cut down trees," said the rabbi. "Especially in times of warfare." He cleared his throat. "Allow me to buy this sapling," said Rabbi Golden, taking out his wallet. "Twenty-three dollars and forty-seven cents. You can say your building's all paid for."

"Pray for it," said Forrest Sanders. "Pray for my shed."

Rabbi Golden's face darkened briefly at this request, and Serena was afraid that he would say something that was not at all a prayer, but then he bowed his head, clasped his hands, and said something quietly under his breath. He stood with, she thought, an exaggerated piety, as though mocking Forrest's request, as though his job also meant being a puppet to give voice to people's petty concerns, and he was tired of this. It was not just Forrest; it was all of them.

Forrest eyed him, waiting.

"Well," said Forrest Sanders. "Hope it works." He held out his hand for the money.

Rabbi Golden counted the money into it. Forrest Sanders's hand closed around it. His dogs circled around him, their pink tongues hanging out. The rabbi picked the sapling up, in its tiny tub. "Good luck, sir," the rabbi said, "with your shed and your saplings." He went to his car and drove off.

Three minutes later, her phone rang.

"Did you hear that?" the rabbi said, cackling into his cell phone. "He asked me to pray for the shed!"

"What did you say?"

"I don't even know," said the rabbi. "That's the first time I've prayed for a shed," he said. "The prayer did it. Not even buying the tree." He paused. "Give it half an hour," he said. "Then go in your yard. The dogs won't bother you."

He clicked off.

She stood in her kitchen, holding the phone. In half an hour, she opened the door to the backyard and stepped outside. Forrest Sanders was now opportunistically moving more of his saplings to the front. He was whistling. The dogs trotted around his yard, tails up; they looked at her.

She walked a slow circle around her yard. She kept walking through the yard, pretending to check the flowers. The yard had a ragged, tangled beauty to it, which she had not noticed for the last two weeks: the orange froth of lantana, the sweet musk of the gardenia, the pure scent of honey in the air.

There was nothing — silence.

SHE DID NOT TELL ANYONE about how the rabbi had helped her. She kept it secret, though he had not told her to — in fact, he would probably have been pleased if she had trumpeted this unique use of the Rabbi's Discretionary Fund. But keeping it secret lent it a greater significance and allowed her to turn it around in her mind and make it whatever she wanted it to be. Dan, her husband, had not believed her, and the rabbi had; it was a simple thing, this trust, but it held enormous weight. She went through the motions of her day — fed the children, bathed them, sat by their doors as they fell asleep. At night, she lay far from Dan in bed as they dug paths into their own separate dreams; she closed her eyes and thought of the way the rabbi stood beside Forrest, the way he stood, in his worn navy suit, to pray for the shed. She wanted to reach forward, take his hand, and lead him into her house. She would tell him her plans for the Southeastern North Carolina Jewish Community Center, or for the rest of the years of her life. It was time to leave the South; it was time to leave America; she wanted to go where anyone was safe from their own thoughts, from the bruised nature of love, from the unpredictable nature of death, from the fear — of her husband, of her children, of her family, of herself — that made her sit up in the middle of the night. Her aloneness felt utter and complete, the world retreating from her. But the rabbi would sit at her kitchen table, listening; she could picture him, with great clarity, sitting there, leaning back, alert and languorous, an arm stretched over a chair.

Finally, his hand would grab hers. She would feel it, his warm, attentive fingers against hers, the steady pulse of her heart in her palm. He would lean toward her and she would feel his lips against hers, urgent, wanting something of her, too, her skin alive, his cheek soft, melting. She was tired of the confines of her own body, her own worn sorrow; now she wanted to fall into him. He would pick her up, gently, and carry her away, their hands finding each other, and there she would be, in the temporary harbor of another person, and she would have that most precious feeling — that the only place in the world where she wanted to be was here.

DAN KEPT THINKING ABOUT THE dogs. They roamed around Forrest's yard, strong, light, as though trotting across clouds, and they gazed at him with a blank, eager expression; they did not bark. Serena was wrong; she had imagined the dogs' jumping the fence, or misinterpreted it, and this thought dismayed him. He had spoken briefly to Forrest, asked him if his dogs were jumping the fence, and Forrest acted surprised at the entire idea of it. "These are good dogs," he said, scratching one. "You just have to give them respect."

Dan stopped his car at a red light. He was across the street from Temple Shalom, and he noticed the rabbi getting out of his car. The rabbi walked with a slim, liquid grace to the door of Temple Shalom. It occurred to Dan that his wife worked with this man every day.

His fingers gripped the vinyl steering wheel to bolster himself against the familiar sense of disorder.

Dan did not want to go to work. He turned the wheel and headed toward the freeway. He drove up the overpass, and for one, two, three exits, he was on the freeway, heading west. The other cars floated by him, and he drove with them, joined in a mysterious race, heading out of town, somewhere, the air a swath along his car. He wanted to understand Serena—was that so much to ask? He wanted to know why she had so casually handed over someone else's credit card, what she had been thinking. How could you be married to someone and not know what was going through her mind? He was beginning to fear that when he drove home she would not be there, that he would walk through the door to an empty house. Hadn't she said something about being ready to leave? He had lived, most of his life, distrustful of what might happen next, and she was who he knew, whom he came home to and believed would be there, even when she was not, even when she was at her desk at work. He had never truly trusted anyone before. There was a heat in his throat, an awful, uncontrollable heat, and the sadness surprised him—he had not allowed himself to feel it the last few months. There had been too much to do, to plan, to move. He had been skating on the surface of this heat, and it could be bottomless. Now he gripped the steering wheel, and he did not want to feel this dark pulling inside of him—it gave him the troubling sensation that he did not know what he would do next. He drove for ten minutes, feeling the speed of the car in his jaw, his heart thrumming, frantic, before he turned to the off ramp and headed to work. He had an idea how to fix what had gone wrong.

THE NEXT DAY, SERENA WAS scheduled to work at the Temple office the whole day; the Xerox machine had taken this moment to collapse, and Georgia sounded like a hostage who needed release. Dan did not seem annoyed when Serena asked him to pick up the children; he said he would take a day off because there was something he wanted to take care of around the house.

When she got home, at dusk, there was an enormous flatbed truck parked in front of the house. In it was a wood chipper, which roared, hoarse, and in its maw spun pieces of tree limb, reduced to dust. She stopped, wondering who was getting work done on the house. Then she saw the tree pieces were being taken from her backyard.

She rushed into the yard. The tall pine tree had been cut down. Its trunk was sliced into round pieces like slabs of an enormous hotdog. In its place was a terrible abundance of emptiness, sky. The whole yard held the sharp tang of pine. A pile of branches sat by the wood chipper, the green needles extending like tufts of fur. She stood, frozen.

"Who told you to do this?" she asked one of the workers. He pointed across the yard. At Dan.

He was standing by the door of the house, watching the tree being dismantled. The children were sitting beside him, watching with a kind of excited interest; they seemed to have forgotten the argument over the tree and were absorbed in the complicated ceremony of its being taken apart. Serena started running; she flew across the yard to him and grabbed his arm.

Her voice cracked. "What did you do?"

He blinked; she thought he looked surprised at her reaction. "Let's talk over here," he said.

They walked to the side of the yard.

"Why did you do this, Dan? Why did you cut it down?" she said.

He looked at the ground and stroked his face with his hand. The odor of pine was so strong she could taste it, bitter, on her tongue.

"And how much did this cost?" she asked. "Aren't we supposed to be trying to save some money?"

He glanced at her, then away.

"I got a good deal on it," he said.

She shuddered and stepped away from him. "I don't believe this," she said. "I don't."

"We need — I wanted to get along with our neighbors," he said. "We don't need this trouble. Now we can all get along."

"But it was a beautiful tree!"

He paused and looked over at Forrest's yard. It was, for once, empty.

"He didn't like it. Maybe it would have fallen. Did we want that on us? Maybe he was right —"

"The tree was fine. I liked it! Why do you care what he thinks over what I do?"

He stepped back into the blue dusk and laughed.

"What's funny?"

"You haven't asked *me* about very much."

"What are you talking about?"

"What do you think?"

She looked at him—he was still thinking about Saks, the card, all that had happened in New York.

The workmen, arms full of slender tree branches, elbowed around them. Dan looked over her head, at a distant point, then back at her.

"It ruined us. Serena. Stop and think for a moment. It did." He wanted to say, *I don't know who you are,* but it would make him sound like an idiot. He could not say this aloud.

She stood on the dry yellow grass, surrounded by the mangle of tree limbs, staring at him.

"You didn't have to steal from them."

"It wasn't—" She did not know how to tell him how separate the world had felt, how she did not feel alive, or real, when she walked into that glittering store, how something had been stolen from her, how she didn't even want the jewelry, really, but instead wanted something they could not sell.

"Why did you do it? Just tell me."

She looked away. How could she express it? She could not think of the correct words. "Some of us make mistakes . . . we aren't so able to—"

"I don't know why you did it!" he said. All of his breath emptied out of his body. "I don't know why you couldn't have stopped."

Her face was hot, and something invisible fractured in her feelings toward him. Turning, she rushed toward the house. Stop? What could she stop? Perhaps that was the harshest loss that had come from the action—not that she had been fired, not that they had gone into debt and had to move, but that she could not explain her loneliness to Dan at that moment, that she could not explain her sense that something deep, irreplaceable, had been robbed from *her.* Now she stood, looking at the tree being taken apart, the branches sawed off, the trunk chopped into circles. It had been a beautiful tree. It was startling how quickly it became a dead pile of wood. She had never felt so separate from her husband. The shriek of the woodcutter was loud, guttural; she stood, frozen, and listened to it.

THE NEXT EVENING WAS THE last October meeting of the board. Serena left the house, clutching her briefcase; she wanted to look crisp, knowledgeable, because she had not been able to sleep the night before. She could not bear to look at the tree stump, to think about what the tree's absence said about anything; when she did see the splintery stump in the backyard, she felt the low, sharp sting of shame.

She was grateful now for the various elements of order—foldout card table, the gray flickering lights, the voices of the other board members—but she was not really paying attention to the business of the evening, the complaints about the High Holy Days ticket distribution, some new zoning issues with the land for the Jewish cemetery. The coffee cake flew off the plate. Everyone seemed starving.

She did not notice that Betty was holding a folder that she repeatedly reached into and shuffled papers inside, and she did not notice that Norman was tapping his fingers whenever Betty made a statement, clearing his throat loudly as though trying to erase her words.

What Serena did notice was the way that Tom suddenly wanted to end the meeting. "Well," he said, briskly. "No more business? Then we're done."

"Tom," said Betty. "We are not done."

Norman coughed, sharply.

Tom's face flickered. "I don't know why you're pushing this, Betty—"

Betty's voice was louder. "I'm pushing it, Tom, because it's true."

Tom cleared his throat; he opened his mouth. "I—we need to have a special meeting." He closed his eyes briefly and then gazed out at them. He did not say anything more. Instead, he passed out a pale blue flyer. It said, *Special meeting next week. 7:00 PM, November 6, Social Hall. There have been some allegations against Rabbi Golden.*

Serena stared at the words. She thought, suddenly, that the allegations were about her, that the rabbi had been caught calling her, late at night, but then she realized, of course, that she had been calling him. She sat very straight, hands clasped politely in front of her, and glanced around the table, imagining they all could see through to her pacing at night, her strange, frantic dialing, her need to hear his voice. She had stalked him; that was what they would tell her, and this time there would be no lawyers. But then she understood that no one at this table could see this, and that the allegations had landed on him.

"A Zip file will be sent to all of you," said Betty, solemnly. "In the coming week. We will address all issues, in full, at the next meeting."

"Meeting adjourned," said Tom. "Shalom!" He darted out.

The board members glanced at each other; the meeting had devolved into something unexpected, wholly new. Serena rushed out the door toward Tom, who was scuttling quickly down the dark street. "Tom!" she said. "What is going on?"

A pickup truck rumbled by, a heavy bass drumbeat shuddering through the air. "We will discuss everything at the meeting next week."

He turned to walk away, and she stepped up to him. "Now, Tom."

Tom looked at her, and she noticed a new expression in his eyes: fear. "People are bored," he said. "Or perhaps they are frustrated by other world events, the situation in Israel. . . . Serena. What would compel a person to attack another good person for no logical reason? Perhaps the members of our congregation who dislike our great rabbi, my friend, secretly hate Jews. The blossoming of a Jewish institution." He gestured toward the enormous buildings across the street, buildings with the size and heft of cruise ships. "Or think. What would the Baptists, or the Methodists, the Catholics, gain if we, the Jewish people, were at war with each other?"

"What are you saying?"

He leaned toward her. "Are we puppets of other people's hatred? Why is brother taking up arms against brother? We have to protect him," he said, and lifted his fist. "Right?"

They were in the parking lot beside the Temple, standing in the pools of the orange light from the lampposts. The orange light falling onto their faces made them look not human but alien. The smell of barbecue rolled off someone's yard, and Serena tasted ash in her mouth.

"Yes," she said.

She got into the car and drove home. It wasn't late, but the road had already emptied, and no one was here; the street was hazy and radiant with the lights from the McDonald's, Bojangles', Hardee's, signs, a lonely nation under the night sky. There were signs from the restaurants and churches set out for the drivers to read: BOGO *Monster Bacon Cheeseburgers Today Only!; Call 986-3728 for Free Pool Installation Estimates; Five minutes after you die you'll know how you should have lived.*

The paper announcing the allegations against the rabbi lay on the seat beside her. She touched it, as though somehow the thin physical fact of the paper would bring her closer to him.

Part Two

Chapter Ten

SERENA'S FATHER ALWAYS TRIED TO be home from the emergency room at Northridge General Hospital in time for dinner. He didn't always make it; the car crash, drug overdose, and bullet wound victims who flew through the electric doors of Northridge General tended to pile up late in the day, so her mother set the table at six, and by six thirty, Serena and her mother and sister would start. But a part of Serena would always be waiting for him, as she tried to plan what she would say to him at dinner that night.

Aaron had pleaded with his parents to leave Germany when he was six; they left just before his aunts and uncles were herded on trains and vanished. He had tumbled through his life in America wondering what had happened, why they had chosen that moment to listen, and what was the extent or limit of his own power. He had become a nurse in the emergency room to accommodate the constant thrumming of his own heart. Now, every day he rushed toward stretchers holding patients whose hearts had stopped, whose necks had broken, whose intestines had been stabbed, whose skin glistened with shards of glass; some recovered, many died. He could never get over the arbitrary nature of suffering in any form; it terrified him, and when he got home he wanted to shield his daughters from all of it.

He whisked in while they were in the middle of dinner, each night a little surprised that they were all merely sitting around the dinner table, healthy and alive. Serena and Dawn looked up at him and told him what they had done that day. "Quick," he said, "what happened to my girls today? What did you win? Serena? Go on. Tell me."

She did not always know what to say. Her father was a tall, restless man with gray curly hair and clear golden eyes that were set on her, piercingly, for that long moment. She could sense that he was a little afraid of her, or of her future, and she wanted to tell him the thing that would calm him.

She had about a minute.

"I won my spelling test," she might offer, ridiculously—it was not something anyone could win.

He blinked. "Excellent!" he said, too brightly. She released a breath.

"Dawn?" he said, and Dawn would present her offering to him. Their father sat, nodding too hard, as though he was not truly interested, or else he was so interested he was about to fall apart.

"Okay," he said. "Great. Win. Keep going."

Nothing kept him in his seat. He jumped out of his chair, added salt to his food, got up to pour the extra off, reheated it; his dinner was eaten mostly standing up. He was extremely deliberate about his food, could not get it to the right temperature. There was a kind of athleticism to the way he ate, as if he were engaged in a race that the others were not aware of. Their mother moved about him carefully; she had mastered a kind of wryness around him. Her job was to translate his actions to the rest of them.

"Aaron, sit down," she said lightly. "The potatoes are better with butter. Don't scrape it off. Aaron, you already have a fork. Aaron, thanks for getting up to look for the salt—can you bring it?"

He tried to listen to their mother, sitting down briefly when she told him to, but he found an excuse to pop up, to roam the kitchen, searching for the ingredient that would render them impervious to suffering. Sometimes he told them about his own day.

"Guess what I did today?" he said. "I held my hand against someone's aorta. Stab wound. I felt his life there under my thumb. I held him alive while the useless doctor dropped the needle he was going to use to stitch him. I felt his pulse jump on my thumb. It was like a grasshopper. If I lifted my thumb, it would be a geyser."

He smiled.

"You can all do that, too," he said, and Serena wanted to believe that she could.

....

AFTER DINNER, HE WOULD SOMETIMES go into the garage to work on his train landscapes. Whoever had finished her homework, or presented a particularly memorable accomplishment that night, would be allowed to help.

Serena's father would go over his plans for his landscape. He wanted to make a landscape that other people would want to see and discuss. He told her about some of the nation's premier miniature landscapes: the Ave Maria Grotto in Alabama, located in an old quarry, a garden of miniature churches all over the world, landscaped, incredibly, into rock. There was Holy Land USA in Connecticut, built by a local attorney, showing a biblical Holy Land. There was a panorama of New York City made for the 1964 World's Fair in which 320 miles of New York were reproduced at a scale of 1 inch to 100 feet.

They stood over his large plywood table, the fields made of Tru-Green vinyl mat, the foam inclines, the trees, the houses and stores and fire stations and office buildings, the tiny people, and the endless winding tracks.

"Where should my trains run?" he asked. "Tell me."

He had written a letter to Harvey Smith, who had been featured in *Model Trains Monthly* and who had won numerous awards for constructing terraced landscapes with Windsor blocks and "reject sand," unusable from construction sites. "I've used forty tons of reject sand on my landscapes," Mr. Smith announced in the article about him; that fact itself impressed her father. Her father tracked down bags of reject sand and blocks, and he set up terraces. He wrote to Mr. Smith: *Why terraces? How did you decide that? Do you have many where you live? Do you have houses? What kind? How many trees? Is it a desert or a forest? Which is better?*

Harvey wrote back, politely, *Dear Mr. Hirsch, I have terraces that measure twenty-five inches to thirty-six-and-a-half inches. Trees cover approximately 75 percent of this landscape. I have seventeen houses, three train stations, and seven other buildings. My landscape mimics the terrain of northern Italy.*

Her father had kept Harvey's letter and taped it up in his garage. He had correspondence from other train aficionados: Barry Jones, who specialized in landscapes with tunnels; Quentin Avery, whose trains moved through "Nebraska in 1889." They could relate the exact number of accessories, the degree of angle to their inclines, the numbers of people, cars, road signs, and the bridges that went up and down. They had clear, specific goals. *I plan to create a multilayer train landscape through several Midwestern towns. I plan to re-create the Swiss Alps with silver glitter and snow made of glue.* Serena was annoyed by the letters, the crisp authority of the other model makers, who seemed to have clear and definite goals and no ambivalence about them. The letters intrigued and shamed her father, who lied when he wrote back to them, *I have added my fifty-seventh handmade tree to my landscape,* he wrote to Barry Jones. *I have re-created a Bavarian forest.* He would not send photos.

The garage had the glamour of a castle, that same dank, cool interior, the musty odor of damp concrete. He bought heavy books with photographs illustrating a particular place, spent hours researching, ordering parts, figuring how to make a particular forest look North American, European, Scandinavian.

Only while her father created the train landscapes did they share the rare moments when he slowed down and asked her what she thought. She stood by the table, telling him her ideas for his landscape, and he nodded, tapping his fingers against the table. She was triumphant in that small room, the light hazy, golden from the bright, bare bulb hanging from the ceiling. She loved him. She was aware of the restlessness she often felt in her family, the understanding that all children gain — that the world has been created without thought of them, and that they are left out of the grand world their parents create — but here, in here, she was in the center of the world. She watched him, whittling a tiny tree, adjusting the TruGreen. She might hold down the turf while the glue was drying, paint a tiny apartment building, place tiny people waiting for a bus.

"Serena. Tell me. What should I make?"

She looked up at him, leaning over his table, hands clasped. What did she know at six, seven, eight? At this train table, instructing him on the placement of the world, she had the solid, immutable sense that he knew she was good. She was aware in some way of the tragedy of the link between parent and child, the fact of their separateness — that he would die before she did, that by creating her, he and her mother guaranteed her a self that would someday be alone. She set her eyes on the tracks, on the trees, trying to figure out what she could say that would make him happy she was there.

"Sacramento," she suggested one day. "Where you grew up." But that was really Berlin, which he refused to build. Los Angeles, where he had ended up. Their mother's hometown, Fresno. Las Vegas. Paris. China.

"Good plan," he said, sometimes. "What should I put there?"

He was listening then. She picked out trees and buildings; they painted them.

THE PROBLEM WAS THAT HE never was able to finish anything. As the landscape gained shape, streets, and neighborhoods, as it began to resemble a place, her father became anxious. He stood in the garage, looking at his creation, and then he began to pace.

"Serena," he said once, when he was abandoning a project on a San Francisco gold rush town in the 1800s, which involved multilevel bridges, rows of shanties, fake gold, special tracks, "I don't like it."

"Why?" she asked.

"I can't get the right dirt. It should be more orange. I don't know how the streams fall. The rocks are not the right shape."

The moment he became a perfectionist was when they stopped. She looked at the table, trying to see the flaws. He walked around the table and began to pluck pieces of the landscape, the trains, off it. She pressed her hands down on it, to protect it.

"But you're almost done!"

"It's wrong," he said, got a garbage bag, and began to sweep his model landscape into it. He stalked around the table, taking apart the landscape. It was as though his anxiety so shamed him that he had an urge to display it so that, perhaps, he would be absolved. He yanked off the TruGreen, peeled off the tracks, the false mountains, the streams made with glue. She stood, trembling, watching him sweep everything into a plastic bag. "Help," he said, and she was so startled by the husky childishness of his voice that she lifted up the train tracks and silently handed them to him.

Finally they stood, the plywood bare again, the TruGreen grass wrinkled, the tracks piled up in a corner, the trains jammed together in the middle of the table. The floor was covered in sand or dirt. She waited to see what he would do next. Her father stood, squinting at the ruined train landscape. He never tore apart anything that she had made. She collected it and put it in the corner to use for the next project. He only destroyed his own work, tossing it into the corner. Finally, he sat down and stared at the blank table.

"Look at that," her father said. "It's nowhere."

THE NIGHT AFTER THE BOARD meeting, she saw an email on her computer with the subject CONFIDENTIAL FOR BOARD MEMBERS. She was in her bedroom; she closed the door.

She closed her eyes for a moment, preparing. Then she opened them.

A) Rabbi does not impart, in general, a "warm and fuzzy" feeling

B) Rabbi did not hug a member of the sisterhood when she said hello

C) Rabbi shouted at a congregant when telling her that she could not rent out the synagogue for her own party on a Friday night

D) Rabbi frequently walks too quickly by some congregants, who try to catch up but are ignored

E) Rabbi said (in a sharp and insensitive tone) that the members needed to think less about social events and more about God

F) Rabbi was heard making a sarcastic joke about his salary and the high price of housing in the county

That was it.

. . . .

THE MEMBERS OF TEMPLE SHALOM'S Board of Directors all moved through the quiet streets of Waring to the emergency meeting. It was November; the sky faded early now, and the bare oak branches were hard silver filaments in the glow of the streetlights. Betty drove her Lexus, her accordion file of evidence beside her in the front seat; she had belted in the folder to keep it steady. Tom carefully steered his Buick, Norman beside him describing his call to the rabbi the night before: "You know how long I talked to him last night? Forty-five minutes. Forty-five! I finally made an excuse to hang up because I didn't want to be, you know, a bother."

Serena was speeding. She wanted to get there. She drove past the sad, bright strip malls that composed the rest of Waring, that made it like thousands of other such cities in America; there was the sense that the town was floating on the erratic whims of global industry, the streets lined with McDonald's and Wendy's and Old Navy and Walmart, and the enormous signs glared, cheerful, insistent, into the dark air. Her car floated past the churches, the conversation they had with the street: Today she saw *God has a word for every situation.* She also saw *If your Bible is falling apart, you aren't,* and *Jesus says: Come and make your home with us.* She gunned the car past the signs, their absurd hopefulness. Clutching the steering wheel, she moved through the cool, starry night.

She thought of the rabbi in front of the congregation, his nylon suit glimmering in the low light. She thought of the way he sat beside her in his office the first time, the breathless intimacy of that gesture, how he had stood with Forrest and prayed for that damned shed, how he had looked at her with his dark blue eyes and seen something worthy in her. The allegations had almost made her laugh in their smallness, and then she wanted to cry. Why were they attacking him? She thought of how she felt beside him, whole, how he sat beside her, how still he was when he seemed to listen.

She parked and went into the room where the board members were sitting quietly in the milky light. Somehow, official allegations against their spiritual leader put them all on their best behavior. Betty had brought a big box of Entenmann's glazed donuts; everyone offered everyone else a donut first. No one grabbed a donut without a nod to his or her neighbor. Betty wore a crisp gray Armani suit and perfume that smelled of lavender. She gave Serena a big smile and squeezed her forearm.

"How are you, darling?" said Betty.

"Upset." It was surprising that anyone could eat the donuts.

"We're all upset," said Betty, looking not at all upset.

"All right," said Marty, "let's get on with it." He bowed his head. "Dear God. Let us serve as the stewards of your congregation, to lead in a way that is responsible and moral and carries out your wishes. Amen."

"Amen," they said.

The donut box was empty.

Tom called the meeting to order. "We have come to judge an individual in our Temple," he said, his voice trembling. "In judging an individual," he said, "you review good and bad points." He paused. "Now, Rabbi Josh is a learned man," he said. "He brings congregants to tears when they hear his sermons. He is a dedicated and hard worker. I am proud to call him my friend, and I find him to be an individual of visionary status. Last year he visited fifteen local elementary schools at Chanukah and performed three interfaith seders while his name was being smeared by certain members—"

"I had dinner with him and Saul Schloman, and he talked to Saul the whole time and totally ignored me and my wife and the other dinner guests," proclaimed Barry Weissman. "My wife was in tears."

"We've lost twenty members I can count because of him," said Betty.

"We've probably added thirty more," said Norman.

"He yelled at Fran Schollman until she cried," said Betty.

"She wanted to plant an organic garden along the right side of the Temple. He said no. Well, he didn't say it—"

"The sukkah generally goes there. He didn't want to crowd the area," said Tom.

"Point two," said Betty, "he screamed at Jennifer Gordon when she entered his office without asking. He stood in front of his desk, leaned toward her, and screamed, "What do you think you're doing, you moron?" Betty looked at them, her eyes bright. "Yes, he did use that word. He shouted, or, she said, screamed, 'This is my territory! Did you ask before you came in here? Did you even think of using your hand to knock?'"

Serena swallowed. "He didn't say it like *that*," she said, hopefully. Most of the others looked up as though they all wished this.

"In fact, he did," Betty said. "I have eighteen incidents recorded—"

Could the rabbi have said these things to the congregants? Could there be some explanation? She could sense this yearning running through the others as well, the desire to explain him, to align themselves with one side of him or the other.

"Perhaps they're a little hypersensitive," said Tom.

"I agree wholeheartedly," said Norman.

"Why are you calling old ladies hypersensitive?" asked Tiffany.

"Don't blame the victim," said Betty.

"Maybe he hates his mother," said Norman. "We have a rabbi who hates his mother."

They all laughed, with relief. Thanks to Norman, as always, they all laughed. Serena was grateful for him; it was as though it had just rained, and the air was clear—there was a sense of thrill in the air, at the freedom to speak about the rabbi's flaws. The fact that this man—who paid his rent through his own alleged holiness—had committed various transgressions made their own mistakes seem petty. He had freed them from the indignities in themselves.

"I must interject," said Betty, "one reason the rabbi was hired was because the other candidate was a fatso. This is in the words of the search committee. They liked Rabbi Golden because—his smile. His hair."

"They wanted someone easy on the eyes on the bima," said Tiffany.

"Ladies! Did you hear his sermon on the settlements on the West Bank? So smart, so subtle—"

"Define *screamed*," said Marty.

"Good point," said Tom. "No one heard it—"

The others looked nervous, unsure which group they could be sorted into—screamer or not-screamer. What had the rabbi done?

What were any of them capable of? How far were any of them from any misbehavior? Wasn't that one reason they had started coming here, to try to somehow lift themselves to a higher place?

"Has the rabbi yelled at you?" Serena asked Marty.

"No."

"You?" she asked Tiffany.

"Well, no."

"The word is *attacked*," said Betty. "These are not small things. Here is a list. These are just the documented ones. "He screamed at Sandra Steinfeld, Gloria Price, Wanda Seymour, Maria Goldenman, Marsha Cohen, Lorrie Mankowitz. They are all women over sixty," said Betty. "He bullied them to the point of weeping. Board members—" Her voice became louder. "It's not just a little yell, it's—an attack. He makes little old ladies cry."

There was a silence.

Serena felt like the discussion was going on in a distant place, and the voices were bent and distorted. Perhaps this was all made up, for some unknown reason; she did not want to believe the rabbi had acted this way. "What about," Serena said, carefully, "asking if he needs help?"

"We did," said Betty. "After several of these incidents, we suggested that he seek anger management therapy."

"Is this covered by the Temple budget?" asked Marty, tapping his pencil.

"No, he's paying," said Betty. "But we don't know if he's going. We haven't seen doctor's notes."

"Has he—hit anyone?" asked Marty.

"No," said Betty, sitting up, "but why should we test that out?"

"We should dock his pay," said Marty. "Money talks. A hundred bucks for each time he starts screaming at someone. Two hundred."

"Someone might think it should cost him fifty," said Norman.

"We told him he should apologize publicly during Yom Kippur service," said Betty. "Get everyone he's made cry up on the bima. Personally atone to each of them. He didn't." Her voice had lost its practiced sunniness and was piercingly clear. "What do we want, I ask you? Do we want to stand up for righteousness to everyone? Do we want to have a rabbi who is cruel to women?"

Betty turned her eyes to Tiffany and Serena. Suddenly there was a demand put upon them. They were, as the female members of the group, supposed to condemn the rabbi.

"Impolite isn't cruel," piped up Tom.

"We cannot have a bully as a rabbi!" said Betty. She stood up. "We condone cruelty if we keep him."

The room was quiet.

"But if we don't keep him, who else would want us?" said Norman. Suddenly he looked tearful. The board members huddled around the flimsy table; the fluorescent lights flickered. "I ask you — if you were a rabbi, would you want us?"

Norman looked out at the board members. He pitied them. He thought of them as his assistants, all of them, even (secretly) Tom; Norman had been a member here the longest, besides Betty, and that had to lend him an authority the others should respect. The discussion about the rabbi was a little hard to follow; the accusations seemed flimsy and wrong. It gave him a jumpy sensation in his stomach, which he wanted to end; he did not want to feel anything else going awry in his body at the moment. He wanted to be fine. The rabbi had made him feel fine last night, while they discussed the organ celebration, fine in that he asked about the biopsy but didn't push. The rabbi knew what Norman could offer. Knowledge. During that conversation about the organ's birthday, Norman had told the rabbi the history of organs in Reform synagogues in the United States, for forty-five minutes, and in those minutes Norman had forgotten his diagnosis.

Norman looked at them and lifted his hand.

"It is imperative that this is kept within *these walls*," said Norman. "We don't want to alarm the congregants. A call to secrecy is in order." He paused. "We should have an oath."

"Norman, are you kidding?"

Tom said, "I propose that Norman and I speak to the rabbi about reforming his conduct toward congregants. We will make our point strongly."

The board members slowly gathered up their notebooks. Betty tapped Serena on the shoulder. "If you have any questions," she said, "don't hesitate to give me a call." She handed Serena one of her business cards.

Serena nodded coolly at Betty. "Okay," she said.

They all walked silently into the night. Serena went out with Tom and Norman. Their cars were parked in the bank lot across the street.

"He's never been mean to me," she said. What did this mean, if anything? Perhaps he *had* done nothing. She thought of him standing by Forrest, buying the sapling, and she could not reconcile this image of him with the one described. What were they seeing in him? What was wrong? For a moment she understood her husband, his relentlessly sunny perceptions of others; there was a comfort in just believing whatever the hell she wanted.

"Or me," said Norman, quickly.

"Me either," said Tom.

"Maybe he only yells at the idiots," said Norman.

"The congregation is going to hate us if we fire him," said Tom. "They're going to say we're a lynch mob." He paused.

"It's the Jewish thing to help him. It's a mitzvah," Serena said, listening to her voice, wondering.

"He is a great man," said Tom, slowly.

"Are you kidding? He's a wreck," said Norman. "Our rabbi is a goddamn wreck."

The three of them stood in the thick, dusky Southern night, the air honeyed with gardenia, and listened to that.

Chapter Eleven

THE NEXT MORNING, THE PHONE rang; it was the vice principal of Oakdale Elementary. There was a problem. Her son had been playing with Ryan on the school's basketball court and, suddenly, Ryan had thrown some pennies at him and said, "Pick them up." Zeb had started gathering them up eagerly, and Ryan had laughed at him and said, "See? See?" to a group of kids, "I told you he'd pick them up."

Pennies. Serena's skin was cold. She had heard about this. It was a Southern thing—they threw pennies at Jews to see if they would pick them up.

Was this real? Was this a joke?

"What are you going to do about this?" she asked the vice principal.

"We have them in the office," the vice principal said, sounding tired. "You can come in."

Serena hurried down the school's brown corridors, past the bulletin boards with the cheerful busywork assigned to children during latency, one board with the announcement *The weather today is:* and the corresponding obedient responses: *Sunny. Cloudy. Rainy.* It was a school that prided itself on accuracy, on its students' coloring within the lines, and the art reflected that particular value—the strict reproductions of yellow suns, gray clouds, zigzag lightning. As she rushed toward the office to her weeping son, she felt the fragility with which the school and the children were propped up on these smiling suns and clouds, the ways in which they attempted to maintain some order.

She arrived in the vice principal's office to find Zeb perched on a plastic chair, his arms wrapped around himself. On the other side of the room sat Ryan, looking vaguely irritated, and his mother, trying to bat her toddlers away.

The scene gave Serena a sudden primal urge to call the police, to upend the vice principal's desk; she rushed to Zeb and held him. His cheek was impossibly soft. "Honey," she said. "I'm here. What happened? Tell me—"

"He threw these pennies down," Zeb said, pushing his head into her armpit. "I picked up five cents. He said it was because I was Jewish. Then he laughed."

"It was just a joke," Ryan's mother said. She looked like she hadn't slept in three days.

"You think it's a joke?" said Serena. "It's a stereotype."

"We don't have stereotypes at the school," the vice principal said quickly.

"He was just playing around," said Ryan's mother.

"It's more than that," said Serena. "It's a stereotype that Jews are obsessed with money," she said, carefully. "It comes from the Middle Ages, when Christians weren't allowed to lend money at interest, so some Jews became moneylenders. But also remember that Jews weren't allowed by law to hold many jobs in medieval times or, later, were kicked out of various countries for no reason, subject to mob violence, and—" She stopped, breathless, wishing she had listened more in religious school, not sure where to go with this brief, incomplete history of persecution. She continued, "But you know, *despite* the stereotype, Jews are not proportionally wealthier than anyone else, and they don't secretly run the world. A lot of bad things have happened in the past because of this. You can't teach your kids this. You can't make things up about a whole group. It's—cruelty."

It wasn't even close to a good argument, and she was grateful that they had no access to the Pepsi employee file, but this was all she could come up with at the moment. They all stared at her, shocked; she realized that this sort of bluntness was not the correct strategy here. Ryan's mother blinked. "Medieval times?" she asked, dazed.

"Now, we know that we can all be friends here," said the vice principal, in a desperately cheerful voice.

"He didn't say sorry," said Zeb.

"Don't get bent out of shape. He didn't mean anything," said Ryan's mother.

This statement felt like a physical slap. "Yes, he did," said Serena, staring at Ryan's mother, who wore the glazed expression of a mother who had made one too many excuses for her offspring. "What are you going to do about this? Shouldn't he be suspended?"

The vice principal hesitated. "Ryan. No throwing pennies at anyone. Let's just shake and get on with it," said the vice principal, the pressure of a hundred meetings in her weary eyes.

Serena wrapped her arms around Zeb's slight body. He did not want to just shake and get on with it, and neither did Ryan. Why had Ryan thrown the pennies at Zeb? Had he sensed some opportunity, some weakness, a difference that Ryan couldn't even express but had somehow heard from someone else? The vice principal and Ryan's mother sat, their faces composed in prim expressions of contrition. How easy it would be to just believe them, but Serena did not. Perhaps she should refuse to shake hands. Perhaps she should go to the school board, the newspaper—what could she do? She was trembling. She pressed her lips to Zeb's soft hair.

"What do you say?" asked the vice principal.

Ryan had now decided to cooperate. He slid forward, his hand offered limply. Her son eyed him with haughty suspicion. Zeb held out his hand, and they briefly touched fingers.

"Say sorry," said Zeb.

Ryan squirmed. "Sorry," he said quietly. Serena looked at the mother.

"This is not. Happening. Again," Serena said, very slowly, to Ryan. His mother clutched her babies and looked grim.

"So!" said the vice principal, clapping her hands together. "Friends."

THAT NIGHT, DAN OPENED THE door to his son's describing, in an excited, high-pitched voice, the incident on the playground. Zeb grabbed his father's legs as though trying to grab hold of a tree, and Dan lifted him, feeling the solid, light weight of the boy in his hands. "He didn't say sorry," said Zeb, quickly, "I got five cents . . . "

"What happened?" Dan asked, confused. "You got five cents?"

"It's not what you think," Serena said. "Listen."

Serena did not even want to look at him since he had cut down the tree. Dan had called the tree removal company propelled by a desire to fix something he could not describe, but he looked at it now, the short stump, and it did not make him feel he had won an argument or even made a particularly important point. The yard was just empty, the sky spreading overhead in a fresh, glaring way. Forrest greeted him with renewed enthusiasm, but he did not seem to be grateful in the way that Dan thought he should have been. He remembered how Serena had stared at the tree as though Dan had killed someone. What had he actually said to her? It was difficult to remember in the whirl of wood dust and noise. It was just a tree; perhaps it could have fallen. Why did she seem to think it was something more? Sometimes he glanced outside and wanted to replace the tree, assemble it back into its tall, stretching height, but then he turned away, quickly, believing that having these thoughts meant he was caving—agreeing with her.

"Listen to your son," Serena said.

He sat at the dinner table. The fixture above the table shone a bitter yellow light. At his seat was a plate with four frozen fish sticks, slightly warm. There was the brisk, chemical smell of refrigerated food in the air.

Dan had not heard of this before. "Did he maybe just drop the pennies by accident?" he asked.

"No," said Zeb.

"How much did you pick up?"

"Five cents," said Zeb. "Almost six—"

Dan paused. "Not bad," he said. "Try for more next time. Or next time tell him to throw quarters."

Zeb laughed. "Dollars!" he said.

"Store up for more YuGiOh cards," said Dan, sawing away at his food. "If he's dumb enough to drop more money."

He smiled, a little inscrutably and, in an odd gesture that seemed borrowed from a sitcom, winked at Zeb. Serena was startled by this response but a little grateful for this strategy. Just say the others are fools. She remembered why she had been drawn to Dan originally; he had the gift of the other view, the wondrous, strange ability to at least appear to calm down. She watched him, mystified; it was as though he lived in an entirely different house. Was this perhaps adaptable? Or was it a mistake?

"Forrest is announcing something great at Scouts," said Dan. "Better than any pennies. Glory awaits. Finish up. Zeb, get in your uniform."

Zeb leapt up from the table and ran to his room. He emerged, tiny, deeply official, in the dark blue shirt, the gold kerchief folded around his neck. The dignity killed Dan; he looked at his son, and he wanted, from the deepest part of himself, to preserve it.

HE AND ZEB DROVE UP to the First Presbyterian Church, where the meeting was held. They parked and made their way with the other scouting families into the building. How happy were the other scouting families! Some brought the whole group—father, mother, siblings—to the meetings; it seemed they could not bear to be kept out of the joy. Why wasn't his family like this? The apparent ease of their happiness was gorgeous and galling. Some of the parents were holding hands.

Dan strode to the front of the room to stand with the other assistant fathers; they tended to explode into laughter at the slightest intimation of wit, and they had complicated and extensive sets of keys on their belts.

Forrest's hand tapped Dan's shoulder.

"Let's get started. Dan Shine, how about you lead the prayer tonight," said Forrest.

Dan stood slowly. Zeb looked up at him. The children and fathers stood on the hard red linoleum and grasped hands. They all bowed their heads. Dan's mind was empty. He had not listened to the opening prayer at Scouts. The boys and parents gripped each other's hands. Dan had no idea what to say.

"The Shema," Zeb whispered to him.

He looked at Zeb. No. Good god, not the Shema. Dan didn't realize he even knew that prayer. Blessed is God. God is one. Dan smiled briefly at him, and then out at the crowd. His heart felt like a butterfly caught in a jar.

"Uh," said Dan. "Let us uphold the, um, Scout motto, do your best—"

Forrest stepped forward. "Excuse me! Heavenly father," he added.

"Um. Yes." Dan cleared his throat. "Heavenly father—"

"Jesus," added Forrest.

Dan swallowed. "Jesus," he said, quickly, "let us hold up the Scout motto and, um—"

"Uphold our service to you," said Forrest.

"Amen," said Dan, quickly. Zeb stared at him. The other scouts murmured amen. Dan had an itch in his throat. He began to cough—once, twice. He held up a hand to indicate he was all right, but his coughs continued. Amen. His eyes were damp; he pretended he was laughing. Some of the parents looked alarmed, and one father stepped up to slap him on the back. Another brought him a cup of water. Dan drank it, quickly; the coughing stopped.

"You all right, bud?" asked one of the fathers.

"Fine, just fine," said Dan, his voice gravelly. He sensed Forrest and the others waiting for him to say something else. Zeb looked like he was about to blurt out something unfortunate, and Dan grabbed his hand and called out, "Let's go, scouts!"

He stood in front of them, hands on hips, trying to look official, while the scouts gathered, a lake of navy blue with gold scarves. Forrest strode up to a microphone and cleared his throat. "Tonight we're announcing the rules to this year's Pinewood Derby!" Forrest proclaimed. "Best one yet. Listen." Forrest held up a small car made of two curved lumps of wood. "This is the model," he said. "You can carve it, paint it however you would like. Watch how this moves." He put the car on a plastic ramp and rolled it; it zoomed down the ramp and plopped against a chair. The boys were mesmerized by the tiny vehicle, as though they were watching the trajectory of their own hopeful futures. "It can weigh three ounces or less. We judge for fastest, best paint job, best shape. Our race is going to be in a month. December fifth."

"A Christmas derby!" a mother called out, and everyone applauded.

"This is going to be the biggest Pinewood Derby on record," Forrest said. "We're combining with Pack 378. Sixty kids. Big trophies. News coverage by WKYX. You can buy the car kits at Walmart or Target or at Craft-O-Rama at the mall. Or you can make your own to Scout specifications."

Hands flew up; there were numerous questions as to the most effective tire, the fastest shape, what grease was allowed, what brands of paint. Dan listened. Zeb stared at the car, engrossed.

As he drove home, Zeb asked him, "Why didn't you say the—"

"I said what they told me," said Dan, quickly.

"Who?"

"I said the Boy Scout prayer. That's all I said." He had not known what to do; he wanted his son to nod. Zeb fiddled with his seatbelt.

"Oh," said Zeb. He was silent. The evening was warm, and Dan rolled down the windows. Zeb stretched his arm out the window and opened his hand to the air.

"You want to win this thing?" asked Dan.

"Yes," said Zeb.

ZEB HAD BECOME HESITANT AGAIN, walking into school; he did not scream when Serena dropped him off, but he stood, watchful, quietly gripping the straps of his backpack while the other children ran across the cool, damp grass into the classroom trailer. She did not know what he was watching for, what made him hesitate; he did not tell her, and she did not want to share any of her own fears with him. "Have a good day," she said, touching his shoulder, her voice swerving into a hopeful brightness; he nodded at her solemnly. Neither wanted to move. She backed up, lifting her hand in a wave.

She headed to the Temple as soon as Zeb was at school and Rachel was at her playgroup; Georgia needed her there extra hours now. There was the usual business of scheduling and paper clips and adjusting who was behind in their dues paying. There was the odor of copy paper and the thud of staplers. She sat at her makeshift desk and wrote memos, took calls; there was the sense that they were preparing for a kind of war.

The rabbi kept himself in his office, engaged in loud discussion on his cell phone, but sometimes he ventured out. She wanted to ask him about the complaints, what had happened, and she wanted to ask him about the pennies, what the next move should be, and when he emerged from his office, she looked up at him. He had the alert expression he wore when he wanted to offer advice.

"How are you?" she asked.

He stopped. "Been better," he said. "And how are you doing?"

He was the only person who seemed to ever ask her this. She took a deep breath and released it. "My son had some trouble at school."

"What kind of trouble?"

"A boy threw pennies at him and told him to pick them up."

"Oh, *no*," he said, with his beautiful, intent voice; he seemed to fully inhabit her outrage, as though it were a coat he could put on. She invited him outside to pick up the mail. They pushed the doors open and walked into the bright sunshine.

"I don't know what to do," she said. "I want to go and push the bully who did that. Really. Just go in there and rough him up."

He laughed. "The Torah has interesting things to say about this," he said. "'Turn from evil and pursue good, seek peace and pursue it.' Psalm 34:15," he said. "But. The Torah also believes in self-defense. God's quest is in 'the interest of the hunted.' Ecclesiastes," he said. "What does this mean? If you don't help the victim, then you are supporting the aggressor."

It sounded as though he had been reading up on this topic in particular. He walked beside her with brisk, deft steps, his rayon jacket falling liquid around his body.

"I think of him sitting in his class and I worry." She stopped. He was walking more quickly into the alley beside the Temple, his eyes on something; she struggled to catch up.

"Is that car parked in my spot?" he asked.

He was staring at the small space marked "Rabbi Golden," bordered by two gold lines. There was, indeed, a car parked in his space.

"I think so, yes," she said.

"Whose car is that?" he asked. He walked up to it and looked at the license. "Florida." His voice was anguished. "Who is it? *Who?*"

"There's an open spot here," she said. There was a space next to it.

"I have no car today!" he said. "My brakes went out. I'm okay, thanks for asking. It's in the shop. I took the bus here. Have you ridden the public bus? It smells like a keg party. It's full of DUIs. But look at this. Who would think it was okay to park in the rabbi's spot? Do they not have eyes?" He stepped forward and suddenly kicked the tires of the car. He kicked them once, twice, three times; the tip of his tan shoe paled with dust. He stepped back and rubbed his foot. "What in god's name are these tires made of—"

"Rabbi!" she said, stepping forward, alarmed. "I'm sure they didn't mean to . . ."

His forehead was bright with sweat. He stopped, took a deep breath, and turned away from the parking spot.

"I'm sure they'd move," she said, "if you asked—"

"Ask? Why should I— Why should— I'm not asking anyone." He stepped back, rubbed his face with his hand, and looked at her. His eyes resembled Zeb's for a moment, the same softness around the eyelids.

"I heard that you had quite a meeting," he said.

The meeting.

"This is what I think," said the rabbi, talking more quickly. He lifted his sunglasses out of his pocket and set them on his face so his eyes were invisible. "I think that some people perceive me to be angry. I can under*stand* that." He enunciated this last sentence slowly, as though he had been coached on it. "But I am not . . . a bully."

"All right," she said.

"I hear people. I tell them what I think."

He was biting his lip. She wanted this to be true, for it to be this simple. But she had to ask. "But is it sometimes true that some congregants have—"

"It depends on your perception," he said. "Maybe they don't like my sermons. Maybe I use too many big *words*," he said, crossing his arms across his chest.

"Maybe they're a little intimidated," she said. "You're the rabbi— they look up to you."

He shrugged. "I think the people behind this are afraid of something else," he said. "They're afraid of victory! They're Southerners.

Suspicious." He leaned toward her. "Can you believe some of them? *You* understand."

His voice became sweet, almost hushed. His face was so clean-shaven it looked raw.

"What do I understand?" she asked. She wanted to understand.

"I have done a lot," he said. "Membership. Through the roof. Friday nights. People want to come! I did this. My first pulpit, mind you. The troops loved me. You should have seen them. We prayed together. I fortified them. They were battling evil. Those SCUDs in Israel. They knew the stakes. Push the army out of Kuwait. *I made them strong.* I told them they were Maccabees. They put down *Halo* to listen to me. None of the other chaplains had that effect."

"But—" she said, softly, "what about Carmella? Or Mrs. Schwartz? They count, too."

He stepped back, lightly, and took off his sunglasses. His eyes looked bare, vulnerable as a baby's in the sun. She felt a swooping pity for him.

"Maybe—maybe you need to count to ten," she said, and flinched; had she really said this to him? The rabbi?

His eyelids flickered, then he assumed a pert, childish expression. "Well," she said, "at least I don't stamp my feet."

THAT NIGHT, AROUND MIDNIGHT, THERE was the turning wail of a siren. It was distant, and then it was approaching, and then there was a click and whoosh and it was parked at Forrest Sanders's door. The street was glowing red. The EMTs hauled in a stretcher.

She waited for ten, fifteen minutes until she saw Evelyn brought out on the stretcher. Forrest was not the emergency; it was as though Serena's murderous thoughts had missed Forrest and hit his wife. Forrest walked beside the stretcher, his hand gripping one side as though trying to hold it up. He climbed into the ambulance, and it flew into the night.

....

DAN HEARD THE NEWS FROM a neighbor across the street: Evelyn had had a heart attack; she spent two nights in the hospital, and then she was home.

He wanted to bring them something. A pie. That's what people did here, brought over pies after disastrous events. He headed to Food Lion, intent on this most blameless of actions: purchasing a pie for the infirm. He stood in front of the prebaked pies — apple, cherry, blueberry — and then chose the most expensive: pecan. That evening, he stood in the cool, blue air at Forrest's front door, his fingers gripping the silver tin. He knocked. Forrest opened the door, slowly.

"Forrest, brought you something," said Dan. "All of us hope Evelyn is feeling better."

Dan was startled by Forrest's eyes, which looked as though they had faded the last few days, as if he had gazed intently at something too hot and bright. Forrest regarded the pie.

"She can't eat that," Forrest said.

"Oh," said Dan, feeling foolish.

"But I can," said Forrest, taking it from him. "Thank you."

Dan heard a cough from inside the house.

"You want to come in?" Forrest asked.

He had never been inside of Forrest's house. It held a shadowy, plastic odor; the rooms were small and dim, the wallpaper brown and covered in pink roses. There was the brisk and artificially sweet odor of strawberry room freshener. The room appeared smaller from the extensive collections of knickknacks: There were porcelain figurines of Jesus as a baby, child, adult, Mary looking beatific; these were set against dozens of metal Civil War soldiers in various postures of combat. The different worldviews in the objects lent the room the sense of an unfinished argument. Forrest switched on a light that cast a yellow glow. Dan saw Evelyn sitting in the corner, perfectly still; for a moment, he almost thought she was a lamp. Her white hair was uncombed and had the stiff consistency of seaweed, and, abruptly, she looked at them, her face blank. Dan walked over to her.

"Evelyn. How are you feeling?" he asked.

"I don't know," said Evelyn.

"She was healthy as a horse, and now this," said Forrest. "I came home and found her on the floor—I thought she was just tired as usual—"

"I worked a double," said Evelyn.

"But she was sweating and then she fainted and I called 9-1-1—"

"You're looking good, ah, young lady," said Dan to Evelyn. Evelyn did not respond to this. Forrest stood, holding the pie. He did not appear to want to offer any to Dan. Dan felt an urge to keep talking.

"Let me know how I can help," said Dan. "You know, I can take over the Pinewood Derby . . . if you want—"

Forrest reddened. He put down the pie and stared at Dan. "You're not taking over the derby," he said.

"I mean I can help out," said Dan.

"You think I need help?" asked Forrest.

"No," said Dan, alarmed. "Certainly not."

Forrest crossed his arms. "I've run those derbies for almost seventy years. I'm the only one in that room who knows how to run it."

Dan nodded, a little violently. "You sure are," he said. Evelyn coughed. Dan nodded toward Evelyn and Forrest. "Let us know if you need anything." His face ached from smiling. He pushed open the vinyl screen door and walked outside.

THE NEXT DAY, WHEN SERENA saw Forrest, he stood, holding the garden hose, watering his impatiens. "Forrest," she called—to ask about Evelyn, perhaps, though she still resented him. He glanced at her and then away. What he was doing was examining the side of her house. She followed his gaze to see if she could figure out what he was seeing—a crack, or mold—but there was only a house. His face looked blanched. There was a draining of light beneath his pink skin. She thought she saw something flicker in his expression: a calculation.

. . . .

BETTY CALLED SERENA AND ASKED her to meet her at the Waring Country Club for lunch. "We need to discuss the whole—situation, face-to-face," said Betty. "I'll treat you. The food's good." The club had been established in 1882, and, like other edifices of the era, it was constructed with white marble, columns, and an elaborate system of fountains in front. The entrance featured the requisite stone sculpture romanticizing the Civil War—the Confederate War soldier crouching beside a bush with a gun, a child bugle player nobly saluting the air, the inscription *To all the brave who gave their lives.* It was as though the war had not been fought over one human's right to enslave another but over the right to engage in leisure activities, whether golf or tennis or swimming. Once you walked in, maroon-shirted employees, all pert and attentive, were on hand to guide you to whatever sports experience you wanted to take part in, with a pro shop to the left and a café to the right. There was a sense of quiet there, the windows overlooking the artificially peaceful green landscape of the golf course. Members floated in and out, sunburned pink men in golf caps chuckling, young mothers herding children in bathing suits to the swimming pool. No one shouted. Piano music was piped in. She waited for Betty to arrive.

Betty walked in, her face blooming in a large smile. "Hi, sweetie," said Betty, hugging her. Her silver hairdo had the frothy consistency of meringue. "So very glad to see you."

They were seated at a round table with a perfect view of the sixteenth hole. Betty was apparently a regular.

"How long have you belonged here?" asked Serena.

"Not long," said Betty. "A couple years. They didn't admit Jews till the 1970s," she said. "Then they had a Jewish mayor, Fred Goldstein, cousin of Sharon, you know her? First one. Jews weren't allowed to hold public office until 1868, did you know that? They couldn't exclude the mayor. She was the first. Until then, you had to have family roots here to become a member. Unless one was, of course, asked." She had brown arms splotched with pink stars, which advertised her affinity for outdoor leisure activities; it was the mark of money. "The ceilings were cracked. I helped smash them open. As a Jew and as a woman asked to join on her own."

Her expression sharpened.

"I've always been a trailblazer," said Betty. "I was the only Jewish girl in my high school. If girls were after a boy who liked me, they'd say, 'Do you know what she is? She's a Jew.' I was thin then. Pretty. It happened often. Some boys I lost, some I didn't. I was the valedictorian, sweetheart. The head cheerleader. I won it all. I was the first girl at Temple Shalom to get a Bat Mitzvah. I was the first Jewish girl allowed entrance into Tri Delt at UNC, 1972. That doesn't include what I've dealt with as a woman. I was in the workforce before any of the feminist stuff. Do you know that when I got out of college, the newspaper had two separate columns for jobs, one for men and one for women?" She took a long sip of water, closing her eyes.

Serena's mother had told her the same thing. That fact had fed into her mother's fears and had the effect of making her withdraw from the workforce. She could not stand up to the idea that others might not take her seriously, but she fiercely wanted her daughters to succeed.

"No one tells me what to do," Betty said. She sat up very straight. "Woman to woman—that has helped me create my business. One point two million in sales last year. I did that! Can you believe it, Serena?"

"That's great." She admired this; how had Betty known how to do this? How did some people shuck off the slights the world threw them and rise to success? Was it something they knew innately, or was it just luck? How had her father had the foresight, as a small child, to know that the storm gathering in 1930s Germany would not disappear? How had he convinced his parents to leave when they did? And how had her mother been, as a child, overwhelmed by the playground in Fresno? Her own parents had admired people like Betty and not known how to emulate them.

She looked at the careful way Betty spread her roll with butter; Betty set her knife on her butter plate gently, the way Serena's mother did. How long had it been since she had spoken to Sophie, her mother? It had been months, since the funeral, since she had had a real conversation with Sophie or Dawn, and she missed them. Sometimes, when she picked up the phone, she heard only a breath on the line—then the other party hung up. Who was there? Was it her mother? Her sister? The rabbi? In some alternate world, her father?

"Tell me something," said Betty. "Do you think you are worth the best, Serena?"

"Sure," she said, playing along.

"I sound like the L'Oreal commercial. But it is true. We women especially need to remember this. Have you ever felt that you are putting up with something bad just because you feel you don't have an alternative?"

Serena glanced out at the golf course, the unreal, velvet surface of the greens. "Sure."

"We have to expect more. Of the world. Of others. And of ourselves."

They had each ordered salads, and the lettuce was pale and lacy, with edible purple flowers ringing the plates. Betty took a deep breath and set down her fork.

"I wanted to meet with you today," she said, "because we can expect more of our spiritual leader. I have had countless discussions with that man about his behavior. I have tried, I tell you. He's supposed to be helping us!"

She had ordered a complex and decorative salad and began to eat it methodically—all the olives encircling the plate, then the slices of cucumber.

"I like him," said Serena, before she could stop herself.

Betty looked up. "Why?"

She tried to make her voice even, reasonable. "He's helped me a lot."

"How has he helped you?" asked Betty.

"With a neighbor we're having trouble with. He somehow solved it! He's . . . never said anything hurtful to me."

"And why not to you?"

Serena looked at the table. "I don't know."

Betty slid back her chair as though she wanted to move far away from this statement. "Because it hasn't happened to you," said Betty, "doesn't mean it can't happen to someone else." She paused. "I didn't think my husband would cheat on me. On *me*?" She laughed, a short, cheerless sound.

"I am sorry," Serena said.

"Don't be. I survived it," said Betty. She sat very straight and flapped her napkin out on her lap with the rustle of a little sail.

"Look," said Serena. "Some people think he has also — done a lot of good. What are we going to do without a rabbi? Who's going to lead services? Aren't we going to lose members?"

"Don't you know, hon," said Betty, clasping her hands, eyes bright, "our Temple is chock *full* of wonderful people who will come together."

"Who?"

"Look at the talent in our Temple," said Betty. "Arnold Rosenbaum can tutor in Hebrew. Genevieve Shapman is a published poet. She can write sermons. The Ritual Practices Committee is ready to go. We are important, Serena. We count. Maybe we won't even need a rabbi! We can save money! Do you know how much we contribute to his pension alone? A man who has bullied numerous old ladies when they have sought spiritual counsel from him?" Betty leaned forward. "In this situation, I believe we have to protect the weak. What did Rabbi Hillel say? If not me, who? If not now, when?"

Serena leaned forward. "Where is he going to go? Have you thought of that? What will he do without *us*?"

Betty put down her fork. "Who cares?" she said. "What is going to happen to us if we keep him? Next time he makes someone cry, it's blood on our hands."

The waiters glided across the room so graceful and precise they seemed like actors. There was the soft clink of silverware. Betty pulled out a list. "I want you to look at this," she said. "People who have filed complaints. Call them."

She handed the list to Serena. They sat in the silence, the members lumbering across the golf course, the false grass shimmering in the sun.

SERENA OPENED HER FRONT DOOR to Forrest Sanders two days later. There was a militaristic air to his stance, as though he were leading a large, invisible army behind him, in service of some great cause she did not know. When he saw her, she could tell that she had loomed large in his imagination as well, that the fact of her own human presence was troubling; his face turned pink.

"Hello!" he said, a little too brightly. "I'm dropping off a flyer."

"Oh," she said.

"We've had some hard times," he said. "You may have heard. My wife was sick. Her heart. They got to her just in time."

He looked at her, closely, as though he believed that her animosity had played a part in this. She knew suddenly, despite their differences — their varying thoughts on Jesus, creationism, magic, evolution — that they shared the ancient belief that their actual thoughts were powerful and could do damage. "I hope she feels better soon," she said.

He cleared his throat. "They say she'll be just fine."

"Well," she said. "That's good."

"It gave me a scare," he said. He shifted onto one leg and rubbed his eyes. His hand trembled; she felt, for a moment, sad for him. Was he here to make amends? Was he making an effort at reconciliation?

"It got me thinking," he said. "Our lives are short." He seemed desperate to sum it up for someone. "I got to thinking about the meaning of life. I got to thinking about this."

He handed her the flyer. It was a red piece of paper with a picture of the Virgin Mary cradling a baby in her lap. It said: *Let's have a meeting to bring Christmas back into our children's schools! December 7, 7:00 PM, Oakdale Elementary School Auditorium.*

"What is this?" she asked.

"I'm doing a little organizing," he said. "My grandson's teacher said they couldn't have a nativity scene in their classroom. Or angels! Or crosses! I'm going to fight it."

She stared at him, the embattled Confederate, the near widower, gleeful in his desire to spread the cause of Christianity. It was not reconciliation. Things had not gone in this direction.

"You're going to fight *what*?"

"Things have tipped too far the other direction . . . we need to give Christmas the respect it deserves," he said. "We are one nation under God. Bring the Christ back into Christmas. We're a Christian nation. The founding fathers said it is so. We've been persecuted, too. Our values trampled upon, ignored!" He was a little gleeful now; he heard something fearful in her voice, and he was clearly enjoying it.

"But why?" she asked.

Her son had walked into school by himself today, calmly, chatting away about YuGiOh cards. It was the first time in a week that he had done so since the incident with the pennies. She did not want anything now to interfere with that.

"I saw something that disturbed me last week," he said. "My granddaughter's school schedule. Did you know that the public school calendar now says Winter Break instead of Christmas Break? And Spring Break instead of Easter Break?"

"I think that's all right," she said. Gently.

He blinked and stepped back and made a sort of laugh-cough that was supposed to be a scoff. "Well, you shouldn't. We're one nation under God. You take away a name, you take away the spirit of the holiday."

He wanted to talk—that was half of what was happening here. It was touching, actually. He had to talk to someone, even if it had to be her.

"I have to go," she said, and stepped back inside.

A small smile crept across his face, as though she had confirmed his suspicions. "Well, Miss Serena," he said. "Have a fine day." Clutching his flyers, he turned and walked carefully to the next house.

Chapter Twelve

·························

FINALLY, THERE WAS THE CALL she had been waiting for. It was not from the rabbi; it was not from Dan. It was not from Earl Morton or anyone who had dismissed her in New York. She was not aware of the way she was waiting for this call. She understood it when she finally heard her sister's voice; a pain, an ache, she had not been aware she contained, vanished. There was a short, cheerful message: "Serena. Miss you! Let's talk. Dawn." There were two more of these over the course of an afternoon, and then more emphatically: "Serena. Please! Get on the phone, now!"

She dialed Dawn's number, and there she was.

"Finally," whispered Dawn.

"Finally?" asked Serena. "I've been calling you. Where have you been?"

"Here and there," said Dawn. "I don't keep track. I've been totally swamped. You know, working." She let that dangle in the air a moment and added, "We're coming."

"Where?"

"To visit you."

Serena held the phone, her throat cool with relief.

"Well. Great! When?"

"Tomorrow. Well. Just for a moment. We're on our way to France."

"Oh."

"I mean, *we're* not," said Dawn. She paused. "I'll explain. We'll be there at ten. It will be good to see you—" There was static. Dawn hung up.

THE NEXT DAY AT 10:00 AM, Serena stood at the security gate waiting for Dawn and Sophie, her mother, to come off the red-eye to Waring. Her mother and sister headed down the stale white corridor,

Dawn in sunglasses, limping but wearing high heels, and their mother beside her, her face pale with exhaustion but her wearing a sweater with French phrases — *bonjour, merci, comment allez-vous* — written across it in gold script. The sight of them made Serena feel buoyant. They were all related. They knew her; there was a primitive value in that. She loved them with immediacy and optimism; it was as though family was merely this, the place where your private strangeness could be understood.

Or where you hoped it could be understood.

Dawn and her mother wandered onto the steel blue carpet of the Waring airport. Serena ran toward them and hugged them.

Dawn had not spoken to her in weeks, but Serena clung to her for a moment, letting her sister's body fall against hers, even though Dawn was much taller.

"I missed you," said Dawn; Serena could not speak, understanding how much she had missed her sister as well. She pressed her cheek to Dawn's long, dark hair, the same color as her own, listened to her laugh, the same sound as hers; she longed to see her sister, the face and hands and arms that were shaped in a way that was closest to her own. There was the hope that they would be more similar than they were, the stubborn optimism that, because they had just, by a matter of months, missed being each other, they would think and feel the same way. There was the bewilderment, the sense of loss, when each had a thought or feeling that the other could not comprehend.

Serena had imagined they would appear different now, somehow, with their father gone; she was aware of how she and Dawn looked similar with age, how the minute differences in their looks as teenagers were erased by the softness in their waists, the heaviness under their chins, the first gray in their hair.

"You look the same," said Dawn, with relief. "A child. Twenty-five. We both do."

She smiled, and she seemed to mean it. Dawn stood, her elbows jutting out as they had when she was a small girl; she had a determined need to see goodness. Their father had loved that about Dawn, the way she mythologized the family, the first-place essay in high school she wrote about her father, entitled "An International Hero," in which she described a father so perfect Serena took it as an exercise in art, but which their father happily accepted as biography.

"What a flight," said her mother. "The turbulence. I thought I would vomit. I snagged some of these on the way out—" She reached into her purse and brought out several silver foil packets of peanuts.

They retrieved luggage and headed into the low, silvery autumn light. Her mother and sister walked beside her. Serena sensed the similarity of their gait, the way she and her mother paused, every couple steps, to accommodate Dawn, who was slower. It was glorious to walk with them together here, in this town where they had landed; whoever they were, they knew her and she knew them.

Waring was about twenty minutes from the airport, and she drove past the county jail— which was, in a perhaps insensitive gesture to the prisoners, situated directly across the street from the airport terminal—past some dead, gray strawberry fields, the first of a parade of junk food outlets, various billboards hawking "Smithson's BBQ Extravaganza" and the upcoming Camellia Festival, and past a billboard that featured a bearded man and the words: *He loves you. www.comebacktojesus.org.*

"What is that?" asked Dawn, lifting her sunglasses and blinking.

"This is the Bible Belt," said Sophie, expertly. "This stuff is everywhere."

"It's medieval," said Dawn. "Really."

"So what kind of job can you get out here?" her mother asked.

Serena tried to think about how to phrase it. "Dan's in promotion," she said, carefully. "It wasn't so easy to find something . . . I'm working at the Temple."

They laughed.

"What can you do at the Temple?" asked Dawn. "Do you have some religious power we are not aware of?"

"Does one actually work at a temple?" her mother said. "Or do you just stand up and sit down, stand up and sit down—"

"Excuse me," said Serena, gripping the steering wheel, "I work."

"Doing what?" asked her mother.

She had hoped they would not ask this particular question. "I'm, uh, helping create the Southeast North Carolina Jewish Community

Center," said Serena, with more enthusiasm than she had intended; suddenly, she wished she had not mentioned it.

There was a heavy and perplexed silence.

"And what is that?" her mother asked.

"Well," she said. She paused. "It's in the beginning stages." She braced herself. It was nothing yet, which meant that it could, in fact, be anything. "It's a place, um, eight thousand square feet, twenty-foot glass windows, uh, sanctuary plus library plus bowling alley, et cetera, where, uh, local Jews can congregate and, well, be together—"

"Why do you want to be around Jews?" asked Dawn.

"I don't really like Jews," said Sophie. "Except you girls and Aaron, and myself, of course."

Serena had somehow predicted this response, but still it was unnerving. Her mother often took pleasure in distancing herself from other Jews, always perturbed by this accident of identity, religious or otherwise. Serena turned to look at her mother, who was picking at a fingernail. "Mom! What do you mean by that?"

"I don't really feel a bond. Am I supposed to? Those ladies at the temple you went to. Singing all those songs . . ."

"Well, you could learn them—"

"I hated that. Blah, blah. Asking who knows what for help. And the rabbis, all pompous fakes."

Serena thought of the last board meeting and gripped the steering wheel.

"But you're not Christian," said Serena.

"God, no," said her mother.

"And you're not . . . atheist."

Sophie paused. "Look. I didn't choose any of this. If my actual life had reflected my inner life, I would have been a duchess in France." Her mother stroked her short gray hair over her ears. "Maybe an elegant Jewish duchess who had escaped the Inquisition. I don't know if I ever felt Jewish, even though everyone in my school thought I was. How does one feel Jewish?" She paused and patted Serena's arm. "But I am glad to hear that you are employed again, sweetheart."

Serena drove past the main strip mall of Waring. Her mother and sister stared out at the unlikely alliance of Wendy's, Bojangles',

Chick-fil-A, the Greek revival Wrightson-Birch mansion, the collection of churches, the pre–Civil War mansions, the long, muscular branches of the oak trees entwined with Spanish moss like long, silvery hair.

"Mom now has a nice setup behind our house," said Dawn.

"Oh," said Serena, both grateful and envious. "Why didn't you want your other house?"

Sophie was quiet. "I was living there and then I was not," she said, staring out the window. Serena glanced at her mother; she had the same frozen, frightened expression that Zeb wore when he contemplated walking into school. The gold lettering on her shirt glittered in the November sunlight.

"Where are you going?" asked Serena.

"Paris!" said Dawn, brightening.

"We're going to the red carpet," her mother said.

It appeared that Dawn had just put together the biggest group of donors yet to raise money to combat genocide in Darfur. The event was to be held at a four-star hotel in Paris.

"It will be a whirlwind trip," said Sophie. "I plan to window shop in the Champs-Elysées and sit in a café and eat some chocolate mousse—"

Dawn glanced over at her mother and began twirling her hair. "Paris is cold this time of year," said Dawn. "No one would want to sit in a café—"

"I can't wait," said Sophie. "I can order in French, and people will not look at me strangely—"

"Mom," said Dawn, and Serena could detect a subterranean edge in her voice, a tone she could not identify. "Don't you want to see Serena's house? How much longer, Serena?"

Serena stopped the car. "Here," she said.

They looked at the house. She had swept the porch, but she had not noticed the streaks of blue mold on the front and side of the house; she had not really seen the weedy front yard, either. Forrest's front area was in full display, trimmed and aglow with autumn flowers, and she suddenly understood why they spent so much time and life force tending to their square of dirt. Their gardens were an attempt to explain something hopeful about themselves. It made it seem that they lived beside sane and pleasant neighbors; as long as Forrest didn't come out, anyway, they were safe.

Her mother and Dawn looked around, concerned. "Where?" asked Dawn, a little worriedly.

"We're here!" said Serena.

She opened the car door.

She remembered, from her last visit, Dawn's home, the three-story brick colonial in Encino with the small in-law apartment in the back. It was the sort of house where there was no sign of the children in the common areas, where the rooms seemed to be furnished in one swoop, an Ethan Allen or Macy's salesperson's vision of what a room should be. There were photos of the family, all professionally taken, hanging in tasteful black frames on the walls, as though the home was a museum.

There was no identity expressed in her own house except, Serena thought, one of panic. There was a musty aqua couch from Goodwill, some plastic chairs they had picked up at Walmart, a card table they were using in the dining room. "Well," she said, walking them through, flipping on an electric switch that spat and buzzed dangerously, "here we are."

There were just three of them, walking through this little house in a strange land. They disappeared into the kitchen in front of her, and Serena had the sudden thought that they had vanished completely. She stepped in and there they were, filling the kitchen, but she was frighteningly aware of how any of them could disappear.

"Well, so here we are," she said. Her mother looked pale; Serena did not know if this was from jet lag or disappointment. "Can I get anyone anything?" she said. "Uh. Coffee, tea—"

They all wandered through her kitchen as though seeking warmth. She gave them each cups of tea, and they sipped it at the table, looking around.

"I'm a little tired. I would like to lie down," her mother said.

She took her mother into her bedroom and set her up on their bed. She pulled a blanket over her mother. Sophie looked small, her shoulders thin, as she stretched out on the bed. Serena put her palm on her mother's forehead. Her mother flinched.

"Rest," said Serena.

. . . .

SHE WENT INTO THE LIVING room. Dawn was standing by the window. She turned around and walked carefully to Serena and gripped her arm. Serena remembered the sensation of Dawn's fingers on her arm when Dawn began to learn to walk again after her illness, after Dawn's leg was paralyzed when she was six years old. Serena was eight years old and did not quite know what to do to help her, but she remembered the way her sister's fingers pressed into her arm as the two made a slow circle around the backyard. A few weeks before, Dawn had raced her through this yard; now she needed help to make her way across it. Serena saw Dawn's arm against her own, both of them the light caramel color of their mother, and for a moment she could not distinguish between them. It was a mere accident of time that they were not each other, and she sensed the varieties of fortune and misfortune that could come to them, and their helplessness in the face of this.

Now Dawn had taken off her sunglasses, and her eyes were a little red. "I need to talk to you," said Dawn.

They went onto the porch. There was one plastic chair on the porch, and Dawn sat on it; Serena stood on the soft wood, which felt unstable beneath her feet.

"It's been a hard year," said Dawn.

Serena nodded.

"You know. I have worked hard. I have set up Mom in the back. We're glad she's there, glad we can take care of her." Serena looked away, for Dawn did not need to say the next thing — she was not the fool that her older sister was, she had not committed any criminal actions, and she had the income and room to care for their mother.

"I've been looking forward to this weekend. I have earned it. We are going to stop genocide, once and for all! Through education and food subsidies. Dad would be happy."

There was an edge in her voice as she said "earned," as though some wages, monetary or spiritual, had recently been diminished. Serena had the sense that Dawn wanted her to say something approving, so she said, "That's good."

"Anyway," said Dawn, "I planned this event and bought Mom tickets, but something's come up." She put her sunglasses on again. "So. Um. Well, this time, I'd like her to stay here."

Serena looked at her. "What?" she said, softly.

"Just for the weekend. You'll have a good time. You can show her around the town, maybe get some, uh, barbecue—"

There was always between them the wariness of being ordered by the other, as though each one's status in the family was somehow so precarious it was important not to let any guard slip. "But—look at her outfit! She wants to go!" Serena said.

Dawn cleared her throat. "We can go another time," she said. "We don't always get what we want." She paused. "Do I? Do you?" Her sister stood up and slowly, leaning on one foot, walked to the other end of the porch. "Don't look at me like that. I try. Guess what. I wanted her to come to Paris. I wanted to do something nice for her. But then."

"Then what?"

Dawn sat down again. She put her hands over her face. "I need to tell you something," said her sister. She flipped open her wallet and brought out a picture of a man. "Him," she said.

Serena looked at the photo. He was a rather handsome young man, with a black dyed spiky haircut and square maroon-tinted sunglasses. He was posing in swim trunks by a hotel swimming pool. Serena noticed that Dawn was smiling in a proud, frightened way.

"What does this have to do with Paris?"

"He's going to be there. Mom can't come."

Serena stared at Dawn. "What?" asked Serena. She felt that she had, as an older sister, failed in some basic manner of protection. "When did this start?"

"Six months ago."

"How old is this guy?" she squinted at the photo.

"Thirty. His name is Mo."

"Why? Dawn! What about Jake?"

"I don't know." It was an "I don't know" with roots that extended back thirty, forty years. Serena could hear Dawn saying this when her father asked her if she had, in fact, committed an array of sibling misdemeanors; she had perfected the dry, flat answer—"I don't know"—which was always oddly accepted. *I don't know.* Serena admired it, really. It allowed Dawn to float above everything.

"Since when?"

"A while. He's embarrassed by me. In some way. I can sense it. I have a sixth sense for that. Like our father. Jake never looks me in the eye. He never offers to wash a dish. Not that I do generally, but he assumes someone will. He has never shopped for groceries. He has never thought once that we are low on milk. He just assumes it will all work. Like a child. I don't feel—valued. Everything just runs, and he assumes it will. So I thought, fuck it. I want something for me."

Serena did not know Jake well; he was a tall, heavy man who developed hotel properties in San Diego, the sort of person who had been drawn in by Dawn's access to charitable feelings; at their wedding, he had sweetly made a toast to "the woman whose goodness shines a light into mine."

"So that's it?" said Serena.

"Mo touches my leg," said Dawn. "He kisses it. He holds it like it is a precious gem." She paused. "Jake never did that."

"Maybe he did it metaphorically."

"He did not."

"What do you want me to say? Congratulations?"

"Maybe." Dawn paused. "It was—well, right before Dad passed away. And then I looked at myself in the mirror one day, and I thought I am a good-looking woman, and why don't I feel right—"

"You are good-looking," said Serena.

"Serena, please!" Dawn said, her voice rising. "This is hard to explain. I feel—alone. I need someone to cherish me. That fills me with peace. I'm sick of being *good*. Twenty years of helping the poor. I keep trying, and it doesn't end—it doesn't! Last week, a child at a homeless shelter in Inglewood took my hand and smiled at me. Guess what. *I didn't care. For the first time.* I wanted him to let go, actually. Find your own mother! I actually thought this! It scared me. I'm doing this to unleash my humanity. To find the *love* in myself again. For god's sake," she said, "I'm trying to end genocide! I just need . . . something else."

They sat on the porch. An enormous pale heron bounced heavily along the air. The sky had clouded over and now resembled a gray mattress. It occurred to her that Dawn might be having some sort of breakdown. Who could she call? Jake? But Dawn did not, in all honesty, seem particularly distraught. She reached into her purse, brought out her boarding pass, and looked it over; she seemed eager to get on with her flight.

"Do you really want to disappoint her?" said Serena. "My god, she's a widow—"

"I know that. She's living with us. I'll take her another time. I will! Say there was—a mistake. The airline. They only printed one ticket from here to Charlotte to Paris. Please. Serena." She looked at her watch. "I have to go back to the airport to make a connection in an hour."

"An hour!"

She was impressed by this, if a little horrified—Dawn's assumption that all would be well, that she could park their mother here and fly off to Europe. It assumed a variety of character traits in Serena that felt warped and unfortunate but that were, perhaps, correct.

"It will be fine," said Dawn. "You will have a good time together! Bonding. I'll be back . . . Monday. Back to normal. Please. I want to tell you about him. I haven't told anyone, only you."

She reached over and touched Serena's shoulder; Dawn's hand was trembling. Serena closed her eyes. She wanted, despite herself, to listen.

"Go ahead," said Serena.

"He gets us fancy hotel rooms," said Dawn. "There's always champagne. He undresses me very slowly. This happens at lunch."

"Okay."

"He writes me poems and hides them in my purse."

"Come on! This sounds totally clichéd. It sounds like *Cosmo*."

"Maybe I like *Cosmo*," said Dawn. "I can't wait to see him. It's all I think about all day—"

"Where is your husband in all this? Where are your children?"

"Doing their own activities. Happy, I think. Happy enough. They don't need to know." She paused. "Those two hours with him—time freezes. I feel him kissing my legs, my arms, everything. I am there. When are you ever there, in a place, Serena? I mean, really somewhere? Not tapping your foot and watching the clock, but aware of every part of yourself, of the other person? Dad didn't know that he was going to die that day. He didn't know he would die any day. I want to try to forget about dying. I don't want to be anywhere else."

She stared at Dawn; she understood this part, the unstoppable quality of her yearning, the desire to stop time, more than she wanted to admit.

Dawn bit her lip. "Sometimes I think—I don't know."

"What?"

"Maybe Dad suspected. Or I could be making this up—"

Perhaps Dawn had accidentally killed him, thought Serena. This idea made her feel a little better for a moment: Perhaps it had not been *her*.

"Besides," said Dawn, glancing at her, "it's not like I committed a crime."

Serena blinked. How did she manage to turn the conversation in this direction? This was not at all the same. "It was—some money on the company's entertainment account ... come on! Did they really need it?"

"It was someone else's dime," said Dawn.

"It's not like betraying your husband by screwing someone in a hotel."

"Well. I want to tell you. You can plug your ears. We met at an event for the homeless. The two-hundred-dollars-a-plate fancy dinner, cream sauces, so that you can feed the hungry. What a hopeless cause. I had rounded up some soap opera stars looking to dignify themselves. They were all flitting around trying not to eat. No one eats anything at these events. They're all on some diet. So the fancy spread goes to waste. He was heaping his plate full of food. He picked a big strawberry off the table. He looked at me and said, 'You hate everyone here.'"

Dawn brushed the hair out of her eyes. "I looked at him, and I thought, how does he know? He knew my bad thoughts. And he didn't care. There was something lovely about that. He offered me a strawberry. The way he handed it to me was erotic. It just was. He slipped me his number. I called it. We met. I felt I was in another universe. I've always wanted to be. He paid that hotel room, I paid the next. He owes me a couple hotel rooms. A little more, too. But it's okay."

She seemed to hesitate a bit, and Serena asked, "What do you mean, he owes you?"

"He's investing in real estate in Cuba. For when Castro dies. It's really smart! He wanted me to go in with him. I put up five thousand. That's nothing for me, really. I'm making three hundred thousand a year. He said he could buy beach property and it would skyrocket."

"You gave him five *thousand* dollars?"

"Don't say it like that."

Serena paused. She could not stop herself. "Is he a male prostitute?"

"Oh, my god!" Dawn turned to her. "Apologize."

"Does he really have a job?"

"Yes! He's vice president at his company! He just has a—*joie de vivre*, shall we say. He's looking for other employment opportunities—"

"Quite a *joie de vivre*," said Serena.

"He's a human being!"

Serena thought of Dawn standing on the red carpet, speaking into her walkie-talkie, with thin, glossy movie stars floating around her, directed where she told them to go; she thought of her sister ascending the stage to receive the Most Likely to Succeed award in high school for her generosity, her perseverance, her silky dark hair; she remembered her parents' expressions at that moment, a wilted, numb relief that Dawn had cleared a path for herself, that she had succeeded.

What did Dawn want, now, of her?

"Please. Please. I know you think I'm an idiot," said Dawn. "I'm not. I'm assertive. I wouldn't give him more money. Unless, of course, it seems like it would be a good deal." She looked at Serena. "Do you think I'm an idiot?"

Dawn's large, golden eyes were on her. This was what her sister was accomplishing, on her slim island of time on earth—afternoons with an opportunist in a hotel, who had the unique ability to fawn upon her leg. There was the problematic supposition that Serena was supposed to protect her. Her parents had never gotten over the fact that they had not been able to get Dawn to the hospital in time, that they could not magically float above traffic, that the doctors had taken them in too late, that this rare and unexpected result—the paralysis of her leg—had occurred.

"Just tell me," said Dawn.

"No," said Serena, and then she was an accomplice. But it was the only answer her sister would hear.

SHE REALLY WANTED TO TELL Dawn not to go. But it was not what Dawn could hear at the moment. And what had she wanted herself, sitting in the rabbi's office, reluctant to leave because each moment was slowing down and expanding? What was her need to sit with him in that dark cluttered room, to have him listen to her? Was the escape that they yearned for merely about stopping time? She saw, in the flush of Dawn's face, the surprising force of her sister's loneliness.

"I really have to go," said Dawn, standing up. "I connect Charlotte to Paris. I think I should just go now. While she's asleep. It'll be easier."

"Well, maybe on *you*," said Serena.

"Maybe on me," said Dawn, and she smiled; her eyes were so lovely, so radiant, their father's eyes. "But why not me?"

It was a simple enough statement, proactive in one context and chilling in another. She stood, trying to think. Dawn was pressing buttons on her BlackBerry and calling a cab.

"I'll meet her back home on Monday. She has her tickets. Tell her we'll go there soon. A month. Tell me everything will be fine." Her sister's thin brown eyebrows flickered.

"Fine," Serena said, reluctantly. They looked at each other. She held her sister, the bones of Dawn's shoulders against her palms.

A cab arrived, swiftly, quietly, as though summoned not by a device but by her sister's unconscious. Then Dawn was gone.

THE PHONE RANG. SHE RAN inside to get it.

The voice was so contorted with cheerfulness, it took a moment to identify it; and then she realized it was Rabbi Golden. He sounded like he was shouting into a device that took your voice and made it sound like an infomercial spokesperson's.

"How are you this fine autumn day?"

"Fine," she said, cautiously.

"No one is here," he said, and his voice was husky again, as though he was about to cry. "And I need help."

"What kind of help?" she asked.

"I can't find the coffee," he said.

Was this serious? "Under the bottom shelf in the kitchen—" she said, patiently.

"I can't find it."

"Well," she said sternly, "look."

"I can't. Without Georgia, I can't find anything. Please. Can you help me?"

"Rabbi," she said, "my mother is—um, visiting, I can't—"

"Serena Hirsch. Please."

There was something in his voice, a real panic that she recognized. She closed her eyes. "Hold on," she said. "You have to wait."

She figured that taking her mother to the Temple briefly to help the rabbi find the coffee would be a way to distract her once she learned that she was spending the weekend in the international capital known as Waring. She sat, waiting for her to awaken.

Her mother came out, blinking, pink-eyed, in about half an hour. She walked into the living room and sat down. Her face was both youthful and ancient after having slept midday; there were translucent pink shadows under her eyes.

"I was speaking French in my sleep," said Sophie. "I remember most of it. It comes back, it really does."

Serena's heart tightened. Her mother had been gifted at languages—French, Spanish, German, Russian, a little girl growing up in the Central Valley of California, the floor fans sitting like airplane propellers in her living room to cut through the heat, Sophie's own mother stricken with vertigo when she was twelve, bedridden, and her father a constant card player, distant. They were second-generation from Russia but would have nothing to do with Judaism, except for Chanukah, when her father liked to gamble. Sophie began learning languages when she was a child, when her mother became ill. When she was supposed to be selling gum and soda and bread to the people of the town after school, sitting by the register, she was instead teaching herself two languages, sending away for the Berlitz program, and she had mastered German and French by the time she graduated high school. Sophie's mother had not appreciated her linguistic abilities. "Don't sound smarter than the boys," she said to her daughter.

Sophie stood along the wire fence of the playground, the children running on the hard gray cement. She was shy. She was not good at the games they played. That was how their mother described her childhood: "They did not know why I would want to speak languages they did not know. What was I saying? I was saying nothing. *I would like some milk. That ball is fast. Recess is almost over.*" Why did they not talk to her? Because she stood by the fence and muttered in French? Because Sophie's own mother was incapacitated and they could see that sorrow on her? Sophie told Serena how she remembered standing against the fence at school, her mother in bed. She said she didn't feel outcast but superior, knowing the languages no one else did. "I felt bigger than them," she said. "*I* was going to fly over the ocean to Paris, I was going to sit in a café and converse with people in French, in German, in anything I wanted —"

"You thought big even then," Serena once said to her.

"I did until my mother died," said Sophie. "Then I felt like nothing."

Sophie had plans. She did not have a scholarship to pay for college, but she moved to the Fairfax area of Los Angeles when she was eighteen, lived with an aunt, started Cal State Northridge, tried to work at May Company and go to school, could not get to her classes in time after her shift, stopped working, ran out of money, dropped out, started again; then her mother died suddenly when Sophie was nineteen.

Serena had always wanted to hear this story — how Sophie tried to go to college on her own, that supreme effort. It was the time when her mother had tried to imagine herself as someone new. "I was the best in my class," Sophie had told her. "I sat in the front row. My teachers loved me. I was on the way to becoming a diplomat. The French embassy. All my class presentations were about what I needed to know for that position. Champagne. I researched manners. Place settings. I asked to work at the perfume counter so I could learn about brands.

Chanel. I was preparing for the embassy dinners. My mother was dead. I did not think. I moved forward. It was the money, darling. I couldn't make enough. I fell asleep during class. One time the bus was late so I missed a final. I failed, and I knew everything! The professor wouldn't let me make it up."

She told these stories to Serena growing up, and Serena was moved by this, her mother's living on the couch of her aunt Ruby in Fairfax, sitting in the front of the classroom, raising her hand, discoursing on champagne in French. It was as though her mother were her, then, or Dawn, but better; she was sitting in front of the room without any encouragement, spraying strangers' wrists with expensive perfume and picturing herself in another country; her optimism then sounded boundless, extravagant.

Now she was here. Their mother was slight, smaller than Serena. Serena sat beside her mother, feeling physically like a man. Her mother had always taken up a minute amount of space; after she had stopped going to college and met their father, she had spent her life stepping aside for him, and this need echoed in her very posture; she sat, knees together, hands folded, at one corner of the couch.

"Do you want anything to eat?" asked Serena.

"No," said Sophie. She smoothed her hair down and looked around the room. "Where's your sister?"

Serena stood up and walked across the room. She felt like an executioner.

"Mom, she had to go," she said.

Her mother looked up at her. "Left? Where?"

She took in a breath. "She went by herself to Paris. There was . . . a mix-up. A problem with the ticket. She wants you to stay here for the weekend. Which is great, which I would love —"

"She went — by herself?"

"Well, yes."

"That's not funny."

"Mom. It's not a joke —"

She tried to take her mother's hand, but Sophie didn't let her.

"No. She had to go alone. Something —" Now she would lie for Dawn, and how smoothly her voice slid into it. "There was an emergency —"

"I thought I was going with Dawn to the red carpet."

"So did I, but apparently—"

Her mother stood up. "I wanted to *go*," she cried. "I know French. I could have been her interpreter—"

"I know. She said you could go with her another time." She'd better, Serena thought. "Soon."

"What emergency? What was going on? I could have helped with the emergency—"

"Mom! I don't know. She said she had to leave. You can go with her soon! Next month, maybe! You can spend the weekend here—"

Her mother sat down. She was breathing heavily. "I did something," said her mother. She set her dark eyes on Serena, expectantly.

"No," said Serena. "She had to work. I want to spend time with you. You can stay with me."

At Saks, she may have been a thief, but now she was a horrible liar. Serena's head hurt. Her mother was still wearing her sweater emblazoned with French words, and slowly she slipped it off, folded it, and placed it on the couch. Then Sophie sat, rubbing her hands against one another.

"Next month," said her mother, softly. "I can go next month." She sighed. "So I'm stuck here," said her mother. "Homeless. I'm a homeless vagabond in—what, Georgia—"

"This is North Carolina," said Serena, suddenly wishing that she had not agreed to this. "You are not a vagabond, for god's sake—"

"Why not?"

"Because you're an honored guest!"

Sophie got up and walked around the house, to the porch; she was checking. Serena folded her arms and waited.

Sophie rubbed her face with her hands. When she glanced up at Serena, her face was calm. "Thank you, honey," she said. "I'm sorry. Maybe I would like some tea."

She brought her mother some tea, and Sophie sipped it. They sat on the couch for a while in silence. There was the feeling that Sophie had been here for days already, that they had endured some injury together; there was, for a few minutes, only the call of an egret puncturing the air.

"What happened to your house?" Serena asked. "Why are you living with Dawn now?"

"My house," said Sophie. "I couldn't live in it alone. I kept hearing him."

"Doing what?"

Her mother smoothed her hair and looked at her.

"Walking around. I woke up at night and heard knocking."

Serena looked at her mother's small hands folded precisely. "Maybe it was a dream," she said.

"It was my home for forty years, and I couldn't live there. It was where *we* lived. I kept waiting for him to walk out of the bathroom, to go into the garage, mucking around with his train sets, to leave his dishes in the sink. I couldn't stay there alone."

"I understand," said Serena, softly.

"I didn't know where I wanted to live. Dawn said come live in her place. I was in a daze. I could barely open a can. One day, I opened my eyes and I was living behind her house. It happened that fast."

"And do you like it?" asked Serena.

"I don't know. It's about seven hundred square feet, and all my furniture is crammed into it. She thinks it's cute, having me there. Look, we have two cats and a grandma in the backyard! I can barely move around. I never know when it's the right time to 'drop by.'" She lifted her hands in air quotes. "She had this romantic idea of Grandma, but now I always intrude. Or I come at the right time for chores. Mom, here's a broom! Mom, can you scrub out this pan? Sometimes I think she just fries sausages to give me an activity. She thinks I want to spend all day watching the kids, as though that would be fun."

"Isn't it?" asked Serena.

Her mother leaned toward her. "All right. For a little while. After, say, an hour, it's kind of a torture. I can do ten minutes of Polly Pocket. Then they should just have the kids play with the prisoners at Guantanamo. Now, that would make them speak."

Serena wasn't quite sure if her mother was kidding or not. She decided, for her own benefit, that perhaps she was. "Then why did you move?" asked Serena.

"She asked me. She convinced me. 'You'll get to know your grandchildren!' I never know when to go over there or when she'll shoo me back to my house."

"That is hard," said Serena, trying to sound gentle.

"Well. At least she was thinking of me."

"I was thinking of you," said Serena. "Live here."

Sophie considered the house and laughed. "I can't live here."

"Why not?"

They looked around the small house; there was no need to answer this.

"I was trying to get to you —" said Serena.

"Trying? How hard were you trying?"

"Didn't you get my calls? Every day, almost, every other day? Then I stopped trying."

"You should have sent a telegram," said Sophie.

"No one answers phones at your house?" asked Serena.

"A telegram would have made me feel special."

"Okay," said Serena, confused. Her mother had never before asked for a telegram. She felt she had fallen short of expectations in a basic way. Her mother looked happier now, having gotten that off her chest. A telegram.

"Well, what do you have to do today?" her mother asked.

"The kids are out in about two hours. I have to go to the Temple, to do some — work."

"I want to make money," her mother said.

"What?"

"A lot of money. You girls — or Dawn, at least — made it. Your father made some money. I never did."

"Good for you," Serena said, clapping the couch pillow with her palm. "Good, Mom!"

"I don't have enough," her mother said.

"What do you mean?"

"Not for Los Angeles. It is ridiculous. What does Social Security buy you there? Your father never bought life insurance. He never thought he would die."

Serena was quiet for a moment, absorbing that comment.

"Mom, do you have enough money?"

"If I stop buying meat," Sophie laughed.

She stared at her mother, ice in her throat. "You're kidding."

She was dizzy. How had her mother ended up crammed into the tiny apartment behind her sister's house? She wanted to send her mother money, to buy her a house that would make her feel as large as she yearned to feel, but at the moment, they did not have even enough extra cash for an airline ticket to bring her here.

"So," Serena said after a while, "what do you want to do?"

Her mother leaned forward, her face brightening. "Peer counseling," she said. "At the senior center."

"Oh," said Serena. "Who's—"

"*I* am doing the counseling. My specialty seems to be recent widows. The first month. One does not need a degree for this—"

She looked at her mother, surprised. "Mom. You're doing this? That's great."

"I just started. I am a font of wisdom, apparently. I say 'one day at a time' with great conviction. I don't get ruffled when they are unable to get out of bed or eat, or when they decide they shouldn't have married the man after all." Sophie sat up, clasping her hands. "I go in wearing my navy suit from Macy's and my bone pumps, and we sit in a little room in the senior center, and, you know, sometimes we have a little group, four or five of us, and I pass a rain stick and one person holds it and says what she feels and we all listen until then she passes it, and somehow I create an atmosphere so that they all want to hold the rain stick, and we hear about how Alfred was a good kisser and how Manny taught his wife to play golf and how Elton left for a year and then came back and how one woman wished Matthew would leave but he didn't—" She paused, a little breathless. "And then they thank me."

Sophie was still, her gaze remote, as though she were trying to hear the echoes of her own wisdom—then her eyes settled on Serena. "Maybe there's some sort of certificate I can get," Sophie said.

"Mom, you should look into it," said Serena. Her mother a peer counselor? Serena was more used to her mother's describing herself as a duchess fleeing the Inquisition. But her mother had done this—it was as though she had opened a box she found in a closet and discovered a new talent. "We can find out—"

"*I* can find out," her mother said, and touched her hair.

Chapter Thirteen

....

THE RABBI WAS SITTING IN his office, waiting for her. The idea of him there, with no one, made her restless. The phone rang again; Serena jumped to answer it.

"We need you."

"Who is this?"

"Betty. Honey. Where are the spare keys?"

"The what?"

"They're going to lock us out. Serena. We're spreading the word. No more secrets. Everyone needs to know. I've been getting calls. The head of the religious school just resigned. She said, and I quote, 'He is wonderful with the children. How dare you harass that great man?' The head of ritual practices quit. She says it's a witch hunt. The people need to know, Serena. No one knows where the spare keys are. They're going to lock us out."

"Betty," said Serena, in the falsely authoritative voice she used to reassure her children, "no one's locking anyone out."

"We can't wait! I'm afraid that there will be members taking sides. Honey. Do you know where they are?"

"In a box on the top shelf of the filing cabinet—"

"Can you find them and bring them home? For safekeeping? I may sound paranoid, but things are going out of control," said Betty. "Counting on you." She hung up.

Serena stared at the phone.

"What?" Serena's mother asked, looking up.

She glanced at her mother.

"We're going to work," she said.

She was apprehensive of bringing her mother to the Temple, but now she had two reasons to go there: to help out the apparently paralyzed spiritual leader of the synagogue, and to find the keys to prevent people—Who? Him? Other congregants?—from locking each other out. How had she landed in the middle of this chaos? She stared at her mother, wondering how she could explain any of these situations to her. Her mother got into her car. The day was brighter now, the clouds breaking apart across the silver-blue sky.

"Where are we going?"

"The rabbi needs his coffee."

"Can't he get it himself?"

She paused. "He's a little distracted right now. I'm the only one who knows where it is."

Somehow, this had the effect of impressing her mother. They drove. Her mother delicately ate some of the peanuts out of the packets she had swiped from the airplane. The air had a peculiarly swampy texture, being both cool and thick.

Serena drove to the Temple. She wondered if Dawn remembered the fear in the house the morning she became ill. She heard everyone wake up, early, around five, Dawn had a temperature, and at first it was nothing. Then it began to rise—102, 103, 104. Her father decided they had to take her in.

It was eight in the morning, and they hit traffic on the 405. Dawn's temperature went up: 105. When they got to the emergency room, there were two heart attacks in process, and it took twenty minutes to get Dawn into a room. Serena remembered her father banging on the doors, yelling at the staff to hurry. He was sure he knew what was wrong with her and the doctors didn't; they had to get her fever down.

For two days after the fever broke, they thought she was fine.

She didn't realize that Dawn's leg was paralyzed until two days later; her father did not believe that either. She remembered him standing in his nurse's outfit beside her bed. "It's temporary," he said to the doctor, standing, arms crossed. "Weakness. I've seen this, Doctor." She remembered the casual way he made this statement, and she noticed the doctor's face flinch, as though her father had taken some liberty that she did not then understand.

The doctor's tone had been sharp. "No," he said. "You don't know. You're wrong."

Her father had stiffened and assumed the same posture as the doctor, trying to absorb his authority. The doctor began to talk about rehab and strengthening her sister's other leg, and her father could not listen; he paced around, running his hand through his hair. "How did this happen?" he yelled at the doctor. "You didn't work fast enough. This is your fault! Yours!"

He sat beside her sister and held her hand; he could not look directly at the leg. "You can do anything," he said to her; she lay in the bed, sipping milkshakes. "You know that? You are Dawn Hirsch, the great Dawn Hirsch, and this isn't going to stop you. I promise that."

He had driven to the hospital fast enough to cool her down, to keep her from seizures, to keep her from further harm. But her father was ashamed, deeply, that he could not have brought her back intact, perfect; he could not bear to look when Dawn came home with a walker, for she was one person he had not been able to save. When she returned home, he sat down with her and with the walker; he tried once to teach her how to use it.

"Let's try it," he said. "Grab the edge and stand up."

Dawn grabbed the silver handle and slowly raised herself up.

"Okay," he said. "Take a step. One. Two."

Dawn started; he stood beside her. His large hands gripped the bar beside hers. Dawn's knuckles flushed white; she took a step. Another. Her father nodded; it was taking all of his energy to keep his expression engaged and neutral. He lasted about three minutes. Then Serena felt his hand on her shoulder.

"Serena," he said, and he looked bereft; his eyelid twitched. "Show your sister how to use this."

"Me?" she asked.

"I know you can do it. I'll pay you fifty cents." He vanished into the garage.

She was proud at first that he had asked her to teach her sister how to walk. She told Dawn to sit on the couch and demonstrated the walker, zooming across the living room. Then she hovered by Dawn, watching her sister grip the walker. Her sister's right leg hung beside her, motionless. Serena did not know what to do other than direct her like a traffic cop. To the right. More to the left. She was afraid Dawn would pitch forward, and of course, Dawn did, and Serena grabbed her arms and slid her hands back on the aluminum bar again. Dawn, to her surprise, listened to her. Her sister already had a core of determination; she gripped the walker and stepped forward and turned right or left or wherever Serena suggested. "Good," Serena said, in a teacherly, high-pitched voice; it was a pleasure to use this voice, to assume knowledge of this thing, walking, to hold knowledge of anything at all. After a week, Dawn could move along with the walker, and then, a few months later, with a cane. She watched Dawn tilt across the lawn, not the way she used to, but with a strange lightness, and then a speed that relieved Serena and frightened her.

And later, when she tried to advise Dawn of the best way to hold her cane, the best way to put her foot down, Dawn looked at her with her clear golden eyes and said, regally, "I know."

THE CAR STOPPED IN FRONT of the Temple. Her mother got out and gazed at the building. The gold doors were bright in the midday sun. Her mother looked disappointed, perhaps, that this was not the Eiffel Tower. But she said nothing as they headed in. Serena heard a rustle in the back, and the rabbi stepped out.

"You're here," he said, hurrying forward. "Serena Hirsch."

Both she and her mother stopped at the sound of her name. He said it hoarsely, rather beautifully, like a plea. Serena was startled by the silence, which seemed to affirm the fact of chaos, not peace, as usually there was the swish of the Xerox machine or the clatter of a Hadassah member's heels; now there was nothing.

"Who is this?" he said. His eyes glinted. "New member?"

"This is my mother, Sophie," said Serena, suddenly wary. "Mom, this is Rabbi Golden."

The rabbi reddened as though embarrassed by a sudden thought. "Your mother," he said. He reached out and firmly grasped Sophie's hand.

The phone rang, piercingly. Once. Twice. Three, four times. It stopped.

"Pay no mind," said the rabbi. "I don't know if it's a supporter or . . . well." He looked at Serena. "So. Tell me. Where is it?"

He seemed childish standing there. She led him to the kitchen and opened a cabinet over the stove. There were several red packets of French roast coffee. He stood, rubbing his hands, while she took one down and handed it to him. "There you go," she said. "Remember. It's over the stove. Here."

He clutched the bag of coffee tenderly, as though it were a baby. "Okay," he said. His hands trembled. He walked over and absently placed the bag of coffee on the counter. He seemed to have no intention of brewing it into actual coffee. She understood that he had merely wanted someone to drop by.

His office had the sharp odor of an animal. His desk was neat, organized in a way she had never seen before. Papers were stacked. Serena's mother had wandered over. She looked into his office, the vast gallery of photos of him, shaking hands like a diplomat.

"Why don't you know where anything is?" Sophie asked. "Aren't you the rabbi?"

He blinked. He turned his gaze toward her, alert.

"I know where God is," he said.

"And where is that?" asked her mother, crisply.

The rabbi opened his mouth and shut it. Serena was surprised; she had never seen him appear shy.

"You'll have to come to my service and listen," he said, in acquisition mode. "Friday night, seven-thirty—"

"I don't go," said Sophie, waving her hand away.

"That's what people say," he said, "until they hear me—"

"Well, it's all—I don't know. Somewhat ridiculous, anyway," said Sophie, her voice heavy with a combination of bitterness and woe. "No offense. I don't know why."

The rabbi stepped back, as though stung by something in the air. His face was pale. His eyes darted past them, longingly, to see if anyone else was coming through the doors.

"Well," said the rabbi, "I have a lot to do. Did you know that? A lot. So, goodbye." The phone rang again. He looked at it. "Stop it! Shut up! Shut *up!*" he said to it. He looked at Serena. "That phone. It's not my job to answer it. I don't want to know who's — Can you just answer it?"

He was tapping his foot, waiting.

"Not today," said Serena, startled, "But I'll be in —"

He whirled around. "No!" he cried. "Not toda-aay. Not todaaa-y," he said. "Where the hell is everyone?" he asked. "Does anyone care about this place? Am I the only one?" He stared at them. "Fine! *I'll* keep the doors open. Thank me. The fools. People are dying! Maybe not here, but somewhere! I'll be here. Here!" He looked as though he wanted to continue, then he turned, strode quickly to his office, and slammed the door.

Serena felt something flash in her, a plain of hot metal. "Rabbi!" she said to the door. "What are you doing?"

She went over and knocked on the door; it remained shut.

She turned to her mother. "What happened?" asked Sophie, blinking. She wanted to get out of there. She had to find the spare keys. She walked swiftly into the office, took the box off the filing cabinet, removed the keys, set the box back on top of the cabinet. The question that occurred to her was, Why would anyone now want to get in? She clutched the keys and slipped them into her pocket.

"Let's go," she said.

They walked out into the sunlight and got into the car. She looked at her mother.

"What was *that*?" she asked, to the air. Sophie slipped into her seat.

"He's an idiot," said Sophie. "Drive."

SERENA NEEDED TO PICK UP the children at their respective schools in an hour, and Sophie wanted to talk about what had just happened. She wanted to continue on the subject of Rabbi Golden. She would only refer to him as "that man."

"What does that man do there?"

"He is, well, the rabbi, Mom."

"That man certainly seems to love himself. All those photos."

"He has those, but usually he's alone —"

"That man should answer his phone. He should — When is Dawn coming to get me?"

"You're going to take a plane back Monday, and she'll meet you at her house then."

Sophie's voice was rising in a way that was familiar; Serena felt like she wanted to duck, to dodge her tone, and she thought, again, of her father. Serena remembered how he was gifted with the ability to sleep deeply, no matter where he was or the amount of time he had been awake. His shifts as an emergency nurse were variable, so he slept odd hours, and sometimes he would wake up not knowing where he was. Her father was a man who needed to be loved in public ways, with song and dance routines on his birthday, with large, loud gatherings, with long, detailed toasts, but sometimes he woke from his sleep angry and puzzled by his relative prosperity, shouting at the jacaranda blooming pale purple on the sidewalks, at the cheerful guise of civilization that was Southern California.

THEY PICKED UP RACHEL AND Zeb. "Your grandmother's here!" said Serena, cheerfully presenting their grandmother to them, whom they had not seen in several months. They looked at Sophie suspiciously, as though she were a stranger, which in some ways she was. This fact pierced Serena. Sophie knelt; she tried to hug first Rachel and then Zeb.

"Hello, darlings," she said, and the children looked at her, let themselves be embraced, looked at Serena as though trying to identify what emotion they should have toward her mother. Serena knelt down, helping them hug her back.

They went to the house. "What are we doing now?" asked Sophie.

"I don't know. The kids are tired. Do you want to play with them?" she suggested, with hope.

Zeb and Rachel now wanted to present extended accounts of what they had experienced that day. "Manuel threw up," said Zeb. "It got on

Keisha's shoes. We had to put our heads down in art. Mr. Stone said we couldn't do art, but Mrs. Johnson's class did. I had popcorn chicken for lunch—"

"Kayla took a unicorn from me," said Rachel, grimly. "The pink one. I didn't get it back."

Sophie sat beside them, listening. She looked both amused and baffled. "Everyone had quite a day," she said.

They all sprawled, exhausted, around the living room. First, Sophie read the children some stories out of a book, and they appeared to be listening. Serena left the room, thinking her mother might play with the children while she made dinner. Sophie settle on the worn couch and observed the children: Zeb set up some trucks and Rachel placed plastic animals in them. They were not playing, exactly, but there was, briefly, a modicum of peace. Dan came home, and they all assembled around the table, and for the course of the meal, at least, Serena had the feeling that she was inside some harmony that she had imagined.

"Show me your good manners, Zeb," Sophie said to him, as he sat on his knees, stabbing his chicken nugget, at which point he rested on his bottom, lifting his fork to his mouth with an elegance that seemed to foreshadow hisself in ten years. Rachel took a sequined flower from Sophie's shirt and slid it into her hair.

Dan listened to Sophie's description of having been dumped here instead of flown to Paris and said, "Sophie. Please. This is the Paris of the American South. Haven't you been to the Wrightson-Birch mansion? Haven't you ordered biscuits at Jimbo's? Haven't you tried the delicacies of this part of North Carolina?"

"What am I missing?" she said, her dark eyes flashing a little.

"Don't you want to raise your cholesterol a bit?" he said.

"God, no, Daniel, I already am on medication—"

"I don't believe it," he said, standing, arms folded, smiling at her. "You? So youthful?"

"Stop, Mr. PR man," said Sophie, laughing.

"You look pretty, Grandma," said Zeb.

"Well, thank you, sir," she said.

"You are pretty!" said Rachel, determinedly.

"*Merci, mademoiselle*," said Sophie, with a French accent.

"Say more," said Zeb. "Say more like that."

Sophie spoke to them in a torrent of confident, beautifully accented French, as they sat around the foldout table, and it was as though they were, if not in France, in another distant city. How much her mother knew! Serena gazed at her; she seemed to contain everything worth knowing. Her children interviewed her mother, and Sophie taught them to introduce themselves in French. They all shook hands with each other and said *bonjour*.

"*Bonjour*," said Zeb and Rachel, leaning on the *j*, their faces lit with whatever she taught them.

Serena and Dan went through the high-pitched slog that was bath and bedtime, and Serena thought about inviting her mother to stay longer—a week, a month—her mother teaching her children French, walking them to school, all of them smiling and holding hands. Other families managed to do it, and she imagined Sophie glad to be here, with them, forgetting about Paris, seeing Dawn's mistake as an odd piece of luck. Could a family re-form itself in this new, hopeful way? But her mother stepped out onto the porch after dinner and sat, looking outside, while the children went to bed, and Serena noticed her mother's suitcase, unopened, in the living room. "Hey," she said. "Do you want to find a place to unpack?"

"Well," her mother said. She looked at her with a guilty expression. "Honey. I don't need to. I want to go home. In the morning."

"What?"

"It's, well, nice enough here. But I do want to go home and sleep in my own bed."

"We can find you a bed here," said Serena. "Um. Somewhere . . . "

"I don't even know where my own bed is," said Sophie. "I wake up in the apartment where Dawn put me, I look at the ceiling, and I think, Where am I? How did I get here?"

"Mom," said Serena, "why do you have to go? We would like you to stay. We can have a nice weekend—"

"No," said Sophie. "No offense, sweetheart. I do want to go. I am looking forward to going home. I will leave in the morning and not bother anyone—"

"Mom. Why?"

Her mother hesitated; Serena did not know what to do to reach into her mother's own restlessness, to calm it. "I feel more confident, suddenly. I have plans. Maybe I can teach French. There is not endless time. This was a lovely night, but this is what I'm doing," Sophie said.

She stood up, quickly, as though to continue this line of thought before it disappeared again, and she put her hand on Serena's shoulder, as if to calm her daughter or make sure she remained in her seat. Serena felt the slight, precious weight of her mother's hand on her shoulder and wondered how long her mother would stand like this — it was about a minute. There was no keeping anyone anywhere, not your mother or sister or father, not anyone at all.

Then her mother went into the bedroom, and Serena could hear her on her phone.

THE FIRST FLIGHT SOPHIE COULD get on was at noon the next day. It was a bright November morning. Sophie sat in the kitchen, a little bewildered while the breakfast whirl went on around her.

After everyone had left, her mother pulled her suitcase into the living room. She was not wearing the sweater with the French writing; she was fully made up and had put on a trim, navy blue blazer and matching pants as though she wanted to believe she was going on another exciting journey. She clasped her hands in her lap and looked at Serena.

"Go about your day," said Sophie. "Ignore me."

"Don't you want to go to breakfast?" asked Serena. "Or maybe look around town?"

"I'm not on vacation," Sophie said. "Proceed."

Serena looked at her mother sitting on the worn couch. Sophie was ready for her next journey, organizing her large purse. She was arranging Ziploc bags of snacks in there — whatever kids' snacks she had drummed up in the cabinet. There was a bag of Cheez-Its, a bag containing Nilla wafers, another containing peanut butter Ritz Bits; it looked as though she was preparing for a large and hungry playdate.

Serena sat at the card table in the dining room. She needed to go through Betty's list. She took out the first page; it was impossible to read Betty's handwriting. She would have to call the members.

Her mother was watching her. Sophie stood up and joined her at the table.

"What is this?" she asked.

Serena was a little afraid of what her mother might say, but she also appreciated the fact that she was interested, so she said, "A kind of . . . an investigation."

Sophie brightened. "Into whom?"

"Well," said Serena. "The rabbi."

Her mother's eyes widened. "What did he do?"

"It's not clear, exactly."

"Well, what do they accuse him of?"

Serena raised her hand and scratched her neck. "Cruelty."

Her mother smoothed the collar of her jacket, as though this revelation deserved a gesture of civility in response. "Well," she said. "That's interesting." She looked intently at Serena. "What is your job in all this?"

"I'm going to call some women and listen to what they are going to say about him. Then we're supposed to decide what to do."

"Good for you," said her mother. "Can I listen in?"

Serena was glad for her mother's interest. "Sure."

Serena set the phone on speaker and dialed the first number: Rosalie Goldenhauer. Age: 82. Temple member: 9 years. Member: Hadassah, Caring Committee, Vision Screening Project. Originally from: Long Island, NY.

"Hello," said Serena. She did not know what tone to take — impersonal, like she was taking a survey, or warmer, like a kind of therapist. "I'm calling from the board of Temple Shalom. My name is Serena Hirsch."

"Hello, darling," said Rosalie. "How are you today?"

"I'm fine," she said. "And you?"

"I am looking out into this glorious day. Do you know what the weather is in New York this morning, dear? Twenty-eight. Do you know what it will be here today? Sixty. Ha!" Rosalie laughed, a trilling sound. "Now, what can I do for you?"

"Well," said Serena, "the reason I'm calling today is, well, I don't want to bother you, but I am conducting an investigation into the rabbi. I wanted to discuss an incident—"

"Oh ho!" said Rosalie, her tone sharpening. "That man should not be called 'Rabbi.'"

Sophie was sitting at the table, hands clasped; her eyebrows lifted. She leaned closer to the phone.

Serena looked at her notes.

"You claimed that at a Shabbat service, he walked by you without saying hello."

"That is correct. Not a hello, not a friendly smile."

"This happened once?"

"Not once. Three times. Once, I think he shrugged when I said hello."

Serena said, trying not to lean too hard into the third word in the sentence, "Is that *it*?"

"Is that it?" asked Rosalie, crisply. "I pay my dues. I expect service."

"So he has not said hello to you three times," said Serena. Sophie raised an eyebrow.

"Not a warm one. Not any." She paused. "I'm a widow. My children don't call. My knees are shot. Sometimes I go the whole day without speaking to anyone. The rabbi at my shul at Long Island was a hugger. He hugged people he hated. Shouldn't a rabbi, of all people, hug people he hates? I deserve a hello. I deserve a hug."

Serena thanked her for her time and hung up the phone.

"She does seem mad about something," said Sophie. "But not a good witness. Next."

Next: Miss Carmella Steinway. Age: 89. Temple member: 5 years. Member: Oneg Organization Committee. Originally from: Charleston, SC.

"Investigate? What, darling, is there to investigate? The evidence is in."

"You allege that he screamed at you at a Hadassah dinner."

"That he did. I recall that Ginger Aretz was in attendance, too."

"Can you tell me what happened, in your own words?" Now she had become an actor in a police show.

"I certainly can. We were having a perfectly pleasant conversation about my granddaughter's Bat Mitzvah, how we wanted to bring all her friends on the bima for a brief hora afterwards, and he said, in a most unrabbinical way, 'That's not spiritual!'"

"What did you say?"

"To each his own, Rabbi," I said, mind you, in a polite voice. Then he yelled, 'I'm sorry, are we worshipping the Carmella religion?'"

"Describe *yell*."

"Like a child," she said. "Then," her voice grew excited, "let me tell you what he did next."

"Go ahead."

"He slapped his hand on the table. He yelled, 'What is this, a Broadway show? You want to drag the whole world onto the bima? Give me a break. You want to have the Bat Mitzvah on Sunday? What else do you do in the Carmella religion? How about bringing a cross up, too?'"

"Then what happened?"

"He threw a glass."

Sophie's mouth fell open.

"What?"

"Or maybe it fell off the table. I'm not sure. I am eighty-six years old. I look up to my religious leaders. He would not stop. All I heard was 'the Carmella religion' over and over. I am not a religion! This was a luncheon! I was trying to eat my Waldorf salad."

Carmella was excited to be interviewed; it took some time to get her off the phone. Sophie was tapping her fingers on the table impatiently when Serena finally put the receiver down.

"That one," Sophie said sternly, "goes on a bit. But she's right. He's making fun of her."

Loretta Stone was next. Age: 72. Temple member: 2 years. Member: blank. Originally from: Cleveland, OH.

"Loretta, I have some questions about the rabbi," said Serena.

"Yes," said Loretta. There was the fuzzy noise of a television in the background; it stopped.

"You lodged a complaint against him last year."

There was a gasping sound; Loretta was weeping.

"Oh, no," said Serena, alarmed. Sophie leaned forward, her hand lifted as though she wanted to place it on the phone to comfort Loretta.

"Excuse me," whispered Loretta.

She listened to the woman's ragged breath, helpless. Serena's palms began to sweat. "I'm sorry," she said. "Miss Stone. What happened?"

Loretta took a shuddering breath. "I sat in his chair."

"What chair?"

"His office chair. I didn't know it was his. My feet were tired." She paused. "He shrieked at me to get out of it. Like this: 'Loretta, get out of my chair!' I just wanted to ask him if the Temple had a cemetery yet. I have diabetes. My heart isn't good. How long do I have here? Where will I rest?" Her voice cracked.

"I'm sorry," said Serena. Her mother's face was grim.

"He looked at me like I was a thief. He is a rabbi. I just wanted to ask him about the cemetery." She sighed.

"Did he say anything else?"

"He sat down in his chair, like a king getting into his throne, and looked at me like I was a bug. He yelled, 'Why would you think you could sit there!' I said I was sorry. I was tired. Could he not yell because it was bad for my heart?

"He said, 'For god's sake, I'm not yelling! Doesn't anyone here understand who I am?' I got scared and thought, Who is he? Is he a special rabbi? Is he maybe a prophet? Who?"

"Then what?"

"I told him my concerns, and he yelled, 'That's not my problem! That's the Cemetery Committee. Ask them why the hell they can't get it together to find a decent home for the dead. Get out of here. Goodbye.'

"Miss. I can't go to him. What is going to happen to me? I don't want him to pray beside me when I die. Who do I go to if I can't go to him? Can you tell me?"

"That's bad," said Serena, "I'll look—"

Sophie stood up and grabbed the phone. "Miss Loretta Stone," she said. "My name is Sophie Hirsch. I'm Serena's mother. Pardon me for listening to this, but I think this man should . . . apologize to you. That is not the way to treat someone. You should . . . I don't know. Trust your feelings."

"Yes," said Loretta. "I agree."

Sophie sat back. Serena thanked Loretta for her help and gently hung up the phone.

"What should we do?" asked Serena.

Sophie shook her head.

"You know what the problem is?" said Sophie, her voice firm. "No one is listening to them. That's why they're upset. You're doing a good thing here. Listen."

Her mother stood up and walked out onto the porch. The morning was white with mist, the magnolia and crape myrtle trees pale, barely visible — Serena went to her mother, and they stood on the edge of the day, silent, looking out as the trees and cars and houses pressed themselves into the air.

Part Three

Part Three

Chapter Fourteen

SERENA GRIPPED HER MOTHER'S ARM as they walked through the airport. She tried to remember the last moment she had held her father's arm in this way—it had been six months prior, and he had been making her a sandwich for the plane. He would not allow her to spend eight dollars on a bad sandwich in flight; he had a theory that the money somehow made it to the oil companies, as all money did. He wanted to separate from anything that had to do with the corruption of the nation; he wanted to lift them all away from it.

She felt her mother's fingers against her arm as they moved toward the security gate. "I'm fine," Sophie said. "I really am. I'm thinking everything through."

"I know you are," said Serena.

They had reached the security gate.

"Do your work at the Temple," said her mother. "Sweetheart. You've had a hard time. But I think you're doing something important."

"Thank you," Serena said; she stopped. Her mother stepped forward and held her. For a moment, Serena could not speak; she felt the precious rise and fall of her mother's breath under her ribs.

"I love you," she said to her mother.

Sophie was silent for a moment and then said, "You, too."

Sophie stepped out of her daughter's arms. Serena watched her as she walked toward security. Sophie stepped carefully out of her shoes and placed them in a plastic bin, and then she placed her blazer and earrings there as well. Barefoot, she walked through the metal detector and waited as the TSA crew inspected her baggies full of Cheez-Its. Then her mother slipped on her shoes, buttoned her blazer, and continued slowly toward the gate; Serena waited, the way she'd wait for her son, to be there in case her mother turned to say goodbye to her. But her mother did not look back; she headed toward the gates, disappearing into the airport's gray light.

LATER THAT DAY, SERENA HEARD a rustling by her front door. When she opened it, she found a new flyer stuffed into the handle. Forrest was walking, with a military briskness, down the street.

Hanukkah? Kwanzaa? What about Baby Jesus? Let's bring our savior back to our schools! December 7, 7:00 PM. Oakville Auditorium.

Where have all the cherubs gone? The holy angels? Crosses?

Santa and snowflakes are not enough! Christmas should be shared with all. Come show your support for Jesus.

There was a color picture of a noble-looking baby wrapped in a cloth. A halo had been drawn in gold ink over his head.

She thought of Zeb and the pennies, and her heart felt like a bomb. She knew whom she had to talk to about this. Her cell phone rang.

"I found you." It was Betty. "Do you have the keys?"

"I got them," said Serena. "Yesterday—"

"Good. I'm glad we have them. The Temple's dividing. Pro and con. I've spread the word a bit. Leaked some documents."

"Betty!"

Serena listened, carried along by Betty's excitement. Action. It sounded so clear and dramatic. But what were they supposed to do?

"Betty," she began, "who are 'they'?"

The landline rang.

"I have to go," Serena said. She hung up and picked up the landline.

"I found you," he said.

It took her a moment to recognize Rabbi Golden's voice.

SHE TOOK THE KEYS TO Betty's house. The guard gave her a map, but it was a joke; the slight variations in the design of the houses and the pristine lawns made every street look identical. The designer of the neighborhood seemed partial to three design motifs—either

Cape Cod, English Tudor, or antebellum mansion. The minimal differences in the structure of the homes, the enforced palette of the colors — peach, sky blue, lemon yellow, foam green — attested to the desire
for order and immortality. It was a long ride through the gated community, but finally she found Betty's home. She stood outside the arching
doors, which seemed large enough to accommodate the entrance of a
basketball player. It was the first time she had seen Betty when she did
not look as though she was about to give a PowerPoint presentation;
Serena was startled by Betty's naked face, and she looked surprisingly
pale, both younger and older, her eyes rimmed with lavender skin.

"Smart girl," she said. "Thank you."

Serena looked into the house. The foyer was a buttery yellow; there
was artwork by Chagall on the walls. Some tall, fuzzy branches were
placed artfully in a slim vase in the corner. The air held the sweet scent
of a peach.

"This is the house that canapés built," smiled Betty, holding out her
arms. "Come in."

Serena stepped inside. "How did you do this?" she asked.

"Crispy chicken bites. Bleu cheese and iceberg mini salads. Apri-
cot Gruyère tartlets . . . " She was buoyant. She touched Serena's arm.
"Marketing, honey. I listened to what clients wanted, I gave them 110
percent —"

"No, really," said Serena, wanting to know something else, something larger. "What did you do?"

"You believe. You create your product. You make sure they know
who you are. You stand up and say hello." She paused. "What kind of
work did you do?"

"Speechwriting. For corporations."

"Did you really? I hate words."

"They're nothing to be afraid of," said Serena, "You just get specific. You think about what people will remember. You make sure to be
short, sweet. When you sell something, anything, you think about how
everyone wants to be included."

Betty was regarding her. She patted the box of keys. "What should I
say about these keys?"

Serena looked at the box. "These aren't just any keys. They're not just keys to the Temple. Pick one up. Look at it. They're keys to who we are."

"I like that. Go on."

It was blather, ridiculous, but she could whip it out: "They are keys to how we define ourselves at Temple Shalom. There's one for each of us. You can turn it the right way, the wrong way."

Betty had tears in her eyes. How far could she go with this? Serena remembered the joy she felt when she finished her first speech for Earl Morton, the slightly unleashed sensation of glee, like she was tumbling down a hill; it was the airy, careless joy that she could really say anything at all, that she could, by stringing together a few phrases, fool others into believing in their accomplishment, confidence. How powerful she felt to merely say anything and have it seem true.

Now she heard her words and winced.

"What doors do they unlock?" asked Betty, her eyes alarmingly curious.

"They unlock . . . " She paused; yes, she was going to say it. "They unlock the doors to our hearts," said Serena, and closed her eyes.

Betty clapped her hands. "More!" she said, stepping into her living room. Large glass windows overlooked the plain that was the golf course. In the far distance, Serena could see tiny figures standing, occasionally swinging clubs over the flat, unnaturally green grass.

"Maybe you could write for me someday. What I could tell my waiters before they head out to serve guests at a wedding. Or what I could tell an anxious client. I have a budget for this. I sometimes don't know what to say."

"That seems hard to believe," Serena said.

"We need to preserve our community," said Betty. "It is small but a lot goes on. The Hadassah does free eye exams at the local schools. The children come for religious school and learn about, um, Jewish topics. The doors open for services. And now some of the people I sit across the aisle from are not speaking to me. My friends. They think this is a frivolous crusade, but it is important! We have to take care of each other."

Serena was startled; Betty's pure gray eyes were free of everything—of condescension, of pity, and, briefly, of need; they merely acknowledged her presence.

"Yes," Serena said.

Betty offered a tour of her professional kitchen, samples of the fig and sheep's milk cheese tartlets she was trying out. It was soon time to go. Serena had another meeting. She drove out of The Orchard, past the guard, through the gates, and back into the main streets of Waring. She had not told Betty about the other appointment she had made.

THE RABBI'S APARTMENT COMPLEX APPEARED empty; the unemployed and rootless did not hang out on the balconies this season. It was late November, and there was a moist chill in the air. The pool was empty and seemed bereft with no one trying to copulate in it; the water was glassy and gray.

Serena paused at the door, suddenly nervous, wondering why she had come here. Who was he? Was this all somehow a terrible mistake? She remembered how she had felt being escorted out of the Pepsi building, how everyone had been afraid to look at her, how the secretaries had turned away; she had been erased down to this one thing: a criminal. No one wanted to see her as anything else. Now, she was gathering information. She was trying to give him a chance, and she also wanted to walk with him into the Southeast North Carolina Jewish Community Center, walk into the building of glass, of light, which he had seen with a precision that no one else here had.

Inside her pocket, she clutched the flyer tightly in her hand. The door flew open after she had knocked several times. The rabbi wore a wrinkled T-shirt and gray sweatpants; his face was gray, unshaven. His eyes were rimmed with red.

"Mrs. Hirsch," he said. "Sorry. Thank you for your help yesterday. I needed help, and I didn't know who to call. Just getting my papers together. A pleasure to see you."

She hesitated for a moment, but it was some sort of apology; he seemed to want to make amends. He held out his hand. She shook it.

His smile dazzled in a curious way; it looked as though he had used whitening strips on his teeth.

"This is where you're working today?" she said.

"I cannot enter the Temple office," he said. "The phones. They ring. Off the hook. I can't bear to hear them." He held open the door. "The disciples can come by here to see me today." He laughed.

In his apartment, there was the soft smell of rotting bananas and the sugary, meaty odor of fast food, curtains that allowed in a thin tangerine light.

"You need anything?" he said, suddenly. "Tea, coffee, water, Mountain Dew?"

"I'm fine," she said.

"Oh." He looked at the landscape of the living room, trying to see it through her eyes; it occurred to her that he had no idea how anyone saw him. He had no gauge at all. He quickly tossed some magazines from the couch onto the floor. "Sit!" he said.

She perched on a foldout chair.

He sat down on the tattered couch. "Why are you here?"

"Well," she said, bringing Forrest's flyer out of her pocket. She handed it to him; his hands looked slender, almost frail, as he held it. "How are you doing?"

He laughed, a bitter sound. "How do you think?"

"We want to solve this," she said, leaning forward. "There must be a way—"

"Right, right, right," he said, rubbing his face. "Solve this. Tell me something new."

She did not have a solution, or she did not think any of her suggestions would be what he wanted to hear. There was quiet for a moment as he read the flyer. He laughed.

"Just make us disappear!" he said. "That old magic trick. In the guise of holiday spirit. Old story. Ancient."

She was relieved, for a moment, by his tone, the clarity of it, the way he said just what she felt.

"What do you think?" she said. "Is this legal?"

"Oh, you can call the ACLU, separation of church and state, the whole shebang," he said. "But you don't need to. You have me."

He leaned back. He was himself, and he wanted to help — she could go to the meeting herself, she could stand up for a more inclusive holiday season, but here it was, the most holy action, perhaps: an offer to help her out. The rabbi sat there in the spangled light coming through his thin curtains.

"We'll convince them, Serena. We will."

He stood up, went into the kitchen, and returned to the living room holding a can of Red Bull. He popped the can and began to drink it. He was quiet for a moment; he seemed to be thinking.

"You know what the fine men and women of the military would say," he said. "Put it in the amnesty closet. Put your contraband there. What soldiers stole from other solders, illegal weapons, et cetera. That's what we need to do. Give the Temple an amnesty closet. People put their little complaints there and walk away."

She knew what he was talking about — Betty's list. She sighed sharply and clasped her arms around herself. His eyes were cool in a deliberate way, the coolness of someone holding back a wave of feeling. She did not want to ask the next question, but she did.

"What if they can't walk away?" she asked.

He shrugged. "And why not?"

She paused. "Because they have felt hurt," she said.

He crossed his arms. "So, they say they have felt hurt. Maybe they hurt *me*. Have you ever thought of that? Have you thought about how a rabbi has feelings? No. None of them think of that. They just think of what they want. They need to forget about it," he said. "You know what the Schwartzes told me about the Eisenbergs when I came to live with them? 'Forget about them. They didn't want you? Forget them.' If she had red hair before, now it was black. If he was a fat guy, now he was thin. They didn't exist. I changed them in my mind. Now I don't know what they look like. I did it, why can't they?"

His voice had taken on a light, almost sprightly tone, which unnerved her.

"They're in pain," she said. "They want you to help them."

His eyes were bright, both stimulated and oppressed by his congregants' errant needs. "Why don't you think for a moment," he said. "Listen to yourself. They are all asking me to do things for them. So are you. Maybe they should be asking God. Maybe they should think about how they can change. Maybe—" he snapped his fingers, as though he had just had a brilliant thought. "Maybe their own relationship with God needs to change."

"But why is it just them?" she asked.

"I didn't say it was just them," he said. "I said—" he shifted on the balls of his feet, like a basketball player. He turned, suddenly, and returned to the kitchen. Now he came out eating half a bagel.

"No one understands what I mean," he said, looking bereft. "I don't know how to say it—"

"Rabbi. Are you planning to lock us out?" she said.

The bagel stopped, midair. "Excuse me?"

"I heard," she said, "that some members of the Temple were collecting keys to lock people out."

He stared at her. "The Temple is my *home*," he said. "I came here when I was nine years old. When no one wanted me! This was where I was wanted. Truly. I never left. Maybe I help guide them to something godlike." He paused. "I wouldn't lock them out. *I bring them in.*"

He took a bite out of his bagel.

"So, when is this meeting?" he said.

"Next week," she said.

"I will be there," he said, solemnly. He wrote down the address and time in his day planner. "Don't you worry," he said. "We're going to announce that we're here."

"Thank you," she said.

"See you then," he said briskly, and headed quickly into the kitchen.

She hurried out of his apartment, away from the smell of rotting fruit, away from the stale amber light coming in from the window, past the empty pool, its currents ribbing in the low wind. She turned once, and she saw him, standing at the window, a thin figure, looking out at the dark autumn light.

Chapter Fifteen

THE CHRISTMAS DERBY WAS SCHEDULED for December 5; it was the November 30th Scout meeting, the final night to construct the cars. The church hall was crowded with various woodworking devices. A couple electric saws were set up at stations, and beige squares of sandpaper littered the foldout tables. Stained glass windows sent clear diamonds of red and yellow onto the wood floor, and there was the sweet smell of fresh wood and the appearance of honest and blameless industry. Dan sat with his son, who penciled in the shape he wanted his car to have. It was a sedan with fins, resembling the Batmobile.

Forrest wandered across the room, watching the parents bend over the cars. He leaned over a long table and said, "Remember. Scouts make it. We will disqualify any cars purchased on the illegal Internet sites. You know what I'm talking about." A murmur shimmered through the troop. "It's not just about cheating. I ask you: What true scout is going to make cars to sell on the Internet? Why are dads who buy these not spending time on their kids?"

"My first year, one dad put mercury in the car, which made it fast, except when the car crashed and spilled mercury all over the finish line. We had to be evacuated because the raceway became toxic," said one father, who glued wheels onto the car while his son crouched under the table and picked his nose.

"We placed second last year," one father said.

Laughter. One said, "They hate being second."

Another responded, "They do? I do." He whispered, quietly, "Screw second." There was raucous laughter behind hands.

"Tyler, you dog, you."

The electric saw screeched, murderous, in the background.

"I just got Harper into the Optimist softball league. I *love* it," Dan heard one father say. "He hit a home run last week. You've got to sign them up early. By seven. You have to get them entrenched. Before they realize they can get out of it. Because by eight they have their own ideas, and you look at the parents who have their kids in this stuff by four, and by eight it's all over."

Dan felt the skin of his arms harden, like armor.

"Hey, Scout, what do you think?" Dan said, holding out the penciled block for Zeb to approve.

His son looked at it. "I don't know," he said, and he darted off.

Dan surveyed the cars already lined up for display. They were a triumph of parental manual dexterity and painting skill. He looked around to see if he saw a single boy making his own car. The boys had mostly dispersed, and it was the fathers leaning, sweaty, intent, over the tiny cars. No one wanted his child to lose. Dan felt camaraderie with these men he barely knew—they were all part of this, the basic engine of the American family. It began with this car, and that would echo in the future on the soccer field, the baseball diamond, the awards assembly, the job interview. It was strange, but it was something to be part of; it was the brute force driving the room.

Forrest came up to him. "Looking good," he said. He held up a car that was so flat it looked like a giant had stomped on it. "This is the car I made for my grandson this year. Dawson. He's coming in from Benson County for the great event. It's a beaut."

Forrest handed the car to Dan. It was light, almost like a wafer. He wondered what kinetic theory Forrest wanted the car to embody.

"Nice," he said.

"Isn't it?" said Forrest.

"Very," he said. He paused. "How's Evelyn?"

Forrest blinked. "Day by day," he said. "She can walk around a little now. She can fix herself an egg. But she was supposed to help me out, and now Jeb Wilson said he can't do timing—"

Dan heard a thin plea in Forrest's voice.

"I can help with timing," Dan said.

Chapter Sixteen

....

THE NEXT DAY WAS A bright, hot December day. The hard sunlight in the kitchen, the summerlike climate, made the day seem as though it were occurring in an alternate hemisphere. It was both cheering and eerie. Dan woke up, put on his work suit, walked outside to get the paper, and came back inside sweating. The sudden change in weather made him irritable. The children put on their shorts and T-shirts again, baffled. It was not like a new beginning, just confusion at all the ways of the world.

Serena had half an hour before she was due to work at the Temple office. She went into her bedroom and made the bed. Dan had left a navy sweatshirt crumpled on the floor; she picked it up and suddenly breathed the tangy, cotton smell. It was an old shirt, one he had owned for years, and to hold the soft shirt felt like containing those years in her hands. She remembered an evening ten years ago, when they were first dating, walking along the West Side Highway, gazing at the enormous boxes of light that made up the buildings in the Financial District. The huge, blazing buildings seemed a perfect backdrop for their new feelings for each other, and it seemed somehow that their love, in its strangeness and newness, gave them a right to be here. They were full of opinions that all sounded correct, and they were talking about the idiocy of Pepsi's most recent marketing campaign or what Hillary Clinton's role in the White House should be or what was the best recipe for spaghetti sauce, and when Serena shivered, Dan set this sweatshirt around her shoulders. They were clasping hands, and he lifted her hand to his lips and very gently kissed it. Holding the shirt now, she imagined this gesture so fully she could almost feel it on the back of her hand.

She sat down on the bed, exhausted.

She turned on her laptop.

The email from Tom read:

Subject: ATTENTION URGENT TEMPLE BUSINESS DISCUSS AND DECIDE

We will have a general meeting of all members of Temple Shalom at 6:00 PM next Thursday evening to DISCUSS AND DECIDE the allegations against our beloved leader. All allegations will be discussed in an honorable fashion. Those who have their gripes will have five minutes each to discuss them. Then we will have a one-time, binding vote. We will remain a strong and unified congregation!

Shalom,

Tom Silverman, President

Blessed to Serve

IT WAS DECEMBER 5, THE evening of the Pinewood Derby. Dan came home early that day; he slipped quickly from his work clothes into his crisp beige uniform and stood with Zeb in front of the mirror. The two of them combed their hair.

"Ready?" Dan asked his son, who was gazing at his reflection as though just memorizing the particularities of his small face.

"For what?" asked Zeb.

The wooden derby car seemed oddly small and light to contain the weight of this particular dream. They all piled into their car for the big event. Dan moved briskly, strapping the timing equipment into the backseat. The children bubbled with excitement. Zeb held his car carefully in his lap. He touched the wheel with his finger, rolling it back and forth. Serena had never seen her son this hopeful; she wondered if Dan's idea was, in some way, right. They traveled through the thin mauve dusk to the room where the tiny cars would roll down wooden tracks to cries of disappointment or triumph.

They arrived early so that Dan could set up the tracks and computers. He did not know what he would get if Zeb won, but just that he wanted his son to win. Or, more accurately, Dan wanted to win. The incident with the pennies had troubled him in a way that he didn't want to reveal to Serena; the joke about the quarters had just come to him, he had said it, and everyone, thankfully, had laughed, but Serena didn't know how he had seen her fear, felt it start to invade him, like a dark wave, and before he joined in on this madness, he made the joke. He was so grateful for the derby! It had presented itself, miraculously, that night, as a distraction, an opportunity. He wanted Zeb to have a memory to replace the other; he could remember this and forget about the pennies. Dan could not bear the idea of his son walking away from this event with nothing in his hands.

Dan had set up the sensors at the top of the track, linked them to the computer, flicked the on switch, and watched the cars zip down the track. Each track had to be set up the same way, to trigger the sensor to start the computer. Serena watched him crouching at the bottom of the tracks, scrutinizing the cars rushing down, trying to identify what made one faster than another. The room was heavy with the smell of cinnamon and nutmeg, and it had transformed into a paean to both spiritualism and materialism. A soundtrack floating out from the walls alternated between the sound of car engines revving up and a chorus singing "Santa Claus Is Coming to Town" and "Little Drummer Boy." The racetracks finished at the bottom of a three-foot-tall papier-mâché statue of the holy infant in a manger, surrounded by smiling farm animals that had been slapped with brown paint by some scouts' siblings who, said one mother, wanted "to contribute to the great event." A halo made of tinfoil hovered above the baby, a plastic doll. Dan had not expected this display; he worried about a car flipping off the track and damaging the various participants in the scene.

"A car will not hit the holy infant," said Forrest, adjusting the animals a bit.

"Are these figures going to affect the aerodynamics of the cars?" Dan asked.

Forrest regarded him with an exasperated expression. "Perhaps they'll help the most virtuous scouts," he said, and he darted off.

Forrest was escorting his grandson Dawson around the room. A man whom Serena assumed to be Dawson's father—he had the same forehead and chin as Forrest—stood at the back. He had a long blond ponytail and was the sort of muscular man who was intently aware of his muscularity; he walked a little lightly, girlishly, holding out his arms, which were covered with tattoos. The tattoos had a theme of breasts and weaponry, and some of the tattoos featured breasts wielding weapons. The other parents carefully left space around him. When a phone rang on Dawson's father's belt, he bolted from the room and did not return.

Dawson was a heavy boy whose flushed cheeks gave him the appearance of someone who was perpetually embarrassed. He had more badges on his uniform than Serena had ever seen on any scout. It seemed impossible to have earned all those badges at his young age. She wondered if Forrest had simply sewn them on in an act of tribute or as talismans against a troubled future. "This is Dawson Sanders from Burgaw," Forrest said. "Most badges for a Cub in the county. Count his badges. Go ahead." The boy did not seem to appreciate the grand introduction and slunk by Forrest, rubbing the car against his bottom lip as though he wanted to eat it.

Was this the answer? What did they all think they would get when they won? Serena wondered. She could see in Forrest's face the same hope that was in Dan's, and in her own, the desire to be lifted from the general sordid nature of their longing. What would they feel when they stood on the winner's podium, clutching their trophies? She thought of her father standing over his train track scenes, right before he destroyed them, and the yearning in his face to create a landscape better than anyone he'd read about in *Model Trains Monthly*, anyone who'd written him a letter. "It's not how I saw it," he would say, his voice rising, as he began to crush the tiny trees. "It's not what it was in my mind." She thought of the way she sat before Earl Morton, waiting to hear what he thought about a speech she had written for him, watching him read it, as though to have her words chosen over the other speechwriters' in the company would somehow finally make her visible. It was the way the scouts were now gathering around the table that displayed all the cars—to merely be born was to distrust the fact of your reality, but to win something was to finally understand who you were in the world.

The cars were set out on a display table for judging in the artistic categories: Most Colorful, Most Original, Best Paint Job. There were cars shaped like a hotdog, an iPod, a spaceship, a gun, a foot. There were various cars with a Christmas theme, Santas, reindeer, a bright gold cross; there was one that had been outfitted with blinking electric lights. Serena was alarmed by the elaborate level of design. Zeb grabbed Serena's hand. He seemed to sense that some ante had just been upped.

"What do I do?" he asked.

"You race," said Rachel.

"How?" He bit his lip.

"It goes by itself," said Serena. She squeezed his hand and felt his slim bones. "It'll be fine," she said.

"But what do I do?" asked Zeb, pulling at his lip.

"Before we get our cars on the track," said Forrest, "before we get into the spirit of friendly competition, let's remind ourselves of the values of this holiday season. I invite you to come up and share some of the ways we celebrate Christmas!" Forrest swung, smiling, around the room. "I'll start. My family comes together, four sisters, eighteen cousins, down here. We spend Christmas Eve in front of a big bonfire in our yard. Then we go to sleep and leave a snack out for Santa, and in the morning, it's always gone. It took me years to believe my mother ate it." Laughter.

There followed several jolly anecdotes in a similar vein. Dan was tapping his fingers, annoyed.

"Can we just get on with it," he whispered to Serena.

"Now, Dan is going to tell us how the Jews celebrate Christmas!" said Forrest.

Dan looked up; he had not expected this.

Dan sat, frozen, for a moment, and then he jumped up and ran to the front of the room. He rubbed his hands together. The room was not particularly diverse, period. There were two black families, one Hispanic father and son, one scout who had been adopted from China, but everyone here had this in common: They were Christian. It was a situation that Serena's father would have, in his odd way, loved. When he felt uncomfortable in any situation, he always took note of fire exits and the quickest ways to reach them. One of his favorite things to point out in a movie theater, an enclosed place that unnerved him, was how many steps it took to get to one particular exit and why it was superior to another. It had aggravated her as a child, though it was also strangely exciting, the idea that at any moment one should be prepared to hurl oneself through a fire exit.

"Go ahead," said Forrest.

Dan clapped his hands together. "Our Christmas is called Chanu-kah," Dan said, drawing out the *ch*, like a gargle, to comic effect. There was mild laughter; Zeb stood up on his knees and looked around to see why they were laughing, and then he did, too. "We have eight days. That's eight days of presents, boys, not just one!" He shook a fist in the air, as though triumphant. "We play with a dreidel. We eat chocolate coins. We, uh, shake graggers. We light candles." He smiled broadly. "Eight days of presents!"

"Well," said Forrest, clapping his hands. There was applause. Dan bowed and walked to Serena. His forehead was damp.

"We don't shake graggers," Serena whispered to him.

He looked at her.

"That's Purim," she said.

"Gentlemen, let's start our engines!" called Forrest, and there was wild cheering. The scouts and their families went to the race preparation table and began smearing tires with graphite. Dan went to stand beside the tracks. His job was to press the button to start the cars moving and the timer running.

"Let's go, scouts!" called Forrest. "Can Will Tyler, Harper Pierce, and Amos Smith report to the tracks?"

There was applause. The boys trotted up and placed their cars on the tracks.

"Ready!" said Forrest. The boys stepped back from the tracks. Forrest shot off a muted starting gun, Dan pushed the button, and the cars were off.

The race took a matter of seconds. The wooden cars zoomed down the tracks, hit the bottom, bounced, and stopped. Numbers flashed on the screen: Track 1: 4.589, Track 2: 4.689, Track 3: 4.903.

"The winner of this race is Will Tyler!" Will Tyler jumped up and down and screamed.

The race continued like this, the little wooden cars speeding down the track, hitting the bottom, the winners and losers separated by milliseconds and for no apparent reason of engineering or skill. The scouts were each allowed three races, and their scores would be tallied, and the overall winners would be announced. The children and parents seemed to be caught up in a great wave, this simplification of their desire. It was its own form of holiness.

Then it was Zeb's turn.

He felt his mother's hand on his shoulder. He clutched the car in his hand and began to push through the crowd. There were so many people, and he just came up to their waistlines as he moved through the forest of brown pants and belts and butts and hairy arms. His father was calling his name. He tried to move in the direction of it, though he was not sure where he was going, and he was distracted by the sour smell of grownups and sweat, but somehow he was moving, and then he was stepping onto a stool and he was at Track 3, standing at the top of the sloping track, which looked endless. His father's hand was on his shoulder, and he did not know what he was supposed to do, or how to do it, but he placed his black car on the track. People laughed at his car; he liked the color black and thought his car looked especially powerful painted that color. He glanced at the others, the elaborate designs on them. He was set up against a car that resembled a Christmas tree and one that, amazingly, resembled a donkey with a halo. He shivered; he felt a huge wave rise inside of him, a desire to conquer these cars, to conquer this audience, to see his name on the screen. He was a little dizzy. He looked for his mother, who was staring at him with a confusing expression on her face, and he saw her holding his sister. Zeb wanted to win. He sensed his father holding his hand over the levers, about to start, and an icicle of fear shot up in his chest. Zeb placed his hand on the car.

His father pushed the button, and the cars were off. Wrightson, Sanders, and Shine. Track 1: 4.321, Track 2: 4.789, Track 3: 4.217.

The screen said, "Winner: Shine."

A roar went up, and Dan grabbed his son and hugged him, a violent hug; Zeb felt as though he were being crushed. He had done something right, and joy blew through him.

Zeb ran back to Serena. She gripped him and felt the exuberance, the quivering in his torso. Rachel, too, was jumping up and down and gripping the car; they were both crazed by it, this triumph, and Serena was, too, this thrill, the prickle down her arms, the shouting inside herself that he won, that Rachel would be next, that next year she would win in the sibling division, that their lives would be all right, and that they would march forward, buoyed up by some skill or luck into a perfect, clear blue sky.

Then Zeb won again. And again.

Dan could not believe it each time he saw his child's name on the board, glowing in green: Shine. It was beautiful, his name, the word, *Shine*, and there it was. Once, twice, three times. Had they inadvertently made a car that was a winner? Or was it all just luck? There was no way to know. He put his hand gently on the boy's shoulder.

At the end, the scouts and their parents stood as Forrest announced the names of the overall winners: individual fastest, and then highest speed over three races. Fifth place. Fourth. Third. Second.

"The overall winner, by oh point eleven seconds ahead of second place, is!" said Forrest.

His forehead gleamed. He wiped it with the end of his neckerchief. He called Zeb's name.

"You won!" yelled Dan, who scooped Zeb up and ran him to the front of the room where the boy, bewildered, was presented with a plastic golden trophy. There was applause, though some scouts in the audience were weeping.

"Next pack meeting in two weeks," said Forrest. The crowd swarmed the refreshment table. Dan looked around at the other parents. They were, depending on their scores, either comforting their children or fondling the trophies they had received. A few parents stepped up to Dan and shook hands in a show of good sportsmanship. "You all are the Andretti family!" exclaimed one. He pretended to be modest. He (oh, right, Zeb) had won.

Dan looked around for Forrest. He felt a tug of gratitude to him for inviting them into this group and wanted to say something to him.

Forrest gazed out at the emptying room. He slowly walked off the podium to join Dawson. His grandson was walking through the room, fingering the cloth badges on his uniform as though to check that they were all intact.

"Where's your vehicle?" Forrest asked him.

"Dunno," said Dawson. His face looked redder.

"Find it," said Forrest.

"I don't know where it is," said Dawson.

Forrest looked as though he were about to launch into a lengthy response to this comment when Dan stepped up. "Great race," said Dan, clapping his hands together.

"Yep," said Forrest, a little stiffly.

"It was close," said Dan.

Forrest laughed, a sound that seemed to have been manufactured in a factory that produced laughter. "Close. Close. Who knows why it happens? My father spent forty-some hours one year helping me with my car, doing who knows what, and I came in dead last. Ha!" He laughed, a strangled laugh. "Every race. I couldn't sleep that night. I thought I'd let him down. Did you know that Dawson woke up at 4:00 AM today? He was so excited."

Dan looked at Forrest and understood his sadness, his beaten expression. "He did a good job," said Dan.

They all unplugged the wires from the computers and set them in the back of the church. Then they went to the car. The lot was empty now; the asphalt sparkled under the gray parking lamp lights.

"What a night!" Dan said. "That was fun." Serena had to agree—there was something energizing about seeing the cars speed down the tiny tracks, about Zeb's excitement. "You made a good car," he said to Zeb.

"I want six trophies," said Zeb, running up beside him.

"I do, too," said Rachel.

The children got into the car; in a sudden moment of harmony, they positioned the trophy between themselves. It was merely a plastic gold cup mounted on a hunk of stained wood, created in a trophy factory, but the letters, in elegant script, said: GRAND WINNER: PINEWOOD DERBY 2003.

Dan started the car. Serena glanced at his face. In the long march of marriage, she had seen his face evolve—from the young confidence of a man whose cheek she wanted to touch, to the gentleness that overwhelmed his face when he first held his children, to the aggrieved hardness that he had worn the last few bleak months, to now. She saw something new in his expression. He wanted to be a boy—she could see it in the structure of his face, in the way it was aging, even in the way the creases emanated from his smile. His face held some innocence or was trying to force itself to a sort of flatness, and, seeing this, Serena was startled.

Chapter Seventeen

THE MEETING AT OAKDALE ELEMENTARY Auditorium was two nights later, December 7. It was scheduled for seven, but audience members began to claim seats at around six. The SUVs, the jacked-up pickup trucks, and the worn-out Buicks and Chevys were parked on the damp, matted grass. Forrest Sanders had come off the Pinewood Derby to prepare for this; he was standing at the front of the school, armed with flyers and now T-shirts, shaking hands as though he were running for office.

Serena walked inside the auditorium alone. The Oakdale Auditorium was like every public school auditorium: dank and sloping and with a heating and ventilation system so flawed that even during the winter everyone was fanning themselves with their flyers to remain cool. The atmosphere resembled a family event, almost jolly. Many people were wearing Christmas sweaters, grand and curious woolen manifestations of trees, reindeer, angels, adorned with tiny bells on the shoulders. Some of the people had made protest signs. There was a sign with Santa with an X through his face and a single tear rolling down his cheek. Forrest's flyer had cast a wide net; the saving of Christmas attracted the vocal members of the far right, the creationists, the pro-lifers, those who wanted prayer in school, people who wanted to define marriage as only between a man and woman. One young woman gripped a sign that said, "What about the Fossil Record?" There were a couple representatives from the liberal side—one was a local midwife who had nursed her two-year-old openly in the school hallway, her large, pale breasts gaily flashed to the students. The vice principal had asked her to please nurse the child in her car, which had led to its own cries and protests. She held up a sign with religious symbols—a cross, a Star of David—that together created a word: COEXIST. There was a sparkling, tense energy in the room, as though the grinding hew of raising children, of preparing meals, of the war news, of the visage of the president proclaiming the war had been won while soldiers were still dying, of the tremulousness of their marriages, of the drudgery of their jobs, could be put aside for this most precious enterprise: a cause.

The rabbi was here. He stood, arms crossed, at the front of the auditorium, looking at the assembling crowd. He had decided to wear his white suit, the nicer one. He wore a tie covered with smiling silver dreidels that had big cartoon eyes. Had he seen any of the irate, impassioned email messages going on about him? If he did, he did not show it.

"Thank you for coming," she said. "Are you ready?"

He leaned toward her. "Ready! This is my version of heaven," he whispered. His face had a menthol scent, not his usual swampy cologne.

"Why?"

"They don't think they want to listen to me," he said. "And they will."

"Tell me how."

"Easy. They want what you want. They love what you love. Trust me. We're here to make friends." He paused. "I need my hat," he said, and he dashed off to his car. She made her way to a row near the front. She was sitting near two mothers she recognized from the school—Mary Jo and Felicia, mothers of two boys in her son's class.

"Clayton pulled two sticks yesterday for badness," said Felicia. "For what? Not being able to sit for the whole story time? When they give them just twenty minutes of recess?"

"School isn't made for boys," said Mary Jo, knitting a tinsel-threaded baby's cap.

"It's not human," said Felicia.

"I wish they had more recess," said Serena.

"I wish they had more *play*," said Felicia. "Kids should be kids."

"Why'd you come out for this?" asked Serena.

"Fun," said Mary Jo, rather grimly. "Fun and joy."

"The children need more of it," said Felicia.

"Bring on Santa!" said Mary Jo. "Bring on caroling! It's the joy of December!"

"Right," said Felicia. "I am chock full of ideas." She looked at Serena wistfully. "I have so much *energy*," she said. "Pipe cleaner nativity baskets. Aluminum foil stars. What do you do with a five-, three-, and one-year-old? I ask you. I don't want to pay someone to care for them while I work. I couldn't earn enough that way, anyway. Can you tell me who can?"

"It's frustrating," said Serena, nodding. The energy of the underemployed mother was forceful and sobering; what were they supposed to do with their unused exuberance and talent?

The rabbi returned, clutching a large fuzzy menorah hat. It was a flat-brim hat with a menorah made of antlers sticking out the top like an enormous fork. At the tip of each antler was a little electric bulb; he pressed a button on a clicker in his hand, and the tips of the antlers lit up.

"Good god," said Serena.

Mary Jo laughed when she saw it. "What a costume!" she said.

"Sho' is," he said, grinning at her. Serena wanted to clap her hand over his mouth. She was horrified by the suddenly acquired Southern accent, for she knew he was making fun of them, but he had mastered it so wholly and subtly the women didn't notice.

He leaned toward Serena. "This wins everyone over every time," he murmured. "They love it. They love menorahs. The living, the dying. Everyone, for some reason, loves hats."

"This is your main argument?" she asked, concerned.

"One," he said. "What are you going to say?" he asked.

She had not thought about this.

Forrest Sanders walked up to the stage. He was wearing not his Scouts uniform now but the gray blazer he put on for church. He looked out at everyone and beamed. This was not a tribute to Christmas, or whatever he was selling, Serena thought—he believed this was a tribute to him. It was, she thought, the misperception that was undoing all of them. He bent toward the microphone. "Welcome, all," he said. "To everyone who believes in Christmas!" There was a great, loose cheer and show of hands. "I've had a busy week," he said. "I'm Forrest Sanders. I ran the local Pinewood Derby for our terrific young men who are our Boy Scouts." There was applause. He held up his hands against it. "No. I love it. It is my privilege to lead these young-sters. And it is my honor to stand up for Christmas and all it signifies when I heard it was being stolen from the schools." More applause. "Now, listen. Christmas is love," he said. "No one is taking it from us!" Rabbi Golden tapped his fingers rapidly against his seat, the rest of his body still as a rock as he watched Forrest.

"Welcome to our organizational meeting to bring Christmas back to the schools," he said. "I would like to thank Chick-fil-A for provid-ing refreshments. Check out the chicken nugget tray near the back! I'm a big fan of the barbecue dipping sauce, myself. Chick-fil-A now offers retreats where folks can work on their marriages. They also have retreats where you can help truth and values move from your head to your heart. They have generously left some brochures in the back."

He took to being a corporate spokesperson almost as fluidly as he took to being an organizer for political action. He sighed deeply and stared at the audience. "My wife almost died a few weeks ago," he said. "And it got me to thinking what's important in life. I am not a wealthy man, folks, nor one who is known in many circles. I will admit that five of my business ventures failed during my life, and *not due to my own shortcomings.*" His face was getting pink with the exertion of these admissions; he looked like he had wanted to let them out, in a formal setting, for a long time. "I'm a hard worker, like many of you. I had to support five children. I tried. When my grandson came home from school and told me that he was not allowed to create a nativity scene in his second-grade classroom, I was mad. What are the values taught in our school system? What's important is this: *love.*" Applause. "Love for each other, love for Jesus. What's wrong with spreading that love this time of year, I ask you?" He opened his arms.

"Nothing!" called Mary Jo, who stamped her feet.

"Some may call our cause silly, but it is important to me. I see it is important to many of you." He shielded one hand over his eyes and gazed out at the audience. "I ask anyone to come up to say what they think our schools should offer in this area. We start with honoring Christmas. We can bring back prayer. We can design our schools in the image it was designed to have. Line up to the right. You can sign a peti-tion in the back." He walked to the front row and sat down.

The support for Christmas reached across racial lines, across economic divides. First on the stage was a trim black woman in her sixties who identified herself as Mrs. Dolores Jackson. "My grandson is a student in the first grade," she said. "He is tested, tested, tested. He does not like those tests! And I see no reason why he should not have the opportunity to pay tribute to Jesus during this holiday season. I have read studies through my church that children who can express their love for Jesus in a school setting perform better on standardized tests. I would also like to add this: Why should he be *denied* the opportunity to declare his love? Jesus is a star! Jesus is our beacon!" She sat down to much applause.

"Amen," said Mary Jo.

Next was a tall white-haired man, a Clayton Pembroke, who began, "I love Walmart." Much applause. "Do you know why? It is not just the good prices. It is not that I can buy pizza and bug repellant and socks in one stop. It is because they are not afraid to say 'Merry Christmas.'" He paused. "I walk into the Gap. 'Happy holidays.' Folks, it's just not the same. I want to hear those words, 'Merry Christmas!' I am boycotting Gap, folks. I want to be able to say 'Merry Christmas' whenever I want, whenever I want it. I want to shout it from the rooftops! Happy holidays, bah, humbug!" He sat down to a standing ovation.

It went on and on. Serena felt the skin on her arms prickle. There were loose interpretations of the Constitution: "I tell you. One nation under God. We all know which God they were talking about!"

There were calls for prayer in the schools: "I ask for a moment of prayer to our Lord Jesus Christ in the morning. Just one moment, heads bowed. Won't that help them get through their day?"

And there was the mother who wanted creationism taught in the schools. "I wasn't here two million years ago," she said. "If evolution is so slow, why don't we see anything evolving right now?" Hearty applause. "If they can teach that theory, they can teach our truth."

A woman stood up and announced, "Some of you may have come from monkeys, but I certainly did not!"

There was significant applause for this statement. It was, Serena thought, the end of reason. She wanted to run. The heat seemed to have been cranked up in the auditorium. She eyed the rabbi, who was sitting, one leg crossed over the other, watching everyone who came up. He seemed focused on them, almost bemused, as though he were trying himself to figure out how to love them. There was a lot of talk about love. She wanted to love, too, and in fact, sitting beside the rabbi, his presence here, she was beating down a different, ridiculous sort of gratitude that floated through her, despite her. He, who saw her goodness. The restlessness of being human would end. And if they could see into her mind, see this peculiar love, see what she was thinking right now, they would all go after her. There would be no debate in this. That would be it.

The love described by the audience seemed too easy, too suspect, too uncomplicated; she did not trust it. Yet they all seemed so happy. They all wanted to bring Jesus into the school. They wanted prayers to start school board meetings, as long as it was a Christian prayer. "If it was a Buddhist monk or something leading a prayer," said one man, "*I'd walk out.*" There was cheerfulness to their certainty, to their idea that this was the right thing to do, that this was the point of the public school system.

There was a pause in the stream of people speaking at the podium. The rabbi turned to her.

"Go ahead," he said.

She stared at him. He had to be kidding. "No," she whispered. "Listen to them. I don't know what to say."

"Sho', you do." He winked.

"I can't."

He squeezed her forearm; her pulse jumped. "Go ahead."

She climbed up the stairs to the podium. She looked out at them. Dolores Jackson was delicately removing a Life Saver from its roll; Clayton Pembroke was texting on his cell phone; Mary Jo had almost finished knitting her hat.

"Hello, everyone," she said. Her throat was dry. "How are all of you today?" she asked. Her voice shook. "I'm Serena Hirsch. My son is a kindergarten student at Oakdale." She felt her voice, a cool pressure, rising through her chest. Her mind went blank, but her voice kept going without her. "He loves it here." Not exactly true. Should she bring up the penny incident? But perhaps that would not really help their case. He didn't exactly love the school, but he would love it a lot less if Forrest and his minions took over. "He walks into school and he feels part of it. He wants to belong." He was not even the issue—frankly, he barely cared; it was her. "We actually don't celebrate Christmas. We celebrate Chanukah." This felt like an absurd declaration—so what? She did not look at their expressions; she kept going. This was what being Jewish was; it was the difference, the other view. It was that small, significant action: opening one's eyes. The first Jew they had ever met. Not an ambassadorship she had wanted. She wished suddenly that she was taller, better-looking, anything to serve as better promotional material. "Christmas is a wonderful time," she said, pandering. "I am a believer in public schools. I hope that the public schools, which are for everyone, can remain, um, for everyone. School can be a place where everyone can belong."

She stopped. That was it. She was a speechwriter, and this was where she should stop. She nodded at the audience and stepped down. There was no applause, which felt unfair. Maybe that was part of the point of praising Jesus—a sure audience pleaser. You loved him, people would love you. The audience was frozen. However, they were schooled in a kind of politeness; she noted that nobody booed.

She went down the stairs, hearing her footsteps ring against the old, shellacked wood. The rabbi was beaming at her in a manner both delighted and condescending, as though she had just finished her Bat Mitzvah. "Thanks," he murmured. "They're thinking. I'll close the deal."

He leapt up, clutching his menorah hat, and hurried up the stairs. She felt protective of him, the way she felt about her children when she released them into the world. He had worn white, she thought, because he understood it would glow in this American institutional fluorescent light, the gray luminescence of schools and post offices and army barracks and jails.

"Friends," he said. "Let me say hey. I am Rabbi Golden from Temple Shalom. We're the Jewish congregation in town." Instantly, she could see how he differed from the other speakers; he was a pro. He stood back from the podium, relaxed. His arms swung by his sides loosely, confident as a game show host's. His white jacket fell, watery, around him. He leaned forward into the microphone and gazed out at the group.

"First, I want to say merry Christmas," he said. "I don't mind saying it. I'll say it again, merry Christmas! I think you folks should be able to say it whenever you want, in your homes, in your churches, in the world. This is a free country! Who could have a problem with that?"

"Merry Christmas," a few shouted back.

"So," he said. "No one wants to take away Christmas. Now, how many of you can throw a spear?"

A surprising number of hands flew up.

"We could have used you!" said the rabbi, his voice bright. "You would have been great Maccabees!" He paused. "Does anyone know anything about Maccabees?" He went into a discussion of the temple and the light, dramatic renditions of Romans breaking in on Jews worshipping and dragging them off to be executed. He strode to the side and dimmed the lights for a moment, and he lit a menorah, one candle after another, a piercing white glow on the stage.

She sat very still, watching him; the stage was butter, and he glided across it. The bravery! It made her breathless. It seemed the essence of his being had evolved around the desire to convince an antagonistic group of his worth; she felt a golden, sorrowful sympathy for him. Her fingers gripped the wooden arms of her chair.

"Happy Chanukah," he said. "And if you ask nice, you can wear my special Chanukah hat."

He lifted up his antler menorah hat and put it on. He looked like an odd sort of reindeer. Gripping the electric clicker, he turned the bulbs on the tips of the antlers on and off. He turned around and did a jig in the watery gray light. The audience laughed, a loud and raucous laughter, as though they were relieved to be laughing at something. It was a joke; it was terrible, she thought, that he was using himself as a joke. But it was working. He wanted to win, and he did not care how.

When he stopped, there was some puzzling scattered applause. What was it for? His desire to be ridiculous? Some bizarre tribute to them? A sense that Jews were actually idiots? Or was the hat secretly a brilliant move, making him somehow, oddly, likable?

"Oakdale is for everyone!" he called as he hurried offstage. "Merry Christmas and happy Chanukah, y'all!"

The antler hat act was, truly, a difficult one to follow. Everyone was suddenly shy. Forrest came up the stairs and said, "Well. I guess Rudolph has some competition!" More laughter; Serena flinched. She heard the rabbi laugh beside her, a sharp, false laugh. "I invite all of you to refreshments in the back. Please sign the petition."

The rabbi sat next to her; his forehead was damp. The audience members got up. Now that their anger had been expressed, they seemed awkward and puzzled. They began to file toward the back.

"What'd you think?" the rabbi asked. "Did they like it? Do you think it worked?"

"Great job," she said, quickly.

"Now's the most important part." He darted to the back to the fold-out tables where the plastic platters of Chick-fil-A nuggets and brownies were spread out. "This is where you make friends," he murmured to her. "By the free food."

The rabbi broke away from her, holding up his arms as though he'd made a touchdown. The audience helped themselves to the dry brown nuggets and warm sweet tea and brownie squares.

It was as though the three of them were candidates for some inexplicable public office, the rabbi and Serena and Forrest, shaking hands with the people who had come. The rabbi had, of course, remembered the small details the speakers had sprinkled into their speeches; he sidled up to Dolores Jackson and told her how he had also hated tests in school; he told Clayton Pembroke that there were good deals right now on Christmas cookies at Walmart.

Serena looked around. The crowd pressed forward at the refreshment table. She hovered around the knots of people, who nodded at her but did not invite her into the discussion; they were all talking brightly about the Camellia Festival fundraiser or the bake sale at First Baptist or the renovation of the bathroom or the science project for Mrs. Landis's class, as though the previous discussion had not happened at all.

Serena walked around them. She was invisible, from their discomfort or her own or both; finally, she inserted herself into a discussion with Mary Jo and Felicia about the difficulty of packing lunches without peanut products, which were banned because of severe allergies among some of the children.

"I don't understand why the allergic kids can't sit in a corner," said Mary Jo. "I can't make another ham sandwich. And Trevor will not eat tuna."

"And peanut butter is *all* that Clara will eat," said Felicia. "What do you feed your son?" she asked Serena.

"Oh, god," she said. "The choices are minimal. Butter on bread? He'd rather have an entire lunch of Chex Mix."

They laughed, carefully; it was straining, this proving one's humanity to one another.

The rabbi had parked himself beside the petition. The paper above it read: *We the undersigned call upon the school board to order all schools to authorize all forms of celebration of Christmas in the public schools, to stop this tyranny of secularism. The U.S. of A. is a Christian nation.* The petition was beside the nugget tray, and the rabbi was making fast progress through the nuggets, dipping them into the orange barbecue sauce. He stood by the petition and watched the audience members float around him, pause, pick up a nugget, not pick up a pen, walk out. Only a few people signed in his presence. Perhaps the people did not want to sign such a petition beside a religious figure, even one representing competing interests, or perhaps they did not want to present themselves as aggressive, or at least not in a public space. She counted how many people signed it: One. Two. Three. Six. Ten.

Ten.

The Chanukah antler hat sat on the floor beside the rabbi. A couple people asked to try it on.

Some people did sign the petition, their eyes averted from the rabbi, who took the opportunity to distract them with a brownie. "Excuse me," said the rabbi, in a honeyed voice. "Can I pass you a brownie?" This dissuaded one couple, who chose a brownie over political action and then darted out.

The hallway emptied; it was just Serena, Forrest, and the rabbi in the hallway. Her head hurt. Forrest was transferring the leftover brownies onto one plate. He picked up the petition, counted the names. He had filled a quarter of one page.

"It's a start," said Forrest, looking up. "You have to start somewhere." He stared at Serena, a sudden, direct gaze.

"Maybe you go somewhere you don't expect," Serena said.

He looked at her, unblinking. "So, Zeb was the big winner," said Forrest.

The race. "Right," she said. "It was a big night for him. He was happy."

Rabbi Golden came up to him before he packed up the remaining nuggets. There were five left. They all eyed the nuggets as though daring the others to grab them, though they were not that good.

"How's the shed?" asked Rabbi Golden.

Forrest looked surprised. "Been a while since I've worked on it," he said. "Sir, I have one question for you," said Forrest.

"Yes?" said the rabbi.

"Do you ever worry about the afterlife?" asked Forrest.

Rabbi Golden scratched his neck and said, "No, sir."

"I know where I'm going," said Forrest. "I know where I'm going to get my reward. How about you? Aren't you worried about—"

"What?" said the rabbi.

"Judgment," said Forrest.

Rabbi Golden rubbed his hand over his face and laughed carefully. "Well," he said. Forrest stood, alone, amid the balled-up napkins and chicken nugget crumbs on the floor. Serena thought he looked exhausted.

"Well, sir," said the rabbi. "Do you need, ah, any help cleaning up?"

Serena was startled; this was not exactly the question she had thought to ask Forrest, but it seemed the right thing to offer. The rabbi was an expert at distraction. There were paper plates and brownie crumbs strewn all over the room. Forrest flinched; he had not expected this.

"No," said Forrest. "I can do that."

"It'll take just a sec," said the rabbi, and he began to pick up plates.

Serena also began to pick up crumpled napkins and empty cups, and toss them into the trash. It was like they were simply cleaning up after a school function. It had that feeling of normalcy. Forrest watched, and his face reddened.

"I don't need any *help*," said Forrest.

Serena knew that tone; she put down a plate and started heading toward the door. The rabbi paused and put a hand on Forrest's shoulder. "Shalom," he said to Forrest, and then he and Serena went outside.

The sky was dark now; the air had cooled, and the grass gave off a sharp, bitter smell. His suit showed its wrinkles as he walked in front of her. She could perceive his exhaustion in his walk — it appeared that he was hurtling forward, the way a child walked after having been awake for too long. At her car, he stopped.

"What do you think?" he said. "Did it help?"

She was shaken by the whole experience, the understanding of what resided in the minds of some of her neighbors. But after all the yelling, not many people had signed the petition. She was touched by his last question, considering the week he was going through. "I think it slowed it down," she said. "For right now, anyway. He didn't get too many signatures."

"Good," he said. "All you can do is present yourself. First step is that they see you. Second is that they remember your name." He looked tired in the dark blue light. "Mind if I sit down for a moment?" he said. She opened the car door. He lowered himself to the passenger seat. He sighed; it was the sound of air being released from a tire.

"I try to help people," he said. "I have a big heart. Those strangers saw it. I believe it. They still want what they want, but they feel a little confused, so they slow down a little. Watch." He stared at the street, rubbing his hands slowly together. "Say," he said, his tone brighter, "have you heard anything about the meeting this week?"

"No," she said, wishing she hadn't.

"I don't understand what anyone wants. Here I try. I am an excellent rabbi. Not just for Jews, but for everyone. I can't tell you how many soldiers I helped abroad. They, who really needed help. Here, they don't understand the chain of command. What is not to understand?

This is the way you do it. A dying soldier gets it. He gets it more than Mrs. Stella Goldsmith, who wants to have a Bat Mitzvah Saturday afternoon, so that Grandma can fly in from Pittsburgh. Or how about Esther Price, who calls me at 2:00 AM to ask me to pray for her dead daughter? Let me tell you. They are full of what they need now. The entitlement of civilians. They don't know."

"What don't they know?" she asked. He could tell her; he could figure it out.

His eyes flashed. "They weren't there when I was in the hospital in Baghdad and they rushed in Private George Martinez. Legs blown off. He wanted a priest. The priest was busy. He got me. First time away from home. He grew up in East L.A., he grew up in church, blah, blah. He had tried to help out one of the shepherds who came up to him with a fake limp at a checkpoint, and *kaboom*. He was pumped up with morphine, and he was holding my hand, and he said, 'Chaplain, I have to tell you something. I never screwed anyone.' He asked me, 'Will I be able to live without sex?' He didn't ask about walking so much. Just about sex. He said he had dreamed about it for years and he was going to do it when he got out." He paused. "He was in intensive care for a week. He asked for me. Even after the priest was around. I think he didn't want to tell the priest he still wanted to have sex. Maybe he was secretly a Jew. I sat by him, and he asked me to pray for him. He asked me to pray for erections. I didn't know exactly what prayer would do for that, but I knew one for healthy bodily functions, so I said that, in Hebrew. He didn't care. He just cared that it was me. *I comforted him.*" He closed his eyes. His face was slack for a moment. "Then he had a heart attack, and that was it."

She closed her eyes. They sat in the darkness.

"I'm sorry," she said, softly.

He lowered his head. "Sorry, sorry. Everyone's sorry. Those kids sent out there not knowing what they were getting into, going for a job, to see the world, all that bullshit. They know there aren't any weapons of mass destruction. They don't have the right suits for them to wear. Those are my children, dammit. I help them. They can sense it in me. They know." He looked at her, his eyes burning. "*I care about them.* They seem tough when they line up and when they stand with their weapons, but I see them crying. I saw one guy crush his toe with his gun to keep himself from crying."

"You helped them," she said.

"I help them. I say help, not helped, because I know the ones who are still there are thinking of me. I still get emails. *Pray for me. I'm taking the road to Tikrit. I have six buddies. Pray for us. Include our legs and arms.* They trust me because I know what they know. Fear. You know what I did whenever I was being shuffled to foster homes? I would lie awake in the new bed. I knew it wouldn't last long. I learned the Hebrew prayers, and I would say them to myself, not knowing what they meant. The families I stayed with didn't know what they meant. They weren't religious; they just shoved me off to Hebrew school. At night, I would wander into the parents' room and watch them. I wanted to see that they did not move. I would say whatever prayer I could — the Motzi, the Kiddush, the V'ahavta. Can you see me, sitting there, saying the prayer of the Torahs over these people? But the Torahs didn't leave. Do you hear me? They didn't move—"

He glanced at her, as though waiting for a certain response. She sat next to him in the darkness. She let out a breath and put a hand on his arm, lightly.

He nodded at her. He sat back, focused on what he wanted to say. "And here I am. My first pulpit. Who do I get? Loretta Stone. Honestly? An old bag. Esther Price. Stella Goldsmith. What do they need? What have they ever needed? 'Just make the Bat Mitzvah Saturday afternoon so my relatives can fly in.' Why not make it Sunday? Monday morning? Why be Jewish at all?"

She sat forward. "But," she said. "They're—"

"They can follow a few rules." His voice started to rise. "I'm the rabbi. I'm the teacher. I don't need them. Witches. That's what they are!"

She closed her eyes. It felt as though the car was rippling. Loretta was a frail, elegant woman in her seventies, as was Esther. "But rabbi," she said, "they're just asking—"

"Really?" She could barely see his face in the soft evening, but he seemed almost to be smiling. "Tell that to George Martinez."

"Yes, but—" she said.

"Is that what you're going to say to our men and women who sacrifice?" he said. "What are you saying? Who's more *important?*"

Her shoulders stiffened. "Does someone need to be more important?"

"Yes."

Something caught in her throat; it was difficult to speak.

The dark sky stretched, cold, over them. She shivered. She was sitting next to him, but she felt like a monster, impossibly tall. "Rabbi," she said, slowly, "you've been through so much. You wouldn't want . . ." she tried, carefully, sensing this might not go over well, but feeling as though her options were slipping. "The board has been suggesting this, possibly, to talk to someone, get a little perspective, someone who could help with these issues—"

He laughed. "The board is suggesting it! The board is suggesting *psychological help?* Who are they? No. It is not me."

The bare trees wound up into the sky, their slim trunks black in the streetlight. She could feel the chill air through her clothes.

"It's not you," she said.

"No," he said.

His cell phone rang. He stood up and answered it. She could hear a torrent of speech on the other end; he closed his eyes. Then he opened them, held up a finger, and swerved into his car. He drove off, pressing more anguish against his ear.

She looked at the darkened elementary school, the sodden fields ribbed with muddy tire tracks. A gauzy swath of stars swept across the black sky. After all the emotion, the proclamations, that had echoed through the auditorium, it was terribly silent; there was no one here.

Chapter Eighteen

DAN WATCHED ZEB CARRY THE Pinewood trophy around with a deep and instant fondness, as though it were alive: a kitten, a beloved pet. The night of the derby, Dan picked up the trophy beside Zeb's bed; he pressed his cheek to it and breathed the cheap factory smell of victory.

They had won. But Dan stared into the dimness of their small, acrid bungalow, and he listened to his heart. He tried to imagine he was feeling joy or relief, but the sensation he had was actually different. The moment that Zeb had won, Dan had been flooded by an immense lightness, a relief; there was a moment when he felt he did not need to yearn. Zeb would be fine; he would succeed in different forums. The morning anguish had subsided. His children would move on to something sparkling and good, and he, their father, had somehow enabled this. They had arrived, an anxious group, and they had left, he felt, cohesive, more of a family. Even Serena seemed to walk more lightly as they headed to the car. But in the quiet of the house, when they had all fallen asleep, he padded around their home.

He felt the same way as he had before.

Worse, in fact. He wanted to run. The victory had changed nothing: They had somehow ended up in Waring, his wife still left the room quickly when he was in it, his brother was dead. He thought of Harold at the intersection in Omaha, going there to meet a girl, killed by a careless driver while he was crossing a street, whereas he had safely negotiated the back roads of Thailand, Columbia, Zambia. Harold, as an adult, became an evasive figure; he never married, got jobs teaching in China, the Ukraine, Peru—floated the world. His correspondence with Dan was brief and kind and enigmatic, and while it left Dan with a desire to know more about Harold's life, he never asked.

Dan suddenly thought about the moment when his mother found out about his father's affairs, when Georgette Ohrbach had seen his father and someone—not his mother—kissing at a deli on Sixty-fifth Street; he remembered that day, remembered how he and Harold crouched, side by side in their room, his brother's heart a hummingbird against his shoulder, while vases crashed in the living room. Harold did not say anything but looked at Dan's shoelaces, which were untied. Harold had just learned to tie a series of knots at Scouts. He leaned down and he tied Dan's shoelaces for him, and they stayed tied. The boys did not know what was going to happen in the other room, but Dan touched the laces, and a relief swept through him. He could walk around without his shoes falling off, and this was somehow wondrous.

Dan thought of Harold standing in the garage beside him. How old had Dan been then? A child, barely older than Zeb. It seemed impossible that Harold had been that young at that moment, for he thought of his brother as immensely old, mature, just then, but he had been so small, eight, nine—Dan had never asked him what that moment had been like for his brother. That night, at 2:00 AM, he sat down and sent an email to Harold's former address, and there was no response, no returned mail, just an electronic note sent somewhere in the universe.

Hello, he wrote. He tried to think of what he wanted to say to him, and it was this:

We won.

He looked at these words and felt like an idiot. What had they won? A trophy for a wooden car? Now he was the sort of person who sent an email to his dead brother.

Dan looked at his family at the dinner table the next night, felt guilty for writing to his dead brother that they had won, where he did not feel like a winner particularly, and he was disoriented. Zeb was glad to have won but seemed to have forgotten it, and it was as though Dan were peering at his family, this group that he had joined and created, through a box of glass; he was trapped inside this box, and he did not know how to get out.

The phone rang.

It was Forrest. He sounded cheerful. He wanted to come and chat about the derby for a moment and wondered if he could drop by now.

"Sure," said Dan; there was an urgency to Forrest's voice that he had not heard before. He put down the phone and looked at his family sitting at the table.

"Forrest wants to come by and talk about . . . uh, the derby," he said.

"He's coming *here*? Now?" Serena asked.

"Apparently," he said.

"Are you kidding?" she said. She did not want Forrest anywhere near here after the school meeting. "Do you *know* what happened at the meeting last night?"

"He seemed fine," Dan said, trying to sound confident. "He just wanted to drop by for a sec. Maybe we left something at the derby—"

Serena stared at him. She did not want Forrest in the house. She thought about what he had said to her and the rabbi: judgment.

"They do live next door," said Dan.

"Two minutes," she said. "Really. I'm going to set my watch."

She set the children up with bowls of ice cream in the kitchen. She closed the doors between the kitchen and living room and stood like a sentry at the doorway. She was glad the room was not very comfortable, so Forrest's visit would have to be quick. Dan pulled the kitchen chairs into the living room, brushed crumbs off the couch. Five minutes later, Forrest knocked on the door. He was dressed in full troop leader regalia, and he was accompanied by Mr. Hester Smith, another assistant leader.

"How are you all?" said Dan, holding open the door into the cool blue evening.

"Hello," said Forrest, stiffly. "Don't want to take long—"

"Come on in," said Dan. "Can I get you folks anything? Soda?" He paused. "Beer?"

"No, thanks," said Forrest. He stood inside the living room, looking around with a determined expression; he seemed to be searching for something specific. His eyebrows twitched. He glanced at Serena, then he sighed, a short, impatient breath, as though she were a particularly troublesome plant that needed to be trimmed.

"Two minutes," said Serena, crisply. "That's all we have tonight."

They all stood, waiting to be directed by some other authority. "You want to sit down?" asked Dan, after a moment.

"Sure," said Forrest. They settled on the broken couch. Hester wore, Serena thought, an empty expression that could be interpreted as boredom or thuggishness.

"How's Evelyn?" asked Dan.

"Up one day, down the next," said Forrest. He rubbed his hands over his face as if he were trying to mold it into a particular expression. Hester tried to smile, but it looked like he was baring his teeth.

"Now, you know," said Forrest, his voice both strident and trembling, "I'm not a man that likes conflict. I like everything to be well between my friends and neighbors."

Serena felt a warning along the back of her neck.

"Well, I'll get right to it. There have been some concerns raised after the derby. Some people, some others in the troop, thought we should have a talk."

Dan blinked. Even the way Forrest sat—straight, prim, folded into place—made him look incongruous in the living room. Dan glanced at his uniform, his badges, the way his hands were folded, and was aware that he knew almost nothing about Forrest at all.

"What concerns?" asked Dan.

"You know, some people are more skilled than others when it comes to making the cars," said Forrest. "Some people are afraid of irregularities."

"Excuse me?" said Dan.

"Being in charge of timing, you see."

Dan cleared his throat. "What are you saying?" he asked.

"I looked at the computers," said Forrest, "and it all seems fine . . . but some people thought you should have stepped aside when your son's car came up . . . "

Serena and Dan stared at Forrest; her face was abruptly hot.

"We won!" said Dan. "Fair and square! Look at his car!" He jumped up and grabbed the car, which was on top of a bookshelf. The absurd black Batmobile. He held it out to Forrest, who took it and rubbed the wheels against his palm.

Serena felt Dan's voice swell in her; she understood his outrage. For the first time in months, they both felt the same thing.

"Well," said Forrest, wiping his brow, "some of the troop members — quite a few, in fact — have gathered to complain that there should have been different rules, that there was no objectivity — "

"It's the timing issue," said Hester.

"That's right," said Forrest.

Serena stepped forward. "We're talking about wooden cars here. You can all be good sports and deal with it — "

"They ask that you give back the trophy," said Forrest.

There was a sudden silence. It was so harsh and uncomfortable it felt like someone had been slapped.

Serena felt her body moving, a kind of hulk, and all she could say was, "Forrest. Stop."

"You know what I mean," said Forrest, standing up. "Coming in. Taking over the derby — "

"What are you saying, Forrest?" Serena said. He looked excited, as though accusation was his best, most natural state of being, that this is where he found some inner peace.

"We don't know you," Forrest said. "We don't know what, uh, the rules are in that Jewish church — "

Dan froze. That Jewish church? Was that how Forrest saw him? It seemed a joke; didn't Forrest know that he hated services, the mumbo jumbo? What the hell did he see? Forrest had made a mistake. But Dan heard the tone in his voice with absolute clarity.

"I can't have this doubt with my assistant leader," said Forrest, now sounding almost merry. "You are hereby relieved of your duty — "

"Forget it," yelled Dan, standing up, his whole body tense. "We quit!"

Serena looked at them — Forrest small, crazy, grinning, Hester standing beside him like a bodyguard, which was, she realized, his intended role, Dan standing, face red, suddenly shocked at this turn of events, which she had tried to tell him about many weeks ago. She wanted them out — Forrest and Hester — before something else happened. "Go," said Serena. "Now." She opened the door.

"Take care, now," said Forrest. His posture was slightly hunched, almost deferent; now that he had accomplished his goal, he was trying to be apologetic.

She shut the door and locked it.

The children were hanging on the kitchen door, watching.

"What happened?" they asked.

"The Boy Scouts just ended!" Dan shouted. "It blew up. Gone." He ran into his room and brought out his uniform and stuffed it into a trash can. It looked like he was stuffing a dead body inside the plastic receptacle.

Zeb looked appalled. "What are you doing?"

"We've quit. We're out. They're—" He stood, trying to think of the right word. "*Boring*. Give me your uniform." Their son trotted upstairs and brought it down—the small cotton navy shirt, the gold neckerchief. It was a costume of decency, of the yearning for order, and they were stuffing it into the trash. The children thought this was an exciting activity and wanted to toss other random items into the trash, and some door of lawlessness had been opened; in went a Barbie, a nightgown, a couple trucks. They threw the items into the trash happily. Five minutes later, Zeb reached in and grasped the sleeve of his blue uniform.

"Can I put it back on?" he said.

Serena was watching Dan. They had won the Pinewood Derby, and now they were kicked out of the Scouts. Could this be happening? She saw Zeb lifting his uniform out of the trash, staring at it, trying to figure out how it might now fit. She touched Zeb's hair. "Don't worry," she said. "You still won. The trophy's yours. The Scouts are going to get boring. We'll do something else that's fun." She looked at Dan with concern; he was striding around the room, hands trembling.

"Screw them," she whispered. "Assholes. I told you. I saw it—"

"What the hell did they think?" he said. The children laughed, astonished. "I mean—"

"Dan," she said, looking at his face, "he's a jerk. I told you—"

She looked at his face again; there was a great strain within it, a reddening, a hardening of his jaw, the sense that he was struggling terribly against something. He looked away.

"I'm going out," he said.

"Where?" she said.

He bit his lip. "Out," he said.

He picked up his jacket. The night seemed so bent and wrong that she imagined doing something impetuous—taking the children to a late movie, running them through a toy store, all of them packed into the car and rushing into the night. But he was not waiting for them. He hurtled out the door. There was ice in her throat. She stood at the door and watched him drive off. The children were looking at her. She waved at the car, to seem normal.

"Where did he go?" her daughter asked.

HE DROVE. HE HAD NO idea where he was going—he just could not be around anyone he knew. His father headed out of the garage with that woman thirty-five years ago; Dan and Harold had watched their father's car move through the shadows and through the garage's electric door, outside; he had wanted to jump into that car with him, put his hands on that woman's shoulders, push her out, and take the seat beside his father as the car rumbled away.

Now Dan's car moved down the wide streets. It was seven, the rush-hour congestion had cleared, and Waring's main drag was a long, dark strip, the headlights cutting luminous paths into the darkness. Dan gripped the steering wheel, opening and closing his fingers, like an anemone, as they began to ache. The cars felt too close to him in the adjoining lanes—he did not want anyone near him. He drove through the milky light to the darkness of the exurbs, circled them, took the interstate briefly, headed north.

SERENA DID NOT KNOW WHERE Dan had gone. She moved through the actions of the evening—the bathing, dressing, story reading—as though this were any night. The children were oddly obedient. The strange events of the evening, the adults shouting in the living room, had made them feel they had to move gently, carefully, through the rest of the night. Serena pressed the sheets around their faces when they went to sleep. As she tucked in Zeb, he reached forward and grabbed her wrist. His grip was hard. His eyes were closed, and he did not speak.

"Are you all right?" she asked him. She sat with him, his hand holding her arm, for a long time until he fell back asleep.

There was no call. Nine PM. Ten PM. She listened for the wheels in the driveway. There were sounds of others coming home from work, from parties, car doors slamming, but not his. He did not answer his phone. Serena lay in bed, listened, got up, checked the children, went back to bed. She got up and looked out the window at Forrest's house; the windows glowed yellow, and his sidewalk was clean, swept of leaves. She locked the door and placed a chair in front of it. Perched on the living room couch, she stared into the dark.

IT WAS 11:00 PM AND Dan was getting tired; his spine was stiff against the vinyl seat, his neck ached, and he had to urinate. He picked up his cell phone to call Serena, but he could not bring himself to punch in the numbers. His palms made wet streaks on the rubber steering wheel. The brake lights of the other cars glowed in front of him, bright red lozenges. What had Forrest said to him? What had he said? Dan's mind was empty. It was something about "the Jews." Forrest thought he had cheated. Guess what? He had wanted to. He sat by that timer and tried to figure out how to favor Zeb—just as, he imagined, all those fathers had done, too. But Dan had not known how to rig the machine. Dan had thought they were part of this group. He had felt pretty good in those meetings, liked the feel of the stiff cotton uniform against his skin, liked the sensation that he and his son were, with the others, flowing down a current to a hopeful place. He had liked the way Zeb ran around with the other Cubs; he even liked the way they stole sugar from the kitchen—how free and careless they seemed. What would Zeb remember from this? Would he remember the night he won, that lightness, or would he remember the scout leader coming by to tell them they were not welcome at meetings anymore? Harold stood, ten years old, wearing that uniform, looking at himself in the mirror. The world was made of paper; you could push your finger against it, and it would tear. On the other side of it was nothing.

Dan drove on.

He didn't know where he was going, only that he had to move; he listened to the vibrations of the car on the road, the thin shriek of wind when he cracked the window; he was focused on the sensation of his hands around the wheel, his back against the seat, the long ribbon of blackness in front of him, and he wanted to be rid of himself; for a pure, strange moment, he thought he understood his father.

At about midnight, he swung his car into a Wachovia bank parking lot, shut off the ignition, locked the doors, and closed his eyes.

THE CHILDREN TOOK A LONG time waking up and then were full of demands: to eat cereal on the floor in bowls, to have several cookies as dessert; Serena allowed all of it, which delighted them.

"Where's Dad?" Zeb asked.

"At work," she said, quickly, lightly; she thought she fooled them. Then she took them to their schools. Rachel hurried into her play-group, but Zeb clutched his mother's hand as they walked into the classroom with the same intensity he had gripped her as he fell asleep. The classroom was its general, pleasant chaos of backpacks being put away and children settling into their chairs, but the tasks, in their regimentation, were strangely beautiful.

Serena got into her car. Her face was slack with fatigue. She sat in front of the steering wheel. The interior of the car felt like an icebox. She drove around their neighborhood, down to his office. Nothing; she stopped at a Waffle House that he liked, ran inside, stared at the strangers in the orange-punch-bright plastic booths. She was a woman looking for her husband in the morning at a Waffle House; she was now one of those sorts of wives. How quickly this had happened.

The cashier at Waffle House was looking at her with curiosity. "Do you want a seat?" she asked, and Serena ran out.

Driving by Zeb's school, the third time, she saw her husband's car.

Dan was standing beside the school playground, the low wire fence that surrounded the jungle gym. He was watching the children. Zeb was running along with a cloud of children, absurdly innocent to the turmoil of his father. A janitor was raking some leaves and eyeing Dan with an alert expression. Serena slammed on the brakes, jumped out of the car, and ran toward him.

"Dan," she called.

He was wearing the same clothes as he had been the night before, exhaustion blue under his eyes.

"Hi," he said.

"Hi?" she said.

He glanced at her briefly, then away.

"Dan. Dammit. Where were you? My god. I was up all night—"

"Look at them," he said.

He was watching their son run. The grass was silver, slick with dew. There was the thunder of sneakers across the pale, dusty yard. The children were, with great excitement, chasing a flat volleyball.

She stood beside him. His fingers gripped the wire fence as though he wanted to hurl himself over it. His hands were red; she put one of her hands over one of his, and his hand was cold.

"So?" she said.

"Look at them."

She watched him. Her skin felt papery and thin.

"I want to know nothing," he said.

She stared at him. He could tell that she noticed only that he had driven away for the night. But he did not know how to tell her that he did not know what to do with that enormous burning inside him; it felt as though it might subsume him.

"Let's go home," she said, quietly. He peeled himself off the fence. His palms had red lines where he had clutched the wire.

"Let's go," she said. She held his arm, and they walked slowly to the car.

He got in. They were together, sitting in the unclean car, quivering. What now? She did not know where to drive them. A coffee shop? A hospital? She was unschooled in this particular chaos. Starting the engine, she decided to pretend normality; she headed home.

The car rumbled down the gray streets, the bare branches now etching the sky.

"Where were you?" she asked. "I was afraid something had happened—"

"I just drove," he said. "I couldn't stay in that house. I didn't want the kids to see me."

"Why?"

"I just wanted him to be happy," he said.

"Okay," she said.

"What did he say?" he said. "Forrest. What the hell happened?"

"I don't know," she said.

"And then they thought I was a goddamn Jew."

Somehow, this made her laugh.

"Look," she said. "He's an idiot. Trouble. I tried to tell you, over and over—remember the dogs! You didn't believe me—"

"Okay," he said, slowly, rubbing his forehead. "Okay."

It struck her how she had been walking through a faint and endless roar her whole life. It was as though the world were an enormous, empty room, and everything she heard echoed through this; in this room there was a roar in which she could never hear anything clearly, and in which no one was able to hear her. It was as though everyone wandered through their own empty rooms shouting, and the sounds that they heard were the sounds of everyone's trying to simply listen to themselves. She believed she could truly hear nothing; she heard the roar that came as she tried to interpret other people's shouting directed at her, and when she spoke to anyone—her parents, her sister, her husband, the rabbi—they heard their own roars in their own rooms. And she understood, then, the profundity and the beauty of the next step—what did it take to actually hear the words of another person, to stop and perceive the pure clarity of another person's voice?

They were home. She parked the car. They walked into the house, and he turned to her as though he had suddenly come to an understanding.

"Why did you do it? Why did you steal? The necklaces, the bracelets, at Saks?"

They had not seemed like bracelets; they had been panic, they had been a way out. She had barely been aware of them as jewelry.

"Everything felt dangerous," she said. "Nothing seemed real. I wanted to go somewhere else."

"What do I get," he said, "by doing what I'm supposed to do? Anything? Does anyone ever notice?" He looked around as though to a ghostly audience. "What do I do but drag myself out of bed every morning? Does anyone ever listen to me? Does anyone want to do anything but wander the house in the middle of the night, running off to that Temple to cure god knows what?"

She did not know what he was trying to see when he looked at her.

"I get up because I can't sleep," she said, softly.

"I'm awake," he said. "Waiting."

"For what?"

"For what," he said, and looked at her. "For what. Waiting to feel like I'm part of a family. Waiting for my wife to come back to the bed. Waiting. Waiting. Waitingwaitingwaiting!" He paused; his voice was raw. "I can't wait anymore."

Her skin was cold; she wrapped her arms around herself.

"I'm sorry," she said.

He looked at her. "Why?"

"For using those credit cards," she said. "That I did all of that." She was; it was a terrible, bludgeoning weight, shame, and she didn't want it, did not want to feel her limbs heavy with it, but she looked at him, standing there, and she saw, for the first time, how he had been hurt. "I'm sorry."

"Okay," he said. He sat down, heavily, on the couch. Neither of them spoke for a few minutes.

"I didn't know who you were," he said.

"Okay," she said. "But you could have tried to talk to me." The feeling of separateness she had had the last few months filled her, and she stared at him. "Why didn't you try?"

She waited. The roaring was in everyone's head. She did not know if her husband could hear beyond it. Finally, he looked up at her; she needed him to say something else.

"I was right about Forrest," she said. "All these weeks. The dogs. The tree. Tell me."

He rubbed his face. "Yes," he said. "I'm sorry. I thought he was —
How could he be —"

He knew. He knew how someone could be not who he seemed.

"But he *was*," she said. "You can't pretend, Dan. My god, you have
to see what's actually in front of you. Here."

They were quiet for a moment. How did anyone hear, see, anyone
else with clarity — was the ability to do that, to accept another, love?

"You know, I never thanked Harold," he said. "He was the only one
who did anything for me. I never thanked him." He paused. He could
not look at her; his hands trembled. "What the hell do you do with all
this?" he said, holding out his empty hands, to nothing, to everything.
"I don't know how to do it."

She put her arms around him. She pressed her hands to his back,
large, muscled, the illusion of his adult body.

"I know," she said.

He grabbed her and held her to himself. She wanted to feel his lips
against hers, that wetness, crushing. They wanted to love each other.
They were imperfect berths, these bodies, and there was a roar in her
ears, and she fell upon him, feeling his muscles in her hands, older
muscles but still strong. He rose up and spread himself over her. She
tasted his mouth, the salty, coffee taste, and she wanted that taste, she
wanted the pressure of his lips, the longing to belong and the history of
their belonging to each other. They handled each other with the hardness and delicacy of couples who have injured each other. She fell upon
him, breathless, the two of them wrestling each other, as though div-
ing through some other substance — water, air — and they rose and fell,
naked, turned over, flesh damp, slapped, grasped, trying to grab onto
the part of each other that would make them feel aware of their precarious standing on earth, and it was that falling, that ease of falling into
him, and into her, that understanding, that made her love him, that
made her feel she was tumbling out of herself. There was his hand on
her nipple and her hand on his thigh, and there was the roaring in their
ears, and there was the dampness of their skin, the long, slick walls that
they tried to conquer. Was that not what anyone wanted, that moment
of tumbling out of one's body, the permission, the legs wrapped around

each other, but the invisible tumbling, the pressing out of her own skin? She loved him; she loved the feeling of him around, inside, her. It was his eyes and his soft breath and the way he gripped her, tightly, the attempt to enter each other's bodies again and again. That was love, that journey, the effort to climb into another, that permission to try it one more time.

They lay, after, in the living room, a little shy. Their limbs draped over each other, caramel, heavy, as though they were full of gold. They were quiet. They looked up and saw this: the trophy. The trophy sat on the carpet, a low golden glow in the shabby room, hoisted onto its glazed wooden stand. It stood in the morning light, this thing they had coveted, on the flat beige carpet. They sat, damp, naked, beside each other, and they looked at it.

Chapter Nineteen

THE TEMPLE MEETING WAS AT seven on December 10, but Betty called her at five to tell her that she was going to have to coach the women who had filed incident reports. Serena was dreading it, the sudden and unplanned nature of this congregational meeting, the vague and complicated goals. There were sixteen women who had filed reports, but only five felt comfortable speaking in front of the entire congregation. "I've tried to convince others," said Betty, "but they won't do it. Loretta Rosenthal can't stand the pressure. She stopped coming to services because she thought Arnold Schwartz kept moving pews to get away from her. Darlene Hochsburg called me crying because she couldn't talk badly about a holy man even if he had been a jerk. She was afraid it would keep her from getting into heaven, though I explained there is no established quote, unquote, heaven, according to Reform Judaism. You coached the executives," said Betty, wanting her allies to have usable skills at this juncture. "You talk to them. Help them figure out what to say."

"I never coached executives."

"Doesn't matter. You know what I mean."

Serena sensed the desperation in Betty's voice, the strain of a queen trying to control her unruly populace; she had appointed herself head of this investigation into the rabbi, and now there was the unsavory task of actually having to present the accusations in front of an audience, many of whom held the mistaken assumption that their rabbi was here merely to lead them in earnest worship.

"Um. There's more," said Betty. "You have to present it yourself."

"What?"

In her haste to get her files together, Betty had tripped and turned her ankle; it was swollen and painful, and she could not walk. "I'm icing it. But I can't walk. On this night of all times. Come over and pick them up. Please."

Serena drove over and retrieved the files. Betty sat on the couch in her living room, her foot propped on a pillow; her face was freshly made up, but she looked wilted and sad.

"Thank you," said Betty, handing her the files. "You can do it. You can be me!" She smiled at Serena as though this was a great idea. "The women are all right. They need this man out! Another thing. Board members should not sit together. Scatter so you seem like part of the audience. Not a bloc forcing an agenda down everyone's throats. Tom's going to have Seymour Carmel run the meeting. Seymour Carmel, for god's sake. Another best buddy of the rabbi. He's just going to try to shut everyone up."

Serena clutched the files, now frightened of the whole enterprise. There was the roaring in an entire congregation's head.

"Do we have to have this meeting? Can't we figure out a better way to solve this?"

Betty looked down.

"I wish there were," she said. "But Tom called the meeting. Now everyone wants to say something. Go."

When Serena reached the Temple office, Pearl, Esther, Rose, Carmella, Loretta, and Lillian were assembled there. They had dressed as though they were about to attend a Hadassah luncheon—they had a desire to make this an occasion that was familiar and also to convince others of their seriousness, and their elegance seemed to be a form of combat. They were in dark silk and polyester dresses from, variably, Belk's and Marshall's and Sears, and these were accessorized with gold clip-on earrings and black pumps.

"Tell us what to do," said Pearl, a tiny silver-haired woman perched, not too steadily, on two-inch pumps. "I'm getting stage fright, sweetheart. To get in front of all those people . . . some have donated money to the Hadassah—"

"Me, too," said Rose. She had worn clip-on earrings in the shape of tigers, perhaps as motivation.

"Let's practice," said Serena. "Lillian. What happened?"

"Where do I start?" asked Lillian. She gripped Serena's arm. The skin of Lillian's hand was soft as a cat's stomach; it had the sweetness of lemon.

"Start with —" Serena paused. "What happened to you."

Lillian began to tell Serena about her granddaughter, who had almost made it to the Olympics. She began to tell Serena what the rabbi had said to her, and then she began, almost willfully, to digress. Lillian began to go off on a tangent describing the money raised during her successful Passover candy fundraiser; Carmella began to rant about her daughter's divorce. They were women in their seventies, eighties, used to saying that it didn't matter, used to pushing down their discomfort, and now that they were asked to say that it did, they were skittish.

This was what they had asked the rabbi:

> Please pray for my granddaughter.
> Can I bring my aunt to the bima during a Bat Mitzvah?
> Can you tell me where I will be buried?

She had, for years, tried to help Earl Morton shape his speeches, tried to find the words that would tell people what they should think. Now her role was different—she was helping Rose and Lillian and Carmella find ways to say what they wanted, what had happened, truly, to them. They responded merely to the admonition to say it. Say it again. Say it another time. Their stories became a kind of chant, the words familiar or even boring, but they were able to repeat them so that they were understandable, so they made sense. They were each encased in the roars in their own heads, but they slowly, carefully, described their experiences. The world somehow came into clearer focus. They merely wanted to be seen. What was it like to truly see someone as a person, to not see him or her as a target or a mirror or a garbage dump? It was easy; it was impossible; it was everything. She could do this—she could stand beside these women and tell them to say what they felt, draw the words from the bottoms of their throats, over and over—and the air in the room was clear, as though at the moment of a birth or death. She thought of the way she had stood with her mother in the rabbi's office, the vibrations of the building after his door slammed shut, the way her mother's hands had trembled as she tried to buckle her seatbelt. "Tell me again," she said to them, and stood in her old corporate suit, but now she felt better in it, useful somehow, as she listened to Rose and Pearl and Lillian and the others tell her how they had been hurt, hearing their stories grow clearer and stronger as they practiced them, until they could say them without stammering, until they could tell her, precisely, what they had hoped to get from the rabbi and how they had walked, tears in their eyes, to their cars, after he said what he did, until all of them felt as though they could breathe, here, in this small room. Serena sat back and listened to them, their silver hair aglow in the fluorescent light.

THEY ALL TURNED AND SLOWLY filed into the hallway outside the sanctuary. The windows of the sanctuary were incandescent with yellow light. She had never seen so many congregants converging on the synagogue. Apparently, announcing that there were allegations against the rabbi was the surest method to bringing them all in.

She walked into the foyer clutching the files, and the building echoed with chatter, the sharp, excitable voices of people who felt someone precious was about to be lost. It was as familiar as the manic quality that came before grief.

She felt a hand on her shoulder; it was Tiffany. "I heard we're not supposed to sit together."

"Let's sit together," said Serena.

"Thank you," said Tiffany. "People are looking at me. I'm not paranoid. They think I want to tear him down and install—I don't know—a priest up there. You know I don't, honey. You know I'm real . . ."

She was sporting a large gold Star of David that appeared heavy enough to cause a brain injury if she swung it at someone's head.

"Where did you get that thing?" said Serena. "My god."

"Jewish jewelry dot com," said Tiffany. She rubbed it against her lip like an Olympian tasting a gold medal.

They entered the sanctuary. Members were filling the aisles, taking their places in the pews. Serena realized that the meeting to reveal the failings of the rabbi would be held in the sanctuary.

"We're having it in *here*?" she asked Tom, who was helping people sign their names to a list if they wanted to speak.

"We wanted to give it a little dignity," said Tom. She saw Norman, a bandage prominently wrapped around his neck, anchored on a red velvet chair on the bima. Beside him was Seymour Carmel, who was tenderly clutching a gavel.

"Dignity?" said Serena. "Shouldn't we have it . . . in another room? Away from . . . the Ark?"

"Better to talk about a holy man in a holy . . . locale," said Tom. "So people know what's at *stake*. Where's our dear Betty? It's getting late."

She paused. "She's not coming," said Serena.

Tom lifted his eyebrows.

"She's not coming? And why?"

"She fell. She can't walk," said Serena, carefully. Tiffany covered her eyes with her hands.

"So why are we going on with this?" asked Tom, sounding rather happy. "Cancel the meeting!"

"No!" said Tiffany. "You can't do that! We have proof!"

"She gave me the notes about the allegations," said Serena. "I'll read them."

"Seymour Carmel will be in charge," he said. He looked at Serena. "You get five minutes."

Tiffany walked her away. "You need more than that," Tiffany whispered. "You need twenty. We'll have to—we'll have to disrupt the beginning. Before things get rolling. I'll yell 'Fire!' or something and get everyone's attention, and we'll stand up, waving our arms, and we'll demand more time—there will be no injustice—"

The tenor of excitement and suppressed rage in the room was building, and she stood next to Tiffany, somehow comforted by her plans for civil disobedience but also discomfited by the fact that civil disobedience might be necessary at all. The room sounded like it contained a thousand chattering birds. It was as though they were all, suddenly, on trial. She sensed, listening to the excited voices of the congregants, that they feared they were about to be robbed.

She needed air. Serena pushed through a side door to the alley. She stood for a moment by the damp brick wall, the bitter green odor of moss. Then her heart jumped.

The rabbi was walking back and forth beside the garbage cans, murmuring to himself. He was wearing his white suit again, though it was now slightly gray, the suit that seemed to be earmarked for special occasions. He was walking quickly by the big plastic trash cans through clouds of flies.

"Oh," he said, looking up. It was a soft, anguished sound. He stepped back and crossed his arms against his chest; it was an awkward motion, as though she had caught him naked. They stood there among the flies, the warm, spoiled smell of the garbage. Her eyelid twitched.

"Well, Serena Hirsch," he said, "guess what I'm doing? I'm praying. Praying for the fools who are going to betray me." He paused. "I guess that would be you."

She tried to swallow; he was right. "No," she lied.

"No?" His blue eyes brightened; she could not bear to look at them. How she had waited to hear his voice in the middle of the night, a treasure, an echo. How afraid she had been, walking through her house, feeling as though she would disappear.

"Aren't you on Betty's side?"

She looked at the list. "Rabbi. I'm sorry—"

"I did nothing," he said.

"No," she said, "not according to them."

His eyes widened; she could tell he had expected to claim her. "There could have been the SENCJCC," he said. "But Betty got to you. Sophie. Rose. Liars. Hysterics." He closed his eyes.

"Rabbi, they didn't know where else to *go*," she said. "They wanted to go to *you*—"

He glared at her and turned quickly on his heel.

"Rabbi. What's wrong? Tell me."

"Wrong?" He rolled his eyes. "What's wrong?"

"Please. Tell me something that would change my mind," she said. "Let's figure it out!" What would help? An answer; an apology; a glimmer of understanding.

A low breeze riffled through the alley; the odor of rot rushed forth, strong, and then subsided. He stopped in front of her. He clasped his hands together, rubbing them; his face was intent and faraway.

What did it mean to be trapped in the roar in your own head? How did anyone listen to anyone?

His face was determined.

"Nothing is wrong. I'm going to win." He turned and rushed inside.

THE PEWS WERE NOW FULL. She watched him leap to the back of the room, shaking hands like a politician on the campaign line. She was just herself now, empty; he simply wanted to gather her for his team. That was what his purpose was, in the Temple, in his life. He had an acute sense of who was on his side; she saw him clapping his hand on the shoulders of certain congregants who pumped his hand, vigorously, bent toward him with concern.

She sat beside Tiffany in the front. Tiffany leaned toward her and whispered, "Look." She opened a handbag. Inside it were the dozens of keys Serena had ordered. Tiffany smiled. "That's something, don't you think?" Tiffany felt a particular attachment to the keys, the necessity of distributing them. No one would keep her from this, if it came to it. She did not know how she had ended up here, in this room, or, for that matter, in this religion, but here she was, and she wanted to make sure everyone else had a way to get in.

Finally, at 7:00 PM, Tom Silverman ascended the stairs of the bima. He clasped the sides of the wooden podium where the rabbi usually stood. "Welcome," he said, thinly, into the microphone, and then, perhaps optimistically, "shalom."

"Shalom," a few ragged voices called back.

"This is an unusual meeting for Temple Shalom. But in my judgment, as president, it seemed wise to do this. It is time to dispel rumors that are going around about a great man. It's time to vote to renew our rabbi's contract permanently—to keep this man on as leader of our—"

Tiffany stood up. "Objection!" She stood up front of the bima. She held up her purse. "This Temple belongs to you! No one can lock you out! I have keys if anyone wants one! I have them here!"

The congregation, used to standing up and sitting down in order to utter the prayers of the various services, looked on, stunned.

"Let's have some order," Tom said, his voice crackling in the microphone. "Rabbi Golden is not going to be present for the meeting. He is going to watch this proceeding on closed circuit television in the social hall," said Tom. "Then he will give his rebuttal."

They all realized then that Rabbi Golden was standing, quietly, at the back of the room. Swiftly, almost majestically, he walked down the aisle to the social hall. He held up a hand as though to silence them, or as though he were riding a float in a parade. There was a palpable longing in the people jammed in the pews. They wanted to go with him. How they wanted him to lead them! Serena saw two people stand and walk with him to the other room—Norman, his throat in a thick white bandage, moving forward with a cane, and Tom's wife, Dora. They gazed out at the rest of the congregants with grim, proud expressions. Serena envied them, their certainty, their pure, simple belief in him, even if she now believed the rabbi was wrong.

The rabbi disappeared through a door.

Then everyone was quiet. They sat in the small room, surrounded by the decor of worship, sitting in the pews, but without an appointed leader, and Serena thought an understanding rippled through them— that they could do whatever they wanted.

Tom looked out at them. "Now," he said, "I'll turn the proceedings over to a member of our congregation who has years of legal experience. Seymour Carmel, former prosecutor for the State of New York, will offer an unbiased legal perspective."

Seymour Carmel happily took his place at the podium. He was a short man of about sixty-five, mostly chest, and he looked out at the congregation with a dazed, almost delighted expression, as though he had finally ascended to the court to which he aspired.

"Here are the rules," he said in a stern voice. "Only members with dues paid up can speak. This is by rule of the bylaws of the congregation." There was murmuring. "Order in the room!" He banged his gavel on the podium, a little too hard. It made a clunking sound, strangely civilian, so that everyone fell into troubled silence. "If not, I have a sergeant at arms, one of our finest members who has come here from Camp Lejeune, who will remove anyone who becomes unruly."

Was this really going on? Serena stared at a tall, shorthaired man on the bima who resembled a bouncer. In a moment of nostalgia or blindness, he was the only one, except the rabbi, who wore a velvet yarmulke on his head. He stood and held his hand in either a salute or a greeting.

The only possible response to this was laughter.

"Stop laughing!" said Seymour Carmel. He lifted the gavel again.

"Why only paid-up members?" shouted someone. "We have a right, too—"

Tom stepped to the podium. "Then pay on time."

A kind of panic fluttered through the congregation; the ease of coup in a sanctuary, of all places, was settling on all of them. There was the incongruous sound of cell phones in the sanctuary, the phones erupting, chirping into errant forms of song. No one knew how to get Seymour or Tom off the bima, especially now that there was a military presence there.

"Everyone who wants to will speak," said Seymour. "Five minutes each. I'm timing. Then the rabbi will give a rebuttal. Then we will vote. First up. Serena Hirsch."

She stood up. Her groin was light with fear. The borrowed formality of Seymour's announcement, accompanied by his brandishing of the gavel, made her now see the tremulousness of religion, this whole endeavor—how the rules were set down in order for people to follow them, as the impulse to chaos was so immense. The gavel was particularly unnerving given her recent experience with the law—she wondered if Seymour could, with his legal expertise, see her criminal activities, her terrible and crooked longing. But he appeared to see nothing. He nodded at her and sat down. Now her crime would be to rob the congregation of their perceptions of a great man.

He tapped his watch. She positioned herself in front of the microphone. Her hands were shaking.

"My name is Serena Hirsch," she said. Her voice cracked; she closed her eyes. "I've belonged to this Temple for three months."

She thought of the rabbi's voice on the phone, saying hello softly in the middle of the night, and she thought of him standing with Forrest, praying for the shed, and she thought of him sitting with his troops in Kuwait, and sitting alone in his apartment, crouching over a pizza box, alone, and she thought of him leaning toward the old ladies and making them weep. She thought of the silence of the phone line at midnight, and she wondered what all the other callers were thinking, what kind of love they harbored in their skins, for him, for their mothers and fathers, for their brothers and sisters and husbands and wives, how they wanted their beloved to be different; she wondered what they craved when they waited to hear his voice in the dark.

"We all know that Rabbi Golden can be a good rabbi," she said. "No. A great one. But the rabbi has another side. This is a list of complaints put together by Betty Blumenthal over the last year. Listen to how he has treated some of the congregants. Maybe it is you. Maybe it isn't you." Her mouth was dry. "We have to figure out what to do."

She read the complaints. Everyone was listening: Tiffany and Mike and Tom and the others, even Seymour and the sergeant at arms, who was methodically squeezing a rubber ball as he sat on the bima. How they all had not been listened to, Loretta and Carmella and Lillian and Rose and Pearl and the others, how they all held these diminishments inside them, curdling, waiting to come out. "And then he slammed the door on her," she read. "And then he screamed at her"; "And then he threw a glass"; "And then he called her a witch"; "And then she began to cry, and he turned away."

There were four pages of this.

Her voice was thin as she started, but then she felt it rise. She had never been aware of how her voice felt in her throat, the way it rose up through her chest; she heard herself get louder as she spoke. She saw the faces of the women she had spoken to; they sat very still, perhaps embarrassed, but there was a relief on their faces that something that had diminished them was being acknowledged.

Then she was finished.

"All right, Mrs. Hirsch," said Seymour. "Next person to speak. Howard Rosenfeld."

She descended the stairs and sat beside Tiffany.

There was no particular order to the following speakers. People had signed up in passion and haste, having heard only a variety of rumors: A naked woman had been found in his office; the Temple was going to shut down; an Orthodox contingent wanted to take over; the rabbi was being railroaded out by an emotionally unstable gang. There was the animal odor of sweat. A tiny, frail man, wearing a yellow bowtie and a brown suit, made his way up with a cane and stood at the microphone.

"My name is Howard Rosenfeld," he said. "I was born in the great state of Kentucky too many years ago to remember. I am a Jew." He looked at the group, his papery face glowing, as though accepting an Academy Award. "I moved here from Louisville forty-five years ago. I was privileged to serve in the Armed Forces in World War Two. I got someone to change my birth certificate. I wanted to crush those Nazis. They didn't want me to be a liberator of Dachau, but I insisted. They were afraid I would get caught and tortured. But I didn't. I won a Purple Heart. Half of my platoon didn't come back." There was respectful applause. "When I got back, I lived on Beaufort Street with the other Jews. This is all to say that I am a proud member of this institution, and I would like my opinions to matter."

Howard looked out at the audience. "I would like to say that the board is being a lynch mob," he said, his voice rising. "This rabbi is a great man. If you could only hear the inspiring conversations we have had on the Book of Genesis. You members of the board should be driven from the congregation." He paused. "I would like to read a quote from Elie Wiesel. 'There may be times when we are powerless to prevent injustice, but there must never be a time when we fail to protest.' Thank you."

There was a surge of applause. Howard made his way back to his seat.

It seemed they were all auditioning to be a leader, a prophet, a Messiah, a Maccabee, whatever side they took, as though the current vacancy in spiritual leadership left an opportunity. There was Sasha Wakowski, who described herself as a local yoga instructor and a healer, and who sang, "Hineh ma tov uma na'im shevet achim gam yachad," with great feeling, and then translated, "Psalm 133. Behold, how good and how pleasant it is for brothers and sisters to dwell together in unity!" It seemed, at this point, a great wish.

Marty Schulman walked up and grabbed the mike. "Stop, everyone!"

he called. "Why are we not getting along? Do you think," he pointed across the street, "*they* might not want us to get along? The folks across the street at First Baptist? What about St. John's? How do they benefit if we don't get along? Think about it."

There was a change in the air—almost a wistfulness—and a hope that this whole fracas could be blamed on someone else.

"Are you suggesting there is an agitator in our midst?" called out Norman, hoarsely.

"No," said Marty, "just think. Since the dawn of our religion, they have wanted us to vanish." Everyone looked moved by the word *dawn*. "Do you think they would be happy if we closed our doors? Don't we all know that they all pray for us?" A murmuring, a ripple of shared anger. A connection. "We must get along. For the survival of our people." He sat down.

It was Norman's turn. He walked slowly to the podium. His throat was thick, heavy from his surgery, a fist in his throat when he tried to swallow. He looked out on the crowd; he did not know as many of them as he had before. It used to be that he knew everyone in the congregation; now many of the members did not even know his name. As he lay in bed after the surgery, he counted how many members of the Temple knew his name. He counted sixty-seven before he got tired. It was not enough. He wondered why his wife Clara had decided not to cancel her plans to cruise the Caribbean, why she had called in just once, yesterday, and if she felt any remorse at all while she sunned herself by the ship's pool. He remembered how the rabbi sat, motionless, attentive, by his bed. The rabbi had gripped his arm and whispered, "Norman. I will pray for you."

Norman looked at the group and said, "My name is Norman Weiss. Many of you know this, some of you should. Rabbi Golden is a great man. I say he is great because he has a true heart and compassion for the ailing. When I was in the hospital, he came to see me every day. I know he is a busy man. But he made the time in his day to come see me, to be there." Norman paused. "How many of you —" his voice caught briefly, "how many of you can say that you have done that?"

There was Donna Steinberg, a therapist, who said, "If he wants to be helped, we should try to help him through this difficult time. If he does not, we should not."

The room grew warm, thick with emotion. Serena's forehead became damp, and it was difficult to concentrate on the voices.

Seymour looked depleted. "We have time for one more speaker, and then we will turn the bima back to the person who knows best how to use it . . . Rabbi Golden. Last speaker—Lillian Hoffman."

Lillian slowly ascended the bima and took her place at the podium. "I have listened to both sides," she said. "I have heard good and bad. Everyone has their ups and downs." Murmuring, nodding. "I had my own experience with Rabbi Golden. I'll tell you this, and you make up your mind if he should be our leader or not."

She leaned toward the microphone. "I wanted a prayer for my granddaughter who died. In May. May eighteenth. She was eighteen years old. Car accident. I think of her when I wake up. I think, perhaps we can have lunch, but then I remember. It is like a weight falling on me. A boulder. Every morning." She closed her eyes. There were reflexive, low sounds of sympathy. "She was an alternate for the Olympics in 2000. Figure skating. I loved her. She was the light of my life." She stopped for a moment. "I went to the rabbi because I wanted a prayer for her. I wanted a special prayer that would . . . " she stopped for a moment. "That would acknowledge the fact that she almost made it into the Olympics. I wanted the prayer because I couldn't sleep."

She paused. "I went to him. He said there was no special prayer. Why was I so special to ask for one, he said. He yelled. It was not for me. It was for my granddaughter. Why do you want to change the religion? I said, I loved her so much. He said it was stupid. He threw me out of his office. He took me by the shoulder and marched me out. I remember his grip on me. Then he slammed the door in my face."

Her voice was quiet. Serena suddenly thought of the rabbi listening to this, in his office, Lillian's telling him about her deep love for her granddaughter, about the Olympics, the triple axels, pirouettes, sequined costumes, and Serena imagined an emotion he could not control flaring up in him: jealousy.

"Who am I supposed to go to?" Lillian said. "I don't know Hebrew.

I can't come up with a prayer. Who is going to give me something to say when I wake up? Who is going to help me?"

With that word, she stopped. She began to make her way down the stairs. Serena jumped up, and Lillian gripped her arm as she walked down. Serena could feel her breathing quickly. Her last words hung over the congregants as she walked back to her seat. They remained there as Seymour took his place at the podium. He lifted his gavel, but the quality of the silence was pure and it seemed dangerous to disturb it. He stood, his gavel in the air.

"The plaintiffs have spoken," he said. "Now we will hear a rebuttal from our rabbi."

HE HAD HEARD ALL OF it. Serena cringed when she thought of him sitting in the other room, where he had been watching the proceedings through the closed circuit television. She wondered whose idea this had been. Tom's? Norman's? Betty's? Who had they been trying to protect by placing him in a different room? What had he thought of all of this?

The members of the congregation sat up as the rabbi walked in. A few members stood up, as if before a dignitary. There was a peculiar imbalance of power in the room; the congregants were still, as though yearning for Rabbi Golden to restore the proper order.

Rabbi Golden strode up to the bima, grabbing onto the podium with both hands. He looked out at them. His face was red, as though he had been running. "Well," he said. "It's been a long day." He laughed, a terrible, strangled sound. "A long night, a long year. I have a few things to say."

She was relieved that he had not been destroyed by the allegations and that he was still up there on the bima in the blinding white suit. A ripple of obedience went through the congregation, almost gratitude; they had seen how easily this place could devolve into a courtroom, a circus, and they all wanted him to ask them to open their prayer books, to fall into that current of murmuring and action that was the service.

"No one ever wants to hear my side of the story. Sometimes when people push me, I want to push back. I'm sorry, but I do. I made a mistake. Having, dare I say—" his voice dropped to a whisper, "standards. Some of you are unfamiliar with that, with the idea that I am practicing a religion. This is Judaism. This is a grand tradition that reaches back thousands of years. I am here to show you how to practice it, how to recognize the holiness in yourselves." He did not look at them, but his body swayed back and forth as he spoke, as it usually did when he was leading them in prayer, the delicate, fluid movements of a boxer. "I have been kind to most of you. You know that I have. I kept a tally. Fifteen people noted the wonderful things that I do. Most of you don't appreciate how I am slaving over your requests, day after day. Is there anyone among you whose phone call I have not answered? At dawn, noon, midnight, 2:00 AM?" He stared at them. "It's *my* house. I work hard at trying to bring you here. The Saturday Torah discussion group? My idea. The men's club? My idea. The Tot Shabbat? My idea. I am the creator—" he stepped away from the podium for a moment and lifted his arms around him, "of this."

The white flaps of his suit fell loosely from his arms; the inside lining was silver satin and gleamed like mirrors in the light. He leaned into the microphone.

"Some—" he slowed down and pointed at the group sitting before him. "Some of you are more difficult than others. Some of you want to *take over*." He clapped a hand on the podium; the sound of the slap rang through the room. "You have a list of *your* grievances?" He said the word slowly, in a sneer. "*So do I*. Carmella, oh, Carmella. Come on. How dare you think you know how to run a service—"

He began pacing back and forth on the flat carpet of the bima, ranting about the congregants. "Rosalie Goldenhauer. You're an idiot. It's true. Oh, you may claim I slammed a door. Maybe I did. Maybe I didn't." The rabbi was suddenly like a lion in a cage, walking back and forth, his voice becoming more rapid; it was clear that he could not stop. He had kept a list in his head of how he had been wronged, how they had disappointed him, his congregants: Lillian. Loretta. "No one," he shouted, "should step *foot into my office* unless I invite them. No one can barge in, no one! Those who do are fools!"

The congregation sat, frightened, rapt. No one moved. It was strangely mesmerizing, this vision of him storming back and forth, demeaning the congregants. It was, truthfully, sad but compelling hearing him call the congregants idiots. More than one. Other names. Witches. Morons. Idiots. He hated some of them. It seemed an impossible fact, that he could hate them! But it was true. Serena watched the rabbi, in his suit, his yarmulke, dressed to lead them, at his lectern, his face drawn into a snarl. "Enough! Fools!" he yelled. He stepped back, pushed the lectern so hard it fell over and broke. It cracked in two, not a small feat. One side of it toppled, and the microphone squealed, and the wooden side fell onto the floor of the bima with a loud, terrible *thunk*. There were a couple cries from the audience; he stood, now himself, before them, looking at it.

Seymour leaned over and picked up the side of the lectern and propped it against a wall.

He had broken Temple property. What would he do next? They all sat, frightened. Serena's arms felt heavy, as though a final hope that he might reveal a sorrowful part of himself, that he could see them at all, was fading. Finally, he stopped. His face grew pink, and he picked up the microphone. "Shalom and good night," he said. The rabbi sank down on a chair on the bima. He closed his eyes.

Seymour Carmel carefully lifted the half of the lectern that was in the center of the bima. The brashness with which he had started the meeting had been replaced with a pale, solemn visage; he looked like a husk. Gripping the damaged lectern with one hand, he brought the gavel down on it.

"The proceedings are closed," he said.

LONELINESS, STIFLING AS THE HEAT, settled on the room. It was unbearable. The doors of the sanctuary were opened, and the congregants filed out into the cool night. They squinted into the bright lights, bewildered — they were bound now in a way they had not been, in a shared shame that they had let the rabbi display himself like this, that they had not known what to do.

Everyone spilled onto the street. No one could stop talking. The streetlights outside the synagogue cast a strange orange glow over everyone's faces. People gathered in excited knots. The synagogue divided into varied streams—those who indentified with the women who had been insulted by Rabbi Golden, who felt they had never stood up to those who had put them down, and those who felt they had, like Rabbi Golden, been unfairly accused. There was the plain fact that they had all probably acted like Rabbi Golden, or worse, at one moment or another, that this was now an opportunity to air those moments, brashly, almost to brag about them, or to murmur them quietly, with shame. "What's the big deal that he slammed a door?" said Melvin Kingfeld. "Just last night I got so mad at my wife I threw a wineglass on the floor. Not at her. Not really. It did land on her foot. Thank god it was plastic. It bounced." Laughter, some uneasy. He said, "Those who live in glass houses . . ."

And Mildred Weinstein admitted, "We stop talking to each other. Hal and I. When we get mad. Nothing. Silence. Once it lasted twenty-six days—I slapped my son when he talked back to me. I couldn't help it, I did." They all had ways in which they had been harmed—by their husbands, wives, children, siblings, and on and on—they all had ways in which they had fought back or shut up. How could they solve it? What was the right way to be? They stood in the dingy orange street-light, and they were, Serena thought, all aware of the timbre of their voices, for there was the sense that others were listening.

The rabbi was standing apart from the crowd. His face was damp and gray, and his head tipped back as he downed a Coke. He looked all at once youthful, revved up, and older; he was surrounded by eight or nine fierce supporters. "They don't *know* you," said one, wiping a tear from a cheek, "that podium was about to break, anyway."

"They knew how to listen in the barracks," the rabbi said. "They all did. None of this. Let me tell you."

They leaned in. They still wanted to be close, the inner circle, no matter what he did, drawn to the invisible glow they wanted to see around him.

The rabbi saw her. Serena watched his eyes absorb her, flicker, and then look away.

Serena walked along the sidewalk to her car. The sky was dark, the heavy silver clouds pressing down on the city. She was alone. The air touched her arms. She heard her breath rise in her throat and fall again. There was, in her head, now only silence.

Chapter Twenty

WHEN SERENA GOT HOME, IT was ten o'clock; everyone was asleep. She sat down to check her email. Already, there were responses to the meeting.

There were numerous exclamations of approval. *Get rid of them all,* wrote George Rushman; *Why are a new member and a Christian, who were sitting together, trying to destroy our Temple?* wrote Joshua Pierce. There were members announcing their resignation: *Mrs. Donna Wetzman, member in good standing for fourteen years, will not pay a single penny more in dues to this so-called religious institution. Shame on all of you for desecrating the bima!* There were also cries of shock at the rabbi's behavior. *To degrade congregants on the bima is not rabbinical,* said Darlene Goldhammer; *it is unacceptable to call any member an idiot. Or a witch. We must all be treated with respect.* The emails flew in even as she read them. There were wistful calls for order: *Is anyone organizing the Chanukah party? Will there be one?*

THE PHONE RANG. SHE PICKED it up.

"Tell me I'm not bad," whispered Dawn.

"Why?"

"Wait." There was the sound of footsteps. "I have to tell you something," Dawn whispered. "I can't tell anyone else. I broke it off. With, you know. Mo."

"Okay. Well. Congratulations." Serena did not feel like cheering.

"You were right."

The phone was cold against her cheek. "How?"

"It wasn't the money."

"So, what happened?"

"He came in one day, and I was waiting for him. He sat down on the bed. He said, 'Dawn, I need to tell you something.' His hands were shaking. He said he was busted. I sat up and said, 'Honey, for what?' He looked at me and said, 'Don't laugh.' I said I wouldn't. What could it be? He said he went to a club the night before and the club discovered he had a fake ID."

"My god," said Serena, now alert, "what is he? A terrorist?"

"It was to buy beer," said Dawn. She paused. "He's twenty."

Serena almost dropped the phone. "What?"

"He's twenty. He's a kid. He said he loved me, but he had been working behind the counter at Bloomingdale's. Scarves. He had dropped out of Cal State Northridge—"

"Twenty?" said Serena. "Dawn . . . couldn't you tell?"

"He was very mature. Not like your average twenty-year-old. He didn't kiss like your average twenty-year-old, believe me, and, well, he dressed like he was thirty and he wore sunglasses a lot—"

"How old did he think you were?"

"I don't know, thirty, maybe, twenty-nine." Dawn laughed. "Anyway, he started crying. He was a kid. He was afraid he was going to lose his job selling scarves if they found out about the ID . . . and then would it be on his permanent record . . . "

"He was using you," said Serena, softly.

"I lost all interest when he said the words *permanent record*. He probably *was* using me," said Dawn. "But I sat there looking at his hands shaking, and I thought, You know what? I was using *him*."

Serena blinked; her sister rarely sounded this clearheaded to her.

"What do you mean?" she asked.

"I thought I loved him. But really I loved the way he loved me."

Serena was quiet, absorbing this.

"And he was twenty. All I wanted to do was find him a job. Or a scholarship or something." She paused. "I felt like an idiot."

"I don't think you're an idiot," said Serena, suddenly wanting to know something. "How did you, uh, do this? How did you decide?"

"I have no idea. Now I was thinking more about if he had enough money to buy books for next semester. Those kinds of thoughts. I wondered if Jake would be able to see it, I don't know what, this craziness—but he hadn't guessed anything about anything."

Serena's breath slowed; she waited.

"So, Jake came home, and we had a nice night, all of us, one of those nights when we all actually ate the same dish at dinner, a macaroni thing, and then they were asleep and Jake and I were in bed, reading, and he turned to me and said, 'I know.' I said, 'You know what?' and he said, 'I know where to go for summer vacation.' I said, 'Where?' He said, 'Cuba.'"

"What did *that* mean?" Serena asked.

"Right. I asked him, 'Why Cuba?' And he said, 'I saw a map you had left in the bathroom. Maybe we should go visit there. Take the kids.' He was serious. He was just interested in Cuba."

"Well, that could be nice," Serena said.

"But actually—it was the most wonderful thing he'd ever said. The strangest, really. I had no idea what was going on in that head of his. And he didn't know what was going on in mine. Thank god. But maybe there was something similar in the way we thought. Do you know what I mean?"

"I think so," said Serena.

"I started crying, and he didn't know why I was crying, and I wasn't even crying for Mo or what I did but just thought that we are all just disappearing, that we would all, to be honest, pretty soon be dead." She stopped. "I just wanted to fall into something, Serena . . . do you ever feel that?"

There was no way to protect anyone, thought Serena. She thought of her sister sitting a continent away in her house in California, holding onto the phone in the dark.

"I think so," Serena said, cautiously. "Dawn, tell me—how is Mom?"

"She's good," said Dawn, her tone brightening. "Guess what she did? She started taking classes at the community college. She did! She said, 'I don't care if I fail a test. I will just take it.' She's taking beginning psychology. She talks about her professors, using their first names."

Serena absorbed this picture, her mother unafraid. Her mother sitting in the professor's office hours was a splendid turn of the imagination, but it was real, not a trick — Sophie had found in herself something new.

"What happened?" she asked, softly.

"Those widows. They love her. They think she knows what to do. I think she likes them thinking that. She loves telling me what she tells them."

Serena pictured her mother sitting, hands clasped, with her peer client. She loved this vision of her mother, the unexpected quality of it. "I'm glad," said Serena.

"Serena. I want to ask you something else." Her sister's voice was soft now, almost pleading; Serena bent closer to the phone. "I was thinking about something . . ."

"Go ahead."

"My leg. Why was Dad always so embarrassed about it?"

Serena gripped the phone; something pressed against her throat.

"He wasn't embarrassed," said Serena. "I think he was ashamed."

"Why?"

"He tried," said Serena, softly. "He wanted to do everything to help you and he couldn't."

Her sister began to weep. "Dawn, please," she said, frightened. She had rarely heard her sister weeping. It was an awful sound; it was as though her family had been organized to prevent that sound from happening, and Dawn, in some silent barter, had agreed not to cry if they would indulge her in any way she asked. Serena tried to remember that morning when her father had tried to drive through the thick traffic, how he had paced, trembling, in the waiting room, how he could not bear being this . . . human.

"He tried," said Serena. "But he couldn't do everything."

Dawn's voice sounded exhausted but clear, somehow. It was a strange sound, that clarity, and it felt like an offering.

"I wish he hadn't been embarrassed of me," said Dawn.

Serena stood, holding the phone, listening to her sister. The colors in the kitchen seemed to brighten, as though the room had filled with sun.

"Dawn," said Serena, "he wasn't. He was proud of you. It was him.

It wasn't you." She wanted to reach out and touch her sister's hand. Her breath shuddered in her throat. "I love you."

"You don't have to say that," said Dawn.

"I want to," said Serena.

"Well, I love you, too," her sister said, and they both held onto the phone for a minute, two, before they said goodbye.

THE FOLLOWING EVENING, THE BOARD held an emergency meeting to vote whether to dismiss the rabbi. The board arranged themselves around the long foldout tables, the fluorescent lights flickering. Their faces looked like hard candy in the light. They had—most of them—been condemned by the congregation, and that made them feel both grateful to see each other and somewhat uneasy. No one had brought snacks, and everyone looked hungry. Tom sat, determinedly stirring a Styrofoam cup of tea.

Her ankle wrapped, maneuvering with crutches, Betty took her seat at the table.

"Dear God," said Betty. She closed her eyes and could not speak for a moment. "We find ourselves at a crossroads. Our community is divided. Our leader is in crisis. Give us, one and all, the fortitude and wisdom to make the best decision to lead our congregation into the twenty-first century. Amen."

There was something in Betty's voice that held them.

"Good job," said Marty. "Thank you."

"We all know what business we have to discuss," said Tom, wearily, "so let's get to it."

"How, may I ask, are we going to function without a rabbi?" asked Norman. "Are we all going to drift apart?"

"For me, it depends on whether he could change or not," said Marty. "He said he likes to push back."

"I don't see that changing," said Tiffany. "He didn't say he would."

"Has anyone heard him say anything ever about changing?" asked Tom. "One thing? Anyone?"

There was a disquieting silence.

Norman sighed deeply. "It's not Jewish to fire him," he said. "It's not . . . forgiving."

"I would like to read a quote," said Betty, holding out a sheet of paper. "If we are going to go on about what is Jewish. From Maimonides." She cleared her throat. "What is complete teshuvah, repentance? A person who confronts the same situation in which he has sinned when he has the potential to commit the sin, yet he abstains and does not commit it." She put down the paper. "He has to abstain because of his teshuvah alone and *not* because of fear or lack of strength."

There was quiet.

"He needs to understand what he is doing," said Betty. "After bullying our congregants, he maligned them on the bima. And he broke the lectern. Enough said."

Everyone refilled their cups of tea. The table was littered with empty sugar and Splenda packets. Serena wondered what the rabbi would think if he could see them, engaged in vigorous debate about him, all of them, in some way, in love with him; perhaps that had been the main point, ultimately, that they were spending all their time not on each other, not exactly on the congregation, but fully, devotedly, on him.

"I will personally allow him to live in my house," said Norman. "He can have a congregation. Starting with me."

Serena was grateful to Norman for this offer.

"Will he even want that?" asked Tom, sounding like he wished he had thought of that.

"I don't care if he wants it. *I* do," said Norman.

"So, who is going to make the motion?" said Tom.

The room was still. No one looked at one another.

"Is someone going to make the motion?" said Tom, raising his eyebrows.

There was the promise of action, and there was the actuality of it; there was the cold certainty of grief.

But then, slowly, across the room, a hand lifted.

Tiffany's.

Her hand was trembling. Tiffany decided to do it. She could see that the others couldn't. They could not remove the rabbi, despite the fact that she saw him as a volatile man and not the leader they needed. She had not grown up Jewish; she could see that this made her freer in this than the others. This gesture would be her gift to them.

"Yes, Tiffany?" asked Tom.

"I move that we end the rabbi's contract," she said, softly.

They all sat and listened to that.

"I second," said Betty.

"All in favor," said Tom. "Raise hands."

Everyone but Tom and Norman slowly raised their hands. Serena felt her hand rising, and it was in the air. There were ten hands in the air.

They had decided.

"The board has voted to end Temple Shalom's contract with Rabbi Golden," said Tom. The room was stale, devoid of air.

"Now what?" asked Marty.

"This is not a day we feel like celebrating," said Tom. He rubbed his eyes with his hand.

They made plans to meet again to assign service duties and write an advertisement for a new rabbi. Tom adjourned the meeting, and they all slowly made their way outside. The air was cold, and the thick, heavy branches of the magnolia trees moved slowly in the wind, which had the low roar of an engine. The tin-colored clouds fled quickly across the black sky.

"Do you think we'll have a Temple?" asked Tiffany, her voice shaky. "Is everyone going to leave?"

They stood on the chilly corner, looking at the large, white walls of the churches across the street. They all wanted the same thing—they wanted a place to go to, a place that would welcome them as they tried to maneuver across their own crooked passages.

"We will be fine," said Betty, clapping hands on their shoulders.

"How?" Serena asked Betty. "And what about him?"

Betty paused. She didn't answer. They stood on the corner, and the cars streamed by them, metal and rubber rattling.

Chapter Twenty-One

ON DECEMBER 13, NORMAN SENT the word to the congregation about the firing of the rabbi through an email, to be followed by an official letter. He did not, in the group email, describe the details of the meeting. But word had leaked out. Almost instantly, the responses began:

> From: Seymour Carmel
> Subject: The Final Insult
>
> It is not enough that the rogue board has decided to unseat the greatest rabbi we have known. It is not enough that they are dismissing him as of yesterday. It is not enough. It is not enough, may I add, that the people who made the motions were A) Not a real Jew, and B) A vengeful woman. Who, may I ask, would want to do this to our congregation? May I ask?

> From: Lillian Hoffman
> Subject: Rabbi
>
> Thank you.

That night, she dreamed of her father for the first time since he died. He was running down the street, wearing a gray suit. He was running from something, and then he was floating over the sidewalk as though he were swimming, using his arms to move himself through the air. She was chasing him, and he turned a corner each moment that she could reach forward, touch his shoe, and she felt herself running too, a familiar action, as though this was all she had ever done, running for something just ahead of her, and then she felt his presence in front of her, his smell, the smell of craft glue and hospital sanitizer and cigars, and she could sense him so fully that she felt a great pain diminish in her. She leapt forward, but he was not there.

When she woke up and understood again his absence, the disappointment was so immense she briefly could not breathe.

FORREST SEEMED TO HAVE VANISHED after his visit to their house. He was spending a great deal of time in his shed. Serena heard a great, determined hammering there, the piercing cry of the electric saw; it was like he was building several dining room sets or constructing shelves for a home library. Two days later, he brought out a large, five- by six-foot wooden sign and planted it on his front lawn. It said, in letters made with blue paint, *"Behold my servant whom I have chosen."* *Matthew: 12:18.* There were yellow rays radiating from the letters.

Through all of this, there was still the daily routine of elementary school. She did not want to drop Zeb off at school after Forrest's meeting, even though it had not been sanctioned by the school; there had been many parental faces that had been familiar there. She looked for them. She walked beside her son, who was cheerfully muttering about YuGiOh cards and raising a small hand to wave at the children in his class, and some of them waved back, all of them marching ahead to their own particular ideologies. Who would the children become? The other parents walked in, polite, dropping off their children, but they were all, in some way, wary. The smiling cutout snowflakes and mittens and the jolly exclamation "Why We Love Winter!" on the corkboards lining the hallways seemed to hold an even deeper significance—to find some sort of common ground among the population here, to somehow help everyone realize that on some level, they were able to feel the same things.

Some of the parents who had attended the Christmas meeting looked at her and then quickly looked away. The mother who had expressed outrage at the idea that she had ever been related to a monkey was now tenderly untangling a knot in her daughter's Hello Kitty shoelaces. The mother looked up at Serena and squinted as though she was trying to recognize her. Apparently, she couldn't remember.

"How y'all doing," said the mother absently; she struggled with her daughter's knotted shoelace.

The teacher's assistant, Miss LaChawn, a young woman with a fountain of brown braids and fingernails decorated with tiny, elaborate gold roses, had the charming tendency of stopping parents with an effusive bulletin about some small accomplishment their child made that day. Serena also noticed that she always wore a delicate cross around her neck. Miss LaChawn touched her arm. "Did you see them?" she said, in a hushed voice.

"What?"

"His R's. In his notebook last night. Works of art. I tell you."

"Yes," she said, trying to remember. His R's. As civilization crumbled. "Yes," she said, grateful to Miss LaChawn, her enthusiasm for this, for literacy.

"All of the students. You should see. The mastery of the R's. It makes my heart sing to see them."

"Thank you," she said. Miss LaChawn was now looking at her with a bit more interest.

"I saw you," she said.

"Where?"

"At that meeting," she said. "The Christmas one."

"Oh," said Serena.

"It was an interesting presentation," she said. "I'll say, enlightening. I'll admit, I for one am for more Christmas. I'm for as much joy as we can bring these children." She looked nervous. "But I wanted to ask you," she said, "if you could bring some of those dreidels in for the class. I've never seen one." She smiled shyly. "It's heartbreak — I mean, heartwarming to see children talk about . . . their home lives." She smiled. "I've never known anyone who celebrated anything else."

"Okay," Serena said. "How many in class?"

"Twenty-two," said Miss LaChawn. "Thank you."

. . . .

AFTER THE NIGHT DAN HAD vanished, the night they had fought and pushed past the roaring in their own heads, Serena found they were polite with each other, careful; both were aware that they were visitors in this marriage, and, perhaps, that marriage was in some ways a form of theater, that each one had made a decision to act as a husband or wife. She crawled into bed with him again, and there was the feeling of his skin against hers, that sensation of cherishing, a tide rising in her chest. He had admitted something to her, his sorrow for his dead brother, and she felt she had gained admission to some deeper part of his heart. She held herself awake, watching his dark eyelashes while he slept; the house was silent but for the creaks in the siding and the sound of his breath, then the sound of hers, beside him. She ached to press herself into his skin, wholly, to inhabit him, and she wondered if she loved him because he gave her a way to fall out of herself, if that was the reason anyone loved anyone, for that brief detour out of one's skin.

Dan was also watching her. Her face, as she slept, was unbearably sweet to him; it was a relief to be able to look at it, to have her beside him again. He was embarrassed that he had driven off the night that Forrest visited them, but he had not known how to stop himself. Forrest's words kept shouting through his head. He kept thinking of Zeb running with the other scouts and then as no longer part of the group, for no other reason but that Forrest didn't want him to be, and he kept seeing that night over in his mind, at odd moments, when he was talking to clients, when he was waiting at a stoplight, when he was tucking Zeb in—he thought of Forrest's pleased face, and Dan's entire body started to burn. In his mind, he was telling Forrest the things he hadn't: Fuck off; Don't do this to my son; Think what you're doing; I didn't cheat, stop thinking that I did; I wanted to make things easy for my son; Don't do this to him.

Dan got into his car and went to work, and nothing made the searing disappear. It had the distinct quality of pain, and he wanted to be rid of it. That night, he stood in their bedroom, looking out the window at the dark yard, theirs and Forrest's, separated by the thin wire fence, and he could not bear it.

"I want to do something," he said. She knew what he meant, just looking at him.

"We can't just sit here," he said. "How are we supposed to sit here? After what he did."

"What do you want to do?"

He swallowed. "Come with me."

They walked in their thin clothes into the backyard. It was the first time they had been alone together, with some shared purpose, in months, and now, instead of going to get a meal or see a movie, they were going to take revenge on the Boy Scout troop leader. Serena could barely see Dan in the dark. The grass crunched, crisp, frosty, under their feet; the dry leaves sounded like the ocean. Dan felt invisible; it was a great, powerful feeling. They stood at the edge of the yard, by Forrest's fence. The dogs were in the house, and the yard was silent.

She stood in the darkness, and she had to admit: There was something pure and thrilling about standing here, wanting to do something to make Forrest feel as they had.

Serena shivered. Dan was pacing back and forth. His hands were trembling; he was staring across the yard. There was something in his expression that she had never seen before—it was in his eyebrows, the curve of his lip. He could not control how he felt; it made him look helpless.

She followed his gaze, which was directed at Forrest's shed. It was completed now, a tidy two-story building, a pale tin roof gleaming in the moonlight.

He knelt and picked up a branch; he threw it over the fence. It soared and landed. He picked up another. Then he hopped the fence. He crept around to the back of the shed, tapping the branch against his hand. She hopped the fence, too. Dan walked around the shed, clutching the branch. He lifted the branch and whacked it against the shed. Once. There was a hollow thump. She picked one up and hit it, too. The shed. The shed that had required a prayer. An icy fear dissolved to giddiness. *Thunk.* The dogs. Nothing. No one was stopping them. The shed echoed like a tin pan when they hit it, but it did not dent; it was like a drum, echoing a sad, helpless song. Serena's arm muscles tensed, the sky above was velvet black and scattered with stars; her breath floated, dragonlike, silver, in the air. Fear and excitement gathered, light, under her ribs. Dan's arm reached back, and *whack*—there was a glistening crack, ringing—a window shattered.

"Shit," he said, looking surprised. Glass glittered onto the grass. Dan turned and hopped the fence, with Serena following him. They ducked and ran back into the house. A dog began to bark.

Dan slammed the back door and they stood, breathing hard. His face was flushed. She looked onto the kitchen floor; glass had cut his hand, and blood was streaming down it. Serena grabbed hold of his forearm.

"Are you okay?" she asked. Drops of blood were falling onto the linoleum.

"I think," he said. She grabbed a dish towel and wrapped his hand in it.

"Is it bad?" she asked. "Does it hurt? Let me see."

He held out his hand. It was not a large cut, but it was deep, and blood quickly soaked the towel. They stood, looking at each other. Her cheeks were cold.

The smell of fresh pine was sharp on her hands. She washed them. They had broken a window; she could hear the shattering in her mind, the strange sound now attached to them, their actions.

"I could have knocked the whole thing down," he said, his tone glad and pained and wondering. "I *could* have done it, you know, I wanted to just hit it down. I could have just beat the whole damn thing into a pile. Not just that—his house. I could take a bat to the goddamn neighborhood—"

"Okay, okay," she said, alert to something in his tone. "Stop." She was ashamed, all at once, that they had done this, that they had leapt the fence and broken Forrest's window. How easy it had felt, how light, in a way, to try to answer him for what he had done. But—what had they done? And now—what was Forrest going to do? She took another dish towel and wrapped it around her husband's hand. The peach-colored fabric, decorated with lemons, reddened.

THE NEXT MORNING, SHE LOOKED outside to see if she could detect traces of their visit, but the yards appeared the same, the sparse grass like cold flat straw, the leaves scattered across the dirt. She could see the window that Dan had broken. It was startling: The building had been injured. Dan was dressed and clutching his coffee by 7:30 AM; the children shrugged on their jackets and marched out into the chilled winter air.

When she returned from dropping the children off at school, she went into her yard to pick up Zeb's sweater, which he had left there. As she walked back, she saw Forrest slowly circling his shed. Her throat was empty, light. She watched him walk, the dogs beside him, tails bouncing.

Forrest stood, clutching one of his saws. His eyes flickered on her and stopped.

"Vandals," he said. The word pierced the air. "Did you see *this*?" His face was red and flushed; he looked deeply old. "I come out this morning, and what do I see? This window? How did this happen?"

She swallowed.

"Maybe a tree," she said, watching him.

He looked up; there were other trees stretching around the yard, but none had been as close as hers had been. His eyes fluttered. "Someone broke my window," he said. "Help me clean it up. That's the neighborly thing to do."

She stared at him. It was as though he was not talking to her anymore, but to some ghostly representative of her—as though that was all he had spoken to ever, she now understood.

"Forrest," she said, "maybe I would help you . . . but why would I want to . . . after what you said to us?"

His eyebrows lifted.

"Do you remember what you said?" she asked.

He stood, whistled a moment. The tune was not discernible.

"*Me?*" he asked.

"You," she said.

A smile flashed across his face, a child's smile, then vanished as though the wind blew it off. He put his hands into his pockets and took them out, placed them on the wire fence.

"You kicked my son out of Scouts, Forrest," she said. Her voice was strangely cool; she listened to it like remote music. "For no reason. Just because you wanted to."

He looked at his hands, and she saw his shoulders shrug. "I had my reasons—"

"You made them up! You just wanted us out. You did this to a *child*," she said. The sky was gray and blank.

His eyelid twitched. "No, I didn't," he said.

"Yes. You *did*."

"Stop saying that," he said. "I love children. Don't you see them watching me every week? They love *me*." He stepped closer to the fence. "They love me because I'm the best scout leader in the county. The state. Maybe the nation."

"But—" she said.

"I've been through some hardships in my life, but I got over it. You wouldn't know. I survived things that would destroy you. I never complained! People love me. I love God, my country, my neighborhood. But then things got—well. You move in, and my trusted pecan tree, which had produced pecans reliably for twenty-two years, suddenly stops. Coincidence? Maybe not. You move in, and my grandson Dawson loses the Pinewood Derby after we tested that car for five hours last weekend. Coincidence? Maybe not." His hands gripped the fence. "You move in, and they change Christmas break to winter break. You move in, and—" his words tumbled over each other, "my wife has a heart attack, my wife who was fine until you moved in, and then I'm sitting beside her in the hospital, wondering if she'll wake up the next day and—"

"Forrest!" she said. "Look. I don't know why any of that happened. But it wasn't us, for god's sake—"

"Then what?" he yelled. "*What?*"

They looked at each other, the sky hard and gray, a flat roof stretching over them; the ground was thin, a mere shell, under her feet.

"I don't know!" she said. "How does anyone know? But I know that you kicked him out—I know that much."

He flinched. "*Stop*," he yelled, his voice raw. His face held confusion so vast it erased everything else. The wire fence stood, flimsy, between them.

His expression crumpled as if he did not know what to say next. Forrest stumbled back suddenly, jerked by an invisible hand; his face was bright red, and she could see a dark shadow of sweat under his shirt. A sound like a laugh and a cry fell out of him. It was the first time she had ever seen him speechless. Forrest scanned the yard, looking at the shed, the clouds, the trees, his hands open, trembling. He was looking at what was leaning against his shed. There was a saw, a pair of pruning shears, and a gun.

It was a hunting rifle, which she had seen in his shed, and which he had brought out today; there was a rag beside it. He grabbed the gun.

She stepped back, first slowly, then more quickly.

A vein rose slightly in his forehead. His hands gripped the gun firmly but also with a kind of tenderness, as though he was yearning for it to tell him what he needed to know. She backed up, one step, two. His blue eyes searched the yard. He opened his mouth and closed it—he did not seem aware that Serena was even there—the gun was pointed toward the sky, pressed against his shoulder, as though this was what he craved finally, this particular posture of authority; he pressed the gun to his body as though it were a baby.

"I did not," he said. She watched him holding the gun, watched for any movement. He backed up. He wanted something, she could see that in his face, wanted to say the one thing that would clarify all of this, that would help him comprehend the disorder in the world. His gaze was both hazy and focused. He backed up more, and then he turned and tripped, his gait tilted as though he were running down a hill. He veered toward his house. "Stop," he said to the air, a chant, husky, almost a sob. He headed toward his house, one leg limp; he grabbed the railing of the two steps that led into the back of his house, dragged himself one, two steps, into his house, and she understood then that Forrest, in all his rage and bewilderment, could not bear to be viewed as anything but good.

THERE WAS A SLAMMED DOOR, the brisk flapping of a hundred wings, Evelyn's hoarse scream, the long, sorrowful drone of ambulance sirens, the dogs trotting, their barks piercing the air, the metallic rattle of the stretcher, the flat, bored descriptions of the paramedics into their walkie-talkies, the wind-rush of traffic two blocks away, the faint buzz of a plane against the sky, the low rustle of the wind, the voice of Celine Dion erupting from a passing car radio, a stray cat crying across the street, the wheeze of Dan's car scraping up against the curb, the shuffle of the mailman putting mail in their box, the bump of kids' bikes on the sidewalk, the doors opening and closing as the neighbors gathered, the screech of an owl gliding over the yard, the branches bending from the weight of the birds, the dogs barking, still barking, padding around the yard after the ambulance left, the innocence of the birds chirping after, their sounds filling the air.

Chapter Twenty-Two

THERE WAS NO SOUND FROM Forrest's house for a couple days. The newspapers were strewn, uncollected, on the front lawn. The wooden sign in front toppled over. It lay like a thin raft on top of the rows of pink and white impatiens. Serena and Dan sat on their front porch, waiting. Other neighbors wandered the street, also wondering what had happened. There was June Trayvor, in her sixties, another determined gardener; there was Pete Johnson, who took his pickup truck out to work before the sun rose and didn't return until it had set.

They were all quiet, wondering in the way people do when there has been a sad event, a rupture in the neighborhood. But they did not know what to say about Forrest.

"I remember," said Pete, "when he called the police on me for renting out a room when I wasn't zoned for it and I needed the money."

"He trapped my cat in a cage in his yard and took him to the animal shelter without telling me," said June, her eyes damp. "I barely got to him before they were going to put him to sleep."

They wanted to hear again about what happened — what Forrest had said to Serena about his gun. They wanted to piece something unknowable together. They were still compelled to describe the myriad ways in which Forrest had hurt them — they were not forgetting that — but their voices were, in his absence, full of wondering.

THEN THERE WAS A STREAM of people gazing out at the world with Forrest's perpetually suspicious or jovial expression stamped onto their faces. She had not seen most of them before; they drove up in pickup trucks the size of fishing boats perched on three-foot-tall wheels. They alighted from these massive vehicles, a couple women in their forties, a gaggle of children, the twenty-year-olds clutching their babies, a couple ragged-bearded men. There were Confederate flags on all of their license plate frames.

His family.

Forrest had died.

She saw the obituary for Forrest Sanders in the *Waring News*: *Forrest Sanders, father, beloved husband, leader Boy Scout Troop 287, has returned to Jesus' arms. Born in Sanderson, North Carolina, he leaves behind his wife, Evelyn, of Waring, daughters Evie-May Bryce of New Makon and Wanda Lee of Autumn Creek, sons Jimmy and Bobby of South Stanford, South Carolina, son Micah of Wallace, North Carolina, son Johnny of Miami, twenty-two grandchildren and five great-grandchildren, six sisters, one brother, sixty-two cousins, and the many people he touched with a twinkle in his eye and a smile for all his years. May he rest in peace.*

THE NEXT DAY, FORREST'S LARGE family streamed in and out of the house. Evelyn did not come outside. The relatives clutched casseroles and bouquets of flowers and walked inside, travelling through their own dominion of grief. June and Pete stopped by Serena and Dan's house and stood, somber, with them. The neighbors wanted to talk about Forrest, the way the living always want to talk about the dead, to find a way to circle and control that monstrousness.

"What happened?" asked Dan. It was all he wanted to ask. Everything had gone by so quickly, without stopping—his mind felt thick, cottony, and he stood shivering a little in the clear, cold sun.

The air felt sharp, cold on Serena's arms, the way the whole world felt after a death—its weight on her skin both too potent and ephemeral.

"The Lord wanted him," said June Trayvor. She sounded a little skeptical. "It was his time."

Serena shifted; this didn't explain what she wanted to know.

"But why now?" asked Dan. "Why would the Lord want him now?"

That came out a little wrong; he blushed, but the others did not correct him.

"I just wonder," said June. "Can someone tell me? Why did he do what he did?"

They looked across the fence at Forrest's family. Then Forrest's grandson, Dawson, wearing his Scout uniform, shot out the door, his face red with tears. "*I wanted his sword. He said I could have it!*" he said to his large, tattooed father, who walked slowly, his shoulders wilted.

Serena watched the boy, the way he clutched his father's hand as though trying to anchor him to the earth; his father placed him in his pickup truck, and they drove away. Sadness rushed through her—she thought of the way Forrest had staggered away from the fence, the sense that he wanted to find something to say, something that expressed a big impossible feeling within himself. What was it? What had he really been thinking? Why couldn't there be a way to see into the thoughts of other people—would that change anything in the way they thought about each other? Or were they all trapped in the peculiar costumes of themselves? The neighbors and mourners gathered on the sidewalk and nodded at each other, all of them standing in the lengthening gray shadows of the trees.

A FEW DAYS AFTER FORREST'S death, after his family had left and the dogs trotted, bewildered, up and down the empty yard, Serena saw Evelyn come out of the house. Evelyn walked slowly, clutching a cardboard box of pansies and a shovel. Serena had never looked closely at Evelyn; the woman had been a shadow, Forrest taking all the heat and sound out of the house so that everything faded behind him. For the first time, Serena studied her—the woman's face held the drawn, stunned expression of someone who had just lost another. Serena stood for a few minutes and then went to the fence.

"Evelyn," said Serena, and the woman looked up. Serena did not know what to say to her. Evelyn was just a worn, elderly woman, just anyone, looking, with a measured expression, at her. "I just wanted to ask—" She paused. "How are you doing?"

Evelyn wiped her hands on her sides. "I'm all right as I can be," she said.

Did she know that Forrest had set the dogs upon Serena and the children? Did she know that Forrest had asked them to leave the Scouts? Did she know that he had picked up a gun during their final argument, to what end neither of them would ever know? Evelyn just stood there, arms loose, her palms gray with dirt.

"I don't know what he was doing in that shed," said Evelyn. "I told him. You're too old for those saws. He didn't listen. He never did."

Serena gripped the fence. "Oh," she said.

"He was running around so much after I was in the hospital. I kept telling him, Forrest, please. Put your legs up. Rest. I kept telling him. That heart attack. It was me."

Serena stared at her. "No," she said, "it wasn't you —"

Evelyn stared at her with pale blue eyes. "I don't know," she said.

They stood on their separate, cold squares of lawn. Evelyn cupped a container of pansies in her hands. "I don't know where the pansies should go."

Serena looked at the older woman, standing, her face dazed, and she understood, wholly, the bleak tenor of her voice. She asked, "Do you want any help?"

Evelyn blinked, clearing her vision. "I suppose so," she said. Serena walked around the fence. The leaves from the maples crunched under her feet. Her own bungalow appear a bit larger when she looked at it from here, and she tried to imagine what Forrest saw when he gazed over the fence.

Evelyn turned a box of pansies over in her hands and handed it to her. Serena took the plastic box, the purple flowers a searing ruffle of color. "How about this corner?" she asked.

She shivered in the brisk air and knelt, digging a hole for the pansies. Evelyn crouched beside her and set the flower in its spot. "There," said Evelyn. They crouched over the cold dirt and lifted the flowers out of the box. "That's good," said Serena, and they began to dig more holes for the flowers. They did not speak, and they did not know each other, but she saw their breath curl, white in the air, and their fingers pressed into the dirt, carefully, as they set the flowers into a row, one by one.

....

GEORGIA WAS TAKING OFF FOR a couple weeks, so Serena assumed her place in the Temple office. Now there were tasks. There were numerous emails from the remaining members wondering which activities were still going on. She checked with Betty to see what, in fact, was still happening. Nothing was clear, but they would have Shabbat services on Friday night. Serena sent this information out. The phone was silent.

She listened for the rabbi's footsteps, even if she pretended she didn't. She had not seen him since the meeting, and she had picked up the phone a couple times, wondering how he was, but she believed he would not want to hear from her. And then she heard them—she knew their particular velocity, as though he were perennially late for an important event. There he was, Rabbi Golden, hurrying through the dimness. He was clutching a large cardboard box. When he saw her, he stumbled slightly, and then he stopped.

"Hello," she said; her voice trembled.

He closed his eyes for a moment and then put down the box. Then he laughed.

"Serena Hirsch," he said. Her name had sounded light, like a balloon, when he spoke it before; now it was the name of someone he did not know. "Happy?" he said. "Now that you're rid of me?"

He shifted from foot to foot, as if to peer into her and see something: how she worked, the internal gears of another person.

"No," she said. He was not their rabbi anymore; they had yanked him down to this status, another civilian.

"You sounded happy when you were reading that list," he said. "You were having the time of your life. Saying every little slipup I've made."

"Rabbi," she said, "no. No. No. It was not—"

"You were wrong. You all were wrong. Every last one of you. You couldn't see one iota beyond yourselves." He took a sharp breath. "Not that you've made any mistakes yourself. None."

She swallowed. "You're right," she said, softly.

He put down the box. "I know who's been calling me at twelve in the morning. I know everything." He crossed his arms stiffly in front of his chest and stared down at her, coolly, like a bodyguard set against blocking . . . what? Her own longings? His? Everyone's? He possessed an immense, lonely energy; it seemed he might topple into her.

"I might ask you, Serena, what did you want from me then? Why did you want to wake me up?"

Her face reddened. "That wasn't me," she whispered.

"It was you. Why?"

He was enjoying this. She could not look at him.

"I know," he said. "You think I did some bad things. But think about what I *could* have done. Think about what any of us could do."

He smiled, a cool, tight-lipped, rather beautiful smile; this was the reaction he was used to eliciting, or the one he wanted to elicit. He wanted only to be loved. They all did, that was their great desire and misfortune. But to react to the rabbi any other way was a form of weakness on the part of the other person.

"We loved you," she said. The fluorescent bulb buzzed, and the air seemed too bright, suddenly, the light almost unbearable. She flushed and then said, "Everyone. Norman. Tiffany. Tom. Everyone. Me."

His eyes widened. He folded his arms across his chest.

"Then why did you do this?" he asked.

His utter bewilderment made her glance at the floor. She was not sure how to answer. "You were good to me. And Norman. And other people. But not to everyone," she said. "And you couldn't see it."

"Well," he said. He stepped back, squinting. He made a soft, chuckling sound and said, "You're all lucky."

She looked at him; she was breathless at the weight of his sadness. He seemed to have heard what he had just said and added, "You were lucky. To have me."

She listened to that.

He put down the box for a moment and smoothed his hands down the sides of his suit. He wore his white suit, the one that he had worn both to lead in holy worship and then to stand in front of them and be condemned. It had, it seemed, been recently cleaned; the sharp, gray odor of dry-cleaning chemicals rose off it.

"You may wonder why I'm wearing this," he said. "Norman asked me to begin another congregation here. He even picked a name. But I have had another offer. I am off to a guest pulpit. I am driving to Wil-cox, South Carolina, in a few minutes. Another congregation is await-ing me. If all goes well, they will hire me. My second pulpit. They will know who I am."

He raised his arms quickly for a moment, stretching, and there was a sudden zipping sound—a rip. The material around his elbow had torn.

"Oh, no!" he said, lifting his arm and looking at the rip. He looked almost as though he would cry.

She stepped forward. "Let me take a look."

He held out his sleeve and she touched the material, examining the tear. "I can fix this," she said.

He eyed her, and the sleeve, and he sighed, sharply. "Okay," he said.

Georgia kept a needle and some thread in her desk, and Serena took it out. The rabbi slipped off his jacket and handed it to her. She took his jacket in her arms and smoothed the sleeve straight out. Her hands were trembling slightly; she wanted to do this correctly. The fabric was thin and soft in her hands. He stood, watching, as she quickly sewed the gash shut.

"Serena, tell me," he said, softly.

"What?"

"They will love me."

He looked at her—he was over forty years old, but his eyes looked so young. It occurred to her that everyone was stuck at a certain age, whether it was two or four or five or thirteen or twenty. When was any-one able to crack out of an age, to evolve to a new place? She knot-ted the thread. She handed the jacket back to him. "Yes," she said. "I believe they will."

"Thank you," he said, shrugging on his jacket, and he looked calmer. He fingered the sewn sleeve. "This too shall pass." He nodded and placed a hand on her shoulder, briefly. "Shalom."

They were simply two people in a hallway; the air was both flat and immensely full. Then he turned and walked out of the building. She stood by the window and watched him walk down the sidewalk to his car. He hurtled lightly down the sidewalk; he was trying to move too quickly for the world to grab him, to pull him to its sweat and grime.

She watched him each slow moment, absorbing him, feeling his presence fade from her. He slipped into his dented orange car, started the engine, and was gone.

SERENA TOLD THE CHILDREN ABOUT Forrest. They were shocked by his death and wanted to know all about it; their interest was fueled partly by the desire to research it, to see how they might find a way to avert it.

"How did he die that quick?" asked Zeb. He tried to snap his fingers. "Like that?"

"Sometimes people do."

"Will I?" asked Zeb.

"I doubt it. He was old—"

"He was mean when he came to our house."

"That is true."

"When will I die?" Zeb asked.

His beautiful, worried face gazed at her. She looked away; she did not want to answer this, at this age—five! Already he wanted to kill his innocence. She pressed the two of her children to her body. Never. She wanted to say never. You will live and live, you will outlast the earth. This moment will not vanish. But each moment melted the instant it happened; they would step out of her arms in a matter of months, they would stumble across the junior high school cafeteria into high school and college dorm rooms and then into middle age and their gradual descent. What would their end be? They stared at her, alarmed. She was going to break to them the news of their deaths. Here it was, at five, already—by giving them to the world, she had sentenced herself to this. She wanted to lie, but they would see through it. "Honey. I don't know. Don't worry. A long time."

Zeb blinked. His face was perplexed and then irate. It was, of course, an absurd answer.

"What about you?" Rachel asked, touching her arm.

"I don't know," she said. They stared at her. "No one knows. We're here now," she said. "Let's go outside."

They clutched her hands as they walked outdoors, and she felt the dampness of their palms against her own. The sky was soft and gray. "Let's clean up the leaves," she said, and they drifted across the yard, picking up the dry brown leaves and setting them in a pile. The air was cold in the way that every leaf and rock was utterly precise; the yard was peaceful, and Forrest's dogs sniffed around his yard, quiet. Evelyn nodded at them as she raked some leaves.

Zeb and Rachel tossed the leaves into a large, round pile. They crumpled large, crinkled handfuls of leaves in their hands. It was all they wanted to do. The pile swelled. The children ran into the pile of leaves, picked them up, and threw them, the leaves floating into the air.

DAN SAT IN HIS OFFICE in front of his computer. He was supposed to edit some copy about the Azalea Maze, but the words kept jumping in front of his eyes; all he could think of was Forrest. Dan rubbed his hands over his face. What had happened? He wondered if he had brought this on when he walked into the headquarters of the Boy Scouts that morning, had brought it on when he shook hands with Forrest, when he laughed with him. What had he missed? Or was it not him at all—how could he have known what Forrest would become? He remembered also how he couldn't stop himself from picking up the stick, there was a terrible purpose in his arm, his body—he remembered just the sensation he had when he stepped into Forrest's yard, the hope that some awful pressure in himself would be released.

He stared at the words on the screen: *The Azalea Maze is a secret path to wonder.*

Everything seemed like bullshit; it was a troubling idea.

He shut off his computer and got into his car. The steering wheel was already slick with sweat from his bare hand. The sky was growing dark, and the electric signs on the chain stores glowed against the deepening blue.

Dan ended up at the Azalea Maze. He walked inside, among the hedges, the damp shrubbery surrounding him, big, sharp walls of green. Dan walked quickly. He was forty years old, and he was unable to tell who was real. He brushed the sharp green leaves with his fingertips, wanting to feel the hardness of the leaves on his skin. The air was cold and bitter and green. What had he even known about his brother, his father, his wife, his neighbor? His neighbor, whom he had trusted, had even liked, had done something cruel to his son, and in his bewilderment, Dan had found himself breaking a window on the man's shed. He had thought he understood how to interpret a smile, a handshake, an invitation—it all seemed so easy. Now it was as though his mind were a crumpled ball; this was not familiar. He did not even know himself.

What was familiar was this—the idea of his walking in, standing in front of a small, hopeless group, telling them how to promote their small virtues; what was familiar was the idea of his bringing Waring to greatness. He could see the entrance to the town, the steel gateway that would be erected, *Welcome to Waring*; he saw the lines of people waiting to be invited inside the town. How everyone loved this, the idea that any place could be simple, admirable, and could welcome them. How he wanted to walk into a place where everyone knew who he was, who waved at him, who murmured his name. Dan Shine.

The green leaves were highlighted by spotlights, carving white patches into the radiant blue. The gardens were scheduled to close in half an hour. The soles of his feet were cold, light. He did not feel like escaping because now he understood that there was nowhere to go. There was only the blunt certainty of himself, his possession of his own consciousness. He did not want to feel; he had never wanted, truly, to feel, the moment he saw his father in the garage, the moment he heard about the death of his brother, the moment Serena became a thief, the moment Forrest had walked into their house to kick them out of the Scouts. Was this what others held, this wildness inside themselves? How did anyone know what to do with it? He envied the bravery of others in managing their feelings, the chaos that came with being human. His feelings were a cold wave rising up in him; he did not know what else he contained that would come out, did not know how this wave could subsume him. He stopped, the tiny spotlights illuminating the sharp green leaves around him; he understood, for the first time, what had driven his wife when she walked into Saks.

....

WHEN HE CAME HOME, HE trotted through the regular motions of dinner, baths, tucking in the children. He felt that she was watching him, that she sensed his dislocation; he wanted to tell her something deeper, even, than love—that he believed he understood what she had felt the day when she walked, bereft, down the streets of Manhattan.

How simple it seemed. But what would she think of him if he said this? He believed she loved him for that ability he had to walk into a room and say hello to anyone, to remake a lonely town into something glorious—not for this Dan Shine, who stumbled, bewildered, through the Azalea Maze and couldn't, for god's sake, even come up with a good term to promote it. No, she would not want to know him, the person who wandered, lost, afraid, through the azalea bushes; he did not want to destroy her perception of the person whom she had chosen to love.

He read the children a story in their room, tucked them in, while she cleaned up the kitchen. Then he walked through the house toward her. She was wiping off the kitchen table. He leaned against the doorway, aware of the wide splay of his shoulders, the fragile pressure of his shoulder against the door.

"I want to tell you something," he tried.

She stopped; she heard something urgent in his voice.

"What?" she asked.

When they had first met, he had been baffled by and how he had admired how she could perceive everything with such precision and clarity—how generous, he thought, she was to love him. She sat in the yellow light of the kitchen, her eyes set on him, alert, waiting. He wanted to tell her that he thought he understood her, and he did not know how to start.

AT SEVEN FORTY-FIVE, SHE DROVE through the darkness, past the churches and cheap motels, past the colorful radiance of the fast food signs, past the proclamations to the drivers: *God Answers Knee Mail; Pray for Our Troops; Welcome, Colgate Sales Conference; Brush up on Your Bible to Avoid Truth Decay; Congratulations, Jeanette Wilson, on her new baby boy!*; *Stop Domestic Abuse! It Happens Once Every Ten Minutes.* She thought of the first time she had driven down these streets, how quickly she had gotten lost in them. *If You Don't Believe in Hell, You Better Be Right!*; *Welcome, Class of 1983 Waring High.* She remembered her hands clutching the steering wheel, the car moving forward into the blanched hot day, the sense that the street that held Bojangles' was identical to the one with Chick-fil-A and Walmart and McDonald's—it did not really matter where she turned, for she did not think she would belong.

But now she believed that she was not alone in this—for she understood that no one felt that they quite belonged to the world. She thought of the rabbi, bending toward the congregants at the oneg, listening to their sorrows and then shouting at them from the bima; she thought of Forrest losing the Pinewood Derby, distributing his flyers promoting the Christian nation after the ambulance took his wife from his house; she thought of Zeb screaming as she walked him into school and Rachel screaming in accompaniment; she thought of Dan, wearing his Boy Scouts uniform proudly, and the desolation in his face when Forrest told them to get out. She thought of Betty and Tiffany and Norman and Dawn and her mother and father, and all of their crooked yearnings, and she thought of the weight of that diamond bracelet in her hand.

Everyone lived in the empty rooms of their own longing, wrangling with their own versions of love and grief; sometimes, if they were lucky, they stepped out of their rooms to meet another person, to try, for a moment, to live in the precious room of another. In time, they all were gone. Serena drove, reading the signs that shone in the night: *Go, Oakdale High Cheerleaders, to the 14th Annual Golden Cup Championship in Jacksonville! Go, Go, Go!*; *Don't Wait! Lose Weight with Jenny Craig Now!!*; *Choose Your Future: Smoking or Non?* She felt the presence of the cars floating beside her, the strangers driving, and she felt a hint of lightness, the hope that they were all united, somehow, in the perilous beauty of this journey. Serena leaned into the steering wheel, watching the glowing lines that measured out each lane.

Serena opened the doors to the synagogue. She was the first one to arrive, and the other board members soon assembled at the front. They each had a job: Betty would light the candles, Serena would lead the Sh'ma, Sophie and Marty would carry the Torahs.

"Do you think anyone will come?" asked Tiffany, hopefully.

"Look at how many came last week," said Tom.

"Maybe we don't want *everyone* to come," said Norman. They laughed uneasily.

They all sat facing the bima, but most of them turned at any sound, looking at the door with eagerness; it was ten to eight, and no one was there.

Then the door opened. They all turned to look.

It was Henriette and Herman Schwartz. The cries of welcome echoed through the room. Then there were others. There was Lillian, who had spoken of her granddaughter who had died before the Olympics. There was Seymour Carmel, loping in slowly, wearing one of his fanciest suits, one embellished with gold braid. Six members came for services.

There were twelve of them total, including the six who had come to run the service. They all sat together in the first two rows. It was eight o'clock.

The pulpit was empty. It was as though all of this—the meetings, the emails, the debates—had all been meant to keep this moment at bay, and no one had wanted to see this, the simple wooden podium, the sight of the microphone stretching up into air.

No one moved.

There was a rustling; Betty stood up. She walked silently to the bima. She lit a match and touched it to the tops of the two slender white candles. The flames took and flickered; they stretched upward like white taffy. They burned, a clear white shuddering in the dim sanctuary.

The six went through the service, each of them with their tasks. Serena tried to sense how the congregants who had come were viewing the enterprise, if they thought this was a serviceable Shabbat or not. But there was no protest, there was merely a quiet as they went through the prayers, the sense they were all part of some machinery, the pure engine that was the Shabbat service. It was designed, she thought, to keep them moving. She was aware of the sharp physical presence of the other members, all of them packed together, the heat of their bodies; Betty's sage-scented hair conditioner and the wintergreen Tums that Tom held in his mouth and the glimmering of Henriette's silvery hose and the way that Florence mispronounced "ha-olam" as "o'halam," and the way that Tiffany held herself especially straight when reading the Hebrew and the way that Marty coughed wetly before he started a prayer. She did not want to be fooled by their similarity to her, in muttering through these prayers, and she wondered why she was murmuring the prayers at all; it was the way any family fooled you, father, mother, sister, husband, child, that they were like you simply because they lived with you, because you woke up with them and ate food off the same plates and kissed them goodbye, and because you had all pledged, somehow, by virtue of blood or choice, that you would care for each other, that you owned each other in some damp and precious way. It was the same trick. But she stood by Betty and Henriette and Tiffany and Norman and Marty and Tom and the rest, all of them left here, in this dim room, to their lives, and she was glad for their presence.

It was 8:25 PM, time for the sermon. Betty went to the podium. "Tonight, instead of a sermon, we're all going to share something now," she said. "Something we want to offer to the rest of us. It's open. Something important to you." Betty paused. "Or whatever you want to say."

Lillian was first. She came up and gripped the sides of the lectern tightly. Then she put on her glasses and peered over the top rims. "Thank you for having me," she said. "I know the last story I shared was a sad one." She looked down for a moment. "Now I would like to share a different sort of story. About my mother," she said. "My greatest influence. Little Rosie from Hester Street. Endured terrible poverty growing up. Her mother had made hats for the czar and died when she was ten. She had the biggest heart. Would invite anyone, Jew or Gentile, in for Shabbat. Made mitzvah balls as big as bowling balls, light as air." Laughter. "I kid you not. I wish she were here today." Lillian's face blanched for a moment. "But the story I want to tell you is about when she let me skip Rosh Hashanah dinner. I was part of the chorus at my high school. We had a performance that night. We were living in New Hampshire at the time, and the nearest temple was two hours away.

We had to go to services the whole day and have a big dinner after, and I asked her if we could skip dinner so I could perform my solo. She said, 'Ask the rabbi.' He was not the friendliest man, so I said no. I said, 'Mom, this is my gift. Please. How will they do this without me?' It pained her, I know, but she said yes. We drove back at probably eighty miles an hour. I rushed in. My mother put her best shawl on my shoulders. It was going to get wet. 'Do a great job,' she said. I got up there, sang, and it was one of the best Rosh Hashanahs of my life. Thanks to my mom."

The members were not sure what to do; they all clapped.

Lillian returned to her seat, and Betty walked up to the podium. "My story has to do with my brother," she said. "Many of you don't even know I have a brother. I did. He was three years older than me. He got polio when I was fourteen. He was a beautiful artist. Watercolors. He loved Sargent. My mother would get him dot-to-dot painting sets, and he would make them look like the real thing. You could have put them in a museum. He kept painting when he was sick, until he couldn't. After my brother died, my parents stopped going to Temple. They just stopped. We celebrated nothing. Not Chanukah, not Christmas, nothing. This was in the South in the 1950s. For three years, I wasn't Jewish, Christian, anything. Then one day, my father found another painting my brother had done. My mother was cleaning out his closet. It took her three years to get to this job. His room had been shut all that time. She found this." She held up a watercolor picture. "We all thought he had painted a picture of our town." Betty paused; her voice was quiet. "It was the last view we had of his world. Dated two months before he died."

She held up the photo of the painting. It was a perfectly ordinary watercolor. A sunset cast a gold light over the entire town.

"Thank you," said Betty. "I will pass this around for all of you to look at."

Norman was next; he came up to the podium and looked out with great solemnity and delight. "I am glad to welcome all of you to these services," he said. "I would like to remind you of the other battles that have been fought. In 1972, the Finance Committee fought the Beautification Committee when they wanted funds to commission the new covers for the Torahs. I was, I will admit, on the side of the Finance Committee, because a pressing need was the care and repair of the basement after a hurricane, and the fear of killer mold, but the Torah beautifiers won, and we put off the basement repair for another year. And here are the Torah covers, still in service. Then in 1979, the Membership Committee had a question about admitting non-Jewish spouses who had not converted. Should we only admit the Jewish spouse to the Temple? Needless to say, this caused quite a ruckus. I took the side against the Membership Committee and with an open heart wanted to admit all members and spouses, *as long as* they vowed to support and fund their children's Jewish education. I'm happy to report that we agreed to admit the non-Jewish spouses, and that we welcome all supporters of the Jewish faith to our doors." His face was a little ashen; he clung to the podium. "I have been here thirty-seven years," said Norman. "I just want to say that battles are fought and then they are done."

He had just heard from the doctor. He would have six months of chemo. He looked out at the members, and he wanted them to know what he had done.

They each went up to the podium. Seymour Carmel ascended the stairs slowly, carrying a large box. He brought out a plastic tray and tilted it toward them; it was filled with compartments, each containing a single, suspended coin. "I would like to show you all my collection of Israeli coins. I collected these with my father. He was a hero in World War Two. He was one of the liberators in Buchenwald. He was gone two years when I was a boy. I watched the newsreels in the Brooklyn movie theaters and tried to see him in them, but I never did. Then he went to Israel and got their first coin and brought it to me. It was the first time I met him. I was eight years old. 'Here you go, bucko,' he said. 'Freedom. If the U.S. of A. tries to kick us out, this is where we will always be able to go.' Two months later, he left my mother. He moved from Brooklyn to Morristown, New Jersey, with a waitress he met when he was having lunch at a diner, and he divorced my mother, and that was that. My mother pretended he was dead. She said the Kaddish for him each Friday night. She went to work teaching kindergarten, and woe to those students, let me tell you." Seymour stopped for a moment and closed his eyes. Then he opened them, his hand on the box of coins. "It was hard to pretend he was dead when he sent money, which he did. Each month. He sent me coins. Sometimes, once a month, he met me in a baseball field and threw some balls with me and gave me these coins. He was not dead. He was alive. He lived somewhere else. I looked forward to those days he would come see me. I waited for them. I didn't really care about the coins. He died when I was in college, and then I started collecting more of these coins. Did you know that I have the most complete collection of Israeli coins in the United States?" His voice cracked slightly. Seymour walked slowly around the congregants, holding out the plastic box. The coins were suspended in plastic boxes, floating in the small squares of air.

Tiffany unfolded a portable plastic dance floor and set it on the bima. "I want to share what got me through my childhood," she said. She tapped a beat on the floor; a clacking sound rang through the synagogue. "I was the champion tap dancer of Elizabeth, New Jersey," she said. She rubbed her leg. "A little rusty now. But when I was good, I was really good. I was in the background of *Cabaret*. The movie. You can see me in one of the frames. I tap-danced because I wanted to do something loud. My house was quiet. It was always quiet. My mother didn't want to get out of her room. I was always in the kitchen, practicing. I could copy 'Singing in the Rain' at age eight." She stood, beaming at the group, tapping a refrain from "Singing in the Rain" onto the plastic square; the sound of the heels rattled through the high ceiling of the synagogue. When she finished, she bowed deeply.

Serena wanted the others to go on and on. She leaned forward, clutching her arms, the inside of her throat hot; she thought she could see inside them, briefly. She wanted to see inside everyone in the world. What they were telling her was so slight, a small sliver of their lives, but she sat, rapt, listening to all of it.

She remembered how it felt to sit beside her father in the garage and look at the trains. She remembered the way the sunlight fell, pale, unearthly, through a crack in the roof, gilding the faded green Astroturf on the train table. She remembered sitting beside him while he stared at the trains. He sat regarding the table, the particular arrangement he had set up there that day. She was going to help him. She waited for him to ask her what she thought, for she always had ideas. The table gleamed with its tracks and towns, but really she was trying to absorb every element of him—the way he leaned toward the table, thinking, the grayish grizzle on his cheek, the way he tapped his fingers together, the way he picked up a bridge and put it down. She sat, primly, beside him, but what was inside her was wild; she did not know what to do with her love for him. That was the final allegation, the first one, truly, in everyone's lives: the fact that you sat beside your father and loved him so deeply and wildly you felt your arms, your body, become light, and you wanted to pass into him, under his skin, or you wanted him to become you—but he sat there, looking at his trains, and you knew he would die someday and leave you here, on this earth, without him. And here you were, saddled with this feeling. You held a love so deep it shamed you. You knew this: A parent put you on earth to some-day leave you, that you and your father, your mother and sister and husband and children, inhabited the same island of time so briefly on earth. You knew this, and you sat there, wanting to be superior to this fact, to stop time, to keep the two of you together, in this quiet room, but your father seemed to know nothing of this, casually moving a few Styrofoam rocks, or worse, did not seem to care, and even had the gall to ask, seriously, "Do you think all the rocks look fake?" You wanted to tell him the right thing. Yes, the rocks looked fake. The entire train setup looked fake. That's why you liked to look at the miniature houses and trees and the tiny, almost imperceptible people, the misperception that you were superior to it all, merely because you were bigger and alive, breathing. He did not know that you were already trying to figure out how to keep him from dying, to break into his body, his thoughts, like a thief, to do everything—to fix his sadness that happened before you were born that you were supposed to be the solution to, somehow. You were supposed to be the solution with your office and your title and all the money you were supposed to make. But you were not. You just watched him pick up the rocks and move them around as you sat beside him in that musty garage, and you tried to match your breath with his.

You sat beside your father, separate, unable to save him, and you sat beside Dan and Zeb and Rachel, and you sat beside your mother and Dawn and the rabbi and Forrest and Betty and Norman, and it was this, the fact that a person sat beside you, that you did not know all of his thoughts, that they were not all ones that you wanted to know, that they could be ones that you hated, that made it impossible to talk to Forrest, that it made it impossible for the rabbi to know how to speak. It was the great curse on all of us, the fact that we did not know each other's thoughts. It was the way everyone knew nothing about anyone else.

But it also enabled love. It was this, the fact that another person lived in a different space and time than you — that no one was you — that created this purpose; it made it possible to love someone else. You were not your father. You were not him, and you were not your mother or sister or husband or child or anyone else, and that was the great lone-liness that divided everyone, but it was also the great purpose, for the drive to be close to him, to know him, to possess him but briefly would be the engine that drove you to him and to everyone you loved. It was the invisible route you each traveled, day by day, and it was what made you sit beside your father while he stared at his train table, what made you stand outside of the school, waiting for your children to run out so you could gather them in your arms, what made you lean toward your husband's lips in the middle of the night, to kiss him and to hear him whisper something he wanted only to share with you. There were so many small, mysterious ways to try to break through yourself, to try to know and love another. It was perhaps why everyone gathered at this Temple, or a church, or any place that tried to be holy — perhaps they were all simply praying to know another person, to take a step from the empty room that contained their own roaring, to step out of their own room for the rare privilege of meeting someone else.

There was a burning in Serena's lungs, but it was not simply loneli-ness. It did not have to be just that. It was also this: It was freedom. It was freedom to feel, to be, to love.

"Serena," said Betty, putting a hand on her shoulder. "We haven't heard from you yet. Go on up."

Serena sat, frozen for a moment. The stiff velvet of the pew pressed against her back. Then, slowly, she stood up and made her way to the podium. She looked at the eleven people. They had all clustered in the first couple of rows; they wanted to be near each other.

She did not know what was going to happen next. But neither did anyone; they were all linked, inextricably, by this, this endless and eternal not knowing, as they walked across this small, lighted room and out the door to their lives.

"I'm not sure what I want to say," she said.

"Just something," said Betty.

There was a beauty to their faces as they patiently waited to hear something about her. The congregants looked at her, waiting.

And then she spoke.

Acknowledgments

I want to thank a few people who helped me in the journey writing this book. First, with endless gratitude, to my parents, Meri and David Bender, for their love and support and openness, and to my sisters, Suzanne and Aimee Bender, for their love and wisdom and good pep talks at crucial times. Also to my cousins, Natalie Plachte and Michelle Plachte-Zuieback, for their warmth and support. To my agents Eric Simonoff and Claudia Ballard for their belief in this book and for patiently shepherding it to a good home; and to my editor Dan Smetanka and the crew at Counterpoint Press for wonderful, uplifting enthusiasm and care in bringing this book to publication.

A big thank you to my friends who listened, read, and helped along the way: Margaret Mittelbach, Jenny Schaffer, Jennie Litt, Katherine Wessling, Timothy Bush, Hope Edelman, Irene Connelly, Paul Lisicky, Deborah Lott, Eric Wilson, Rebecca Larner, Sandy Brown, and to my mother-in-law, Frances Silverglate, for careful and helpful reading. To everyone at UNCW, and especially Rebecca Lee, Dana Sachs, Nina de Gramont, David Gessner, Virginia Holman, Wendy Brenner, John Jeremiah Sullivan, Clyde Edgerton, Sarah Messer, Sheri Malman, and Emily Smith, for friendship and support at crucial moments. And thank you to Tom Grimes, Edith Pearlman, and Craig Nova for their generosity.

And, finally, to my son, Jonah, and my daughter, Maia, two beautiful gifts, whose presence enriches and instructs me every day. And, of course, to Robert, for the theory of the saint, the general, and the soldier, for being my partner in the factory of odd thoughts, and for, really, everything and more.

Printed in the United States
by Baker & Taylor Publisher Services